OPERATION THRALL

AN ALICIA YODER NOVEL

M.A. ROTHMAN

STEVE DIAMOND

PRIMORDIAL
PRESS

ALSO BY M.A. ROTHMAN & STEVE DIAMOND

Alicia Yoder Series:

- New Arcadia

- Operation Thrall

- Vatican Files

CONTENTS

CHAPTER

ONE

About one hundred twenty miles south of the Amur River—and China's border with Russia—winter had the city of Yichun in its icy clutches. The bitter cold had blown south from the Arctic, and even the snow complained as it squeaked under the general's footsteps, sounding very much like he was walking on Styrofoam.

Two People's Liberation Army soldiers snapped to attention as the general approached a lonely unmarked building. One of the men turned and swiped his ID on a badge reader, and a whoosh of air burst from the seams of a heavy metal door that slowly yawned open on silent hinges.

General Hong strode past the soldiers and climbed down the steps leading into an underground concrete tunnel, a hidden entrance to a research facility that he'd co-opted for very specific research needed in the defense of the Chinese homeland. None of today's political apparatchiks out of Beijing even knew this place existed, and only a hand-picked crew of PLA soldiers and research scientists were given access to the site.

As the door at the top of the steps sealed shut, the lights in the corridor flickered to life and a hidden generator whirred. The general's ears popped as the pressure in the tunnel changed, sealing him and everything else inside the facility away from the outside world.

As far as the public was concerned, air defense systems research was being done at this site. Few knew the truth. The real work here, both research and testing, had been underway ever since his predecessor had absconded with old Soviet weapons intelligence around the time of the fall of the Soviet Union.

Hong and his peers had grown up on the tales of the Russians' absolute supremacy in the world. Even though their economy was held together by baling wire and duct tape, the science they'd pursued was top-notch, and their military might was a source of national pride. China, despite all its public-facing bluster, was decades behind the rest of the world in such things, and it was only in the last decade or so that General Hong felt China had come into its own.

It was General Hong's life's mission to see the faux glory of the Russian past become the true glory of China's future.

They would be a nation to be feared.

Today, the chief scientist at the site promised that he'd have a demonstration that would put China in its rightful place in this world.

Hong approached a second metal door, his breath coming

out in jets of steam in the chill air. Before he reached it, clanking noises sounded as a heavy metal barrier lowered behind him. Hydraulics slowed the two-ton barrier's descent as it settled on the ground, sealing him off from any possible retreat.

Two soldiers stood guard on either side of the door ahead. They stood behind bulletproof glass, but trained their suppressed QCW-05 bullpup submachine guns at him through thin slots in the transparent barrier.

A robotic voice crackled from a speaker mounted in the tunnel's ceiling. *"Please verify your identity. Attempts at unauthorized access will result in termination. You have sixty seconds."*

Hong walked up to the metal door and pressed his hand on its cold surface. A green glow leaked from under his splayed hand, followed by a metallic click.

"Identity confirmed. Welcome, General Hong Zuocheng."

Hong pulled his hand away. The sound of metal smoothly sliding against metal whispered from the wall as the heavy metal door dropped slowly into the ground.

On the other side stood Dr. Shen Ping, the head researcher for the site—and an old schoolmate of Hong's.

His friend smiled and waved him forward. "Zuocheng, you're late as always. You won't believe what that colonel of yours brought back from Taiwan."

"I expect it's something interesting, especially with all the effort they used to keep people away from this, whatever it is. Is it a bioweapon?"

Shen's expression was grim as he shook his head. "Not in the way you're thinking."

Hong raised an eyebrow. "I hate riddles, and you know it. What is it that these bastards have been cooking up?"

"It's easier if I show you. You wouldn't believe my explanation." Shen walked toward an unmarked door. "Come with me. You'll soon realize why they kept this under wraps."

Hong looked through a glass wall into a small room. A birdcage, or what looked like one, hung from the ceiling, but there was no bird inside. Just a plant with shiny purple leaves.

"A plant?" Hong said. "This is the weapon?"

"It's not what it seems," Shen said. "That greasy-like coating oozing from its leaves is highly toxic. Anything that comes close to it and takes a sniff will immediately discover its effects."

Hong took a step back.

"No need to worry, Zuocheng," his friend said. "The chamber is completely isolated with negative pressure; nothing in there will come out. The plant's toxins are more than five times as lethal as the botulinum toxin, which is deadly at concentrations of less than five nanograms per kilogram. A single drop of that oily coating could kill half a million people."

There was a single door at the far side of the chamber, and at that moment, it opened. Two men were shoved inside, prisoners by the looks of their clothing, and the door slammed closed behind them.

"What the hell?" one of the men growled, trying to reopen

the door, to no avail. His voice came through a tiny speaker in the observation room's ceiling. He couldn't see the researcher or the general; the glass they looked through was one-way.

Yet the other prisoner was clearly aware of his observers. He butted his head against the glass and yelled, *"I know some-one's back there! You can't just leave us down here in this dungeon of yours! Someone will find us!"*

Both prisoners turned their heads toward the ceiling at the new sound of a whirring fan.

"Watch," Shen whispered eagerly.

Both prisoners began rubbing at their noses. Then one of them fell to the floor, clutching his chest, while the other leaned against the wall, wheezing.

"The toxin is similar to VX nerve gas. It's an ACH inhibitor, meaning it causes the muscles in your body to lose their 'off' switch." Shen paused for a moment as the second man collapsed into a fetal position. "The toxin causes their muscles to contract constantly. Within minutes, they'll be dead."

Hong watched the men struggle. One of them tried to extend an arm toward the whirring fan blowing across the leaves of the plant. His fingers and wrist were contorted, and the muscles in his arm twitched.

"Amazing," Hong said. "VX isn't nearly as strong as this." He turned to Shen. "Colonel Xi gave you all of the intelligence he collected, yes? Did the Taiwanese have a plan for weaponizing this for use against their enemies?"

"They had a plan. With safety measures built in to prevent unexpected disasters. It's actually quite clever."

Both of the prisoners had stopped moving. Shen pressed a

button on the wall and spoke into an intercom. "The demonstration in test room A is complete. Raise the temperature to eighty-five degrees, wait two minutes, then have the subjects removed."

"*Understood.*"

Shen released the button and smiled at Hong. "You're wondering about the temperature. That's the safety measure. The toxin decomposes almost immediately at any temperature above seventy-eight degrees. Watch."

Hong waited. After a few minutes, the door in the chamber opened, and two guards entered, wearing no masks or protective clothing. As they began dragging out one of the dead men, Hong looked up at the birdcage. "The fan is still blowing."

Shen nodded. "We would normally turn it off, but I wanted to prove the point. The temperature has deactivated the toxin. If those guards went right up to the plant and took a big whiff, they'd have a problem, but in the time it takes the aerosolized toxin to travel through the air to them, the higher temperature is sufficient to have rendered the toxin safe."

Hong pressed his lips together as he watched the guards remove the second body. "The attacks would have to be done during the winter."

"Not necessarily," Shen said. "Regardless of the temperature, you can spread the spores of that plant everywhere across enemy territory. The spores are non-toxic, and they can be spread like any other seed. Then, when the temperature drops and the plant has taken root, that's when things get interesting."

Hong frowned. "We can't allow this weapon to remain in

the hands of a rogue province. We can't trust what the Taiwanese government might do with it."

"Agreed. Have you read my proposal on how to eliminate this threat?"

The general nodded. "You want us to sneak back onto the island and burn that site to the ground."

"It's the only way to make sure that the plant and its spores are eliminated. It won't be easy. It was hard enough for Colonel Xi to get us this sample and the intelligence, and it will be twice as difficult to go back now that they are no doubt more suspicious."

"Difficult, but not impossible," General Hong said. He allowed himself a small smile. "In fact, I've already given Colonel Xi the go-ahead to deploy the Dragon's Breath Protocol."

"I am relieved to hear it."

Hong looked through the glass wall at the benign-looking plant hanging from the ceiling. "You said you have a plan for adapting this in some way. It's something we can use?"

Shen grinned. "Oh yes. I am certain we can make good use of what our comrades in Taiwan have come up with."

Alicia Yoder doubled over in pain, clutching at her abdomen, for all the good it would do. The cut branches she'd gathered to make shelter for herself and her dad fell to the rain-soaked ground. She leaned against the nearest tree and sank down, scraping her back against the bark. For a moment she forgot to breathe, then took in two quick, gasping breaths to steady herself.

The trip to the Catskills should have been a good test of her survival skills. Instead, barely eight hours in, Alicia wasn't sure she'd make it through the night.

The pain started maybe a month or two ago. The nausea didn't affect her much. Neither did the occasional back pain. But then the hot, angry pain moved into her abdomen and spread across her pelvic region.

She felt those early pains anew just a few days ago and took the agonizing drive straight to Georgetown University Hospital in DC. The visit led to an ultrasound, which led to the discovery of tumors on her ovaries. This in turn meant a CT scan, a CA-125 blood test, and a biopsy.

Test results were still pending.

Alicia pushed herself back to her feet, and the nausea sucker-punched her. She lost the two pieces of toast she'd forced down that morning. *Whatever*, she thought, wiping her mouth with the back of her hand. *The bread sucked. Who uses sourdough bread for toast, anyway?*

She took slow, deep breaths until the pain and the desire to hurl subsided. She didn't want her dad to see her weak. She didn't want *anyone* to see her weak. That was a lesson she'd learned at a young age on the streets of Hong Kong, a lesson that had been reinforced in New York City. *Never show weakness.*

She lifted her face to the sky and let the rain patter on her face. It felt good. Maybe it could wash away her worries.

It didn't.

Tumors.

The doctor had said that ovarian cancer in premenopausal women was uncommon, but the words had offered little relief. Something inside her clearly wasn't right, and it was getting increasingly harder to ignore—or even to bear. All she could do was wait for the test results to come back.

She retrieved the branches from the ground. They felt heavier than before, her arms like lead. She ended up dragging them instead, along with her tired body, back to the camp. The branches, the shelter, they didn't even matter. Her mind could focus only on the worrisome possibilities that those tests might reveal.

Levi Yoder—her adoptive dad—had already built the frame of a lean-to, and he had a small fire going. He frowned when he saw her dragging the branches.

"Alicia, if you won't take something as small as this training seriously, how..."

He trailed off as those piercing blue eyes took her in. Then he stood quickly and rushed to her side.

"Alicia?"

"Sorry, Dad. I... I'm not feeling so hot. Must be a cold or something."

She hadn't told him. Hadn't told him any of it. Didn't need him worrying about her when he was off saving the world from terrorists, or whatever mission the Outfit sent him on next.

"Why don't you sit down for a minute?" he said. "I got this."

Levi gently helped his daughter to the forest floor beneath his handmade shelter, then laid the branches onto the frame of the lean-to, forming some semblance of a roof. He jogged out into the trees and returned a few minutes later with pristine cuttings that filled in the gaps and kept nearly all of the rain out.

Alicia chuckled to herself despite her exhaustion—a frequent companion these days. Even at her best, it would have been a serious project to find the right components for the shelter and put it all together properly. For her father, this sort of thing was second nature. And somehow, even in the woods in the rain, he always looked put together, like he'd just stepped out of a Cabela's advertisement.

He sat down next to her, keeping his eyes on the small fire. Normally he wouldn't have done that. *Don't look right at the fire*, he always said. *You can't afford to have your eyesight impaired if you're in a situation where survival is key.* She assumed he was now breaking that rule for her benefit. Looking away from her, trying to give her a measure of privacy where none really existed.

Alicia rested her head on his shoulder, loving him for the kindness he'd always shown her and her siblings. She wiped away a tear before it could roll down her cheek. "Thanks."

She felt his smile without having to look. "Hey, neither of us wants to be soaked to the bone when we go to sleep."

She shook her head at the answer, but said nothing. They both knew that wasn't what she'd thanked him for. His tact—especially when it came to family—was a skill Alicia hadn't managed to learn quite yet.

"How are things at the Outfit?" Levi asked, changing the subject.

The Outfit was an agency that didn't officially exist, although it was part of the federal government... sort of. Levi had been doing the occasional assignment for them for some time now, and recently they'd recruited Alicia into the agency as well. When she first walked into the Outfit's US headquarters—their secret, underground headquarters—she felt like she was in the movie *Men in Black*, where nobody knew anything they didn't absolutely need to know. Sadly, as far as she could tell, the Outfit had nothing to do with aliens. That would have made things much more interesting.

"My six-month evaluation period is nearly up," she said. "They supposedly fast-tracked processing on my SF-86. I should get my Top Secret clearance squared away a week from now."

"No interim? Nice. The Outfit does have a way of skirting around the rules that others have to follow."

"Can I ask you something about the Outfit, Dad?" Even after working with the Outfit for nearly six months now, the shadowy society still remained an enigma to her.

"Shoot."

"You said they've been around since before the Revolutionary War, right? Pulling strings and keeping our government on the straight and narrow—"

"I wouldn't go that far," Levi interrupted.

"Don't believe in miracles?" Alicia joked.

He hesitated for a brief second. Had she imagined it? "I can get behind a miracle or two," he said. "But keeping the government... how did you put it? On the straight and narrow? Yeah, that's one miracle that's *never* happening."

Alicia laughed, letting the conversation push her worries into the background. "Fair enough. But still, they're obviously pretty powerful. And that's an understatement. I just don't get it. Like, how long does a full TS clearance usually take to process?"

"Two years."

"And I'm done in three months. With my background?"

"Yeah, well, the fast-tracking is the Outfit's doing, but your background isn't an issue. No search will ever turn up anything about your real background. When I adopted you, I pulled some strings. You have a carefully fabricated and very official backstory going all the way back to your birth."

Alicia hadn't realized. After Levi had saved her and the other girls from the trafficking ring they'd been captive to, she hadn't asked questions. Somehow, despite everything, her adoptive father's ongoing kindness surprised her.

"Well... that's awesome. Same for the others?"

"Of course. But that's not your question. What about the Outfit do you want to know?"

"How about everything?"

Levi laughed. "Not sure how much I can really tell you. I'm just a contractor, you know. I don't begin to know everything about what goes on in that place."

"How about this then: why do I even need a clearance? It's obvious that they run by their own set of rules anyway."

"That I can answer. While it's true that the Outfit gets around the classification rules on plenty of occasions, you still might find yourself on another agency's team that demands proof of clearances. It's simply easier to have it than not to."

"Makes sense," Alicia said.

"What else?" Levi asked.

Alicia smiled impishly. "Did they kill JFK?"

Her father laughed, long and loud. Like just about everything with him, the laugh was warm and endearing.

"No idea," he said. "Ask Mason."

Doug Mason was one of the directors at the Outfit. If anyone could answer deeper questions about the agency, it was him. Not that he would, of course. Secrecy was the lifeblood of that place.

The rain relented and the clouds above thinned to give them a peek at the stars. Away from the city, they were so bright. To Alicia, they seemed full of hope and promise.

Then she felt a growing tightness in her lower abdomen, and the fear and dread wormed their way back into her mind.

"I'm going to go get some more wood for the fire," her father said. "Build it up a little." He stood. "We've had a long day testing your survival skills, and you've done well. Since you're feeling sick, let's not push things with any nighttime drills. We'll just enjoy the outdoors tonight, then get back to the city early. Give you some time to prepare for your final review with Mason."

Alicia felt another pang of dread. For all she knew, a message from Georgetown University Hospital would be waiting for her. *Don't show weakness.*

She forced a smile—she was a professional in the art. "I'm not worried about Mason," she said. "It's the shrinks."

"Psych evals?"

"Once a week."

"Just remember, any time they ask if you're sleeping well—"

"Like a baby. Couldn't be more rested."

He pointed both fingers at her.

"Don't do that," she said.

"What?"

She exaggerated the gun fingers. "Makes me remember just how old you really are."

He grinned, flashing perfect teeth. "I'm young at heart." He gave her gun fingers again with a wink and walked off into the woods.

Young at heart. He'd said it as a joke, but the truth was, he didn't look a day over thirty, and Alicia knew he was closing in on fifty.

Droplets falling from the trees above splashed onto the roof of the lean-to, lulling her into a comfortable haze. With her eyes closed, she took in a few deep breaths. It wasn't the meditation her father frequently practiced, but close enough for her. She'd never been able to figure out how he did it, locking out everything around him.

Her peace lasted only a few minutes before the guilt kicked in. Regardless of her pain and exhaustion, she shouldn't be just sitting here, doing nothing, while her father was off collecting wood for them. For that matter, why was he not back yet? Collecting wood shouldn't have taken him this long.

She crawled out of the shelter and pushed herself to her feet. Pulling her jacket tighter around her, she headed off in the direction her father had gone. The rain had stopped, but the chill of the forest air wormed its way through every gap in her clothes. They didn't fit as snugly as they used to. The nurse at the hospital had told her she weighed one hundred and twenty-five pounds. Alicia hadn't commented on it, but that meant she was down nearly twenty pounds from just a few months ago.

Despite the chill, she did love walking among the trees in the Catskills. They didn't judge her. Didn't look at her with pity or commiseration at her upbringing. Nor did the forest remind her of the claustrophobic alleys and filthy beds that had been her life on the streets. The trees didn't care about her past, her present, or her future. They simply existed.

She walked for nearly ten minutes, following signs of her father's trail. The occasional footprint in mud or newly broken branch guided her footsteps. Her father usually worked harder to cover his trail, one of the skills he'd been teaching her. She wondered if that was because he was worrying about her. He didn't need to go this far for wood; maybe he'd taken a walk to clear his mind.

In truth, she never knew what he was thinking. In some ways they were more alike than blood relatives, even though they weren't related by even the tiniest drop of blood, but in other ways he was a total mystery.

Low, murmuring voices made her stop short and step behind a balsam fir. She edged forward, moving tree to tree toward the sounds. The quiet talking resolved into two distinct voices as she drew nearer—one unfamiliar, the other belonging to her father.

"Narmer, just answer the question. What are you doing out here?" By her father's tone, it was obvious he was agitated.

"Can't a man enjoy a bit of nature? Levi, you know how I am about the forest." It was a man's voice. Old. And... somehow gauzy, almost as if it wasn't completely there. Yet this Narmer came off as oddly playful.

Alicia had a knack for voices. Being able to judge a person by their voice, hearing their intentions in their tone, had saved her on more than a few occasions as a kid.

"No," Levi said. "Not you. Not after all these years. Someone like you doesn't just show up."

Alicia walked closer, careful not to let even the smallest twig snap or creak underfoot, until she could see the two men. Her father held an armful of wood for their fire, but he stood ready, right foot back and his weight balanced between it and his leading foot. Alicia could practically feel the tension in his body, ready to explode at any moment.

The old man in front of him, on the other hand, wore a lazy smile. His clothes were threadbare, but he didn't seem to feel the cold. He had an eyepatch over one eye, and one leg was gone below the knee, with a wooden peg in its place. *An actual pegleg.* The man couldn't have stood out more in this place... or, she supposed, this time. Everything about him felt out of place, as if he didn't belong in this world.

The old man lowered himself to sit on the trunk of a downed tree, set a polished wooden cane next to him, and sighed. He looked up at the forest's canopy, and when he spoke, it was with wistfulness. "You know, Mr. Yoder, where I grew up, we didn't have forests like this. Just... sand and desert scrub. Even sand and deserts have their stark, flowing beauty... but I think I prefer the green. In my travels I've seen nearly every forest. I never grow tired of them."

There was something off about him. Alicia felt a shiver up her spine as she flashed back to one of the characters from *Men in Black*. She half-expected this old man's skin to slough off and for a giant cockroach to emerge from the skin suit he was wearing.

"Why are you here?" Levi asked again.

The old man sighed. "My time is coming to an end. I came to see if you'd reconsidered your place in history."

"My place in... are you joking? I'm out here training with my daughter. I don't believe in any of your nonsense. I told you that years ago."

"I had children once. Wives." Again, the wistfulness. "A curse, wouldn't you say, to outlive your wives and children? Though I suppose it doesn't have to be. Burdens and gifts are often the flip side of the same coin."

Levi stiffened with anger. No... Alicia recognized it for what it truly was. Rage.

"You don't get to lecture me about *loss...* or *gifts*." He spat the last word. "I don't have time for riddles, old man. My daughter doesn't feel well, and I'd rather spend my evening in her company than yours. Tell me what you want."

"Time. Yes. For most people it is finite. But not quite so for you. And yet you refuse to believe. Do you not look in the mirror? Has not every benefit I mentioned to you been verified?"

"I'm done listening to you." Levi turned to walk away.

"Wait." The iron in Narmer's voice stopped him in his

tracks. "Here. Take this."

The old man held up a piece of paper. Thick parchment, and even from where she stood, Alicia could see the texture. It reminded her of old papyrus she'd seen on display at the Met in New York City.

"I'll be here for a few more weeks," Narmer said. "Come see me if you change your mind."

"I won't."

But Levi walked back to the old man and snatched the paper from his outstretched hand. Then Levi calmed all at once, his rage vanishing, replaced by sadness, and he bowed to the old man. "Goodbye, Amar Van." He said something more in a language Alicia didn't recognize before walking away.

Alicia kept behind the trees, unmoving. Her father obviously knew this old man. Obviously respected him by the way he'd bowed at the end. But his wariness, hostility even, couldn't have been more obvious. Just who was this... Narmer?

"Do you intend to stand behind that tree all night, young woman? Or perhaps you would humor an old man and come introduce yourself?"

Alicia cursed silently, wondering what had given her away. A scrape of her coat against bark, maybe? Maybe she'd snapped a twig and not noticed? Walking back to the warm fire appealed to her tired mind and body, but curiosity about the old man won out. She stepped out from behind the tree and walked forward.

Up close, the man looked even more ragged than he did from afar. His clothes were not just threadbare but motheaten, hanging off his body like the tattered remnants of a burial shroud. He patted a spot on the log next to him. Alicia knew she should walk away. Should *run* away. But the man had an odd magnetic effect that pulled her close until she sat beside him.

"Who are you?" she asked. "How do you know my father?"

"I met him years ago. When he was trying to find himself. In those days he still carried grief with him."

"Grief? About what?"

"That's a question for your father, I believe." His laugh carried a dry brittleness. "My name, young woman, is Narmer. I've gone by hundreds of names over the years, but that one is the truest I have. The one I think I would like to carry with me to the afterlife. And you, my dear?"

"Alicia. Alicia Yoder."

He patted her on the leg. "It is good to meet you, Alicia."

"How did you know I was there?"

"I heard you breathing."

Alicia scoffed, and before she could think to keep her mouth shut, she said, "Impossible."

"Oh, my dear, you truly have no concept of what is possible and what is impossible." The words were a rebuke, but they weren't said unkindly. Then the old man sniffed the air, and his eyes fell to Alicia's abdomen. "Ah. You have my sympathy."

"I don't know what you mean," Alicia said. But she did know. He couldn't possibly know she was sick... especially down there.

"If you say so." He smiled at her then, and his expression turned to one of curiosity. "Tell me, my dear, do you believe in miracles?"

"I... I don't know. I'd like to believe they're possible." Alicia didn't know this man in the slightest, but something about him made her want to continue talking with him. "I think... I think sometimes people go *looking* for miracles... and that doesn't seem like a smart play."

"Oh? Please explain."

She nodded. "Nowadays I think people are looking for the easy score or for wish fulfillment without ever having worked for those so-called miracles. Frankly, I think people need to work hard if they want anything good to happen. And if you're going to work, always try to do your best. If someone is working toward a goal, I believe they'll find opportunities open up for them that might not have been there had they not been earning what I like to call sweat equity. It's then up to them to grab onto the unexpected opportunities. It may seem to a lot of outside observers that miraculous things happen to people, but often I believe that luck comes to those who work hard. Sorry. I don't know if that makes any sense."

"It does to me." Narmer stared off in the direction her father had gone. "There are also those who experience a true miracle, and yet refuse to acknowledge it for what it is."

After a moment of quiet, Alicia frowned. "Narmer, how do you know my father?"

"Your father is a special man. He was given a gift. I'm sure you've noticed he's a little different than most men? Tell me, Alicia, do you want to be special?"

"No." The answer came out instantly, without hesitation. "Not unless being special means I can help more people. Otherwise, what's the point? Like, what does being special even mean, anyway?"

"Indeed. That's a question that demands contemplation." Narmer patted her on the leg again. "Well, I've taken enough of your time. Go to your father. Spend time with him." He pointed at her abdomen. "And don't worry too much. I'm sure you'll be fine." He pushed away from the log and limped off into the forest without another word or backwards glance.

What a strange man, Alicia thought, watching him go. And it suddenly dawned on her that he hadn't answered any of her questions about how he knew her dad.

It wasn't until he'd walked into the shadows and disappeared that Alicia realized she should have been more concerned about him. He was old, barely dressed, and hobbling on only one good leg in the middle of the forest. Could he even find his way safely to the nearest road?

With a deep sigh she rose and followed after him.

She'd barely walked a few feet when out of the same shadows Narmer had disappeared into, a tiny cat appeared. Black as night, with bright golden eyes that seemed to drink in the starlight, it walked straight up to her, curled around her left ankle, and began to purr.

Alicia reached down and picked it up, cuddling it high against her chest. It wasn't a cat, it was a kitten, small and thin, like it hadn't eaten... maybe ever. It was starving.

There was no sign of Narmer in the shadows. Not even a single track from his pegleg. Alicia shook her head in confusion, then made her way back to camp and to her father, wondering what she should tell him about her encounter with the old man.

CHAPTER

TWO

"So how was your trip?"

Alicia shrugged. "Not bad. I wasn't feeling too well, so we cut it short."

"I'll say. You look pale." Rebecca Baker popped the trunk of her car and put Alicia's pack inside it. "You're probably anemic and need more iron in your diet. Have you tried colloidal silver? Stuff works on everything. Seriously. I take it to keep the flu away. I haven't had strep once since I started taking it six years ago."

The woman prattled on, but Alicia didn't mind. During the train ride, she'd gotten a call from the hospital. She didn't answer, couldn't deal with it right then. She let it go to voice-mail. And had spent every minute since thinking about it. So she was more than happy for Becca to take her mind off of things.

Becca was her neighbor across the hall in their apartment

complex, and the woman had taken to Alicia like a mother hen. She'd lost her husband of forty years the previous November to a stroke, and was probably lonely. She was also incredibly sweet—and one of Alicia's only friends.

They pulled out of the Acela train station parking structure in DC and headed to their apartment building on Wheeler. Becca talked the whole time, filling every opportunity for silence with recommendations for herbal treatments for sickness, her latest recipe discoveries, or how she'd found a TV station that ran *The Ray Bradbury Theater*. Alicia smiled and nodded, but didn't really engage in the conversation.

The kitten was curled up in her lap the whole time, sucking on its tail. The little black bundle of fur always seemed to be curled into a circle like this.

"I didn't know you were a cat person," Becca said.

"I'm not," Alicia said. "I found him out in the forest. Couldn't just leave him out there. I mean... look at him." She rubbed the kitten behind its ears.

"You won't get any argument from me. You know I love little fur babies. Did I tell you I've been training my little sheepadoodle to talk to me?"

Alicia raised a disbelieving eyebrow. "How do you do that?"

"I'll show you when we get upstairs."

"How old is your dog now?" Alicia asked, not really caring, but not wanting to be rude to her friend.

"She's two. Well... in human years. In dog years? I have no idea. I don't know that I believe the whole seven-to-one dog years thing. No. I don't know about that."

Alicia smiled as the older woman spun off into some article

she once read on "dog years." Had Becca always been this chatty? Alicia cringed as she imagined the lady's poor husband having to listen to that for forty years.

They pulled into Becca's covered parking spot, and Alicia started to pull her bag from the trunk, but Becca wouldn't have it. Her friend insisted on carrying it to the elevator, where she punched the button to the third floor. When the door slid open, they headed down the hall. Becca's apartment, 310, was directly across from Alicia's, 311. Becca opened the door to 310 and waved for Alicia to enter.

Alicia felt torn. It was either go into her friend's place and have her ear talked off, or go into her own apartment and check the message waiting for her on her phone.

She went into Becca's place and took a seat at the kitchen table.

Becca already had the gas stove on and a teapot going. Her little black dog, Brees, stood up on her hind legs next to Alicia trying to get a view of the kitten. The kitten reached out a paw and swatted at Brees's nose. Alicia chuckled and reached down to scratch the dog under its chin.

Becca had named the dog "Brees" after the former quarterback of the New Orleans Saints. The woman was a diehard football fan who loved the Saints almost as much as she hated the Washington Commanders.

A few minutes later, Becca brought over two mugs of hot apple cider, steam rising. She sat down, blew on her own mug to cool it, then looked at Alicia for a long moment. "You don't look well, Alicia. Are you okay?"

The question caught Alicia off-guard. Her friend rarely took the direct approach.

"Actually..." She decided to be honest. "No, I'm actually not okay. I have a pain in my abdomen. I got it checked out at Georgetown before I went on the trip with my dad, and they did some tests, and now I'm waiting for results." She paused. "That's not true. I'm not waiting. I think they have the results already. I got a message from them during the train ride, but I haven't listened to it yet. I'm... afraid to."

"I'm so sorry. Need me to do it for you, sweetie?"

From anyone else, the question would have been nosy. From Becca, it was an offer of kindness.

Alicia shook her head. "No... I appreciate it though." She took a sip of the cider and changed the subject. "So you're training Brees to talk?"

"I certainly am! Look over there. You see that mat with the buttons sticking out of it?" Becca pointed to a mat on the floor by the sliding glass door to her balcony. The mat was made of different colors of foam hexagons, and seven big round buttons stuck up from it, each with a simple picture on it.

"I got my little Breesy these buttons from BabbelPet. I just record an easy word into each, and my sweetheart can press one to tell me what she wants." She looked down at her dog and pointed to the buttons. "Go tell Mama what you want, Breesy. Tell Mama what you want!"

To Alicia's astonishment, the little dog walked over to the foam pad, looked down at the buttons for a long moment as if considering, then pressed one with her paw. Becca's voice came through the button's speaker, saying, *"Ball."*

Brees looked up expectantly.

"Wow," said Alicia. "That's really cool. She really knows what that means?"

"Oh, sure she does! My little pupper is amazing. She knows *ball*, *outside*, *treat*, *now*, *play*, *stick*, and *mama*. She uses that last one to get my attention, then presses one of the other ones to tell me what she wants. I saw it on the internet. Some bigger version with like, thirty buttons. I swear, that dog was having a full-on conversation with her owner. Breesy seems to have maxed out at seven, but she's still a smart little one, aren't we now, Breesy?"

"That's... that's actually pretty awesome," Alicia said. "I had no idea."

The cat suddenly squirmed in her lap, then jumped down. It walked over to the buttons, stared down at them, then batted idly at one. Nothing happened. As if realizing that he must not have hit it with enough pressure, the kitty reared up and slammed both front paws onto the button.

"Outside," said Becca's voice.

Brees backed away from the cat, whining.

The kitten repeated the call for "outside" and looked up at Alicia.

Becca whistled. "Ha! The little fella wants to play too! I doubt you can train a cat to do much of anything it doesn't want to, but if you want, I have a bunch of extra buttons that I can give you. Brees won't need them." She said this last bit in a low voice, as if afraid Brees would hear and feel insulted. Then she vanished down the hall and returned with a box containing two more of the foam hexagons and several buttons.

"Thanks, Becca." Alicia doubted the cat would actually use the buttons, but she didn't want to be rude. "And thanks for the ride and for the cider. But I think I should go home and listen to that message."

"All right, dear. You let me know if you need anything. Anything at all. I'm here for you."

"Thanks, Becca. I know you are. You're the best."

Alicia gave the older woman a tight hug, grabbed her bag, then scooped up the kitten.

She'd stalled long enough. It was time to get the news she'd been dreading for days.

Alicia stared at her cell phone, too afraid to touch it. Next to her, the kitten curled up again into a little circle, sucking on his tail. For some reason he reminded her of a bagel.

"I guess that's what I'll call you. Bagel."

The cat looked up at her, cocked his head, then walked over to sit in her lap. Within a minute he was again curled up into a little ball, the tip of his tail stuck in his mouth, purring as he closed his eyes.

"I guess the name fits you, doesn't it."

The purring got louder.

Alicia took a deep breath and looked once more at her phone. She quickly played the voicemail before she could change her mind.

"Hello, this message is for Alicia Yoder. This is Dr. Kim Reynolds.

We got the results for your biopsy, blood tests, and CT scan back. Please give our office a call as soon as you get this."

The message ended.

"That's it?" Alicia said. "They couldn't be bothered to just tell me what's going on?"

Her anger wasn't fair, and she knew it. She should have realized. Of *course* they wouldn't be so careless as to deliver important medical info in a voicemail.

She dialed Dr. Reynolds. After five rings, someone picked up.

"This is Dr. Reynolds's office. Lance Andrews speaking."

It was the doctor's assistant. Great. The guy always sounded condescending.

"Hey, Lance, this is Alicia Yoder. I'm returning the doctor's call. She left a message saying my results were in."

"Give me one moment. I'll see if Dr. Reynolds is available."

The line stayed live, and Alicia heard muffled scratching noises. Lance must have forgotten to hit the hold button.

"Hey, Kim. Alicia... der's... You want me to... her?"

Another voice responded, but Alicia couldn't make out the words.

"Okay, I'll tell... tomorrow. Do you want... positive for ovarian cancer? Okay... leave to... "

The words crashed down on Alicia like an anvil.

Positive for ovarian cancer.

"Miss Yoder, are you still there?"

Ovarian cancer.

"Miss Yoder?"

All the moisture in Alicia's mouth vanished, leaving her struggling to form a coherent word.

"Y-yes."

"Dr. Reynolds is in the middle of a consultation that she can't put off. She apologizes. She needs you to come in tomorrow to go over the results. Is the afternoon fine? Say, two p.m.?"

"What's... what's going on?"

"I'm afraid that's best discussed with the doctor. Are you available at two p.m.?"

"Yes."

"Then we'll see you tomorrow at two."

Alicia hung up, her hands shaking. Tears fell from her face onto the kitten in her lap. He looked up at her, gold eyes filled with concern, then nuzzled her stomach.

Ovarian cancer.

She brought up her dad's number, wanting desperately to talk to him, but stopped. How would he react to the news? Why put him through this too?

She put the phone down, moved Bagel to one side, and pulled her computer onto her lap. A few searches told her how bad it was.

Stage Two had a five-year survival rate of seventy percent.

Stage Three's survival rate dropped to thirty-nine percent.

Stage Four... only seventeen percent.

She shut the laptop and leaned back.

She probably wasn't farther along than Stage Two. Right? The odds were good.

She tried to convince herself the odds were good.

But even if she survived, there was no way the Outfit would

let her remain as an operations agent and go out in the field again. Chemo would destroy her immune system. The Outfit couldn't send someone medically compromised into the field. They probably wouldn't even let her be a desk jockey.

Her promising new career was over. And that was best-case scenario. She didn't want to think about worst-case.

She lifted Bagel in her arms, walked to her room, and curled up in bed.

Hot tears flowed down her cheeks until she fell asleep.

Dreams were a funny thing for Alicia. When she was younger, she never had dreams, only nightmares. Nightmares of shadowy men and women towering over her with red, glowing eyes. After being rescued from the street life, those nightmares largely faded away, only to be replaced by a different kind of nightmare: anxiety-raising scenarios about failing a test or somehow being in class with no clothes.

But even those faded in time. Now her dreams, when she remembered them, were usually nice, innocuous dreams of nonsense.

She'd forgotten the taste of real nightmare-fueled fear. Not just anxiety. *Fear.* Now it returned like a bad penny.

At first, it was only a feeling. Foreboding and dread doing their best to suffocate her. Then the dream took shape. Massive, fleshy tumors swallowing her, bit by bit. The tumors turned dark, and they had the same glowing eyes as her abusers. Alicia tried running from them, but her feet sank into a ground made soft from the cancer's poison, holding her fast.

She recognized the nightmare for what it was, but her sleeping mind wouldn't let her escape by waking up.

The tumors faded away, replaced by the old man in the woods watching her, telling her she would never be special and she would never help anyone ever again.

Those words hurt worse than the cancer.

She even had a nightmare about Bagel. The kitten crawled onto her stomach, sniffing and then pawing at her abdomen. Alicia knew he was trying to get to the tumors under her skin. In the dream, Bagel was just a dark silhouette, but he still had those bright, brilliant gold eyes.

The cat pawed at her skin, but not enough to scratch it. Then he made a gagging sound and threw up on her exposed belly. The vomit looked like liquid gold, and it spread all across her stomach, shifting and moving in the dark like a living thing.

Sunlight stabbed into Alicia's eyes, waking her. As bad as she'd felt in the Catskills with her dad, she felt so much worse now. Every joint hurt, from her fingers to her toes. Her muscles ached, and her head throbbed worse than any hangover she'd ever felt.

Bagel licked her cheek. The poor thing was probably hungry.

When Alicia rolled out of bed and tried to stand, her legs

gave out underneath her, and she crashed down onto the wood-patterned laminate flooring she'd installed the previous summer.

She was so weak. Weak and... feverish.

She wiped hot sweat from her face and gave up on trying to stand. It was hard enough just to get up onto her hands and knees. She settled for crawling to the living room, looking for her phone. Bagel followed cheerfully beside her, rubbing against her side. Alicia couldn't even find the strength to shoo the kitten away.

The phone was on the coffee table, right where she'd left it. She grabbed it and called Becca.

"Hey there, Alicia! How are you this morning?"

"Please..." Alicia's voice came out in a rasp. "Please come... over... please..."

Less than a minute later, her neighbor knocked at the door. Once. Twice. Then the woman let herself in with her spare key. When she saw Alicia on the floor, she rushed to her side. Becca's hand felt cold against Alicia's forehead.

"Oh, my dear. You are burning up! I don't need a thermometer to know you're way too warm. Let me help you onto the couch."

Alicia let herself be pulled and rolled onto the couch. Becca was a lot stronger than she looked. A moment later Alicia felt a cool washcloth pressed to her forehead.

"Thank you, Becca." Her voice came out thin and raspy, barely audible.

"I put a tumbler on the table next to you, straw and all. You need to sip on that." The older woman sounded worried. "You might need to go to the hospital. You're absolutely burning up."

"It's just a fever," Alicia whispered. "Probably from the cancer."

Becca stayed quiet for what felt like an eternity. Alicia opened her eyes to look over at her, and even that was a struggle. Had her eyelids ever felt so heavy? She found her friend sitting on the floor next to her, one hand stroking her hair, the other wiping her own tears away.

"I'm so sorry, Alicia. What... I mean... where?"

"Ovaries."

"I'm so sorry," Becca said again.

"Do me... a favor?"

"Anything, honey."

Alicia waved a tired hand at her kitten. "Get Bagel some food? Pay you later."

"Bagel, huh? Cute name. I'll go get him something right now. You just lie here and get some rest."

Alicia faded in and out of fever dreams for the rest of the day, alternating between sweating through her clothes and shivering under three blankets. At some point Becca helped her into the shower, where she sat on the tiled floor letting the water wash over her for the better part of an hour. She didn't feel any sense of embarrassment or modesty when the older woman came to help her get dressed. Those feelings had been driven away long ago during her time on the streets.

"Looks like your fever gave you a rash, dear."

Alicia looked down through bleary eyes. Sure enough, a huge, angry rash covered her entire abdomen. The placement of the redness seemed like it should mean something to her, but her mind was too exhausted to think, and she pushed the feeling away.

The next day Alicia's mind felt clearer, though that was a low bar. She could actually walk unaided now too, more or less. Becca brought over more food for Bagel, who was doing his best to eat twice his weight in tuna. The kitten already seemed to have grown, though that was probably a trick of her fever.

She managed to call to get some pho delivered from the local Vietnamese place, Pho-nominal. She'd found in the past that chicken noodle soup didn't do it for her when she was sick, but pho always did the trick. Especially with a little of her homemade chili paste.

After finishing off the leftover broth, Alicia downed a few ibuprofens and some Tylenol. Despite her improvement, she still felt like she had the world's worst flu. Every movement brought with it aches and pains. Worst of all was a ringing in her ears that just wouldn't quit. She was familiar with tinnitus —she'd fired pistols and rifles without ear protection—but this was like tinnitus on steroids. Like the ringing was mixed with a weird sort of static.

And *loud*.

In fact it was so loud that she missed the buzzing of her phone. Fortunately she saw the screen light up, and grabbed it when she saw Dr. Reynolds's number on the caller ID.

She tapped the phone to answer. "This is Alicia."

"Hey there, Alicia. This is Dr. Reynolds. We missed you at the office yesterday. I'm just calling to see if everything is all right."

"I'm so sorry, Doctor Reynolds. I came down with something. I've barely been able to stand since the night before last. I spent all day yesterday down for the count."

"I'm so sorry. Can you tell me your symptoms?"

The doctor was all business. Alicia even detected a little worry.

She took a sip of water and cleared her throat. "Uh... bad fever. Aches and pains everywhere like you wouldn't believe. Couldn't even stand up yesterday. Could barely think straight or open my eyes. Constant headaches. And now I've got this ringing in my ears that won't go away."

"Alicia, that doesn't sound good. You need to be cautious about high fevers. You should have someone take you to the hospital. Especially given all the symptoms you're describing."

Through all the pain, fever, and general feeling of garbage, anger burned to the surface, white-hot. "Cautious? Listen, I'm feeling terrible and after talking with that condescending assistant of yours, who was utterly useless, I'm at my wit's end. Can you just tell me what's going on with those damned tests?"

Alicia regretted the outburst almost instantly. She'd always had a temper. Always expected people to give their best, and hated when people cut corners. She knew yelling at the doctor wouldn't do any good. Her father's disapproving frown came to mind.

Screw it. This was her life and her test results.

Dr. Reynolds sighed. *"I understand your reaction, and I'm sorry you're feeling as sick as you are. I'd really rather do this in person, but Alicia, the tests show—"*

"Ovarian cancer? Yeah. Tell your assistant to actually hit the mute button next time he puts a person on hold."

There was a moment of silence on the line before the doctor spoke. *"I'll... I'll have a talk with him. But regardless of the poor manner in which you were given the news—"*

"Overheard."

"—the fact remains the same. The biopsy and blood work confirm that the growths we found are malignant. Cancer."

"What stage? Don't sugarcoat this, please."

"The CT scan showed the tumors aren't just on your ovaries. They've spread, and are large enough to spot through the imaging. This puts you in Stage Three."

"Less than a forty percent chance of making it five years," Alicia said. "What... what are my options?"

"Don't fixate on those numbers; there are always new treatments that improve those survival rates. That's why we wanted you to come in yesterday. To go over some of this. We need to get you started on chemotherapy treatments as soon as possible. We can have our oncologist, Dr. Sandoval, get this all set up and squared away. I suggest a consultation as soon as you're feeling up to it."

"All right. Give me a couple of days and I'll see where I'm at. Is it the cancer that's causing these symptoms right now?"

"Fever, nausea, aches and pains... all of that is pretty common. But... not at the level you're describing. And not the ringing in the ears. Then again, everybody is different."

Alicia closed her eyes and let out a long breath. "Sorry I was short with you, Dr. Reynolds. It's been a day."

"No apology needed. Just come in as soon as you can."

As Alicia hung up, Bagel crawled into her lap. The kitten was a needy little beast.

"And what do you want?" Alicia asked.

The cat gazed at her with its golden eyes. There was something mysterious in those glowing orbs. Like liquid gold, their color seemed to flow.

Liquid gold.

The dream came back, hazy at first, then clearer. Alicia pulled up her shirt, vaguely remembering the rash. There was no rash now, but a wide patch of flesh on her abdomen looked irritated, and when she put her hand on it, the skin was hot to the touch.

She looked down at Bagel. "Was that a dream? Or...?"

She couldn't even finish the thought. It was absurd.

Three days after the fever had hit her like a dump truck full of bricks, it vanished like it had never existed. And in its absence, Alicia felt... *wonderful*. No aches. No pain. Zero nausea. All the fogginess clouding her brain was swept away as if by a strong ocean wind. The world seemed brighter, more vibrant.

She sat up on the couch, planting her bare feet on the wood laminate flooring. Curling her toes, she felt the grain, and for some reason it brought a smile to her face.

"Food."

The sound of Becca's voice came from one of the BabbelPet buttons.

"Food. Food. Food. Food."

Bagel was slamming his front paws repeatedly on the button.

Alicia looked over. Sure enough, the kitten's bowl was empty. Becca had said he'd been eating a ton. He must have been severely malnourished when Alicia first found him, because in just three days he'd filled out substantially. He no longer even looked like a kitten anymore, but a full-grown cat. Maybe he'd just been in desperate need of twenty cans of tuna.

She stood, carefully, then straightened with surprise when she felt no aches at all.

Bagel hit the button again. *"Food."*

Alicia raised her eyebrows. "Jeez, you're persistent, aren't you? Well, I better not keep His Royal Bagel-ness waiting."

She walked to the kitchen, feeling a bounce in her step that had been gone for months. After popping the top from a can, she dumped the tuna into Bagel's bowl. The cat pounced on it, eating it all within seconds, then looked up at her while licking his lips.

"Well, all right... I guess I can give you another."

She popped another can into the bowl, and Bagel attacked this one at a slightly less ravenous pace.

With her cat occupied, Alicia hit the shower. While she was in there, she examined her abdomen. The redness and irritation was completely gone, and her skin was back to a normal healthy color. She was thin, though. The last three days had taken a lot out of her.

And yet now she felt good as new.

Too good.

Instead of happiness, she felt dread at the thought. This was the calm before the storm. She still had a veritable death sentence hanging over her. She needed to start treatment… now.

The minute she got out of the shower, she grabbed her phone and called Dr. Reynolds to make an appointment.

CHAPTER
THREE

General Liang Feng walked along the line of subordinates, studying them for visible signs of weakness. Weaknesses could be exploited. And if he could detect such a weakness, so could his rivals in the People's Liberation Army.

Nearly all of the men and women were scientists, personally recruited for this project. For the last three years, they'd been sequestered in an underground facility in the Heilongjiang province, hidden from satellites, drones, and prying western spies.

Three years could feel like an eternity, Feng imagined. Not that he cared. The comforts of scientists meant less than nothing to him. They either did their required jobs, or their families would be transferred to the reeducation camps in Xinjiang. Only one fool had dared challenge his mandate on secrecy. A scientist by the name of...

Feng couldn't remember the traitor's name. Not that it mattered. That scientist didn't exist anymore. And his family rotted in a camp, waiting their turn for testing.

"Good," he said to the assembled workers. "Another day to show your value to the PLA. Another day working toward our shared goal of a dominant China."

None of the men or women spoke. They knew his rules.

"General Liang. The report for this week." Shen Ping, his head scientist, bowed and handed over a red folder, then bowed again before stepping aside.

"Very good. Let us see what progress has been made."

Feng opened the folder and flipped through the reports. Most of the science was beyond him, but he couldn't let anyone see that. He nodded at the occasional graph, then pulled out the summary paper and skimmed to the bottom.

RECOMMENDATION: PROCEED WITH LIVE TESTING.

His breath caught. "So we're ready?"

"Yes, General," Shen said.

Feng let a smile spread across his wide face. He snapped the folder shut. "You all have done well. Very well. As a reward, you may all have one day to meditate and relax your minds. I'll ensure we have special rations. You have done this country proud. You have done *me* proud." He waved the folder at them. "Please, you are dismissed. Enjoy your day of rest and come back refreshed to start with the next phase of the project."

He spun on his heel and left the room, taking the long underground hallway to the elevator leading to the helipad.

Live testing. Finally. After all these years, his plan was

finally reaching its end. He would make fools of the other generals. Of the politicians.

Then all the world. They would all tremble.

CHAPTER
FOUR

Despite the short notice, Dr. Reynolds agreed to see Alicia that afternoon. The doctor met her at the office door and escorted her to an examination room where another doctor, Dr. Sandoval, was waiting.

The oncologist.

A cancer doctor.

Alicia explained how she felt, and her related worries. Anyone else would have celebrated an improvement in health, but to Alicia, these positive changes just meant the other shoe was about to drop.

The doctors went over her test results with her: her ultrasound, the bloodwork, CT scan, the biopsy.

Dr. Sandoval looked at Alicia with a curious expression. "And you're saying that the pain you were recently has abated?"

Alicia nodded. "I'd caught the flu and had a terrible time of it, but once my fever went away, so did all my other symptoms, including the pelvic pains."

"Well, let's take another look, and see what's going on."

Dr. Sandoval had her lay back, and he performed another ultrasound.

"It's a little easier for me to talk you through it live," he said.

He placed warm jelly onto the business end of a wide transducer, then pushed and pulled on her abdomen to get the best view possible. After a few minutes, a look of confusion spread across his face.

"Dr. Reynolds, can you take a look at this?"

Alicia felt a stab of worry. She'd been right to come in. Was the cancer even worse than they'd thought?

"What's going on?" she asked.

Sandoval held up a single finger and smiled. "One second, Miss Yoder."

He pointed to a blob on the screen. "Right here, Kim. Small cysts on the ovaries. But nothing like the images from the previous ultrasound." He clicked a button and spun a trackball on the ultrasound machine, then clicked again. "Barely three centimeters."

Dr. Reynolds shook her head. "That's... not possible," she said. "I don't get it."

Alicia propped herself up onto her elbows. "What's going on?" Logically she understood. Her tumors had evidently... shrunk? That was good. But the doctors looked worried. That seemed bad.

Sandoval ran a hand through his thinning gray hair and

shrugged. "Miss Yoder, your scans and bloodwork all indicate cancerous growths on your ovaries that have spread into your lymph nodes. A fairly typical diagnosis of stage three ovarian cancer. But this..." He waved at the screen shot from the ultrasound. "This tells a different story. Either your tumors were never that big to begin with, or they're shrinking at an impossible rate."

He frowned. "Before we start making proclamations, let's do some more tests. Another CA-125 blood test. Another CT. I don't want to get your hopes up here, Miss Yoder, but there's a chance that your outlook may be better than we first thought. And I don't feel comfortable scheduling chemo until we've got a better handle on your condition. Are you up for a few tests?"

Five hours later, Alicia drove home feeling lighter. They'd poked and prodded her until she grew bored with the whole thing, and the test results wouldn't be back for another two days, but she'd now decided she didn't care what the tests said. Her body felt different. Better. The exhaustion she'd felt for months was gone, leaving her with more energy than she knew what to do with. Her stomach even growled, and she realized she was legitimately hungry. If not for the light ringing in her ears, she wouldn't have had anything wrong at all.

A week ago she'd barely been able to make the hike to a camping spot in the Catskills. Days ago she couldn't even get out of bed. Now she felt like going for a run... and she hated running.

As the scenery sped by, she took it in almost as if seeing things in ways she never had before. Everything had more contrast somehow, the leaves on the trees had sharper edges, the colors were brighter and more distinct. The blue of the sky had more depth to it, more beauty. She couldn't explain it or rationalize it, but literally everything around her was brighter. The details crisper.

Maybe her mind was playing tricks on her. A second lease on life was bound to give anyone a brighter outlook.

She pulled into the drive-through of the local burger joint, the Patty Melt, and ordered a double cheeseburger with sautéed mushrooms and onions, extra fries, and a vanilla custard with peanut butter and brownie chunks mixed in. When they gave her the grease-spotted bag, Alicia knew she wouldn't be able to wait until she got home. She pulled around, parked, and tore into the food.

"Holy crap."

She closed her eyes and leaned back into the seat. Had a burger ever tasted so good? She reached blindly into the brown bag and grabbed some fries to shove in her mouth. "Dang. I'm stuffing my face just like Bagel does."

Before she had time to process how fast she was eating, the wrapper of the cheeseburger lay in her lap like a forgotten carcass. The custard disappeared just as quickly.

For the first time in months, life was good.

Two days later she was back in Dr. Reynolds's office at Georgetown University Hospital. Dr. Sandoval was once again with her, and both doctors looked baffled.

"We don't know how to explain it, Miss Yoder," Sandoval said. "The blood came back clear of the antigens we saw in your earlier sample, and your CT showed none of the growths we captured in the prior scan. Do you feel up for another ultrasound?"

"Sure, why not?"

Ten minutes later, both Reynolds and Sandoval were staring at the monitor in disbelief. "There's... nothing," Reynolds said. "Even the smaller cysts are gone."

Sandoval shook his head and rolled his chair to Alicia's side. "I don't know what to tell you, Miss Yoder. I just don't know. I've been practicing medicine for forty years, and I've witnessed a lot of weird stuff, but this may be the wildest thing I've ever seen. Simply put, we are seeing no signs of any cancer. Not in the CT, the bloodwork, not in the ultrasound. Maybe your first round of tests was the perfect storm of poorly functioning equipment and lab errors. Or maybe..." He shrugged.

"But I *was* having symptoms," Alicia said. "Exhaustion, for one. And severe pain in my pelvic area."

"Are you still having pain?" Sandoval asked.

Alicia pressed against her lower abdomen and shook her head. "No. Not at all."

Sandoval spread his hands wide in a show of defeat. "In

that case, I can only apologize for what seems to have been an egregious error on our part. Miss Yoder, you're perfectly healthy."

Alicia looked from Sandoval to Reynolds, then back again. *These people are lucky I'm not the litigious type.* "So... that's it?"

"That's it," Reynolds said. She seemed a bit annoyed, and Alicia wondered if the doctor was taking the fall for the supposed mistakes.

Sandoval held up a hand. "How about this, Miss Yoder. Over the next few months, be especially cognizant of your body and how you feel. If your pain returns, come back in and ask for me directly. Otherwise, maybe come in, say, six months from now. Deal?"

"Deal," Alicia replied.

She sat in the parking lot of the doctor's office for a half hour, staring out the windshield without really looking at anything. Finally she wiped the tears from her face, took in a deep shuddering breath, and chided herself. "Enough of that."

The last week had been a rollercoaster of emotions. She'd been told she had less than a forty percent chance of surviving the next five years. Now she'd been told all was well and good.

And it wasn't just what the doctors had told her—it was what she *felt*, too. That fever had really done a number on her, but after she recovered... the changes were extraordinary. She could see better than she had before—not just sharper, but there were more hues of color, gradients in everything from leaves to water to paint. Smells, too, were sharper and more distinct, and she found she could pick out the scents of different ingredients in foods. And her hearing had improved too. She felt more balanced, more in tune with herself.

She felt like she'd been tuned up by the world's best mechanic.

And she was now sure it wasn't just her imagining things. In fact she'd tested it. That very morning she'd gone to her local range to throw some rounds at a target with her Sig 229. Even when she'd run the target all the way to the end, she could still see the ten-ring clearly. Absurdly clearly.

She'd handled the weapon better, too. Managing the recoil had been a breeze. She pulled out her smaller, snappier 365X and found it was easier as well.

What was going on?

Then an odd thought occurred to her. Her father always seemed like he could hear better than anyone else. He had always seen things before she did, and detected scents that she'd never even caught a whiff of. Whenever she'd asked about why his senses were so sharp, he was always dismissive about it. But the words of the old man from the forest, Narmer, wormed their way into her mind.

Your father is a special man. He was given a gift. I'm sure you've noticed he's a little different than most men. Tell me, Alicia, do you want to be special?

Her phone buzzed in her pocket, making her jump. She pulled it out and looked at the caller ID. Her sister.

"Hey, Gigi, what's up?"

"Just checking in on my favorite sister."

"Then you should be visiting Paula at the farm."

Alicia and her adoptive sisters had lived with Grandma Yoder on her farm in Pennsylvania, and knowing them, most of her sisters would probably stay in that Amish community and never leave.

Gigi laughed, and the sound made Alicia smile. Even on the streets, Gigi had been the one to keep the other girls' spirits up. Her laughter was contagious. *"Hey, are you home?"*

"Just at the doctor's office, why?"

"You okay?"

"Yeah... I'm actually feeling great. You around, or something?"

"Leaving Harrisburg now. Should be rolling into DC in two or three hours. You up for some dinner? I have some cool news for you."

"Sounds good. Anywhere you want to go?"

"You pick. Dad's going to meet us. Give him a call and let him know where, 'kay? Text me the address. Hanging up. See you then."

Alicia stared down at the phone. That girl was a whirlwind.

Of the twelve girls her father had rescued and adopted—not sisters by blood, but sisters in all the ways that mattered—only Alicia, Gigi, and Samantha had left the farm. Alicia had moved to DC six months ago to be closer to the Outfit's headquarters. Gigi had set herself up in Pennsylvania, and Samantha now worked for a Department of Defense contractor down in Bethesda as an accountant.

The others... well, Alicia didn't think they would ever leave the Amish community. They'd seen enough of the world.

She dialed up her father, and he picked up on the first ring. *"Gigi call you?"*

"Yeah. Some big news, apparently."

"It better not be about that pathetic boyfriend of hers. Unless she's saying she dumped him."

Alicia laughed. "Remember when you told one of my dates, 'If you don't treat my girl with respect, I'll come visit you. If you hurt her, I'll make sure you're breathing through a straw. You *capisce?*' Oh, man. I thought he would piss his pants. Never did get a second date with that guy."

"Huh. I wouldn't have said that in front of you."

"I was listening from the hallway."

"You're sounding... better. You over whatever had you under the weather last week?"

"It's a long story, Dad. After we eat with Gigi, I need to ask you a couple of questions."

"Of course. You can talk to me about anything, you know that."

"I know. When are you hitting town?"

"Two hours. Where are we meeting?"

"Remember that barbecue food truck I took you to a few months ago after that business in China? I've been craving brisket."

"Great choice. See you there. And I swear to you, Alicia, this better not have anything to do with her boyfriend."

"I'm engaged!" Gigi flashed a diamond ring.

Seeing her father's expression, Alicia clamped her hand over her growing smile.

"Wow," her father said. "That's, uh... that's something."

"I know, right?" Gigi said, oblivious.

"To Curt?" Dad asked, obviously hoping she'd changed boyfriends in the last month.

"Of course! I'm going to be Mrs. Curt Franklin."

Alicia wrapped an arm around her sister's shoulders and gave her a squeeze. "That's great, Gigi. When's the date?"

"Valentine's Day next year. It'll be so romantic!"

Dad nodded slowly, but didn't say another word. He was saved when a young blonde wearing an apron brought out a tray filled with food and placed it in the center of their picnic table.

"Here you go. Three brisket sandwiches, some pulled pork, and St. Louis-style ribs. Mac on the side. Three bottles of Mexican Coke. The boss also threw in a couple sausages. Let me know what you think!"

With her last words, she winked at Dad, brushed a hand on his shoulder, and headed back to the food truck.

Alicia and Gigi shared a look, but her father hadn't noticed. He already had a mouthful of brisket.

"Man, I love this place," he said.

"Yeah," Alicia said with a grin her sister shared. "Smokin' Steve's is the best BBQ around. The help's not too bad either."

Dad's eyes narrowed. "What are you going on about?"

"Oh, come *on!*" Gigi laughed. "You didn't notice the waitress? She was obviously flirting with you. In front of us!"

"Me? I'm old enough to be her father. Shoot, I'm probably

older than her dad."

"But you look like you stepped out of Photoshop," Alicia said. "It's a good thing you already have someone. You're completely hopeless."

He shrugged and took another bite. Around the food, he said, "I am what I am. Now if you don't mind, less talking, more eating. Letting this food get cold would be a tragedy."

They spent the next few minutes eating in silence, enjoying every smoky mouthful. The mac and cheese had little bits of sweet pulled pork in it, and Alicia could taste the three cheeses the owner had put in the sauce: sharp cheddar, parmesan, and gouda. And the smoky flavor was done expertly, not too strong. When she took a bite of one of the ribs, the meat came right off the bone.

"Peach and..." she smacked her lips, "habanero. This might be the best sauce I've ever had on rib."

"Ain't that the truth," Gigi said. "For me, though, it's the pulled pork. The pieces with bark are perfect."

"I wonder what the owner uses," her father muttered, popping a piece of shredded pork shoulder in his mouth. "Honey? Agave?" He shrugged, then stabbed some of the brisket that had fallen from his sandwich with his fork. "But for me, it's always about brisket. Salt, pepper, and a little garlic. Nothing else. Doesn't need any frills."

"Easy, there, Dad," Alicia said. "You go any further with that brisket, and I'll have to tell Lucy."

He chuckled, then grabbed one of the sausages. "So what else is going on with you, Gigi?" He was clearly avoiding the topic of her sister's engagement.

"Well… that's the other thing I wanted to tell you two."

Alicia put down her fork. Her sister's face had suddenly taken on a guilty expression. "What did you do?"

"Do? Nothing! This is all good news. But I know you're going to freak out—"

Dad's eyes narrowed at his sometimes-flighty daughter.

"Spit it out," Alicia said.

"Well… Curt and I are going to China. Tomorrow morning."

An unnerving silence held the moment hostage until Alicia said, "China? You?" She switched to Mandarin. "Have you already forgotten what things were like the last time you were there? And you're willingly going back into that hellhole?"

"I haven't forgotten anything," Gigi replied, also speaking Mandarin. "I think about it every day."

"Where in China? Hopefully no place where you'll need to speak Cantonese. I kept telling you to improve your Cantonese, but you never listen—"

"It never mattered before! When will I use Cantonese in Pennsylvania? Why are you always such a hardass about—"

"Enough." Their father cut them off in perfectly spoken Mandarin. It wasn't so much his command as it was the tone with which it was spoken. "Gigi, Alicia is just worried about you going back there. So am I. That country is not a great place to visit right now."

"Or *ever*," Alicia said, remembering her recent mission in northern China.

Her father gave her a *knock it off* look, then turned back to Gigi. "You have a good reason, I assume?"

Gigi nodded and spoke softly in English. "I'm going there to report on the concentration camps. My YouTube channel has over twenty thousand followers now, and they want to hear the truth, not just some sanitized trash from the mainstream media. You guys both know how it is over there." She glanced at Alicia. "We were lucky that Dad got us out of a horrible situation. But how many thousands of kids are trafficked every day, and the media is too busy being shills to the politician of the week? The camps in China are one of the main sources of trafficking, and we hear almost nothing about it because news outlets and politicians are too busy getting paid to cover it all up.

"And yes, I *know* it isn't the safest place," she continued. "But Curt has a contact over there we can stay with. This contact has family members who have been disappeared into the 'reeducation camps,' and he says there's all sorts of shady stuff going on there. Torture, obviously, but he said there's rumors of other things happening too. Imagine the good I could do if I can expose some of that. CNN, NBC... none of them care. But I do."

A small smile pulled at the corners of their father's mouth. "Why am I not surprised that you, of all the girls, decided to become an activist?"

"I'm not a hair-on-fire crazy person, Dad," Gigi said. "It's just... I want to do something that I think could help people. This is the way I want to help."

Alicia gave her sister a side hug. "Sorry, sis. I just want you to be careful. And safe."

"I will be."

Dad took a swig of his Coke and cleared his throat. "Are you going to livestream from there?"

"No way, I'm not suicidal," Gigi said. "I'm just going to get the footage—interviews, B-roll, and all that—and bring it back. We're going as tourists. The information-gathering will be done on the sly."

"What airport are you leaving from?" their father asked.

"Harrisburg International. Flight leaves at two. Why?"

"Don't go through security until I get there. I have a guy who can get you a special storage device. It's got a hidden partition that can be biometrically locked and unlocked. He'll be able to key it to your fingerprint. As long as you always hide the partition when you're not using it, no one will know it's there, even if they look. So keep all the... inflammatory stuff in the hidden partition, and all the bland tourist stuff will be easy for the customs inspectors to see and review. Just in case."

"Thanks!" Gigi's eyes narrowed. "What do you mean, you 'have a guy'?"

"A friend. Don't worry about it. Just wait for me."

"Twenty thousand followers," Alicia said, steering the topic away from Dad's clandestine resources, which she had an inkling about. "I hadn't realized your channel had taken off. That's awesome."

"Curt's degree is in marketing and media relations. He's pretty good at it all. I'm just the pretty face with a lot of passion." Gigi winked and took a bite of pork. "Don't worry. I won't forget you guys when I'm famous."

Gigi drove away, leaving Alicia alone with their father. The sun had gone down, and the fall chill had begun to seep through Alicia's light hoodie. But she didn't mind. It felt good, and the smell of the smoker attached to the back of Smokin' Steve's food truck filled the air. Oak. It was weird how she could tell from the smell.

"So what did you want to talk about?"

"Dad, don't freak out."

He frowned. "Nothing good has ever come after those words."

Alicia forced a smile. "Dad... I was pretty sick when we went to the Catskills."

"I know."

"No, you don't. I'd been pretty sick for a couple months before that. I didn't tell you about it. It was...bad. I went to the doctor and got checked out right before we left. The test results were waiting for me when I got home."

"Results?" He barely breathed the word, a furrow between his brows.

"They diagnosed me with stage three ovarian cancer." Alicia held up a hand to ward off a response. "Don't worry. I don't have cancer. Dad, I got better. In, like, five days. Completely better."

Her father pressed his hands to his temples, then clasped them behind his neck. He stood, walked off a few steps, then came back. His expression was unreadable. "Cancer doesn't just go away, Alicia. Was there some mistake in your diagnosis?"

Alicia nodded. "That's what the docs are saying, with a lot

of wringing of hands and backpedaling. But I saw the test results. CT scans confirmed my lymph nodes had also been affected. The ultrasound showed big tumors on my ovaries. My bloodwork also came back positive. Dad, they even did a biopsy. There's no way *all* of those tests were goofed up. And then when I got home, I got really sick. Like, *I'm going to die* type of sick. Crazy fever, massive aches—"

"Hold up." His expression was troubled. "This all happened right after our trip?"

Alicia nodded.

Her father's jaw tightened, his eyes reflecting the nearby streetlights, giving them a preternatural glow. For a second, his handsome face took on a murderous expression, one that she'd never seen before. "Alicia, this is important. Did you see anyone else in those woods?"

Alicia nodded. A wave of guilt washed over her. She should have told her father that she'd met Narmer. She should have told him right away.

"An old man," she said.

"Narmer?"

She nodded again.

Her father muttered a stream of profanity. "Tell me everything he said to you."

Alicia recounted her meeting with Narmer from start to finish, as well as she could remember.

"He asked me if I wanted to be special, Dad. I don't remember *exactly* what he said, which is weird since my memory is really good recently. It's strange. I can easily visualize everything I've encountered lately."

"*Special*. He said that?" Her father frowned. "Tell me more about that fever."

"It was terrible. It happened the day after I came back from the woods with you. It was like the worst flu I've ever felt. I could barely even open my eyes."

Her father put his right hand on her shoulder, and his tone was serious. "Did he give you anything?"

The question startled her. "No. I don't think so. Why?"

"He didn't give you anything at all? Maybe like a necklace, or an old Egyptian symbol. An ankh?"

Alicia tried to figure out where he was going with this. "No, nothing like that. I don't think... wait! When he left, I tried to follow him into the woods. That's when I found the kitten. I named him Bagel, by the way."

"That damned cat." Her father clenched his fists, and she heard his knuckles pop. "I should have known that old bastard was going to do something like this. Those golden eyes on that kitten were the clue."

"Golden eyes..." Alicia hesitated. "Dad, I had a dream about Bagel. I dreamt that he puked up some gold-colored liquid on me. On my abdomen, right where the tumors were supposed to be. The next day I had the fever, and a rash right in that spot. Does that mean something to you? Dad, what's going on?"

His head tilted a little to the right as he looked at her, and she could practically see the wheels turning in his head. "You and I need to talk." He motioned for her to follow him. "In the car. We're heading for Albany right now. You'll tell me the rest of your story, and I'll tell you mine. Then we'll get some answers from Narmer himself."

CHAPTER
FIVE

Levi finished his story on the way. He told Alicia about his dead wife, the ankh that had triggered a horrendous fever, his walk-about, and the way he felt afterward. It all seemed like a lifetime ago.

To anyone else but his daughter, he would have sounded insane. And to anyone but him, his daughter's story would have sounded just as crazy. But he didn't doubt her, not for a second. All the things that she was experiencing—the fever, the enhanced senses, the memory changes—they were identical to the process he'd gone through years ago.

And the truth was, he could tell just by looking at her. He'd noticed a change within his daughter the moment he'd met her by the food truck. The pale shell of the girl he'd taken hiking just a short while ago had vanished, and his Alicia was back. She looked vibrant, her complexion full of life and energy. And when he'd given her a quick hug, he'd sensed something else—almost like... like a warmth flowing from her.

Perhaps he shouldn't have been surprised. Him meeting Narmer, and then her finding that stray cat at almost the same time. He should have put two and two together. Cats were a big thing in ancient Egypt. Narmer had planted it. He'd used it to infect Alicia with the same curse that Levi was living with.

He thought back to the time, years ago, when he triggered his own transformation. When he first found the ankh...

Levi lifted the ankh out of its box, and almost dropped it. It had an unexpected greasy feel to it that made it hard to hold on to. He tightened his grip. It became oddly warm to the touch.

The world seemed to slow as Levi's neck and face flushed with heat. His heart began pounding. A burning sensation crawled up his arm, and he felt a searing pain in his hand. It was as if the thing was attempting to burn through his palm.

It suddenly dawned on Levi: drop the stupid thing.

His hand unclenched, and the heavy object dropped onto the wooden table with a loud thud.

Levi's chest was tight, and he struggled to pull in a deep breath. He winced at the throbbing pain climbing up his arm and spreading across his chest and the rest of his body. There was no blistering yet on the palm of his hand, but he knew it would soon follow. The flesh there was red and angry with whatever it was that the ankh had slathered on it.

Levi began to sweat as he wiped his hand with a handkerchief...

· · ·

Soon after that, he'd succumbed to a fever that he was sure would kill him.

But it didn't.

It left him revitalized. He was a new person. His cancer in remission. But his wife still dead.

He'd tried to figure out what had happened to him. To understand it. He'd hired the world's leading researcher to examine his blood. The results only led to more questions. Questions he didn't want the answers to.

Roaming through his body were millions of tiny things that must have come from that golden dust that his skin had absorbed from the ankh. The very idea of it made him turn away and never look back. He didn't want to think about these microscopic things coursing through his body.

Nanites were someone else's problem...

And now, they actually _were_ someone else's problem. His daughter's.

The more he thought about it, the more convinced he was that the cat had done to her exactly what the ankh had done to him.

Conflicted didn't begin to describe how Levi felt. That Narmer would do this to his daughter... it was a gross violation of trust. And yet, the old man's actions _had_ cured Alicia's cancer...

Levi pulled his car to a stop in front of the address Narmer had provided him in the Catskills: the Park Manor Hotel in Clifton Park. The building was painted in that hotel gray that was supposed to stand up to time and the elements, but really only made it look cheap and rundown. He didn't need to look at the scrap of paper again. His memory was clear, and he could see the old man's flowing handwriting, as much artwork as it was the simple presentation of information.

"Room 202," he said. "I imagine he's expecting us."

"Is he dangerous?" Alicia asked as she unbuckled her seatbelt.

"Everyone is dangerous given the right situation."

"That's not what I asked."

"I know."

Levi pushed his door open and felt for the knives under his loose polo. He wasn't expecting trouble, but then again, that was precisely when trouble could show.

"Keep your eyes open," he said. "Take this seriously. Like it's a mission from the Outfit."

"Understood."

They headed inside. The lobby was clean enough to make up for the rain-stained outer stucco. A quick elevator ride took them to the second floor, and they walked down the hall to room 202. Levi knocked on the door and leaned in to try and hear movement. The *shuffle-thump* of Narmer's pegleg coming from inside confirmed it was the right room.

The lock disengaged, and the door cracked open.

"Come inside," said Narmer. "I'll let you get the door."

Levi pushed the door open the rest of the way and walked inside first. He took a quick look inside the bathroom on the right, clearing it, then did the same to the closet on the left. The room was clean, if ugly. The pattern of interlocking ovals on the carpet clashed with the rigidly ordered ovals on the wallpaper.

Narmer wore the same ragged clothing he'd had on in the

forest. He waved to three chairs he'd set up; yes, he'd been expecting them. Both of them.

"Have a seat," the old man said. "Forgive me for not offering tea. I'm afraid I don't quite have the energy these days."

The three of them sat. "We're here to..." Levi paused as he struggled with his surging anger. He took a deep breath and let it out slowly. "I know what you did to Alicia."

"I didn't do anything," Narmer said with a tired expression. "I sensed an issue with the one you cared for and offered an opportunity." He nodded at Alicia. "And she took it."

Levi opened his mouth, but Narmer silenced him with a cutting wave of his hand.

"In truth, I only went out there for you, Mr. Yoder. But as always, you rejected what fate has placed in your lap. It truly is more gift than curse. But your daughter was in need, and I can sense that my gift has benefited her." His good eye flicked to Alicia. "Tell me, young lady. Do you find your situation... improved?"

"You know it is. Was it Bagel's doing?"

"Bagel?"

"The cat. The cat you left for me to find, right? Did he cure me?"

"I suppose I may have had a hand in your meeting of... Bagel. An interesting name." Narmer smiled. "As to whether the cat cured you... yes and no. He was just a delivery mechanism. In my time, cats were seen as guardians of a sort. I rather think the one you now call Bagel makes a good match for you.

Keep him close. He will be with you throughout your days. Treat him well, and he will certainly do the same for you."

"Why did you come back into my life?" Levi asked. The question came out more harshly than he'd intended, but something about the old man put him on edge.

Narmer pursed his lips. "Would you rather I let the sickness eat her from the inside out? That's no way to live or die. You know the truth in my words. You especially."

Levi said nothing. But he knew.

The old man folded his hands in his lap. "I'm dying. Finally. It has been a long time coming. All I wish for now is to see my gift and blessing passed on to someone who will accept it and do good with it. Nothing is done on a whim or without purpose. Fate drives all actions, and this is something I truly believe. This gift has fated us to actions that are today unknowable, but enables us to act in the distant future, hopefully for the good of humanity. And it is my final wish to bestow a blessing upon that person who I pass the torch to. Much like the Olympic torch is passed from one runner to the next, I would like to hand off this responsibility to another."

He turned to Alicia. "Young lady, I'd hoped to pass this blessing to your father, but... he doesn't believe I am who I say I am. He thinks my words are exaggerated superstition. And I won't force it on him. But let me tell you a few things that you must understand."

He reached to the nightstand and took hold of a water bottle in a shaking hand. After a sip, he continued.

"I wish I had years to teach you. There is so much for you to learn, and so little of my time remaining. I hardly know where to start anymore."

"Hold on," Levi growled. "I don't—"

"Dad, I want to hear what he has to say." Alicia looked at him with a pleading expression.

Levi closed his eyes, breathed in deeply, and slowly let out his breath. "You're old enough to make your own decisions. I trust you won't make a foolish one."

"The basics," Alicia said to Narmer. "Please start with the basics."

Levi looked at Alicia and felt a surge of pride. Most people in her situation would have fallen apart. She was calm and even accepting of the adversity she'd faced, and now, with Narmer, she showed a strength of curiosity that he'd never possessed. She was in a different place in life than he was in when he'd first met Narmer. He'd met the man after suffering the loss of his wife. Alicia still had her youth and enthusiasm; she wasn't bitter and jaded by life. He still wanted to interrupt and tell her not to listen to the old coot, but it wasn't his place to do so. This was her life. Her story to live.

"Some of what I'm going to tell you may seem fanciful," the old man began. "And though, as I said, your father claims not to believe me, I suspect that deep down he knows the truth of my words.

"I was born over five thousand years ago in what is now known as Egypt. The same gift that has kept me alive for so long now keeps you alive. And your father. Coursing through your veins is a magic of sorts. I'm not one who can explain such things, but if you wish, I can connect you with people who can. What I *can* tell you is what the magic *does*. You will find that you are now immune to illness. As you have seen, even the poison called cancer cannot hold sway over you. The magic in your blood—"

Levi interrupted. "He means nanites. Not magic. That's what covered the ankh, and it's what was in whatever the cat puked up on you."

"Nanites?" Alicia said. "Like, tiny microscopic robots?"

Levi shrugged. "That's what the scientists explained to me when I asked them to study my blood."

Narmer cleared his throat. "As I was saying, this *magic*"— he gave Levi a sour look—"will heal all things that ail you. Moreover, you will find that your lifespan is extended far beyond normal human expectations."

"How long?" Alicia asked, her eyes wide with curiosity.

"I'm unsure what the limits might be, but I'm one example of what such magic can do. Yet even so, the magic has its limits." He pointed at his half-leg and his missing eye. "You are not impervious to violent harm. It can maim you, and it can kill you. You are simply more resistant than most."

Alicia turned to her father. "I've always said you look really young for being almost fifty."

Levi shrugged. "Now you know why. But it's not some hocus-pocus like Narmer would have you believe."

"It's nanites," Alicia said. "But how does that even work?"

"I don't know. The scientists found them and were puzzled by them. I didn't ask them to continue to research it. I didn't particularly care to learn more."

Narmer shook his head. "Such a loss that you lack the interest—"

"It's not a lack of interest, old man," Levi said. "What's in me is there, and there's nothing I can do about it. I don't see the point in dwelling on it. I have far better things to do than navel-gaze about how special I am."

Narmer shrugged. "As you will." He shifted his gaze back to Alicia. "*You* seem interested in learning, however. I suggest you visit a colleague of mine. Here." He handed Alicia a neatly folded piece of paper made from the same thick, textured papyrus as the note he'd handed Levi back in the woods. "Go see him when you get a moment. He'll be able to explain things better than I can. Then you might truly understand what has happened to you."

Alicia hesitated. "Why?" she asked.

Narmer smiled at Alicia like he was her doting grandfather. "Why you, you mean?"

"Yes."

"Do you remember what you said to me in the forest? About being special?"

Alicia shook her head.

"You said, 'Not unless being special means I can help more people.'" Narmer grinned. "That told me much about you as a person. You want to do good. But good is not something that happens overnight. Not long-term good, I mean. It happens over time. Sometimes a very long time." He glanced at Levi. "Little victories over years that slowly turn the tide and make our world a better place. Oh, there will be opportunities, moments, when you can make a large difference in the world.

But to make a true, lasting impact, it will take a lifetime—maybe even many lifetimes."

"What are you getting at, Narmer?" Levi asked.

The old man ignored the question. "Do you truly want to help this world, Alicia?"

"Yes."

"Very well. This world will need you, years from now. Lean in a little for an old man, please, so I may give you my blessing."

Alicia hesitated. "What are you going to do?"

"A simple touch on the forehead." His voice sounded weaker. Like a stiff breeze would carry it away into whatever afterlife the man believed in. "Please."

Alicia leaned closer and closed her eyes. Levi leaned in as well to get a better look. Narmer extended a wavering hand. He held it an inch from her forehead, closed his eyes, and took a calming breath. Then his hand steadied, and when he touched Alicia's forehead, Levi saw a brief glint of golden light.

The old man withdrew his hand. "There. All done."

Alicia opened her eyes. "That's it? Is there a mark on me now?"

Narmer's sudden laugh caught Levi by surprise. "Nothing like that. A simple blessing is all. Use it well, Alicia Yoder." He turned to Levi. "I know you choose not to believe me, Levi. But one day you will."

Then he broke into a fit of coughing that sounded like his lungs would tear in half.

Alicia grabbed the water bottle and held it out to him. "I thought you said you never got sick."

"Misspent youth," Narmer said with a weak grin. "I'm

afraid I've caused too much trauma to this vessel over many years."

"Are you really thousands of years old?" Alicia asked, almost in a whisper.

"I have not intentionally deceived you in anything I've said." Narmer pushed the water away and took Alicia's free hand in between his own. "I am sorry, Alicia. I had hoped to carry this mantle to... well... I suppose it matters little. Go do your good in this world." Then he winked and tilted his head in Levi's direction. "And see if you can drag the unbeliever with you."

Midnight came and went, but Alicia couldn't sleep. She lay in bed, staring up at the ceiling while absently stroking Bagel's head.

Their drive back to DC had passed in silence as she tried reconciling Narmer's claims with what she knew of science. Her dad had said that tests revealed he had nanites in his blood. And from what she knew, nanites were a real technology. They weren't anywhere near being ready for real-world applications, she didn't think, but they were a real thing. At least in labs.

So... it was possible.

Theoretically, if these nanites could truly fix anything in her body that needed repairing, the aging process would effectively halt. And there was proof of that. Her dad. Not a gray hair on his head or a wrinkle on his face. He was fifty, but looked thirty.

Narmer's words about the world needing her, on the other hand, seemed like blatant mysticism.

She had the address of the old man's colleague committed to memory. The guy was just outside of DC. Alicia wanted to go immediately, but tomorrow she had a final interview and psych eval with the Outfit, and she wanted to make sure she passed. At least she thought she did.

When she'd first been recruited out of Princeton to join the Outfit, she'd been ecstatic. Apparently they'd been wanting her dad as a full-time asset for quite some time already, but something had held him back, and he'd only served as an occasional contractor. As was often the case, he was tight-lipped about why he'd made the choices he'd made. But for Alicia, full-time sounded awesome.

Until now. Now she wasn't so sure.

The strange, almost romantic notions of becoming a private investigator were stronger than ever. Especially after seeing the Outfit's Machiavellian scheming during the mess between China and Taiwan a couple of months earlier. For them to callously manipulate one of their own agents... it had planted a seed of doubt in her mind. She wondered how Agent Xiang was doing. And where he was. He'd promised to be in touch.

That was another thing about the Outfit. Its agents were dispersed across the globe, with only occasional stops back at headquarters for debriefing. Did she want that kind of life?

Her bedside clock read 2:05 a.m. in red, glowing numbers. She rolled onto her side so the clock would stop taunting her.

Bagel stood, stretched, then moved in closer and curled up near her chin. The cat seemed larger than ever. If he had the same nanites in his system, did that mean he would live longer as well? She hoped so. Everyone should want their pets to live forever.

A siren wailed somewhere outside, a far too common occurrence in DC. A small smile briefly crossed Alicia's face as she entertained the idea of going out and solving crimes like some sort of superhero. But the notion passed quickly. On the ride home, one of the few things her father had said was to warn her that although she'd heal faster, hear and see better, and have slightly better reflexes, physics still won out in the end.

"You're a buck forty. A guy weighing two hundred plus will throw you around like a rag doll, especially if he's trained. Remember what happened when I had you spar with Tony." Then he'd pointed two fingers at her head. *"And Narmer's gift won't help you if you take a bullet to the face."*

Extraordinary strength would have been useful, she thought. You can't have everything.

Bagel poked his head up, his glowing eyes staring at her. Then he nuzzled her cheek and laid back down. His purrs eventually lulled her to sleep.

CHAPTER

SIX

Doug Mason looked up at the knock on his office door. Lara Torres poked her head in. "Sir? Are you ready for me?"

"Get in here, Torres." Mason waved the analyst in and pointed at the seat across his desk. Torres was a junior analyst, but despite being only twenty-five, she'd taken to her job like a fish to water. With time and experience, he had a feeling one day she'd be supervising much of the Outfit's intelligence gathering for one of the foreign sectors.

He drummed his fingers on his desk, trying to will the answers he sought into existence. Torres had sent him a bunch of data, including hundreds of transcribed phone calls and emails coming out of China, but the intel package seemed like a jumble of random documents to his overworked mind.

"Torres, I know you were here late getting this compiled for me... but I confess I'm having trouble following what you're getting at here in this stack of data."

Torres gathered her dark, shoulder-length hair into a ponytail and secured it with a purple scrunchie. "I'm sorry I didn't have a chance to organize it into a formal report, sir. I've just got a bad feeling about what we're seeing. Call it the Spidey sense in me."

She leaned an elbow on the chair's armrest. She looked as exhausted as Mason felt.

Mason frowned. If Torres thought something felt off, he believed her. She had an uncanny knack for piecing together seemingly unrelated clues and finding needles in giant data haystacks. It was why he'd poached her from the CIA.

"Walk me through it." he pulled up the only document that made sense to him and projected it onto the eighty-five-inch touchscreen TV hanging on the wall. "I've looked at everything you sent, but walk me through it as if I have no background on this. No assumptions."

Sometimes just hearing the information presented triggered connections and understanding in a way that reading a document couldn't.

"No assumptions. No problem." Torres smiled. This wasn't the first time they'd had this dance. She pointed at the screen. "A little context then. A few months ago, a bunch of *mierda* hit the fan in China." Torres had come over from the CIA with language that might embarrass a sailor. Mason had suggested that she tone it down in the workplace, and her form of toning it down was replacing the English swear words with the Spanish equivalents. "One of General Hong Zuocheng's goons exfiltrated secrets from Taiwan, and soon afterward, the general was deeply involved in what looked like the beginnings of a revolution within the upper echelons of the Chinese government. That's when you threw me to the wolves."

"Thrown to the wolves?" Mason said with a grin. "That's not how I remember it."

She shrugged. "You put me on a so-called task force to keep an eye on China. And while everyone else in the group was busy tracking Chinese nuclear weapons data, along with the spies being sent to the US to sex up our politicians, I was keeping an ear to the ground.

"Hong is dead now, taken out by one of our guys, but that doesn't mean his influence just vanished. I flagged any chatter with his name and got a hit a couple of weeks ago." She nodded at the image projected on the wall. "This was the first domino for me."

"And here I was hoping Hong's rogue faction died with him." Mason let out a sigh. "We've got fires all over the place."

"Anything interesting?" Torres asked.

"Most of it I can't talk about, but there's some cartel activity south of the border around Sonora and Chihuahua that has ICE losing their minds. If I recall, that part of the world is your family's old stomping grounds."

"Sonora? Say the word, *jefe*, and I'm there. I'm from Guaymas."

Mason raised an eyebrow. "Don't even try. You're just trying to get off of the China oversight task force." With a click on his mouse, he pulled up the second page of data on the wall screen. "Go on. What are we looking at here?"

Torres let out a dramatic sigh, then pulled out her tablet. "I've left it in Chinese for you, since you asked."

"Languages are full of nuance in their native form, and translation software tends to miss that."

"I'm not arguing. Give me a second, though. Regardless of nuance, *I* need the translation."

Mason rubbed his eyes and waited for her to pull up her own copy of the data. When he started his career, there weren't automatic translation services, so he'd made a point of mastering a variety of languages, and doing so had saved him uncounted hours waiting for translators to convert intercepted transmissions into English. Spanish, Portuguese, Russian, and Chinese were all part of his repertoire.

"You'd do yourself a favor if you picked up a few additional languages," he said. "Chinese in particular."

"Maybe if I were in the field. But as I can get translations in any of seventy-plus languages in seconds, I don't see the point otherwise." She looked up from her tablet and smiled. "And if I have questions on *nuance*, I can ask someone like you."

Mason harrumphed. "Just tell me what I'm supposed to take away from all this. I'm guessing the paragraph that got your attention is this one, right?" He highlighted it on the screen:

With the unfortunate death of General Hong Zuocheng, a void in special operations leadership has left the PLA without needed guidance. This letter is to serve as official authorization for the promotion of his subordinate, Liang Feng, to the rank of general. He is respected by the troops in his command, and will lead them well.

"That's the one," Torres said. "By itself, it's pretty straightforward. But the language is interesting, right? Nothing in it suggests the higher-ups in the PLA or the government knew Hong was staging a coup. He was using the pretense of war with Taiwan to push his policies in place and to have his rivals disappeared. You'd think if they knew, this letter—this *internal* letter—would have been a lot more condemning. Instead, they're acting like Hong was a *pinche* hero."

"What about this Liang Feng. Who is he?"

"Nobody remarkable that I can tell. Worked with General Hong for years, going from one minor assignment to the next. Nothing to suggest him as Hong's logical replacement. I included a few pictures of him in the package. He may or may not be important. But this next part is where things get really interesting."

"I'm all ears."

Torres swiped on her tablet. "Pull up documents two through ten."

Mason projected the requested pages. They looked like fairly standard requests to and from various elements in the Chinese political system.

Torres stood and walked to the screen. "These are logistical requests from years ago. The first four are troop movement requests to the Heilongjiang province. Not super surprising since that's up by Russia and North Korea. The remaining documents are requests for a contingent of scientists. All are separate requests from Hong, all hitting different desks for approval."

"You're saying he was trying to keep the requests off the radar."

"Yep. And the funny thing about all these soldiers and

scientists is that there's no record of a final destination. They get into Heilongjiang, and it's like they don't exist anymore."

"Their destination is probably a black site. Something off the record."

"Evidently."

Mason frowned. "Why is a general in the People's Liberation Army recruiting scientists and shoving them into some godforsaken black site in Northern China?"

Torres shrugged. "I don't know, sir. I haven't been able to track down what purpose those scientists have in Hong's schemes."

Scanning the documents, Mason shook his head. "These requests aren't even recent. For all we know, the black site has already disbanded and the scientists have gone back—"

"The site is active," Torres interjected with a knowing grin. "And so are the scientists."

Mason cocked an eyebrow. "Spill it."

"You *did* authorize me to use whatever means at our disposal to gather data." The analyst looked almost sheepish. "I got some of our in-country folks to do some dumpster diving outside General Liang's personal residence."

Mason maintained a neutral expression, but he'd done some dumpster diving himself when looking for intel.

"I sent you a PDF scan of the receipts," Torres said. "Did you look at that?"

"I did, but..." Mason pulled it up and stared at it again. "What's this supposed to show me?"

"These are UnionPay receipts," Torres said, "which isn't on

the same network as Visa and Mastercard, so I got Brice's help on getting a backdoor into the Chinese banking database."

Brice was head of research—the Outfit's version of Q from the James Bond movies. A computer expert, inventor, and one of Mason's best hires out of the private sector.

"When he finally got me into the database, that's when stuff got exciting," Torres continued. She leaned forward, her eyes widening and her Spanish accent thickening as she spit out her report in a rapid-fire barrage. "All these receipts are from stores and tea shops outside a tiny airfield outside Beijing. I put together a script that could operate through the portal Brice opened into the Chinese database, and from that I was able to cross-reference Liang's UnionPay receipts to a bunch of other expenses. One of those expenses was for the general's cell phone account, and that gave me enough to track down the general's cell phone tracking data. With his cell phone data, I had the equivalent of GPS locations for our general nearly every thirty minutes.

"I then noted that after our illustrious general stopped at a tea shop near a military base, his cell phone stopped talking with the cell tower for almost four hours before coming back on the radar. Unfortunately, we don't have camera access in the vicinity of the military base, but he must have taken a military transport from there, because after those four hours of silence, he reappeared eight hundred miles away. Want to guess the new general's travel destination of choice?"

"The Heilongjiang province?"

Torres nodded. "The same place where the scientists and

soldiers were moved three years ago. You know... where they all vanish."

"You're smiling," Mason said. "I take it there's more?"

She nodded. "There's more. As I've noted, the general seems to have this thing for tea shops. So I did a lookup for any other credit cards used in purchases in the same shop within five minutes before or after the general made his own purchase. Of course I got hundreds of hits, but two of the credit card numbers showed up across more than half a dozen transactions."

"Meaning you've found two other people who are likely with the general."

"Exactly. One of the cards belongs to a high-level staffer in the PLA, which makes sense. A general having tea with one of his officers. But the other name on the card isn't even a member of the military. He's a professor out of Zhejiang University, one of China's top universities. And..." She grinned. "He happened to go on a leave of absence about three years ago."

Mason's eyes widened. "What was this professor's specialty?"

"It's not something I'd have expected. He's a specialist in botany and plant pathology."

"That *is* unexpected." Mason sat back in his chair and frowned. "Anything else?"

"A bit, but it's all pretty sketchy. Rumors, unsubstantiated."

Mason made a rolling motion with his hand. "What have you got?"

"Well, as you know, the Utah Data Center monitors just

about all incoming and outgoing calls from the continental US, but only recently have we managed to capture a good percentage of phone traffic out of mainland China. We're talking about mostly ground-level civilian conversations, but still, key words will pop up in the heat map. If I isolate the analysis only to the region of Heilongjiang, we pick up talk of prisoners. Zeroing in, it seems there are rumors of prisoners being shipped in from the concentration camps in Xinjiang. People being disappeared."

"Xinjiang? That's in the northwest part of China... isn't that where the Uyghurs are?"

"Yes. Though to be clear I have no confirmation about any of them being moved. Still, why would people in the northeast be talking about folks they probably never heard of who live thousands of miles away? I need to do more data-gathering."

Mason minimized all the documents, getting them out of his view, and leaned back in his chair. "All right. I like the direction you're heading in. I'll send word to the task force leader and tell him to give you free rein on following this line of investigation."

"Pursuing it might be expensive, sir. Not only in dollars, but also in risk. I'm not sure—"

Mason cut her off. "I like both your tenacity *and* your caution. Don't let one get the better of the other. You have really good instincts, so follow them. Who knows, maybe someday you'll be another Jack Ryan."

"Who?"

Mason groaned. "You youngsters are killing me. Go read some Tom Clancy. Point is, I need you to run this to ground.

Doesn't matter to me if nothing comes of it. Frankly, if you come to me in a week and say, 'Hey it's all good,' I'll be thrilled. But I don't think that's going to happen. I'm never that lucky. Were you here all night?"

"Yeah."

"Then first thing I want you to do is get out of here and get some sleep. Then you can come back and hit this with fresh eyes."

"Of course. See you tomorrow then, boss-man." Torres rose from her seat, but at the door she paused. "Are you going to send an agent over there?"

"Depends on what you turn up."

She nodded and left the room with a wave.

When she was gone, Mason pressed his thumb against the biometric sensor on the top drawer of his desk, disengaging the lock. He pulled a blue folder from inside, unlabeled and with no distinguishing marks. On top was a stack of documents all pertaining to Alicia Yoder. Psych evaluation reports. Travel records. Her final security clearance adjudication. All of it was in order. Nothing concerning.

Beneath that were reports from Lucy Chen and Agent Chris Xiang regarding Alicia's performance in China months earlier. Both gave glowing recommendations, but he'd expected as much. He'd been paying particularly careful attention to Alicia's progress. What she'd accomplished in that Taiwan-China mission was much more than could have been reasonably expected of someone with her experience. She was very much her father's child, even though she'd been adopted.

She'd worked well with others. Excelled under stress. She

still had much to learn in terms of finesse... but her father had been right. She'd needed the real-world training to get her on the path to being the asset Mason knew she could be.

He then flipped through her recent medical reports. Ones that she hadn't informed him of. These... were a concern. In fact, they made none of the previous documentation worth a damn.

His hopes for her had been high. Higher than for any of the other new recruits.

But cancer... At the end of the day, that was the only thing that mattered.

Stage three ovarian cancer.

Of course, he couldn't tell her he knew about it. People tended to get upset when they found out their medical records weren't as protected as the doctors and lawyers said. HIPAA meant exactly nothing to the Outfit.

But today, right now in fact, she was doing her monthly physical exam within the Outfit. The last two hadn't gone well. This one would go even worse. It would confirm, officially, what he already knew unofficially. And in a few hours he'd have to give her the bad news.

He tapped a key on his keyboard and brought up the video feed of her physical exam. She was on the treadmill. According to the timer, she'd been on it for twenty minutes. Mason frowned. She didn't seem to be faltering or slowing down. Not like last month.

He continued to watch. After another few minutes, the treadmill tilted to a much steeper angle. This was supposed to wind the agent and push their stats to their limits. But Alicia kept going. He checked her heartbeat and oxygen monitors. They were both well within their normal ranges.

Alicia was cruising through this test.

Mason flipped back to the prior month's exam results just to be sure, then looked at the video feed once more.

What the hell was going on?

CHAPTER

SEVEN

In all her years, Alicia had never enjoyed running. She didn't understand the supposed zen people felt. All she'd ever heard from those sorts of people was how clear their minds were while their feet pounded the pavement. Not Alicia. Running brought back bad memories, and her mind fixated on them step after step.

Today was different.

She felt *light*. Each step felt firm and sure. Even with the annoying sensors stuck all over her body to measure her muscle movements, heart, and lungs, she'd never felt so comfortable while running. So free.

Alicia caught a frown on the face of the lab-coat-wearing man overseeing her test.

"I'm going to increase the speed and angle on the treadmill in three... two... one."

Alicia felt the change, and adjusted her pace with ease. It all felt natural. Despite the oxygen mask, she grinned.

After a minute or so the man announced, "We're going into the final leg of your test in three... two... one."

Alicia again picked up her pace to keep up with the treadmill, and with each stride, she felt an exuberance she'd never before gotten from running. It was almost like she was getting high. Was this the "runner's high" she'd always heard of, but never experienced?

Before she knew it, the test was over and the treadmill slowed gradually before eventually coming to a complete stop. Alicia stepped off the machine and waited patiently as the lab tech pulled all the sensor tabs off of her. Breathing hard, she handed him the mask and bent over with her hands on her knees.

She was sweating like a cow, but unlike in her last session, she didn't feel like puking... in fact, she still felt exhilarated.

"How'd I do?"

"Seriously?" The lab tech was an older man with white hair and horn-rimmed glasses. He pointed at a bank of monitors, each one showing graphs and numbers. "Whatever you've been doing, keep it up." He flipped through her chart and shook his head. "You blew last month's tests out of the water. If I didn't know better, I'd say you were sandbagging us." He gave her a wink.

Alicia laughed nervously and shook her head. She couldn't give an explanation that would make sense to him or anyone else—anyone but Narmer and her father. "Nah," she said, "just been putting in extra work on my own lately."

"I'll say. Good job. Now if you'll follow me, we'll get you going on the next segment."

"What? There's more?"

The man pointed at a door at the back of the room. "Through there, if you will. And hurry, this entire sequence is timed."

Alicia walked through the door and into a long room that looked like a three-lane indoor pistol range. The tech pointed her to the far right and barked out instructions as he donned hearing protection.

"Let's go, Miss Yoder. Station A, put your ears and eyes on. The clock is running."

Alicia rushed over to the right lane and put on her hearing protection and safety glasses.

"Now grab the gun belt and put it on." The tech's voice came loudly over the speakers in the room so she could hear him even with the ear pro.

She snatched the gun belt from a hook on the wall and wrapped it around her waist; it seemed to have been sized for her already. She drew the Glock from its holster, checked the round indicators on the magazine, verified it had fifteen rounds, pushed the mag into place, and racked the slide before holstering the pistol.

"The AR-15 at your station has a magazine loaded with ten rounds. You have five targets. Put two into each, center mass. The range is hot."

With her hands still shaking from the sprint and feeling the thud of her heart racing, Alicia dried her hands on the bottom of her shirt.

A *beep* sounded almost as if a shot timer was being held up to her head.

Alicia grabbed the AR, and the world seemed to slow for her as she replayed the deadly ritual she'd done so frequently that she'd committed it to muscle memory. Slamming the magazine home, she pulled the charging handle, flicked off the safety, and opened fire.

She dropped one shot between the third and fourth targets as she rushed, but she didn't pause. The entire first station took six seconds, and she knew it could have been faster the moment she set the rifle back down on the table.

"Station B, center lane. Six slugs, two to each of three targets."

Alicia raced to the next lane and grabbed the shotgun, which she recognized as a pump-action. Without even thinking, she held the action release button, pumped the slide to load a shell, and aimed downrange at the three silhouettes. It took her only three seconds to clear the shotgun targets, with zero dropped shots.

"Station C, left lane. Five targets. Mozambique drill on each. Two to the body, one to the head."

Alicia moved to the next station and drew the Glock from the retention holster. She missed the headshot on the first target and knew that she was rushing her shots, to the detriment of accuracy. Still, she couldn't get out of her mind that the clock was ticking.

She slowed just a bit on the second and third targets, this time making all her shots. On the fourth she wished she had a red dot mounted on the pistol like she did on her 229, and again she missed the headshot. The last target went perfectly as she rode the recoil from the second body shot up to the head.

The slide locked back, and another loud *beep* echoed across the shooting range.

"Hold your shots, the range is going cold."

With her heart thudding loudly and feeling almost as winded as she had been on the treadmill, Alicia blinked, realizing the test was over.

She dropped the slide on the empty chamber, holstered the pistol, took off her ear protection, and then turned to look at the tech, who gave her a quick nod.

"How'd I do?"

"You dropped three shots in total. Not bad. Your time through the course was reasonable."

"*Reasonable?*" Alicia snapped. She couldn't help but frown at the word. She thought she'd done better than simply reasonable.

The tech shrugged. "Hey, I'm just administering the test. But if you want to know what I think, I think your groupings could have been a bit closer together on both the rifle and pistol portions of your test. You rushed some of your shots, and that led to you missing some critical hits that could make the difference between an instant kill of your opponent or simply leaving them injured—and thus a danger to you and others. Could you have done better? I should think so, but it could also have been worse. So 'reasonable' is my nice way of saying you did okay."

Alicia harrumphed at the older man. "You're sounding very much like my father."

The tech smiled and bowed his head in her direction.

"That wasn't meant as a compliment," Alicia said. "Am I done?"

With an amused look, the tech shook his head. "Not by a long shot. That's just the end of the current timed sequence. Are you ready to move on?"

By the time her testing was over, Alicia could barely stand. The three-gun course had led to drawing from concealment and putting three shots on target from five, ten, and fifteen yards. This time with a Beretta 92FS. From there she ended up running standard FBI obstacle courses, and dragged dummies for hundreds of yards. No rest. No water. The whole time the tech simply jotted notes in his notebook, and the few times she asked for some feedback or comments he simply told her how far behind the fastest times she was. She didn't know if he was trying to motivate her or knock her down a peg.

Regardless of whatever was supposedly coursing through her blood, she wasn't superhuman. She still needed more practice with firearms of all kinds, and she knew she had a long way to go in the stamina and strength departments. She hadn't yet gained back all her lost weight and muscle.

After she'd finally been allowed to shower and rehydrate, the tech passed her off to Dr. Sarah Weller, Alicia's least favorite person in the Outfit.

The shrink.

"Tell me, Alicia, how does it feel to finally be nearing the finish line of your probationary time?"

Feel. Everything was about feelings with this woman.

"I'll be glad to move on to full employment," Alicia said. "Not that I don't appreciate all the training, and I know it's to ensure my safety and the safety of others, but I'd really like to be out there doing some good."

Weller made a note on her legal pad. Did she actually write anything down in that notebook of hers, or was she just drawing cartoon images of Cowboy Bebop? Either way, each and every time the woman scribbled something, it made Alicia feel like she'd said something that would cause her trouble in the future.

"You seem rather focused on 'doing good.' You've used that phrase multiple times in our sessions over the last six months. Would you call it an obsession?"

"Would you?" Alicia clenched her jaw in frustration. After having spent hours being pushed to her physical limits, her patience was waning. She pulled in a deep breath and let it out slowly. This was probably just another part of the test.

Can the candidate resist the urge to throttle the woman in front of her despite being asked a myriad of inane questions?

Weller's thin lips compressed into a manufactured smile. Everything about the woman was thin and sharp. "Do you think it matters what I think?"

Alicia sighed and leaned back in her chair. The seat barely had any padding, and the backrest was too low. Probably all intentional. "Am I obsessed? I don't think so. But then, that's what you'd expect an obsessive person to say, right, Doc? I just want to help people. Is that a problem?"

"Not at all. But what about the cost of helping? In the Outfit, oftentimes you'll be asked to take a life to protect another. Or to protect the best interests of the country. Is that something you're willing to do?"

"I should think my actions on my training assignment in the Far East would answer that question." Alicia shrugged and clasped her hands in her lap. The chair didn't have any armrests either. "But yes. I'm no stranger to making tough decisions."

"Let's talk about that. I assume you're referring to your past, back before you were adopted, when you were living on the streets?" Weller clicked her pen twice and held it poised above the notepad.

Alicia pressed her lips together and tried hard not to exhibit any outward reaction. Every line of questioning from this woman eventually led to this topic. Yes, Alicia had been trafficked out of Hong Kong and had been forced to work the streets as a preteen. And now this woman *really* wanted to dig into it.

"Dr. Weller, I'm sure you never had to live on the streets, but I can assure you that my sisters and I all had to make tough decisions to survive. I'm familiar with having to make tough decisions."

"Your sisters. You feel responsible for them?"

"Every day."

"Why?"

Alicia recalled Gigi's words at dinner. "We were lucky that

my father got us out of a horrible situation. How many thousands of kids are trafficked every day? And hardly anyone with the power to make a difference cares. Well, I do. I care about the girls I went through hell with, most of whom will never leave the Amish community they now live in. Because why would they? What has the world done for them?

"I care about all the other people out there without hope, because I've felt hopeless. With the Outfit, I feel like I can make a difference. For my family. For strangers I haven't met yet. For this country. And yes, even for myself."

"That seems very noble."

"Not at all. I just recently realized I have a lot to offer this world."

Weller scribbled something on her legal pad.

"One last question," the shrink said. "I read through the mission notes on your last assignment in Taiwan and then in China. That was quite the training mission, wasn't it?"

Alicia shrugged. "I suppose so."

"I've been evaluating the mental health of the Outfit's trainees for almost two decades now." Weller pointed at Alicia with her pen. "And in that time, I've read through the notes for many training missions. I can say that the mission you went through and the resulting violence that it entailed was quite unusual. With all your past trauma, and the violent nature of your training mission, how have you managed the stress? How have you been sleeping?"

The response came automatically. "Like a baby. Eight hours a night. Really, Dr. Weller, I've never felt better."

"I see." Dr. Weller scribbled on her notepad once again.

"Well, that's all the questions I have for you. Thanks, Alicia. I think we're done."

"So..." Alicia made a rolling motion with her hand. "Did I pass?"

"Pass?" Weller tilted her head. "What do you mean?"

Alicia sighed. "I presume you'll be making some recommendation to whoever decides—"

"I will be making a report." The psychiatrist had a stony expression. "You may go now."

Alicia knew that nothing good would come of her pushing for more information. She stood, gave Weller a nod, and walked out of the room, hoping that nothing bad would come from that woman's report.

"I admit, Alicia, I didn't see this coming." Doug Mason nodded at a stack of reports on his desk. Alicia didn't know what the papers contained. Results of her evaluation, for sure. But the stack of documents was awfully... large.

"Sir?"

Mason tapped a finger on the smooth surface of his desk. Alicia saw the reflection of the Outfit's director on the polished desktop. It was an old wooden desk, but Alicia wouldn't have been surprised if it had some James Bond–style surprises in it.

"I have your results from the evaluations," Mason said. He tapped again. "According to your physical, your vitals were all in a good range. And your fitness scores were impressive."

"Thank you, sir."

Mason smiled, but it never fully reached his eyes. "The thing is, Alicia, we've been tracking all these same statistics since we first recruited you six months ago. And do you know what they show?"

Alicia shook her head.

"They show an interesting pattern, Alicia. Slow improvement, then stagnation until we sent you on your training mission. From there, a slight dip, then more stagnation. *Then*, for the last two months, a steady decline." Mason leaned back and folded his arms, studying her. "What do you make of all that?"

"Which part, sir?"

Alicia knew exactly what he was getting at, but she chose to play dumb. She wasn't about to willingly share any details of her cancer scare... after all, it didn't matter anymore.

Mason, as always, held no expression that she could discern, nor did his tone of voice give anything away. "After a mission such as the one you had, your lack of improvement in our drills could be explained as being due to the time needed for recovery. Your mission *was* physically taxing. But for the life of me, I'm having difficulty with the steep decline in performance we saw in the last two months. And now, a sudden unexpected surge in performance. Let's start with the two months of poor results. I've got to ask, are you all right? Usually results like that indicate you're nursing an injury or a sickness of some kind."

Being very conscious not to lie, Alicia fought to keep her expression neutral. "I'm completely fine, sir. In fact, I just went by the doctor's office a couple days ago for a checkup. I was given a clean bill of health. Honestly, I feel pretty awesome right now."

Mason nodded. His eyes strayed to a blue folder he'd set to the side of the stack. "That's good to hear, I suppose," he said. "Clean bill of health, you say? Why'd you go in to begin with? Were you feeling sick?"

"Not really. Just some female stuff that had me concerned, but I'm better now." Alicia said this with a straight face, because it was true—at least, that's how it had all started. When she first went to the doctor it was due both to abdominal pains and the fact that she'd stopped getting her period. There was no chance she was pregnant, so she was worried. But now, she was better in every meaningful way. Hell, even her damned period had come back—with a vengeance.

The director stared at her with his silver-hued eyes and said nothing for a full ten seconds. Then: "What about the sudden improvement today?"

"To be honest, sir, I had no idea how I'd done in my previous evaluations—nobody was willing to share that information—but I think subconsciously I knew I hadn't done my best, and I wanted to push myself. I was feeling pretty good yesterday and pushed as hard as I could. I just imagined my father yelling from the sidelines to 'go faster' and stuff like that. It seemed to have worked."

Alicia frowned. "I am sorry about my poor performance prior to yesterday. Maybe it was because I'd lost weight and didn't realize I wasn't eating enough. I'm now focused on getting my meals in like I should."

Again, none of this was a lie, but she was skating on the edge of deceit, and her stomach rumbled its displeasure.

Mason frowned. "I appreciate the improvement in your attitude, but Alicia... this just doesn't make sense." He stared at her for a long minute, then nodded once, more to himself than to her. "Your results on the most recent tests were solid. I wouldn't call them outstanding, but they're better than what most agencies require of their operators. Your weapons handling has improved over the last few months."

"My father has been working with me on live-fire sessions when he's in town," Alicia said. "Though I have to say that may not happen quite as often with the ammo prices going through the roof lately. I've had to resort to non-live drills."

"Oh?" Mason's eyebrow arched a bit, a first sign that his face wasn't sculpted out of stone. "Like what?"

Alicia blew out a slow long breath. "What *haven't* I done? I tried the laser systems—you know, the ones built into a mock bullet that has a laser in it? They work okay. Mainly though I've been doing a lot of draw-from-concealment to first shot—dry-fire of course. I can't carry legally around DC, but I've been practicing anyway. I moved to appendix carry. Quick draw-stroke for me."

"Interesting. I know a lot of our agents have begun carrying that way as well. Easier on the shoulder. Do you have any shoulder issues?"

Alicia shook her head.

"What are you using to practice? That Sig 226 I showed you a little bit ago?"

"Two-two-nine. A tad bit more compact. The larger pistols are harder to conceal."

Mason leafed through his stack of papers and pulled out a single sheet. "Let's see here... looks like you tested yesterday with a Glock and a Beretta. Any issues?"

"Not really. I thought I'd like the Beretta better, but the Glock felt a little better in my hands."

"Good to know. You shot both well. Dropped a few shots in the drills, and I see your splits were a little slow. That's not a big deal right now, though. I'd like you to get better with more pistol types. Glock, Beretta, CZ. Even Springfield. I also want you to take a look at the QSZ-92."

"What's that?"

He tapped on his keyboard, then spun his monitor around to face Alicia.

On the screen was a gun she'd never seen before. "My question hasn't changed."

"It's a Chinese pistol common in the PLA, and probably will be adopted by their law enforcement. Many of them are still using revolvers, and replacement parts for them are getting harder to come by. In fact, brush up on revolver shooting, too. A lot of Asian countries still use them. Would help you blend in."

Alicia suppressed a smile. Mason sure sounded like he had plans for her. "Are you thinking of sending me that way again?"

"You'll likely end up assigned to that region, yes. You speak a few of the languages—"

"And I'm Asian."

"And you're an *American* who happens to *look* Asian," Mason corrected her with a tone of amusement. "I'll be straight with you, Alicia. I half-expected our conversation to go in a different direction today. But you seem to have the grit and drive needed to be an asset to the Outfit. I also have glowing recommendations about you from Agent Xiang and Lucy Chen. I'm sure you understand that it was your father being associated with our organization that got you in the door, but it's you and your performance that will keep you here. You still have a long way to go, but I think your father is right."

"Right about what?" Alicia asked.

"He said that you operate best under pressure. In the real world, you'll find plenty of chances to test that. And given the improvement in your evaluations, I think you'd be a good fit as an agent with the Outfit, assuming of course that you still want to be a part of the craziness that that entails."

"I do."

Alicia responded immediately, knowing that this was what she'd wanted for quite a while, but she felt some nagging doubts regarding that decision. Some of the Outfit's decisions lay in the gray zone of morality and righteousness—at least, that was the way she saw it. She knew of at least one assassination that the Outfit had been directly involved in, and there were surely countless far more dubious things she didn't know about. Then again, almost all actions have consequences, and at times, heinous acts are required to avoid even worse outcomes. This was something Alicia had thought about over many sleepless nights after her training mission. There was likely no organization out there that would perfectly fit her own sensibilities, but the Outfit provided a big opportunity to do good in the world.

"In that case, welcome aboard," Mason said. "I have a feeling you're going to do a lot of good work for us. There will be a few papers for you to fill out next week. Your clearance already came back, with no issues… not that we would have allowed for anything from your past to interfere." He stood and held out his hand. "I'm happy to have you on the team, Alicia."

Alicia pushed up from her chair and took his extended hand. "Thank you, sir."

"Now why don't you head home. Nowadays it's frowned upon to make comments like this, but I'm going to make it anyway: go get yourself something to eat. You need to put more meat on those bones. Maybe a nice barbecue. I'm sure you know of a nice place or two."

Barbecue. The comment seemed innocent on the surface, but knowing Mason and the network of spies the Outfit had, it dawned on Alicia that he might even know about Smokin' Steve's and the conversation she'd had the last time she was there…

As she turned to leave, she stopped. "Mr. Mason?"

"Yes?"

"Has there been anything crazy going on in China recently?"

A frown creased Mason's face. "Besides their everyday existence?"

"Right. I mean… well, since everything that happened when I was there with Chris Xiang… I mean… "

"Has the government gone off-rails again? Not yet. Why do you ask?"

"It's a personal thing. My sister, Gigi, and her boyfriend are going over there." She checked her watch and saw it was just after five. "In fact, they're in the air right now."

"Why on earth are they going to China? That's a terrible idea."

"So something *is* wrong over there?"

Mason laughed. "China is *always* a bad choice, especially in the post-Covid era. I'm not a fan of their lockdowns and such, but then again, we weren't that much different at times. Is this about her YouTube channel?"

A chill raced down Alicia's spine. "You know about that? Never mind, of course you do. Yeah, her idiot boyfriend has a contact over there who says he can get her some exclusives on the concentration camps or something. Supposedly his contacts are full of talk about things happening that I haven't seen anything about in the media. Anyway, she wants to get some interviews and expose what she can."

"That's foolish, if you ask me. Especially for a civilian." Mason frowned. "Out of curiosity, what part of China?"

"Gigi didn't say. She said she'd be in regular contact, though."

"Well, when she calls you after she lands, ask her where she's going, then let me know. If there's anything 'crazy' going on there, well... let's cross that bridge if we come to it."

Alicia felt a surge of relief just hearing that Mason wanted to know. "Thank you, sir. I appreciate it."

"No worries." He sat back down behind his desk. "Enjoy your weekend. I'll see you on Monday."

EIGHT

"Hey baby girl, how'd the tests and interview go?"

As soon as Alicia got out of the Outfit's HQ, her dad had been her first call. "Pretty well, I think. It was more intense than I expected. Heavy, physical tests followed immediately—and I do mean immediately—by shooting drills."

"Keeping the stress levels high. Also keeps the blood pumping to simulate prolonged active engagement. I know SWAT teams all around the country do similar things. Other countries, too. They do the thing where they have you go through an exhaustive physical regimen, then end with something that requires small, precise motor control. It's pretty effective. How are you feeling?"

"I'm completely exhausted," she said with a laugh. "After all that, I had my appointment with the company shrink. She tried getting under my skin, but overall, I managed to keep my hands on my lap and not strangle her."

"That was nice of you."

"My talk with Mason was a little weird though. I think he suspects something."

"What do you mean?"

"He had records of all my previous physical evaluations, and he brought up how I'd been noticeably declining the last couple of months. Then asked why I was suddenly all good again. He specifically asked if I was healthy."

Dad was quiet on the other side of the line for a few moments. *"Hmm. It could be an innocent question. Think about it from his side of the table. You see a specific trajectory of data, then it reverses itself. I'd probably have asked about it as well."*

Alicia frowned. "Is the Outfit monitoring us? I mean... all the time?"

"Why do you ask?"

"I don't know... I just got a feeling he knew stuff and wasn't tipping his cards to let me know he knew. It's weird, but even his comment about me needing to gain some weight and maybe eat more barbecue... that didn't feel like a random remark from him."

Dad let out a sharp laugh. *"With Mason, nothing is said without a purpose. Barbecue, eh? Well, you know as well as I do that he's not wrong about you needing to put some weight on. As to whether the Outfit is monitoring us outside of the offices... of course they are, at least to a certain extent. But to what degree is the question. For me, being a contractor means I have a little added buffer between the Outfit and myself. For you? Who knows. Just keep it in mind. In the grand scheme of things, the Outfit has good intentions. But they'll get to their results by any means necessary, as you already know."*

"Right. I suppose I do."

"Regrets?"

"Not really," Alicia said. "I'm still figuring stuff out. All this change I'm going through…" She hesitated, realizing she was on the phone. "Well, things are different now. Being part of the Outfit… you know how it is. It makes a girl think."

"I definitely don't know what a girl thinks about. No men do."

Alicia could almost hear his smile. "Ain't that the truth. I guess I just wonder if this is the right move for me, long-term. It wasn't that long ago I was studying neuroscience at Princeton. And now what? I'm trying to be Jason Bourne?"

"Who?"

"Doesn't matter." He almost never understood her pop culture references. "My point is, I'm still thinking all this through. But in the meantime, I'm full-blooded Outfit. Mason said they'd likely assign me to operations in the Far East."

"Makes sense. You okay with that?"

"I'll be fine, Dad. I'm not thrilled they used my past to their advantage before, but I have to live with it. I have the scars reminding me of it, so I can either run from it, or just deal. And you know how much I hate running."

"That's my girl."

"Did you see Gigi off?"

"Sure did. Gave her a care package my guy Denny prepped for me. She's got twenty-two hours of flight time ahead of her. With Curt."

"How was the future son-in-law?"

Her father let out something between a low growl and a breathy sigh. *"He was… present."*

"You didn't give him the 'dad talk,' did you?"

"No. I'll save it for when they get back. Anyway, your sister said she'd give us a call when she landed. She's landing in Beijing then taking a local commuter plane to Harbin in Heilongjiang."

"Harbin, huh? Up by Russia and North Korea. Never been there."

Her dad went quiet for a couple of seconds. *"Since I have you on the line, I also wanted to let you know I'll be out of pocket for a few weeks."*

"The Outfit sending you somewhere to save the world?"

"Some undercover work. It'll be a simple job, but it's strictly black bag and my comms will be monitored. I won't be available for a bit."

"No worries, Dad. Thanks for letting me know. I'll try not to start any international incidents while you're gone. I think I'm going to keep things pretty chill for a bit. Get used to... well... the job and the rest of the stuff, you know. Be careful, okay?"

"I'm always careful."

"Sure you are. Well, I've got to get home and take care of Bagel. I swear that cat has major separation anxiety issues. He screamed for twenty minutes when I tried to leave this morning. Then he started spamming the 'No' button."

"Button?"

"Oh. Becca gave me some buttons that pets can use to communicate. It's kinda cool. But Bagel seems to have adapted to them a little *too* well."

"Well, godspeed with that," he said with a laugh. *"Alicia, you're going to be fine. The Outfit is going to teach you a lot. Don't*

let your doubts get to you. Remember what I told you when you first joined up? You have nothing to worry about."

"Thanks, Dad. Love you."

"Love you too."

Bagel was sitting in the middle of the floor when Alicia returned home, his golden eyes silently judging her, almost scolding her for leaving him alone. Alicia had stopped at the store on the way home to get him more food, and she set the bags on the kitchen counter before kneeling to scratch the cat behind the ears.

He dodged her hand and walked quickly to his buttons. *"Food. Now."*

"You've got a one-track mind, Bagel. Maybe I should get rid of these buttons, huh? What would you think about that?"

Alicia swore Bagel narrowed his eyes, then the little beast spammed another button. *"No. No. No. No. No."*

Alicia held up her hands in mock surrender. It almost seemed like the cat had answered her question, but there was no way. "Whoa there. Okay. I'll just get you some food, okay? Can you give me a sec?"

"Yes."

It was Alicia's turn to narrow her eyes at the black monster. The response was too coincidental. She popped some food into Bagel's bowl and took a step back, staring down at the cat. There was no possible way it had answered her.

Bagel no longer ate his food like the world was about to end, but he was still a demanding little thing. As he made his way through the tuna, Alicia caught side glances from him, like he was seeing what her reaction was.

When he finished eating, he sat back on his haunches, looking at her expectantly.

"Bagel..." Alicia said. "Do you understand me?" She felt stupid even saying it.

Bagel licked his lips then looked at the buttons. He walked to them, unhurried, then looked back at Alicia. In what she could only assume was protest, he then turned his back completely on the buttons and crossed the room to jump onto the couch. The entire time, her cat never broke eye contact.

"You little punk," Alicia said. "I know you did that on purpose. If you were a kid, I'd send you to your room."

Bagel closed his eyes and went to sleep.

It was impossible, wasn't it? Be it cat or dog, they couldn't communicate *that* well. Could they?

But what did "impossible" even mean anymore? Two weeks ago, Alicia would have said a present-day cure for cancer was impossible—and the medical establishment would have agreed. But science was in a constant state of evolution. What would have been considered magic and theory to her father growing up was now commonplace, accepted science and technology.

Bagel obviously had the same nanites in his system that Alicia had in hers. What might those nanites do to an animal? They improved her memory, which meant they had some effect on the way her brain functioned... so they could be doing something to the brain of the cat, too. Not that he was ever going to start talking to her like an animal in a bad Disney movie, but not all communication was vocalized.

She sat on the opposite side of the couch from Bagel. Bagel wasn't the only one who could be petty. She turned on the TV, flipping from station to station until she came across a baseball broadcast. The Nationals were playing at home against the St. Louis Cardinals, with the home team up 3–2 in the bottom of the seventh.

People around DC loved their sports, and with their football team a perennial disaster, most focused on baseball this time of the year. Alicia had never much liked football. In China, it had either been soccer or baseball played on the streets, and she had gravitated toward the latter. Alicia loved baseball. Just the sound of it on the TV calmed her. In person, it was heaven. Overpriced hot dogs and nachos. The crack of the ball hitting the bat was a sound of pure magic that couldn't be replicated in other sports.

Her dad had taken her to her first Major League game shortly after her adoption. Just the two of them. New York Yankees against the Oakland Athletics. A picture taken of the two of them on that day still hung on her wall. She'd cheered for both teams, feeling happy just to see a game in Yankee Stadium. She'd since gone back for the paid stadium tour —twice.

Her sisters thought she was nuts for loving baseball, but she had taken to the American pastime like a duck to water. It was her thing, and it was a thing she shared with her father, which made it even more special.

Idly, she wondered if her hand-eye coordination would make her a better hitter and fielder. In season, she played in the local co-ed softball rec leagues, always as a shortstop. She was curious to find out.

Alicia focused on the game and sighed contentedly. The murmuring of the crowd felt like a comforting white noise that eased her toward sleep. Right before her dreams took her, Bagel crawled across the couch and curled into his customary circle in her lap. All was forgiven.

CHAPTER
NINE

"I hate long flights," Gigi said, stretching. "And I hate customs even worse. We were there for *hours*."

Curt took off his hat and ran a hand through his thick blond hair. He smiled, pulling her into a hug, then kissed her forehead. "I hear that. We've been going for nearly twenty-four hours straight. I'm so dang tired."

"You should have slept on the plane like I did."

"You mean *snore* on the plane like you did? Nah. I'm good. The old lady across the aisle from you on the LA-to-Beijing leg asked me to suffocate you as a favor to the plane."

Gigi slapped him playfully on the shoulder. "She did *not*."

"You're right." He smiled again. "I confess, that was just me thinking it."

She laughed. "Good thing you didn't follow through. You know my dad would track you down, right?"

Curt shivered, then tried to act like he hadn't. Gigi knew

better. Everyone who tried dating one of Levi Yoder's girls had the same reaction. "Man, your dad. Did you see how he looked at me at the airport? Does he *know* how scary that look of his is?"

"He's just protective of us. Can you blame him?"

Curt shook his head, then put the hat back on. It was a gift from Gigi, with the Philadelphia Eagles logo on the front. Gigi wasn't into sports, but Curt was a diehard fan.

"Does he know you told me everything?" he asked.

"No. I'll talk to him at some point. Before the wedding."

Gigi didn't like secrets in any case, so of course she'd told Curt about her past as a victim of child sex trafficking. After all, he was the man she'd be spending the rest of her life with. The only concession she'd made—because she knew her dad would insist—was to tell Curt he couldn't tell anyone else. Her father had said most people wouldn't be able to separate her past from her present—they'd see her always as a victim, and that was the last thing she now identified as.

"Think you could take care of getting a taxi?" Curt asked. "I mean, you *do* speak the language."

Gigi smiled and flagged down a taxi, then told the driver in Mandarin that they needed to be taken to the train station. They threw their travel bags in the trunk and got in the back seat. They'd opted against bringing actual suitcases, instead going with large duffels that they could wear like backpacks.

She'd never been to Harbin before, and her cursory internet searches only brought up pictures of the Saint Sophia Cathedral and the Harbin Ice Festival that happened every January. Both looked fantastic, but that's how China was: a façade of incredible experiences and vistas covering up a country operating on lies, corporate espionage, human trafficking, and corruption. The Triad, politicians, and military all played their part. In a way, it reminded Gigi of Mexico. A country that, if it had a constitutional republic like the US, and a shred of honesty, would likely be the richest country in the world.

The sadness of it nearly overwhelmed her, and that sadness only increased as they passed destitute children and adults, elderly people working on the sides of the road. A haze of pollution hung in the air—Curt had to put in eyedrops to counter the irritation.

"Man," he said. "This place is crazy." It was his first time traveling abroad, so to him every sight was new and wonderful. Gigi wished she shared his enthusiasm. When they passed by Sophia Square, he said, "What the heck? Those buildings look Russian."

"A hundred years ago, this place was one-third Russian," Gigi said. "Now there are hardly any. Apparently China signed a treaty with Russia to have it turned over to the PRC in 1949 or thereabouts. I think it's just a museum now."

"Dang. Don't get me wrong, it looks awesome. But it looks way out of place."

He wasn't wrong. Sophia Square just looked wrong. The Russian cathedral was beautiful, but around it were concrete buildings desperately masquerading at being higher class, looking like they had been pulled randomly out of a grab bag and set to surround the museum. Yellows, whites, and grays... nothing brought the buildings together, like kids that hated each other but were forced to stand next to one another for a photo. If Gigi walked up to those buildings, she knew the storefronts would look fine—the place was filled with tourists, who needed to be impressed—but outside of the touristy areas, she knew the buildings would be on the verge of collapse.

The thought brought up memories of her childhood before she was taken to work the streets in America. She lacked even a single memory of her real parents, but she remembered the orphanage, the kids, the people... and she felt a bit of nostalgia being back in the country. She'd loved China, and she had room in her heart to love it once again. But not today. Not this version. Her adoptive father had never had a kind word to say about China, and she knew why. As much as she loved the country of her birth, she hated it equally for what it did to its citizens.

She reached over and took Curt's hand, and he gave it a squeeze.

They arrived at the Harbin West Railway Station a half hour later. The building was massive, surrounded by a sea of concrete. The bright orange-red of the brick façade shone in the afternoon light, making it an eyesore. The taxi pulled to a halt, and she paid the driver and tipped him double the fare. When he smiled his thanks, he had barely any teeth remaining to show. He waved and tore out of the parking lot. Gigi hoped he was headed home to see his family.

"Hey, are you okay?"

Gigi blinked, realizing she'd been staring off after the departed cab for too long. "What? Sorry, I... I kind of zoned out."

Curt stepped in close. "In all the months we've known each other, this is the saddest look I've ever seen on your face."

"I'm sorry. Is it really that bad?"

"Maybe just to me. You're always so bright and upbeat. But not here. It's like this place is casting a shadow over you. And don't apologize. You've got nothing to be sorry about. The way I see it, you're the one owed the apology. From this whole place, for making you feel this way."

She gave him a hug. "You're the best, you know that?"

"I have my moments. Let's go get ourselves tickets. I'd love to ride on one of those cool high-speed trains, but I doubt the one we need is one of those."

"Bummer," Gigi said.

"I hear they have them in Japan. Germany, too. How about a honeymoon there?"

"Which one?"

"How about both? My parents' treat."

Gigi grinned. "Do *they* know the honeymoon is on them?"

"Actually, yes. Babe, they *love* you. Hell, I'm pretty sure they like you more than they like me."

Curt's parents were good people. His dad, James Franklin, was a successful prosecutor in Philly, and his mom, Sally, wrote trashy romance novels under the pen name Patricia Gasp, making an absolute killing. They lived a fairly posh lifestyle, though they didn't flaunt their wealth.

Gigi knew that her own family was fairly well off too, just in a less obvious sort of way. Dad had set aside college funds for all of his adoptive kids, Grandma Yoder had the farm, and they were never lacking what they needed. Whenever Gigi had wanted something that Grandma Yoder didn't know anything about—like a laptop for school— Dad had taken care of it. He'd ask her a million questions first, but inevitably he'd bring what she wanted on his next visit.

Curt's experience had been so different from hers. She had all her sisters, whereas Curt was an only child. She couldn't imagine what that would be like. Lonely, she thought. But his parents had treated him like a king, and once Gigi had come into the picture, they'd welcomed her into the family with open arms.

She winked at Curt. "Well of *course* your parents love me. What's not to love?"

Their train curled around west of Harbin, then headed north toward Bei'an. It wasn't a high-speed train, but it moved fast enough. Gigi sat by the window on a cramped seat, with Curt next to her, slouched down as far as he could. He had dozed off, head resting on her shoulder.

Gigi checked her phone. She was glad to see she had reception, though it wasn't great. "Time to test that international phone plan," she muttered, and dialed up her dad.

The call went to voicemail. He didn't have a message for his mailbox, just a single *beep*.

"Hey, Dad!" She spoke in Mandarin so the surrounding passengers didn't think they were some tourists who were easy marks. "Just wanted to let you know Curt and I got here. We're on a train heading to Bei'an. We'll transfer from there to head east to a small town called Yichun where Curt's college buddy lives. It's a little weird being here, but it's all good. Give me a call when you get a sec. Love you."

She hung up, then dialed Alicia. Her sister picked up on the second ring.

"About time," Alicia said. *"I was wondering if you got... Shanghaied."*

Gigi covered her mouth to keep her laugh from being too loud. "How long have you been waiting to use that joke?"

Alicia switched to Mandarin too. *"All day. What's up?"*

"I'm on a train heading north from Harbin to Bei'an. It's a little tight in here."

"Understood. Nosy neighbors?"

"Who knows? I just assume they all are. The things we learn from Dad, huh?"

"How are things? Is it weird being over there?"

Gigi let out a long breath. "Very. I'm not sure if I'm supposed to be happy, angry, or sad. It's kind of freaking Curt out."

"How's he handling the culture shock? Has he ever been outside the States?"

"No. First time. He's doing well, though. I think he sees the cracks in the veneer, but he's still a little wowed by the strangeness of it all. We went by this cathedral in Harbin that used to be Russian. I think his head almost exploded with the culture clash."

"Just so you know, sis, I think Curt's a good guy. And I think Dad

will too once he gets to know him. I think you two look good together. And he's obviously devoted to you."

A surge of emotion welled up in Gigi. "You think he will? Dad, I mean? He just... I don't know."

"Don't worry about it. Seriously. Not for another second. I'll work on him."

"Thanks, Alicia." Gigi quickly brushed her eyes to make sure no tears fell. "That's... you're awesome."

"Anything for you. You know it."

Gigi smiled and nodded, even though Alicia couldn't see it over the phone. Her sister was tough as nails, always pushing her to do more and do better. Relentlessly so at times. But at the end of the day, Gigi could count on Alicia for anything.

"I tried calling Dad first, but he didn't answer."

"He's incommunicado for a few weeks on a business trip. Don't worry. So what's your agenda?"

"Bei'an, then a small town called Yichun. Curt has an old college friend up there."

"Seriously? How'd that happen?"

"They met in a marketing class at Penn State. They bonded over some books they both read. Some super geeky stuff. I don't know, I'm not exactly the reading type."

"And then the guy goes back home to Nowhere, China? Sounds like he was sent to the States by the government."

"We all agree on that." Gigi looked around the train, choosing her words carefully. "Apparently he's pretty contrarian though. Probably why he lives where he does, you know?"

"Makes sense. This the guy who's going to put you in touch with a bunch of people to interview? What's his name?"

"His name is Song Wen-gin, but I guess he went by Wes at Penn State. And yeah, he's going to... show us around."

"Just be careful, Gigi. And call me on the regular. Or send me video messages. Whatever."

"Will do. Love you, sis. Talk to you later."

Gigi hung up, then held the phone up to take a video of the countryside passing by. She preferred the trees and rolling fields to the buildings in the city.

Curt stirred and sat up, rubbing the sleep from his eyes. "We there?"

"Not even close."

"Dang. Feel like I've been asleep for hours. Did I hear you calling your family?"

"Yep."

"Good, good." He looked out the window for a minute, yawned, and leaned his head on her shoulder again. "I'm just gonna..." He was asleep again before finishing the sentence.

Gigi wished the train would go faster. Now that she was here, unease had settled over her like a smothering blanket. She wanted to get the interviews, get the footage she needed, and get home. Alicia was right: this place was a hellhole. Maybe not for everyone, but definitely for her.

She put her phone away and pretended to stare out the window. Really she was watching the other passengers in the window's reflection. Some gave her sidelong, curious glances. The Chinese girl with the blond American was bound to draw some stares. But most of these people just looked tired. Worn to the bone. Gigi would have loved to interview them for her YouTube channel. The human-interest angle would have been powerful. But not here. She couldn't know who was *really* watching her.

Settling back in her seat, she let the landscape fly by. They'd be in Yichun tonight, and then she'd get her story.

She had a feeling it would be a good one.

CHAPTER

TEN

Alicia hung up the phone and tossed it on the bed next to her. It was four a.m., and every sane person knew nothing good happened before nine a.m. Gigi must have forgotten the time zone difference. But the early morning call wasn't a problem. Hearing from her sister had put Alicia's mind at ease.

Still, now that she was awake, Alicia's mind wouldn't let her fall back asleep. She rolled out of bed and walked to the living room, Bagel following closely behind. She connected her phone to a Bluetooth speaker on the countertop and turned the volume down low so as not to wake the neighbors. Then she scrolled through her playlists waiting for something to pop out at her, and stopped on Earth, Wind & Fire. She hit play and began putting herself through a series of stretches, then core exercises.

The song "September" flowed into "Let's Groove" and "Getaway," then her personal favorite, "In the Stone." She loved the funky, almost Caribbean, acid jazz groove to it. The music washed her away, and she let herself drift in its current from song to song, exercise to exercise. Her father could sit for hours in silence, meditating, but Alicia had never picked up the skill. For her, music took her to that peaceful, inner calm. The genre didn't matter, though she usually preferred jazz, funk, and a little metal depending on her mood.

Ninety minutes passed easily in a blur of music and exercise. At the end, a thin layer of sweat covered her, but instead of feeling tired, she felt energized. Maybe there was something to all those crazies out there who got up at three a.m.

"*Water.*"

Alicia whipped her head around at the button's squawk. Bagel had a paw lifted hesitantly over the pad of buttons, like he was trying to decide what to say next.

"You need some water, Bagel?"

The cat snapped its face up to look at her, and he looked... annoyed. He quickly hit another button. "*No.*" Then, "*Water. Mom.*"

It was a moment of truth. The night before, she'd moved some of the buttons around to see if Bagel's button pushes were random, or if he actually was able to understand her.

"You want me to get some water?"

Bagel looked down at the foam pad of buttons, searching for the correct one. He moved over to the opposite side where Alicia had moved the "Yes" button, and hit it once.

"*Yes.*"

Bagel managed to look proud of himself—and somewhat judgmental of Alicia.

She pointed a finger at her cat. "Busted. Those nanites made you into a super cat, didn't they? That's it. I'm taking a shower, and I'm going over to that guy Narmer recommended. And you're coming with me."

Bagel showed no reaction to this pronouncement, but when Alicia went into the bathroom, he followed, close on her heels.

She took her time in the hot water and steam. There was probably a study out there talking about the tragic consequences of hot showers after working out, but even if so, it was worth it.

When she stepped out and wiped the steam off the mirror, she looked at her reflection—and did a double take. Something had happened to her tattoos. The outlined pony logo was gone, and the buffalo man had faded like it was thirty-year-old ink.

"What the... Bagel, are you seeing this?"

From his perch on the closed toilet seat, Bagel swished his tail.

Alicia opened the bathroom door to let more air in and get rid of the steam. Maybe she just wasn't seeing clearly.

But she was.

The Deftones ink simply didn't exist anymore. It wasn't like laser tattoo removal where you still saw where the design had been. No, it was more like a rewind button had taken it away. And the other tattoo looked like a ghost of itself, spotty and faded.

"Would you look at that, Bagel. What do the nanites have against a little ink?" She shook her head. "Well, I guess I'll have to amend my personal file with the Outfit and say I had these removed or something." She knew they kept track of distinguishing marks on all their agents.

Bagel calmly walked across the living room and sat in front of the door, liquid gold eyes regarding her with impatience.

"You're right, just one more question for Narmer's guy."

Narmer's "colleague" operated out of a dingy strip mall. As Alicia pulled into the parking lot, she paused to check the address on the paper again. She didn't need to, as she could remember it perfectly, but she'd somehow expected... more.

The sign at the address read simply: *Clinic*. It was sandwiched between an old record store and some place called "Fat Boy Donuts."

"Yeahhh..." Alicia said slowly. "I'm not feeling this, Bagel."

The cat jumped to the dashboard and looked at the building without concern. Alicia realized she was talking to the cat like it was a normal person. Was this the first sign that she was becoming a crazy cat lady?

She stayed in the car, watching a slow trickle of customers enter the donut place and leave with small white bags or flat boxes of pastries. The record store wasn't open yet.

Bagel jumped into her lap, then stood up and pawed at the window.

Alicia sighed. "If you say so." She grabbed the cat, then pushed her door open and walked up to the clinic. The windows were tinted so heavily she couldn't see anything inside.

When she tried to pull the door, the heavy glass didn't budge. She took a step away to look at the signage.

24 HOURS

APPOINTMENT ONLY

Mounted to the right of the door was a call box. Alicia pushed the button.

A tired voice answered. *"What?"*

"Uh, I'm here for an appointment," Alicia said.

"I don't have any appointments scheduled today. Go away." The voice sounded like it belonged to an old, uncaring woman from Brooklyn.

"It's really important."

"I'm sure it is. The oxy pill mill is down the road. We don't do that stuff here. So please get the—"

"Narmer sent me."

The voice went quiet for a long minute, then the door buzzed and the magnetic locks disengaged. *"Come in."*

Alicia pulled the door open and stepped inside. The place didn't look like a clinic; it had a single bank-teller-style window with a shade drawn, and a plain door to one side that presumably led to the back. That was it. No chairs, no magazines, no piped-in Musak.

The shade zipped up, revealing a stunning redhead in her forties. She had to have been a model at some point. Still could have been, easily.

Alicia walked to the window, which looked like it was made of the same bulletproof glass that bank tellers sat behind in the inner city. "Uh yeah, I just spoke with someone at the door. I have an appointment, sort of."

Red grinned. "That was me. The voice throw you?" Her voice had now lost the accent and was instead low and sultry. It reminded Alicia of jazz club singers from old movies.

"That was you?" Alicia said.

Red cleared her throat, and the voice was back to a chain-smoking old lady from Brooklyn. "Better to keep out the riff-raff." Then she switched back to her regular voice. "You said Narmer sent you. Pretty bold. That name got you in the door, honey, but that's as far as it takes you without more proof."

Alicia pulled out the scrap of parchment he'd given her, with the address on it. "He gave me this."

Red tapped on the counter. "Put it in the slot."

Alicia dropped it in the money slot at the base of the window. "He said he had a colleague here who could help me."

"Did he now?" Red held the paper up to the light, like she was looking for a watermark on a C-note. "This does look like his writing. You could have forged it, though. Anything else?"

"No. He just gave me that paper... well, and I suppose my cat, Bagel." Bagel had curled up in her arms, but at the mention of his name he popped his head up, opened his eyes, and stared at the woman through the window.

Red smiled, revealing perfect white teeth. Alicia had considered the other woman beautiful before, but this was just unfair. It was a good thing Red used the old lady voice, or there'd be a line of straight dudes and gay women for miles.

"Honey, you should have led with the cat. I can tell by the eyes. Come on back, I'll buzz you in."

The woman dropped the shade back over the window, and a few seconds later opened the door leading to the back. She stuck out a hand as Alicia approached.

"Name's Lorna Phoenix."

Alicia took the hand. "Alicia. Phoenix? Is that your real name?"

"That's my *nom de plume*. No offense, honey, but I don't know you."

Alicia shook her head. "Hey, no worries. I get it. It's just... it kind of sounds..."

"Like a call girl? Yep. That's where I got the name." Lorna waved Alicia to follow her down a short hallway. "I spent a couple of years as a top-shelf call girl in New York. The kind only the elites might have access to, if they're lucky—and very wealthy." She looked Alicia up and down. "You could clean up in that environment, honey. There are quite a few men and women who go for the tall, Asian look. Chinese?"

Alicia nodded.

"Grow your hair out long, you'd be beating them off with a stick."

"It's easier to maintain if it's short," Alicia said. "And besides, it's harder to grab hold of this way in a fight."

Lorna gave Alicia a heart-stopping grin. "Oh, I'm going to need to learn *all* about you. But first we need to have a little chat about our mutual friend, Narmer."

She pushed open a door that opened into a luxurious suite that would have put the penthouses in most high-end hotels to shame. White marble tile covered the floor, with streams of dark blue rock accenting it. The walls were dark gray, stamped with a pattern of narrow bricks. From the center of the ceiling hung an actual chandelier.

When Lorna saw Alicia's stare, the bombshell said, "Got that in the Czech Republic. Oh, don't be put off by the room. I basically live here, so I'm going to make sure I live in absolute comfort."

"You live here... between a donut shop and a record store?"

"Honey. Those are fronts. I mean, Juan next door actually does make donuts. And Harry does sell quite a few records. But they don't really make money. Both places break even, which is just what I want to see. Just enough traffic to ward off suspicion, and not enough money to bring an audit down. Lends to the strip mall mystique."

"I guess it does."

Lorna sat down at a table made from charred wood, with a blue epoxy river cut through its middle. "Have a seat, and—" She sneezed. "Sorry, I'm allergic to cats. Anyway, have a seat. How about I break the ice by telling you about my favorite topic —*me*—then you tell me how you met the old man. Deal?"

"It's your house. Your rules."

"Well. I told you about the call girl thing. That came as I was paying for med school. My specialty was in blending technology and medicine. I was doing the usual research thing, trying to get my work noticed for funding by Uncle Sam, but no one gave me the time of day because I looked like a model. Oh, they all *noticed* me, but they just wanted to take me home. After all, there's no way someone can be beautiful *and* smart."

She rolled her eyes and continued.

"I had hundreds of thousands in loans, and no one would

give me a legit job. So I ended up connecting with a shady getup in New York. I help them patch up their guys, do the occasional call, and I got all the loans paid off in a year. Another year after that, my furniture is made out of stacks of hundreds. But it was pretty sketchy."

"How'd you get out?" Alicia asked.

"I ended up being arm candy for a world-class hacker for the Met Gala. He took a shine to me and offered to get me out. I had stupid amounts of money squirreled away, and I was done being a call girl. I wanted to get back into science and medicine. He made me a new identity and purged the old one."

"And Narmer?"

"The old coot read my papers. Just showed up at my doorstep one day—after I had a new identity. He's never told me how he pulled that off. Said he needed someone who thought outside the box like I did to study his "gift." I thought he was full of it. Who believes a guy saying he's five thousand years old?"

"So you're the 'colleague' I'm here to see." It was a statement more than a question.

"I pretty much have to be," Lorna said. "There's nobody else here."

Alicia felt her cheeks get warm. "I need to apologize, because I just did what everyone else has always done to you. I assumed you were the receptionist and pre-screening me for the doctor."

"That's okay. Believe it or not, I get it." Lorna sat forward, leaning her elbows on the table. "Your turn. How do you know Narmer?"

"I don't *know* him, I just... met him," Alicia answered. "Our encounter was mostly accidental, I think. He was there to see my dad."

Lorna held up a hand. "Who's your dad?"

"Levi Yoder."

Lorna's eyebrows climbed her forehead. "Well now. I've heard of him. Narmer had high hopes for him. Wish I could meet him. He's your dad? Sorry, having a hard time seeing it."

"Adopted. He rescued me and a bunch of other girls from traffickers in New York's Chinatown. Then he adopted us all."

"Glad you got out in one piece. Most don't."

Alicia knew the truth of that statement all too well.

"Anyway," she continued, "Dad and I were doing some survival training in the Catskills. I... can't really say why. Dad was off in the woods, and I heard him talking to someone, so I eavesdropped. After my dad went back to our campsite, Narmer somehow heard me hiding, and we ended up talking." She stroked Bagel's head. "He left me with this cat."

"Were you sick?" Lorna asked.

The question caught Alicia off-guard. "Yes. I didn't exactly know for sure at the time, but... yeah."

"Diagnosis?"

"Ovarian cancer."

Rather than the look of pity Alicia had grown accustomed to, Lorna just looked excited. "That Narmer. Guy's a big softy." She pulled a tablet from a drawer on her side of the table and unfolded it "How much of the cancer is left?"

"It's gone entirely. And it's only been a week and a half."

Lorna took notes. She didn't seem the least bit surprised by this miracle. "And what changes have you noticed? Other than not being sick anymore, of course."

"Better eyesight, hearing, and smell. And my memory is nearly perfect."

Lorna nodded as she typed on her tablet. "All the usual effects. Anything else?"

"Well, improved stamina. I recently took a physical and did better than I used to. I think better hand-eye coordination. And just this morning I noticed something weird. My tattoos are vanishing."

Lorna looked up from the tablet, still unfazed. "Interesting. I haven't encountered the tattoo thing before, but only because no one with nanites has had them to begin with. It makes perfect sense though. The little things that are going through your cells, they're cleaning up any imperfections. The ink that was used by the tattoo artist is derived from various heavy metals such as antimony, beryllium, and whatnot—all of which doesn't belong in your system. So it's being broken down and excreted. Go on. What else?"

Alicia rubbed the back of her neck in embarrassment. "Well... my breasts aren't quite the same size. They're a little bit bigger. I was always told they were underdeveloped from malnutrition and... from the treatment I had when I was on the streets."

"I've got good news, honey. If their size was due to artificial factors like malnutrition or mistreatment, those soft tissue issues will probably get straightened out as well. Of course, if you're short due to malnutrition, you won't suddenly start growing to catch up to your genetic potential, because that part of your growth pattern is in the past. But beyond a few exceptions like that, the nanites will repair whatever they see that 'needs repairing.' They appear to have some kind of artificial intelligence, and they use DNA composition as a template for what *should be*, then do what they can to maintain your body in that state."

"That's... wild."

"I'll say. Way ahead of anything the scientific community has even dreamed of. Can you show me the tattoos?"

Alicia set Bagel on the table and pulled up her shirt, exposing the skin where her tattoos used to be. She pointed to the one that was still somewhat visible. "A week ago this ink was dark and crisp. And I had another tattoo over here, and it's gone as if it never existed."

Lorna examined the spot where the tattoo used to be. "No sign of a blemish. The nanites are repairing your skin as they get rid of the foreign matter. You know, I met one guy a few years ago who had fragments of a bullet in his hip. The little bots attacked the fragments and broke them down into nothing. So not surprising they can handle a couple of tattoos. Sorry about the ink though."

"I'll live."

Lorna laughed. "That's an understatement. Now go on. Any other changes? No matter how small."

"Only one other thing I can think of. I've had a ringing in my ears ever since the stuff got in me."

"Like tinnitus?"

"A little. It's like that mixed with... have you ever heard the old dial-up modems? It's like that."

"I remember that sound. I lived through those days, honey." She put the information into her tablet. "Next question: how did Narmer deliver this gift to you?"

Alicia nodded to Bagel, who had curled up right there on the table. "It was this little guy, actually. I'd just heard the news about the cancer, and that night I had all sorts of nightmares. In one of them, Bagel puked a bunch of gold stuff all over my stomach. I figured it was just a weird dream, but then I had a horrible fever for a few days, like the worst flu you could imagine. And I had a rash right where the gold stuff had been in my dream."

"The fever is normal," Lorna said. "The bigger the issues, the worse the fever. Basic physics. The nanites generate heat when they work, and the more they work, the hotter your temp gets. Sounds like your cancer was pretty advanced."

"Stage three."

"Did you go to the doctor when you felt better?"

"I did," Alicia answered. "They were blown away. They blamed the cancer diagnosis on bad tests."

"Can you blame them? They can't conceive of any other explanation. Cancer doesn't just 'go away.' I would have concluded the same thing in their shoes."

She typed a few more notes on her tablet, then set it down and looked Alicia in the eye.

"Okay, I'll give it to you straight. Narmer is legit. Which you should have realized by now. He let me infect him with all sorts of diseases and poisons. His blood nuked them all, and then the nanites repaired any damage done. He also cut himself a few times for my benefit. It wasn't like the comic books—his skin didn't close up while I watched—but I was pulling out stitches on closed skin within a few days instead of ten days. And then a few days after that, I couldn't have told you where the cut had been. And he tells me the healing was even faster when he was younger."

"Speaking of that, can you tell how old he is? Medically, I mean?"

"Not medically, because medically, his body is *not* five thousand years old. But I believe him, for what that's worth. Or at least, given the way his body repairs itself, there's no reason why he couldn't live to be that old. As long as he avoids major trauma, you know, car crashes and decapitations and whatnot. Don't go thinking you're immortal. You're not."

"I wasn't thinking that." The truth was, Alicia wasn't even comfortable with such a thought.

"Good. Now, let's talk a little about your mental enhancements. You mentioned a 'nearly perfect' memory. You may be selling yourself short. For example, tell me how many people walked up to the donut shop while you waited outside. And yes, I saw you just sitting there in your car."

Alicia replayed those minutes. And the experience really was like *replaying* what she'd seen. In her mind's eye, every detail was as visible as it had been the first time around.

"Seven," she said.

"And how many had hats?"

Alicia smiled. "Three. A fourth had one tucked into his back pocket."

"Slick, right? It's going to be that way from now on. Any book you read? You'll remember all of it. Every page. Though that kinda takes the fun out of doing re-reads. The reason your memory has improved so drastically is because of how our memory system works. As we see things, it's like drawing a line in the sand, but with an electrochemical marker. If it isn't refreshed, it takes very little for that Etch-a-Sketch memory system of our brain to wipe it away. But when we study things, when we *try* to remember by repeatedly reading things or rehearsing, we draw deeper and deeper lines in that sand, making it harder for the memory to go away. Make sense?"

Alicia nodded. "Perfect sense. Actually, I studied neuroscience at Princeton."

Lorna smiled. "A girl of beauty *and* intelligence. I think we're destined to be best friends. Anyway, the nanites seem to be aware of that electrochemical mechanism, and they work to maintain what has been drawn in that mental sand of ours. That's why you can recall things from a mere fleeting glance, while the rest of us can't remember what we had for breakfast."

"What about the ringing in my ears?" Alicia asked. "That doesn't seem to be an enhancement. Frankly, it's an irritation."

"It should be temporary," Lorna said. "I've only seen this twice before—interestingly, both times in women—and in both cases it passed in time. My best guess of what's happening is that you're detecting nearby synaptic firing. You're basically hearing the electrical signals that are firing inside other people's heads, kind of like we do when we've got a patient hooked up to an electroencephalogram—but you're doing it without any wires or a quarter million dollars' worth of equipment. Your brain is now a receiver of sorts."

Alicia was flabbergasted. "You're saying I'm reading minds?"

"Let's say... not *yet*. Unless hearing an irritating buzz counts as reading minds. Are you familiar with an EEG?"

Alicia shrugged. "I've studied the underlying science, but I don't really know how it's used in a clinical sense."

"It's pretty simple. During the procedure, electrodes consisting of small metal discs with thin wires are pasted onto the patient's scalp. The electrodes detect tiny electrical charges that result from the activity of the patient's brain cells, and these charges are fed into a computer. Effectively, we're tracking the electrical activity of someone's thoughts, and there's evidence to suggest that we might someday be able to 'read someone's mind' from these electrical signals. But right now we're just barely scratching at the surface. A lot of research is required to translate that activity into meaningful thought.

"However, the other two women who had this ringing in their ears, they found that in time their brains were able to glean some meaning from the noise. Like they'd gained a legitimate sixth sense. One woman was a club boxer, and she said she was eventually able to anticipate her opponent's next blow in a fight. The other was able to sense when someone was focusing on her, even in a crowd. I will be very interested to find out what you get out of it."

"Wow. I can't tell you how much I appreciate learning about all this. It makes me feel... more in control. And not so alone. Narmer really didn't tell me anything. I got the impression he was too tired."

"How did he look?" Lorna asked quietly.

"Not great. He had the shakes pretty bad, and an awful cough. His voice sounded... thin. Almost empty."

Lorna's expression darkened. "I wish he would just spend the rest of his time here under my observation."

"He was pretty fatalistic," Alicia said. "He kept going on about making sure he passed on his 'blessing,' and that I'd be needed some time down the road."

"He said that? Did he give you his blessing?"

Alicia sighed and leaned one elbow on the table. "That's what he said he was doing, although the 'blessing' was just a touch on the forehead. I didn't feel anything then, and I don't feel any different now from before. Is this blessing a real thing, like the nanites?"

Lorna shook her head. "I don't know. He talked about wanting to give it to your father, but he was worried because 'Levi is an unbeliever.' I guess he decided you're not. But as for what the blessing is... no idea. I would, however, like to find out. Do you mind if I take a blood sample?"

"Of course. I pretty much assumed you would."

"And do you live far from here?"

"Not far at all. I live on Wheeler Road."

Lorna flashed another perfect smile. "I'm telling you, girl. Fate. So you could come back in a couple of weeks? I'd like to track changes over time as the nanites continue their work."

"I'd be happy to do whatever helps with your research—as long as you tell me what you learn," Alicia said.

"Don't worry, I won't keep secrets. I'll take a vial today, but come back in a couple of weeks. I'll even take you to dinner.

And no, I'm not hitting on you. There's just something about you I find fascinating."

"You make me sound like a science experiment." Alicia smiled to pull the sting from her words.

"The most interesting people always are. So, two weeks? Dinner and a blood draw?"

Alicia laughed. "Sounds like a perfect first date."

"I told you, it's not a date." Lorna smiled, then grew serious once more. "Did Narmer say how long he had?"

"No. Just that it's not much longer. Given his tone, I got the feeling it was imminent."

"Damn. I wish I could call him."

"You don't have a way to contact him?"

"I do not. I have to wait for him to call me. Or send me people like you."

"Are there many of us?"

"Not really. And most of them are already a couple hundred years old. Until you and your dad. That's partly why your blood is fascinating. I want to see if there's a difference." She rose from her seat. "Wait right here. I'll bring in the phlebotomist kit and all that fun stuff."

While Lorna was gone, Alicia got up, picked up Bagel, and walked around the room. The décor was a mix of old and new. A huge flatscreen was mounted on one wall, but flanking it on either side were two impressionist paintings. They looked like genuine Monets, both of which should be hanging in the Met or the Louvre. She could see the brushstrokes, and with her enhanced vision, the colors radiated from the canvas in a way that caught her attention.

"What do you think, Bagel? Should we call the feds? Get a reward?"

The cat yawned in her arms.

"You're probably right. If we did that, we'd never be able to see them like this again."

"Admiring the art?" Lorna said. She'd come back with a tray of vials, rubber tubing, and other blood-drawing equipment. "The one on the left is 'The Artists Garden at Giverny.' The right is 'La Japonaise.'"

"Aren't these in museums?"

"Some incredible forgeries are. Boston and Paris." She set the tray on the table and beckoned Alicia over. "One of the first people Narmer sent my way is a forger. He says he's seven hundred years old, so he's had a lot of practice. Replaced the originals with fakes, and passed me these. You can come by and see them whenever you like. Now let's get a quick vial."

Alicia stuck out her right arm and let Lorna work. While the vial filled, Lorna said, "Wanna hear my conspiracy theory?"

"Who doesn't love a good conspiracy theory?"

"That's the spirit. You know how witches in folklore are said to have familiars? I think that originates from someone who had the nanites, and so did their pet. Like Bagel here. Narmer told me he's used pets before, like he did with you. So, people noticed the 'witch' lived for way too long with the same pet, and boom. Urban legend and folklore." She pulled the vial away, and pressed gauze on the skin before removing the needle.

Alicia grinned. "It's interesting to think how much stuff like that could just be misunderstood science."

"All of it, I think," said Lorna. "I don't believe in mysticism, but I do believe in science. And your cat—" As if on cue, Lorna sneezed. "Whether you want to think of him as a familiar or not, your cat has the nanites, which means he'll be upgraded too."

"I swear he knows what I'm saying."

"Probably does. The nanites made his feral little brain better. See if you can teach him stuff. It'll be a good experiment."

Bagel looked up at Lorna and meowed.

"Was that a good meow or a bad meow?" Lorna asked.

"I'm not sure," Alicia said. "But I can find out. Speaking of experiments, I've got these cool buttons at home..."

CHAPTER

ELEVEN

"Tell me about Yichun," Gigi spoke in English. She kept her voice low. The blinds in Wen-gin's tiny apartment were drawn, and the door locked with a chair shoved under the handle, but you couldn't be too careful.

A tired smile spread across Song Wen-gin's face. It wasn't a smile of happiness, but of resignation. "What do you want to know?" His English certainly had an accent, but was probably was good enough that they wouldn't need to do anything special with the closed captioning, which would make things easier in the post-processing. "This town is older than your country. It was originally all rice fields. But then it became a waystation for Chinese military traveling to Russia or Korea. The rice fields faded away, replaced by barracks like this one."

He waved a hand around, then stood, walked to the wall, and scratched it with a fingernail. "Cinderblock. Two rows deep with a thin layer of insulation between them. It does little in the middle of summer or winter. But they could be built quickly. Though this particular building does have *some* charm —mainly because of the fried-chicken restaurant on the first floor." He grinned, wide and bright.

Wen-gin seemed perfectly disarming and relatable. Gigi shouldn't have doubted her fiancé.

She looked over her shoulder to make sure Curt had caught it all. Curt had his DSLR in hand, partly to move around to get different angles of the interview, but mostly so he could quickly move and hide it should anyone come knocking unexpectedly.

Gigi turned back to their Chinese host. "You've been to the US before, right?"

"I went to Penn State."

"And what did you study?"

"Information Systems with a minor in Marketing. It's pretty common. The Chinese government gets us into school in the West. We get placed in companies like Apple, Google, Tesla. That gives us an opportunity to gain access and take as much information as we can before coming home. Standard corporate espionage."

"Where were you placed when you graduated?"

"Sony. In their gaming division. But I never went."

"Why is that?"

Wen-gin shrugged. "A lot of reasons. My mother got sick. The risks my government asked of me were too great. I guess you could say I became disillusioned. I came home, and the government cut my family off. Punished us."

"In what way?" Gigi found she was leaning in closer. The way Wen-gin spoke sent an unexpected shiver down her spine.

"My brother was a scientist. He was whisked away to help with a secret project. They never let him come home. He just vanished. Then they disappeared my mother and sister to a reeducation camp. Blacklisted me from any meaningful employment. I can code, and I have a pretty good handle on marketing. But they put a black mark on my record. No one will hire me for those jobs, or they'll be punished like I was."

"How do you know your family ended up in a camp?"

"They snuck messages out. My sister is—was—very beautiful. I'm sure she used that... you know. To get her message out. Everyone knows there are always bargains to be made. Not unlike the American prison system."

Gigi agreed with a single nod. "When we arrived, we noticed a heavy military presence. Is this normal around here?"

"No. It's been getting heavier for the last few months. I wish I knew why. There are all sorts of rumors flying around. There's supposedly a military site close by, but none of the PLA will confirm it. My neighbor upstairs was out after curfew—"

"I'm sorry, Mr. Song. There's a curfew?"

"Nine p.m. Again, standard practice here. During COVID, we weren't even allowed to leave our homes, so freedom with an early curfew is still better than the alternative. But like I was saying, my friend was outside after curfew, hunting. Small game. He saw the PLA driving animal transport vehicles through town. But instead of cattle, the trucks were loaded with people."

"From the camps."

"Maybe. It's hard to say. It's entirely possible the military grabbed up a building or neighborhood. Wouldn't be the first time."

"Any idea where the facility is?" Gigi asked.

"None. Yuze—the friend I mentioned—hid as the vehicles drove by. He saw the people packed in them, but he didn't follow. He's not suicidal."

"Any chance he'll speak with us?"

Wen-gin shrugged. "It's up to him. I'll ask. Not many people here will talk to you on the record."

"Because of retaliation?" Gigi asked.

No fear showed on Wen-gin's face, just sadness. In the weak light of his apartment, his eyes were dark, sunken pits. "I already know I'll have to flee before your piece goes live. Anyone who talks to you will run as well."

Gigi felt a pang of guilt. On the one hand, Wen-gin—Wes— was the perfect person to put on camera. He was handsome but worn down, and the contrast was perfect. His words were believable. But the flip side of the coin was how this interview would end his future in China. "I'm sorry, Mr. Song—"

Wen-gin interrupted her. "Don't be. I've been planning on getting out for a while now. I have a cousin in South Korea. You have to understand that I love China. But I hate the corruption. Maybe you can shed a little light on the situation here. Your mainstream media spends all its time making excuses for our leaders instead of holding them accountable. And by the way, you can call me Wes. I found I rather liked the name when I was Stateside. Who knows, hopefully I can make it back at some point. Though... maybe somewhere quieter than Pennsylvania."

Gigi gave Curt a quick glance, and he answered with a sad

smile. She understood, now, why the two had become friends. She gave Curt a cutting motion, and he turned off the camera.

"Thanks, Wes," she said. "I think this'll get some serious notice."

"It's the least I could do." He sat forward, elbows on his knees, and rubbed his face. "Honestly, I've been going nuts here. You know how crazy it is that I just want to sit back and code the UI to some phone app? But I'm not allowed."

"So what are you going to do once you get to your cousin's place?" Curt asked. "He's in Seoul, right?"

Wes stood up and walked over to his small kitchenette. "Yeah. There are some outfits there that will get me papers so I can work. They know the score when it comes to situations like mine. I'll be able to code again, and even do a little marketing." He filled a glass with murky water and took a drink. "I won't get paid like a Korean, but it's better than being here."

"What about your family?" Gigi asked. "How will you get them out of the camps?" She wished she hadn't asked the question as soon as it left her mouth. And at the same time, she wished the camera were rolling, which gave her another pang of guilt.

"I won't." Wes took a long drink, refilled the glass, then emptied it again. "I got another message from my sister. My mom's gone. She died of a fever six months ago. And my sister... well, the message was pretty clear. She'd decided she was done living that way. Suicide rates are high in the camps."

"I'm sorry," Gigi said.

Wes shrugged. "If I was the only one with a story like this, maybe I'd feel sorry for myself. But my story isn't unique. It's not even unique here in town. I know a dozen people who have been in my shoes."

"Doesn't make it easier," Curt whispered.

"No," Wes said. "It doesn't."

An air-raid siren wailed, cutting through their conversation. Gigi checked her watch, and saw it was nine p.m. "Curfew?"

"Every night, about an hour after sunset." Wes went to the door and pulled on shoes and a dark jacket. "There's a rumor another convoy is passing through tonight. Feel like taking a field trip?"

Gigi ran to her bags and pulled out a dark hoodie and knit cap. Curt did the same. They'd figured they'd need to run around in the dark while they were here, so they'd packed accordingly. Wes waved them to the back of the apartment. It didn't have any rooms, but calling it a studio apartment felt like giving it undue credit.

Wes pulled the shade to the back window and slid the glass aside. It was a tight fit for Curt, but they managed to squeeze through. Wes led them along a narrow walkway of metal scaffolding, then up three flights of stairs to the roof.

Intermittent clouds passed over Yichun, but the night was still bright. Streetlamps throughout the town winked out, cut by whoever controlled the city's power grid. External building lights went out soon after, then entire structures went dark. It was like a forced brownout.

"They turn off all power at night?" Curt asked in a whisper.

"Every night," Wes confirmed. "It's just another form of control. But it also makes it easier to sneak around. Now, watch. If the rumors about a convoy are true, we'll know in just a bit."

Wes sat down against the short wall that served as a lip to the roof and stared up at the sky. With the city lights gone, the patches of sky showing through the clouds cast the land below in soft, blue light. Gigi sat against the wall too, saying nothing, unwilling to interrupt the peaceful silence. Curt raised his camera and took B-roll of the dark city.

Gigi pulled her thin jacket tighter against the chill. What was going on here? The early curfew and the shutting down of power was more than a simple control move. The Chinese military was hiding something, and this alleged transportation of prisoners was only part of the whole picture.

Without lights or electricity, the town's silence was deeper than usual, and allowed Gigi to hear the distant rumble of diesel engines. She popped up on one knee to peer over the low wall.

One by one, light poles flickered on. Not all of them, but specific ones, all in a row leading through the city.

"Looks like the rumors were true," Wes said.

"They light up the path for the trucks," Curt said, still filming. The effect of a specific route lighting up held a measure of dread rather than hope.

"Their road doesn't lead by this building," Gigi said. "It looks like it goes by one building to the north. Can we make it in time?"

Wes waved them to the emergency stairs. "We'll have to run, but I think we can make it. Just keep quiet."

They ran to the stairs and took them two at a time until

they reached a ladder leading to street level. No one popped their heads out of nearby windows. They must have known better. *Plausible deniability?* Gigi wondered.

They sprinted across the road between the buildings, then around to the emergency ladder. It wasn't down. Curt laced his fingers together and held them for Wes. Wes put a foot into Curt's hands and let himself get boosted up to grab the ladder. Wes pulled himself up rung by rung until he could use his feet to push him the rest of the way, then disengaged the ladder. It rattled down, the sound thundering in the night.

Gigi waved Curt up first. He'd be able to climb the stairs quicker and get the convoy on video if she was too slow.

This time someone did poke their head out a window on the second floor, a teenage girl, eyes wide with worry. Wes put a finger to his lips and made a shooing gesture to get them inside. She nodded and disappeared, the curtain closing behind her.

As Gigi reached the roof, she moved in a crouch to the side facing the lit street. Curt was already there, kneeling as low as he could while still looking over the edge, the camera peeking over the side. Gigi slipped in between Curt and Wes, then poked her head over the lip of the building. Thankfully all the light poles were lower than the top of the building, and all pointed down onto the street. The chance of anyone seeing them against the skyline was low.

A series of trucks rumbled into view. The first few carried a few soldiers, but the middle four trucks in the convoy were packed, standing room only, with men, women, and children.

They wore threadbare garments, and a few had blankets pulled over their shoulders.

They looked like the pictures of Jews who'd been rounded up in the Holocaust and loaded into train cars.

"Holy shit," Curt breathed.

"It's worse than I thought," Wes said. His face was etched with sadness. "That's a lot of people. Before it was just two trucks, partially full. What's going on?"

"Are there any work camps up here?" Gigi asked.

Wes shook his head. "Oil is to the southeast. There are some rice fields to the north, but they aren't of the high-volume variety. And there aren't any other reeducation camps up here."

"So where are they going?"

Two trucks with soldiers completed the procession. Behind them, the lights used to guide the convoy into the city began blinking off, but new ones blinked on ahead in the distance.

Wes pointed at the lights. "I know this city well. I can't tell you their final destination, but I'll be able to tell you which road they take out."

They watched in the darkness until the last light again winked out to the northeast.

"Strange," Wes said. "There's nothing out that way. Some small towns, low-yield rice farms, that's it. The road then turns north and heads to Russia, and there's no way the trucks go that far."

"Why not?" Curt asked. "Maybe they have camps there, too."

"No," Gigi said. "Russia has more eyes on it than even China these days. If they had camps, we'd know. That would be all over the news, and so would Chinese convoys crossing the border."

"Well there must be *something* out that way," Curt said.

Gigi nodded. "A military base. Something off the books."

"If that's true, you'll never find it," Wes said. "They'll shoot you before you even get close."

"That's okay," Gigi said. "We have the convoy on film, and the direction. We can make some inferences for the video when we get home."

"Come on," Wes said. "We should get back to my apartment. Most of the folks here are good people, but there's always loyalists who might turn us in for an owed favor from the government, or for a promotion or release for a family member somewhere."

They took the stairs as quietly as they could manage, and snuck back into their friend's window. Wes lit a gas lamp and some candles, giving light to the dark room. He pulled out some bread and dried meat from a pantry and passed it out.

"Sorry it's not much. With the electricity cut for the evening, I don't want to open the refrigerator."

"No problem," Curt said. "Is there a local market we can hit tomorrow? We'll go stock you up."

"By *we*," Gigi said, "he means *me*. He'll just draw attention and make sure we pay too much. I'll flash my smile and get us discounts. What kind of stuff do you need for your trip to South Korea after we leave?"

"Dry goods, probably," Wes said. "I'll be on the road for a couple of days to get smuggled across the border. There's a flag on my passport. So anything non-perishable would be wonderful. Thank you." He leaned forward, hesitating. "Curt, I was... well... I..."

"Just ask, dude. I'm going to say yes."

"Curt," Gigi said in a low voice. "You can't just—"

"Babe, it's okay." Curt put a hand on her knee and smiled. "Wes was my best friend at Penn State. He's like a brother. If he needs something I can provide? Of course I'm gonna help a brother out."

"Thanks, Curt," Wes said. "The thing is, I'm not the only person who is going. Like I said earlier, anyone who talks to you on camera will have to leave too. They... well, they'll need food too."

"How many folks do you think would be willing to go on camera?" Curt asked.

"I have a dozen people lined up, so it could be as much as twelve. And if I buy too much all at once, it'll draw suspicion. If we split it up, and go to different stores on different days..."

"No problem," Curt said. "Just get us a list of what you need. That okay, babe?"

Gigi smiled and gave Curt's hand a squeeze. "Of course." She'd been worried that Wes would ask for help crossing the border. Or getting into the US. Food was no problem.

"Let's pull up the footage of the convoy," she said.

Curt pulled out the camera. Gigi parked over his left shoulder, and Wes over his right. Curt hit play, showing the shutdown of lights across the city, then the path of light poles as they lit up. Gigi had to give Curt credit. The shots were clear, and they were framed in a way that seemed to heighten the feeling of fear and uncertainty already present. He froze the video at one clear shot of the soldiers in the second truck, converting the frame into a still. He did the same with a few frames showing the prisoners.

"Send that one to me," Gigi said as Curt created a still from a shot of a mother with her arms wrapped around the shoulders of her daughter. Both mother and daughter wore fear like a mask. "If that doesn't get people talking about what's going on here, I don't think anything will. I'm going to send it to Dad and Alicia."

"You can't," Wes said. "All internet traffic here, including emails, is monitored. If you send those, you may as well turn yourself in right after."

"My father set me up with a few tricks before we left. Some ways to hide our footage and pictures on a storage device, and a way to securely upload small files without being tracked. Call me paranoid, but I'd like for some people we trust to have these pictures. I don't think we'll be able to upload full videos with this method, but stills should be fine."

"I'll load everything to the computer," Curt said. "You can handle the hidden drive. What time will the power come back on tomorrow morning?"

"Nine a.m.," Wes said.

"Good," said Gigi. "We'll send the pictures tomorrow morning, then we'll interview some more people. We should just interview a few people doing regular stuff, too."

"Street food vendors," Curt said. "Everyone watches that stuff online, and it's pretty innocuous."

"Good call," Gigi said.

She turned to Wes and gave him a hug. "Thank you, Wes.

This means a lot. We'll get your message out, and we'll get you all the food you need."

Wes blushed from the hug. "I'm just glad you've been able to get some good material. It's all going pretty well so far."

"Yes, it is," Gigi said. "I have a good feeling about all this."

CHAPTER
TWELVE

"How do the trial runs progress?" asked General Liang Feng. He stood atop an embankment, observing twenty workers wading in rice fields below him. The workers moved in unison through the rows of plants, harvesting the crop.

"Progress is better than we could ever have predicted, General," Shen Ping replied. Even outside of the facility, Shen still wore his white lab coat.

Feng nodded his approval, hands clasped behind his back. The morning air felt cool against his face, and he wished he could have felt it on his neck and back. The uniform was particularly stifling this morning. A bead of sweat trickled down from his hairline under the flat, military regulation cap, but Feng didn't move to wipe it away. He wouldn't show weakness.

"Dr. Shen," he said, "you know I dislike having to guess. Unlike my predecessor, I am data-driven. 'Better than we could ever have predicted' does not answer my question." He stretched one hand to point at the line of workers. They were a mix of men, women, and children, though from this distance their ages and genders couldn't be determined.

"Of course, General. My apologies, sir." Shen opened the folder he was holding and pulled out one sheet of paper to hand to Feng. "We've tested the serum on one hundred subjects so far. As you can see from the second bullet point, the mix is 34% adult male, 33% adult female, 16% adolescent male, and 17% adolescent female. The ages within the adult mix have been spread out as well."

"Have you observed group-level differences?"

"Not yet, sir. Not by age or gender," Shen said. "However, it has only been ten days. I suspect we will find discernable differences in reaction to the serum in the long term. It is inevitable."

"How has their work been? Any problems?"

Shen shook his head. "No, sir. No problems. They are docile. The group you see below has been working for thirty-six hours straight. No food and no water. They no longer take breaks. And they are easily trained. A group of soldiers with experience showed them how to harvest the rice, and when we placed them in a row in the rice field and told them to harvest, they followed instructions immediately. The subjects are highly suggestable."

"Suggestable and *obedient*." Feng smiled and turned his attention to the report in his hands. "I don't see anything here telling me how fast the serum can be produced."

"Extremely fast, General. The main ingredient grows

rapidly and can be produced in any lab across the country if you desire it."

The General frowned. "How fast is that?"

"With the ingredients and staff that we have on hand, we can produce one hundred doses every three days. Obviously we can speed things up even more with more qualified people and resources."

"Any side effects?"

"None so far." Shen opened his mouth, closed it, then said, "General, I'm a little concerned by the lack of eating and drinking. Their bodies will eventually collapse. I know you said to chemically inhibit those needs, but—"

"Have any complained? Revolted?"

"No, General. But—"

"Then I do not see the issue, Dr. Shen."

"General Liang, my concern is a dwindling workforce. We can work them as much as we see fit, and they won't cause any issues. That's the point of the serum. But they are still mortal. We don't know how long they will work without fail. At some point, without nourishment of some kind, they will collapse. We need to take care of them, just like we care for any tool, or we risk running out of workers."

"This is why I had more shipped in last night," Feng said. "I presume they arrived?"

"Yes, General. The transport arrived at two a.m." Shen checked his reports. "Two hundred and sixty-three individuals. Where were these from?"

"One of the camps."

"I see."

"Is there a problem, Doctor?"

"N-no, General." Shen always stammered when Feng asked that question. "I just like to know so I can track different variables."

"Very good, Doctor. Tell me, beyond general labor, do you foresee any other applications for those given the serum?"

"I wouldn't expect so, General. Definitely not military. Their docility would likely not make them good soldiers. They would follow simple orders, but I fear anything requiring the complexity of a soldier's orders would require constant monitoring and, for lack of a better term, hand-holding."

Feng frowned. "That's unfortunate. I suppose we can't have everything though, can we, Dr. Shen?" He pursed his lips in thought. "We'll have to see about experimenting with variants of the serum to get better results. But Doctor, could not one of these subjects be trained to, in theory, press a button?"

"Easily, General. Why?"

"I'm theorizing the viability of capturing enemy combatants and turning them into suicide weapons against their own people." Feng cast a sidelong glance at the scientist. "Do you think this is doable?"

"If the general wishes, I believe this could be accomplished easily."

Feng noted that the doctor's face had gone pale. The man lacked imagination. If it wasn't for his results in constructing the serum, he would have been replaced long ago.

"Good, Dr. Shen. Very good. I will provide as many bodies as you need for your testing."

"Sir, where will you pull the subjects from? We can't empty the camps without others noticing."

Feng smiled and patted Shen on the back. "That won't be a problem. The Heilongjiang province is filled with little towns no one will miss."

CHAPTER
THIRTEEN

"All right, Bagel. Let's see what you can do." Alicia held up a picture of her keys and slowly said, "*Keys*. You got that, Bagel? *Keys*." She put the picture face-down. "Now, get my keys, Bagel. Get my keys."

In the days since returning from Lorna's clinic, Alicia had been busy. Pistol drills with every pistol the Outfit had on hand. Sparring with men and women—her size, smaller, and larger. Reading up on the Chinese and Korean intelligence reports Mason passed her. Studying maps of every Asian country.

But today was about her cat, and seeing if her suspicions were correct.

"C'mon, kitty. Get my keys."

Bagel stared at her impassively. He seemed like he understood, but he wouldn't execute the command. He licked his lips and hit one of the BabbelPet buttons. *"Treat."*

Alicia leaned back in her chair and folded her arms. "I don't know about that, Bagel. You've got to work with me. You say you want a treat? I'm not sure I believe you."

"Treat."

"Okay. I can make that happen." She leaned forward and held up the picture again. "But first you have to do something for me. Get me my keys, and I'll get you a treat. Everybody wins." She suppressed a wince. She sounded like a TV cop questioning a witness.

Bagel let out an annoyed meow, but then he jumped up on the counter and grabbed her keys from the tray where she'd put them after coming inside. The cat jumped back down, keyring held in his jaws, and stared up at her.

"Holy. Crap." Alicia stood and fist-pumped the air. "There's no explaining *that* away, Bagel. You *do* know what I'm saying. You little devil! You, Bagel, are the smartest cat on the planet."

She laughed and put her hands on her head in disbelief. "This is crazy. And awesome. Bring the keys here, Bagel."

But Bagel just cocked his head to the side, and with the keys still in his mouth, pressed the button again. *"Treat."*

"Holding my keys hostage, are we?" Alicia shook her head. "Fine. I'll get you your dang treat." She pulled a cat treat from her pocket, wrinkling her nose at its fishy smell. "Here. An even exchange."

Bagel bounded into her lap, dropped the keys, and snapped the treat from her fingers.

"Well played, kitty. Well played. But we're just getting started. Now that I know you understand me, it's time to see how much you can retain, and how well you can communicate."

Alicia checked her watch and was surprised to see it was already midnight. She'd barely eaten. Bagel, on the other hand, was stuffed. He had refused to participate in any experiment without being given a treat, and now he lay sprawled in the middle of her living room floor, asleep and purring so loudly he might as well have been snoring.

The experiments, while costly in terms of cat treats, had been illuminating. Bagel could not only fetch anything he was shown a picture of, he remembered commands and pictures from hours before. Which meant the applications for her little sidekick were potentially incredible.

The field of buttons on her living room floor—she'd ordered a bunch more after her meeting with Lorna—were a problem though. There simply weren't enough buttons in the world, or enough space in the living room, for a cat that could legitimately communicate. And the cat wouldn't be able to talk to her at all when the buttons weren't around.

So, part of tonight's exercise had involved teaching her cat the beginnings of Morse code. Bagel placed his paw on her leg, flexed his toes for a dot, and pushed on her for a dash. They'd started with the basics: *yes* and *no*. Teaching the golden-eyed monster all the words he might need to use would take... well, a long time. Months, at least. But it would be worth it.

She heard banging from somewhere down the hall outside her apartment, accompanied by unintelligible yelling. It must be Friday. Time for the Bernards' regularly scheduled domestic dispute. Mary Bernard was a high school English teacher who coped with the kids she had to deal with by drinking herself to sleep at night. Patrick Bernard was a three-hundred-pound rent-a-cop who manned a toll booth. He had the red nose to prove that he, too, was an alcoholic.

Together, as the saying went in the building, they were no saints.

What was the issue this week? Had he slept around again? Had she spent all their money on bad boxed wine from the local supermarket?

Alicia once again thanked the powers in the universe that the two didn't have any kids at home. They'd had one daughter, but she'd wisely split once she'd turned eighteen, and had never looked back.

The pounding got louder. Becca had probably already called the cops. If she hadn't, she was calling them now. Alicia estimated fifteen minutes until officers arrived.

A typical Friday. The officers knew the Bernards by name.

A moment later, the banging down the hall changed, like something solid had been slammed against the wall. Alicia got up, padded barefoot to her door, and cracked it open just in time to see Becca step out in her flower-patterned nightgown, cell phone in hand.

"I've called the cops, Patrick," Becca called down the hall. "They're on the phone with me right now, and officers are on the way. Put down the stick and have a seat in the hall. No use making this worse."

Alicia peered down the hall. The "stick" was a black baton. He shouldn't have had it. Patrick was obviously drunk, uniform shirt untucked, his bad combover hanging limply over one ear. He swung the baton against his apartment door, connecting hard and sending chunks of veneer flying.

"I know he's in there!" Patrick yelled in a drunken slur. His hand wavered as he pointed the baton at the door. "Bitch's got her new *man* in there. I'm going to tear his head off!"

From inside the Bernards' apartment, Alicia heard the sounds of Mary crying.

Becca stepped forward. "And you think doing that will win Mary back? Boy, you've got another thing coming." She still held the phone to her ear. "Nine-one-one, are you hearing this? What? How am I supposed to go back into my apartment while this guy is out here making a ruckus?"

Patrick pointed the baton at Becca. "You drop that phone and go inside, you old hag." His bloodshot eyes fixed on Becca, angry and fevered. This was about to go sideways.

Alicia stepped out into the hall. "Becca, get back here! Let the police handle this."

The older woman ignored her. "I'm not going to be pushed around anymore, Patrick." Becca put her other hand on her hip in defiance. "I think it's time for you to leave."

"And *I* think," the drunk turned and took a step in Becca's direction, "it's time for you to be taught a lesson. I'm sick of your dumb voice. And you always getting in my business."

Patrick smiled, and a little drool spilled over his lower lip.

He took two staggering steps forward, faster than Alicia thought possible in his condition, and backhanded Becca, who hit the wall and crumpled.

Hot rage flooded Alicia. She sprinted forward, closing the gap between her and Patrick in seconds. The wife beater saw her coming and swung the baton like a baseball bat.

Alicia ducked low and felt the baton pass just over her head. She tucked into a roll that carried her behind the man, then popped up and stomped on the back of his left knee as hard as she could. The man screamed in pain as his knee bent sideways and collapsed under him. He swung a wild backhand at her, but she evaded it with a quick sidestep.

She grabbed the drunk's arm and yanked it backwards while bringing her knee up hard into his shoulder. The shoulder popped, wet and loud. Patrick screamed again and fell face-first to the dirty hallway carpet. The baton fell from his fingers and landed at Alicia's bare feet.

She picked it up and brought it down hard, twice, on his left kidney. He'd piss blood for weeks if he was lucky.

She used the bottom of her t-shirt to wipe off the part of the handle she'd touched, then tossed the baton behind him, out of reach, and headed back toward her apartment.

Patrick made a feeble grab for her ankle when she walked by. She stomped down on his fingers and felt the bones snap under her heel, but she didn't stop there. She grabbed him by the combover to hold his head up, and threw everything into a punch to his jaw.

She left him whimpering on the floor while she walked to Becca's side.

Behind her, the door to the Bernards' apartment opened, and Alicia heard a gasp. "What did you do to my husband?"

Alicia turned slowly. Mary's face went ghost-white when she saw Alicia's expression. "Mary," Alicia said coldly. "It's time for you to move."

"It's not my fault he's a dick!"

"Maybe," Alicia said. "Do you have another guy in there?"

Mary hesitated, then gave an embarrassed nod.

"Then you're part of the problem," Alicia said. "Because you know when Patrick gets home. You instigated this one. Now get back inside your apartment and wait for the cops to get here."

Alicia turned her back on the woman and turned her attention to Becca. The older woman was trying to shake away the cobwebs.

"Alicia? What happened?"

"You tried playing hero, Becca. You should have known better. Walking up on him like that just escalated everything."

"I know. I'm sorry, Alicia. I'm just so sick of their fighting. And so sick of the cops not being able to do anything." She lifted a hand and touched the right side of her face where she'd been hit. It would make a nasty bruise by the morning. Then she looked past Alicia, and her eyes widened. "Alicia! What happened?"

"He hit you and paid the price," Alicia said. "Don't spare a moment of pity for either of them. You can take them out of the trailer park, but you can't take the trailer park out of them."

"But... your cancer. This can't be healthy for you to—"

"No cancer. It was a mistake at the hospital. But don't

worry about me. I need you to sit right here. No moving. You might have a concussion. Let's let the cops sort this all out."

Becca would be fine. Alicia kept her talking while they waited for the officers to arrive, and the woman spoke clearly without any confusion. Her eyes focused normally.

"I'm sorry, Alicia. I shouldn't have walked up on that idiot." Becca kept shaking her head, disappointed with herself. "I messed up, didn't I?"

"You did. Becca, you got lucky. What if he'd hit you with the baton instead of his hand? It probably would have killed you." Alicia took her friend's hand. "You know better. The police have told everyone in this building not to get involved beyond making the call. These types of situations are extremely dangerous, even for cops."

"Apparently not that dangerous for you," Becca said. She once again looked at Patrick's crumpled form. He'd passed out from the booze and the pain.

"I was lucky, too," Alicia said. "I took advantage of him being plastered. If he'd been sober, he could have done some damage to me."

"Uh-huh. What exactly did you do to him?"

Alicia patted Becca's hand. "Nothing he didn't deserve." In truth, she could have done worse, and the drunk would have deserved that too. Alicia had no tolerance for bullies and abusers.

She'd learned a few things about herself on her mission in Taiwan. In many ways, she'd always thought of herself as a softy. She cried in movies and TV shows, and got misty-eyed at weddings. But in Taiwan and China... over there she'd learned she had a comfortable relationship with violence.

The elevator dinged, and the doors slid open to reveal three officers from the Metropolitan Police Department, which serviced most of DC. Alicia recognized one as Sergeant Hector Gonzalez. He took the lead, walking briskly to stand over Alicia and Becca.

"Purcell, throw some cuffs on Mr. Bernard," Gonzalez said.

"Dang, Sarge." Purcell pulled out his cuffs and looked down at Patrick's unconscious form. "This guy's going to need medical."

"Doesn't change cuffing him. Lang, call it in."

"Sir." Lang grabbed her radio. "Dispatch, this is unit 2052. My partner and I are on scene at a domestic dispute. We need an ambulance at our location. 2425 Wheeler Road, Apartment 315. Subject in custody. White male, large, late forties. Beaten pretty badly. We have a supervisor on premises."

Alicia had always found police procedure interesting. In most departments across the country, they'd gotten away from the rapid-fire numeric codes to reference what they were responding to. Now they'd simplified the verbiage so everyone could understand everything. It was necessary: here in DC alone there were dozens of law enforcement agencies, and they couldn't all use their own unique terminology.

As Purcell put cuffs on the unmoving Patrick, Alicia wondered how many people would be throwing a fit if they saw a badly beaten, unconscious man being restrained. Most people didn't get it. They didn't see how often injured suspects played asleep, only to suddenly "wake up" and take the cop's gun. It happened more than ever made the news. Of course, Patrick was white, so no one would care. Such was the hypocrisy of people's judgment of law enforcement.

Sergeant Gonzalez squatted down next to Becca and took off his flat cap, revealing salt-and-pepper hair that matched his graying mustache. "Ms. Baker. Ms. Yoder. Another Friday night with the Bernards, I see." His eyes narrowed when he saw the mark on Becca's cheek. "And things escalated." He pulled out a small notepad. "I'm going to take a few notes if that's all right. We'll need you both to come down and give official statements later."

Becca nodded, and Alicia said, "That's no problem. What do you want to know?"

Hector pulled out his pen. "Just walk me through it. You first, Ms. Baker."

"It's Friday," she said. "You know how it is. I hear pounding on the door down the hall, like usual, but this time it's way louder. And I can hear him shouting."

"What about?"

"I couldn't understand him. I poked my head out and saw him hitting the door with that stick-thing on the floor behind him." She hesitated, looking sheepish. "Then I... well, I made a mistake. I called 911, but then I came out into the hall. I shouldn't have. I was just angry. He got mad and hit me. I don't remember much after that."

Hector's eyebrows wrinkled in concern. "Did he hit you with the baton?"

Becca shook her head. "His hand."

"When the paramedics get here, I'll have them evaluate you for a concussion."

"Oh, you don't need—"

"They really do," Alicia interrupted. Becca didn't like asking for help, and even though Alicia could tell she was fine, the cops had to do their thing. "Let them do their job, Becca. Besides, that hit was a solid one."

The officer turned his attention to Alicia. "You saw Mr. Bernard hit Ms. Baker?"

"I did. I heard the pounding just like Becca did. When I peeked outside, I saw her walk by. Patrick got mad and back-handed her pretty hard. At that point, I feared for her safety, so I got involved."

His eyes flicked up to look at Patrick. "Involved. Right. What exactly did you do?"

"I got behind him, took out his knee with a kick." A medical exam would show all the damage, so there was no use in Alicia leaving stuff out... with the exception of the hits with the baton. "Popped his shoulder when he swung the baton at me. Then I broke his jaw with a punch. He was incapacitated after that."

Hector struggled to cover a smile. "You know, we haven't been able to make anything stick with Mr. Bernard. His wife always vouches for him. This time we have him on aggravated assault on the both of you. I hope you'll help us out with this."

"I didn't just 'fall down the stairs' like Mary," Becca said. "I want him rotting in jail."

"I agree," Alicia said. "And just for added color, Patrick was yelling that Mary had a boyfriend inside. She came out right after I dropped her husband, and she admitted to me that the boyfriend is in there."

"Thanks for letting me know. I'll have Lang get her statement, and Purcell will talk to the boyfriend." He looked down the hall and shook his head, obviously tired of dealing with these people. "Doesn't he come home at the same time every Friday?"

Alicia nodded. "Mary knew what she was doing."

He stood and put the notepad away. "You ever think of joining law enforcement, Ms. Yoder? We could use someone with your... tenacity. And your clear thinking."

"Not my thing," Alicia said, letting a small smile show. She winked. "Plus, I don't think I'd pass the background check."

Hector laughed and put his hat back on. "Ms. Yoder, I would personally make sure no one had an issue with any speeding tickets on your record. Do you need anything from medical?"

"No," Alicia answered. "I'm good. Not a scratch."

"In that case, you can head back to your apartment. Or if you want to wait here with Ms. Baker, that's fine too. I'd rather her not move out of caution."

"No problem," Alicia said. She smiled at her neighbor. "How about I go get you some water?"

"Thank you, Alicia. You're the best."

Alicia walked back to her apartment. The other neighbors now stood in their doorways or out in the hall, watching the proceedings. Alicia's blood still pumped hot in her veins, and she allowed a victorious smile to spread across her lips. She felt good. The physical beat-down was just the icing on the cake.

The true success of the night was getting their drunk neighbor off the streets. Becca would press for the guy to go away for as long as possible.

All of Alicia's training had been hard work, but tonight, she'd used it to actually make a difference. Narmer's words came back to her:

Little victories over years that slowly turn the tide and make our world a better place.

FOURTEEN

The setting sun cast a crimson light over the rice fields surrounding the military facility in Heilongjiang and made the sky seem as though it were bleeding onto the ground below. It reflected off the water, making the workers look like they were wading in ponds of blood.

After a brief return to Beijing for one of the useless military summits, General Liang Feng returned once again to oversee his experiments. It was an obsession for him, filling his thoughts both day and night. He barely managed three hours of sleep last night due to the excitement he felt at witnessing the progress. The serum, which had been taken from a dissident military project in Taiwan and perfected by his Chinese scientists, was working. Having an army of tireless workers would increase production, cementing China's hold on the global rice market. And with the workers not needing any sustenance—

and with a nearly endless supply of them—the profit margins were astronomical.

The unintended benefit of military application was the icing on the cake.

Being able to use the serum to control people into being human shields or as delivery mechanisms for explosives had opened Feng to a massive range of options to explore.

He breathed in deeply of the cool air and smelled the mild funk coming from the farming community. He was watching the workers from his usual berm, well out of range. Nearly all of them were religious or political dissidents from the reeducation camps, but a few came from tiny villages no one knew existed, or the homeless no one would miss in major cities. Over the last week, some of the workers had collapsed, dead before they hit the ground, but until that time, they'd worked eight days straight. Shen was already adjusting the formula and dosage to compensate better for body weight and age, and he had given it to the new batch of test subjects from the week before.

The next step would be long-term application. If Shen could get the subjects to work for *months* at a time, practically around the clock with only a limited caloric sustenance, the quantities of people needed over the years would go down dramatically.

"General Liang?"

Feng turned to see his head scientist approaching. "Doctor. I wasn't expecting another update from you tonight. How does our experiment progress?"

"General... I'm worried."

"About?"

"The serum is perhaps... too effective."

Liang laughed and pointed at the expanse of workers below. "Some of those workers have been down there for nearly two weeks straight. I'd say the serum is working as intended."

"Do you not see the difference in the workers, General?" Shen bit at his lower lip. "They aren't as orderly as they were before. I did an autopsy on a few of the dead chil—"

"Stop." Feng cut the air with a hand. "I don't want to know the results. I need to be able to talk as if I'm unaware of any potential problems. And the health issues of people like... these," he frowned like he'd eaten a piece of rotten fruit as he looked down at the unmentionables, "do not concern me."

"I understand, General. But... some of the children. They are very small, and the fields are large."

Feng turned away from the rice fields and narrowed his eyes. "Are you saying you've lost some of the subjects?"

Shen didn't answer, and wouldn't meet Feng's eyes.

"Shen?"

"We are missing... some. And when they die, we don't know how it will affect the rice, or the water."

"How many?"

"Fifteen that we know of."

Feng shook his head. Only fifteen? Fifteen children hardly mattered. They were likely floating in one of the fields below. Even if they wandered off, where would they go?

But though he didn't care, Feng had appearances to maintain, even to Shen. "How could you be so careless?"

"I apologize, General." Shen bowed deeply. When he

straightened, he opened his mouth to speak, but a confused frown made him stop. He pointed past the general. "What are they doing?"

Feng's eyes followed Shen's arm. A small group of subjects had dropped to their knees and looked to be drinking from the rice pools.

"I thought you said they didn't have urges to eat or drink," the general said.

"They don't. This is strange. That rice field has our first subjects in it. I... don't understand."

Even as they watched, more workers in that section of the rice fields dropped down into the shallow water, one by one. Shen muttered something under his breath, and Feng realized the scientist was counting, stopping, then counting again.

He's timing the gap between each person falling to their knees. He never got to thirty.

He made his voice cold, commanding. "*Shen*, what is happening?"

The scientist stopped counting and ran a hand through his thinning hair. "I'm not sure, General. We segregated the workers based on size, age, and gender to better track the effects of the serum. And we gave them the shots in order within those subsets. I think... I think the smaller subjects are having an adverse reaction, and I think they're having it in the order in which they received their serum dosage."

"If the smaller people are having the reactions first, then shouldn't the children be the ones we see behaving strangely?"

"General, that's what I tried to tell you earlier. There aren't any children left. They've either all died or disappeared." He stared down at the subjects slurping at the ponds. "But I never saw the moment *when* they died. It very well could have been... like this. This is very troubling, General."

Feng glared. "This is a problem for you to figure out, Shen. I am disappointed in your lack of supervision." The truth was, the general still wasn't concerned, but again, appearances mattered. "Is there anything else?"

"We've also isolated some of the subjects so we can verify the work on the anti-serum."

"Good. We need to have everything ready before I announce the project in front of a private meeting of the National People's Congress. They'll want to know we have the anti-serum on hand and tested." Out of the corner of his eye, Feng looked at Shen. "The anti-serum *does* work, correct?"

"Oh yes. That was the easy part," Shen answered. "It reverses the effects... up to a certain point, anyway."

"Live or dead doesn't concern me. I just need it so the politicians feel 'safe,' but eventually I'll need to demonstrate its effectiveness. I want to hear that that will not be a problem."

"It will not, General."

"Excellent. I—" The general stopped mid-sentence as he glanced down at the rice fields again. "What on earth?"

The workers had begun... attacking each other. Indiscriminately splashing through the rice fields, tackling the others. The attackers didn't scream or yell, and the attacked didn't seem to even notice. Their bodies all went down in soundless clumps and churning water. The most chilling aspect of it all was the lack of sound. That somehow made it all the more horrifying.

"General." His voice quiet in the twilight, Shen took two steps back. "General, we need to leave. I'll notify the soldiers to come put down this... uh... action. But you should leave in case their unrest spreads."

Feng nodded, unmoving. It wouldn't do to show the nervousness he felt. Unease crept its way through him. "Yes. I suppose you are right. They lasted two weeks. A good starting point. Be sure to burn the bodies after the soldiers put them down."

"Yes, General." Shen backed away even further.

Feng turned sharply on his heel and followed after, careful not to look like he was on the verge of running. His leisurely steps turned into a quick march, which turned into a run the moment he made the mistake of looking back.

Dozens of the workers were clawing their way toward the two men at the top of the embankment.

Gigi thanked the shop owner for the dried fruit, stowing it in her backpack. The days had all begun blurring together. Curfews shutting down the power at night had the effect of shutting down life and personal control. Likely just as intended. No other convoys of prisoners passed through Yichun, which left Gigi and Curt with only interviews to try and conduct.

Wes had had about a dozen interviews lined up for them, but only three showed up. Gigi couldn't blame the ones who canceled. Their lives were worth more than the good they could potentially do by exposing the truth to a bunch of Westerners. Westerners who couldn't do anything to help them once their identities were exposed.

She wanted to reassure them and offer them promises of protection... but she couldn't, so she wouldn't. In their place, would she have done anything different? Probably not. That simple admission eliminated any frustration she felt at being stood up for the tenth time.

The good news was fewer interviewees meant fewer supplies she and Curt needed to buy. The less attention they drew to themselves, the better.

From what Gigi had gathered, the city had been fairly friendly and carefree in the past, but today its citizens walked on eggshells. It was almost as if the whole town was stuck in a horror movie, and if they moved or breathed, the unknown boogeyman would find them.

Except the monster that people feared wasn't unknown, and it wasn't imaginary.

Gigi stopped to buy a few *baozi*, yeast-risen buns stuffed with shredded pork, from a street vendor. Though she spoke Mandarin fluently and wore clothes similar to what everyone else wore, the city's denizens still gave her a wide berth while casting sidelong glances her way. They somehow sensed something different about her—as if she didn't belong. Would they have been so standoffish without the military presence and control?

Curt mostly stayed inside. The one time he'd ventured out with her, two PLA soldiers spent the entire day following them around. So now he focused on his video editing so they could get their footage together for future uploading.

They'd dropped numerous photos in the secure storage device Gigi's father had set up for them, and on a few occasions —when they got a steady cell phone signal—they'd uploaded via a VPN to a secure portal her father had access to. But each time, she'd spotted the same unmarked van driving up and down the street, as if they'd detected their transmission signal. She knew she couldn't be too careful with communication here. So although she'd typed up notes regarding what she'd been experiencing and the overall weirdness of the city, for now she'd simply queued it for upload whenever it felt safe to send. She wanted to call Alicia, but decided that was out of the question.

As Gigi walked through the city, she *felt* the quiet settle around her before she truly realized that an eerie silence had in fact engulfed the town. A shiver slid down her spine, and she felt like her breath was slowly being squeezed from her lungs.

Ahead, in the middle of an intersection at the northern edge of town, stood a single child, a small girl. She wore filthy worker's clothes that looked to be nearly falling off her. Water stains reached her knees, like the girl had been working in a shallow pond. *One of the farm workers from the rice fields?*

Gigi pulled out her phone and took several pictures using various magnification levels. The little girl didn't move other than to seemingly sniff the air as people walked by her. She twitched, like she was suffering from some kind of spastic episode, or maybe she was overwhelmed by all the people around her, even though they gave her a wide berth.

A small, almost silent voice in Gigi's mind said a single word.

Run.

The little girl took two shambling steps forward and reached out to grab a passerby, a middle-aged man in a suit. He slapped the girl's hand away, started to yell something at her, then shut his mouth with a click that Gigi heard from a hundred feet away. The businessman then hunched his shoulders and backed away from the little girl as quickly as his loafers would take him without running.

A scream shattered the silence.

Gigi couldn't tell exactly where it had come from. It seemed to come from everywhere and nowhere all at once.

Then the source of the scream came around the corner at a flat-out sprint. A young woman, with a boy in ragged clothes hot on her heels. And though the woman screamed, the child ran silently, no shouts for the woman to "get back here." Absolute silence.

As Gigi watched the scene through the zoom on her cell phone, the look on the child's face froze her blood.

His expression was flat and emotionless. Almost alien. Like his face was a Michael Myers mask worn for effect.

The boy flung himself at the fleeing woman, bringing them both down to the asphalt. The woman fought back, punching the boy hard enough to throw him off her. For a moment he lay there in the middle of the road, stunned, then he pushed up to his hands and knees, a drizzle of blood spilling from his lips.

He rose to his feet slowly, mechanically, and staggered toward the woman, who seemed too stunned to move.

"Run!" someone screamed in Mandarin. Gigi didn't know if she'd yelled it herself, or if someone else had. Somewhere in the flurry of action, Gigi had switched from photo to video and hit the record button.

Another person ran around the corner, then another. Ten more. Behind them was a pack of children, chasing their prey like rabid dogs. An athletic man ran by the ragged little girl who still stood in the intersection. The girl arched her neck as if breathing in deeply—then sprinted after the man, faster than she had any right to be.

Gigi knew she should have run when that little voice told her to.

Instead, she filmed. Whether it was out of morbid curiosity, fear rooting her to the spot, or the need to prove how jacked up this town and country were... Gigi kept filming the unlikely predators and their prey.

The little girl leapt onto the back of the fleeing man, her weight throwing him to the ground. She clung to him like a leech, then opened her mouth wide, bit down on his cheek, and ripped upward fast, her teeth holding a piece of bloody flesh.

"Oh shit."

The action broke the spell, and Gigi turned and sprinted away, screams following behind her.

FIFTEEN

"Uhh... Torres? Can you take a look at this?"

Lara Torres suppressed her desire to murder Mason. She was tired of dealing with these *pendejos*.

The Outfit's the premiere clandestine agency, he'd said. *We only recruit the finest from around the world*, he'd said. *I'll send word to the task force leader and tell him to give you free rein on following this line of investigation*, he'd said.

Why did I ever leave the CIA?

She blamed herself. Being good at her job and aggressive had consequences. She once heard it said that the reward for success is getting the added work others failed at.

Now she clenched her jaw to keep from unleashing a string of profanity at the other analyst who'd been assigned to help her. Crystal Howard. Supposedly Crystal had been poached from the NSA, but Lara had serious doubts whether the woman could even tie her own shoes without someone showing her how. Crystal was older than Lara by more than a decade, yet always needed a second opinion. On everything.

And worst of all, she dyed her hair blue.

Never trust someone who dyes their hair a strange color, Lara's grandmother used to say. *It poisons their brain.*

Lara used to laugh off the old woman's crazy advice. Not anymore.

"Sure," Lara said, forcing a smile. Crystal flinched. *I need to work on that fake smile*. Lara rolled her chair around to the other woman's cube.

"You had me looking for weird communications in Heilongjiang?" Crystal said.

"That's right." It was like speaking to a toddler. Lara wondered if she should get a sticker sheet of gold stars and put them on this lady's forehead when she managed to do something right.

"How weird is 'weird'?"

Lara let out a long, slow breath—struggling to filter what she wanted to say into something that wouldn't turn into an HR event. "Good lord, Crystal, just tell me what you have. There aren't enough street tacos in the world to prevent me from... just spit it out, please."

"Oh! You like street tacos, too?"

Lara's hand strayed to her waist, where she'd begun appendix-carrying her pistol. But she'd locked it in the gun locker upon entering the facility. A small blessing for Crystal.

"Crystal," she said as calmly as she could. "Tell me what you have?"

The woman nodded. "Reports of people going crazy and attacking other people. Lots of biting. Kids are chasing everyone and tackling them."

"Sounds like a normal day at day care."

"It's not a day care. It's a Chinese city called Yichun. And it's not isolated incidents. There are hundreds of reports in the last few hours."

She turned to her screen and ran a query on all messages with the words *bite*, *attack*, and *chase* in all their variations. Hundreds of text messages and phone calls scrolled past, the transcriptions translated to English.

Lara gestured for Crystal to move aside, then sat in front of the monitor and scanned through it all. It seemed a group of kids—the number varied from report to report—was running through the streets like a pack of jackals, attacking people at random.

Lara pointed out at the timestamps. "It looks like they locked down all communications for the entire prefecture at around noon, local time."

Crystal nodded. "That's what it looks like to me too. All phone traffic, text, email. It's like the place was unplugged."

"That definitely qualifies as weird." Lara's computer beeped, notifying her of a priority message. "Hang on, Crystal." She rolled back to her machine. The flag showed a foreign transmission—an encrypted text message hitting the personal account of one of the Outfit's agents. The Outfit monitored all of their assets' communications.

The communication was a video sent by text message. It originated from a civilian cell phone in China, but the phone had a Pennsylvania number attached. Lara quickly did a reverse lookup of the number.

Yoder. Gigi Yoder.

"Oh, you've got to be kidding me."

The message was transmitted to one of the Outfit's secure cloud portals, which then forwarded the data to two people. Levi and Alicia Yoder. The elder Yoder's account was frozen, a common precaution the Outfit often took when people were deep undercover.

"Lara, is there anything you want me to—"

"Wait!" Lara waved away Crystal, then watched the short video. "*Hijo de...*" She watched it again just to be sure her imagination hadn't taken hold of her, then pulled her cell out to call Mason.

"*What's up?*"

"Sir, we have a situation."

No sigh of resignation like she'd always received back at the CIA. Mason's response was all business. "*What have we got?*"

"Sir, where's Alicia Yoder *right now?*"

Alicia circled to her right, keeping distance between herself and Julie Hill, her opponent in today's sparring match. Hill wasn't much older than Alicia, but she had been an agent with the Outfit for nearly two years already.

Hill jabbed with her left, then lashed out with a right hook that Alicia saw coming and caught by lifting her arm to cover that side of her head. She countered, quick as lightning, catching Hill with a glancing blow on the side of her protective headgear.

The sound of static that Alicia had been hearing whenever she was close to someone had become less pronounced, but occasionally a burst of noise would fill Alicia's ears, and it did so now. The sound caused her to wince—and briefly lose focus on the fight.

Lorna had said that Alicia would eventually learn to interpret the staticky sound, and find the meaning in it. She claimed it wasn't much different than the signal of an old dial-up modem. Well, Alicia's brain wasn't interpreting crap at the moment.

Hill took advantage, launching a flurry of punches. Alicia barely caught the first in the combo, and took the second on the chin. The third would have taken her square in the nose, but she ducked just enough to catch it on her forehead instead.

She staggered back, then danced quickly to the left, taking herself out of Hill's range. The other woman cut off her retreat, circling to corral Alicia in the corner of the boxing ring. Alicia took a leg kick to her knee, but kept her footing.

The static spiked in her ears again, and this time Alicia made sure not to flinch. She kept her focus as Hill launched another combo, and Alicia was a heartbeat quicker as she stepped into a push kick, planting her right foot into Hill's solar plexus. Hill's first punch caught only air, then she was forced back.

Alicia pressed her attack, pivoting and throwing a quick, powerful inside low kick just above Hill's right knee. Hill's leg gave just enough. Alicia hit twice quickly, left then right, then spun with the momentum from her right hook to launch her elbow into the side of Hill's head. The speed of her attack, coupled with the low kick that threw the woman off balance, dropped Hill to the mat.

Outside the ring, Alicia would have followed with some kicks to the face, or circled around behind the downed opponent to choke them out. But here, she backed away as Hill held up both hands in defeat.

Hill shook her head, then pushed herself slowly to her feet. She grinned and held out a fist. Alicia bumped it with her own.

"I don't know how you reacted so fast to that last combo," Hill said as she pulled off the headgear. "It was like you were reading my mind. And that spinning elbow would have knocked someone out in the wild."

"That's kind of the point," Alicia said with a grin, then deflected the other part of Hill's comment. "And don't sell yourself short. That one flurry nearly put me down. I lost focus for a second."

"Oh, I noticed. You all right?"

Alicia waved the concern away. "Headache. A little tinnitus. Nothing crazy, just wasn't expecting it."

Hill nodded her sympathy. "I know that feeling. I've got the same thing from being on the decks of aircraft carriers." She pulled off the half-finger MMA gloves. "Same time next week?"

"You know it. Maybe we do a little grappling next time?"

"You got it. See you around, Yoder."

Hill left for the locker room, and Alicia took a seat next to the boxing ring and pulled off her own gloves and headgear. Sweat covered her from head to toe, but she felt energized.

And curious. Had she reacted better to that second flurry not despite of, but *because* of that noise in her head?

She replayed that moment in her mind. The world had almost seemed to slow down. In the heat of the fight, it really was as if she'd somehow known what her opponent was about to do. Perhaps that was a dump of adrenaline. Or she'd gotten lucky. But... what if there *was* something to the static?

If it was a thing, it certainly wasn't a conscious communication. She hadn't "interpreted" the static, as Lorna had claimed. Not as words, anyway. But had she understood the meaning all the same?

Despite her fatigue, Alicia wanted another fight. She wanted to explore whether this was an actual advantage that she now possessed.

Instead she grabbed a towel, wiped away the sweat, and ran the towel over her short, sodden hair. A nice warm shower sounded like the perfect way to end the day.

Every day since officially becoming an agent had been filled with training, training, and then more training. Sparring, pistol and rifle work, and general endurance. While she appreciated the chance to get her body back in the shape it had once been in before her sickness had begun chewing away at her muscle mass, there was only so much training a girl could do before the beginnings of boredom took root.

Somewhere out there, a situation brewed that she could resolve. Or help resolve, at the very least. Instead, the monotony of her daily routine had her wondering when the Outfit would stop being a glorified gym and switch her over to something more interesting.

Her phone buzzed deep inside her duffel bag, beneath the clothes and intelligence briefs she'd been tasked with studying. In truth, she'd already memorized the intelligence. They included after-action reports—AARs, as Mason called them—from her mission to China a few months earlier, as well as dossiers on various Chinese functionaries, including the new general who'd replaced the old one Xiang had killed. One careful read by Alicia had ensured the information would stay locked in her mind forever.

She dug through the bag and pulled out her phone. "This is Alicia."

"Alicia, I need you to come to my office immediately."

It was Mason.

She looked down at her sweat-soaked tank top. She'd cooled off, and now just felt sticky. "Sure. Let me go grab a shower—"

"Immediately doesn't mean in fifteen minutes, Yoder. Shove that towel in your duffel bag and get over here." He hung up.

Alicia frowned at her phone, then looked up to the nearest corner of the gym, near the ceiling, where a camera pointed straight at her. She understood the constant, internal surveillance to a certain point, but something about the way Mason used the feeds to watch her rubbed her the wrong way.

She gave the camera a small salute that might, accurately,

have been interpreted as mocking, threw the bag over her shoulder, and jogged out of the gym.

The halls in the Outfit's headquarters were very plain. Neutral gray walls, flooring that looked to be made of bedrock. No photographs or art. The Outfit didn't spend money on the frilly things, but the result was an impression of impermanence, which stood at odds with the history of an organization that had existed since before the founding of the country. For some reason she couldn't explain, Alicia associated the lack of décor with a lack of soul.

As she fast-walked down the corridors, she recognized many of the faces she saw, but knew very few of their names. At some point she'd ask for files on the other employees and skim through them. At least then she'd know who people were.

Her skin tingled with excitement as she drew closer to Mason's office. His tone hadn't been the normal faux-friendly he normally used with her. He'd sounded a little... worried. Did they have a new mission? Something they needed her for?

Am I actually ready for a mission? Hell, what expertise am I bringing to the table other than being Chinese and speaking like a native?

Maybe it wasn't a mission. Maybe it had something to do with her father.

Anxiety bloomed within her as she hurried down the corridor.

Outside Mason's door, Alicia paused and took a second to collect herself. The dread of the unknown, and the brisk walk, had her sweating again.

She knocked, opened the door, and poked her head in.

Mason sat behind his desk, staring up at the huge panel monitor hanging on the wall. From where she stood, Alicia couldn't see what was on the screen. A young Latina woman occupied one of the two chairs opposite the director, a laptop in her lap, and she, too, was looking at the wall screen.

Mason waved Alicia in without even turning his head.

As she stepped toward the desk, Mason pointed up at the screen. "Alicia, can you tell me what exactly your sister is involved with in China?"

Alicia didn't know what he meant. "She went there to do some guerilla newscasting. Footage and interviews. Is this something from her YouTube channel? She said she wasn't going to…"

Alicia trailed off as she turned her gaze to the screen. It looked to be a still frame from a video, and it was grainy—likely shot on a phone. Depending on settings, phone videos weren't meant to be projected on such a large screen.

She immediately recognized the city of Yichun; her mission into China had brought her to the same city, though only as a place to gather supplies. The people in the image were in mid-stride as they ran from something. Some wore masks, but Alicia saw fear in their eyes. Others had mouths open wide in silent screams. Their terror looked primal. Real.

But not everyone was fleeing.

"What's going on here?" Alicia said, confused.

"You'll see. It gets better," the woman said. She had long, dark hair that Alicia envied.

"Alicia," Mason said, "this is Lara Torres. She's one of the

Outfit's analysts, and has been looking over some of the business in China you were at least tangentially involved in. Lara, this is Alicia Yoder... though you already know that."

Alicia nodded at the analyst. "Nice to meet you, Lara. What do you mean, it gets better?"

"Check this out." Torres tapped a key on her computer, and the paused video resumed.

The room filled with recorded screams, stuttering and fuzzing, much like the video, which had gaps and missing frames. But for several seconds, the video cleared and ran clean. And it was now clear what the people were running from.

Children.

The terrified adults were being chased by children.

"Here comes the crazy," Torres said.

One of the children— a girl in ragged clothes, running quicker than a child of her size would have been expected to— jumped on the back of a fleeing man and rode him to the ground. The girl's mouth darted down, clamped on the man's cheek, and ripped away a grisly chunk of flesh.

Torres paused the video at the moment when the girl's face lifted to the sky, the bloody prize in her teeth.

"What... what did we just watch?" Alicia asked, horrified.

"You tell us, Alicia," Mason replied.

"Why would *I* know anything?"

Then Alicia recalled what Mason had said when she'd walked in the room: *Alicia, can you tell me what exactly your sister is involved with in China?*

"What does this have to do with Gigi?" She looked from

Mason to the screen, then back again. "Are you saying Gigi is there?"

"Alicia," Mason said, "when was the last time you checked your phone?"

Alicia pointed at the duffel bag she still had slung over her shoulder. "A few hours ago? I've been training all morning. Pistols, then running, then sparring."

"Check your phone, Alicia," Torres said.

Alicia sighed and pulled her phone from her bag. It showed a notification of a missed call and voicemail, then a forwarded message with a video attachment from the Outfit's secure portal.

She played the voicemail.

"Alicia... pick up... the phone. Something's wrong here. They're experimenting... and the military has the town on... lockdown. It's a mess. I'm sending you a video. We need... help."

From her breathing, it sounded like Gigi was running as she recorded the message. Alicia thought she heard screaming and yelling in the background, too.

She then played the video—and instantly realized why Mason and Torres were asking her about Gigi. It was the exact same video that was on Mason's screen.

She ran a hand through her damp hair. "What is this?" Alicia realized she'd been pacing back and forth in Mason's office. She stopped and held the phone screen up for Mason and Torres to see. "What's going on over there?"

"We don't know," Mason said. "What did your sister tell you before she went over to China?"

"Just what I already told you just now, and what I told

you after my final evaluation." Alicia dropped the phone on top of her duffel, ridding it from her grasp like it held a disease. "She went to China to do some news coverage for her YouTube channel. She had a line on some pretty shady stuff no one was talking about. Her fiancé has an old college buddy living out there who said he could show them a bunch of stuff."

"Like what?" Torres said, leaning forward in her chair.

"Trafficking. Some typical military overreach. Some connections to the concentration camps they have throughout the country. She didn't give me much beyond that."

"When was the last time you spoke with her?" Mason asked.

"The day she landed," Alicia answered. "She called me from the train." Alicia closed her eyes, partly to block out the image on the huge screen, partly to help bring up the conversation again in her mind. "She, uh... she landed in Harbin. From there a train to Bei'an, then she was headed to Yichun, which I found to be ironic, since I was there for part of my mission in China."

"That matches the geolocation data I collected," Torres said. She nodded up at the screen. "The messages you received from your sister came from Yichun, but the whole place is now shut down. All electronic communications of any kind, including phone traffic, has been cut off. Your sister must have sent that just ahead of the lockdown."

"So whatever's going on in this video," Alicia said, "was bad enough for the government to throw the kill switch on communications."

"That seems to be the case," Mason said. "Is there anything

else? Did she get in contact with you any other way? Maybe through one of your father's friends or contacts?"

"No," Alicia answered. "I haven't heard anything. However, my father set her up with access to a secure portal, which is how she would have gotten the video out. Let me check if there's anything else."

She picked up her phone again and went through her emails. With everything she'd been going through, she hadn't been paying attention to emails at all. Sure enough, buried among hundreds of unread messages were a handful of innocuous-looking notifications about files having been sent via the secure reflector Dad had set up, all sent within the last day or so.

Those files included dozens of photos. They showed transport vehicles, some filled with the Chinese military, others packed like cattle cars with what looked like refugees and prisoners. Men, women, and children.

"Oh, Gigi. What did you stumble into?"

"Feel like sharing with the class, Alicia?" Mason asked.

"Of course, sorry. Though I'm sure you already have access to this stuff since you obviously have access to the video." Alicia forwarded the emails to Mason. "You should have them in your inbox now."

Mason put several of the photos up on the wall screen. Then he frowned and shifted his gaze to Torres. "These came in yesterday... why didn't you tell me about these?"

With her face turning red, Torres exploded with a stream of expletives in Spanish. She stopped herself and let out a dramatic sigh. "I'm sorry, boss, I didn't see these until just now.

I'll be clearer with the people helping me on the data-gathering side."

Alicia was looking at the photos, focusing on the expressions of fear, sadness, and hopelessness that had been captured expertly by the photographer. She remembered Gigi talking at some point about how Curt took care of principal photography and videography; she could see now that he knew his stuff.

One picture showed a captive woman with her arms wrapped around her daughter. It could have been the cover shot for *Time* magazine... not that they cared about actual news and journalism anymore.

Torres pointed at a photo. "Is that girl the same one in the video biting someone's cheek off?"

Alicia shook her head. "No. It's not the same girl." Alicia could recall in her mind a crystal-clear image of the girl in the video.

Mason pushed up from his desk and walked closer to the screen. "It looks like your sister stumbled onto something way more serious than some run-of-the-mill exposé, Alicia. I'd wager these people are political prisoners from the 'reeducation' camps."

"How can you tell?" Torres asked.

"The clothes?" Alicia asked.

Mason nodded. "The clothes, indeed. All fairly uniform from person to person. Threadbare. Likely issued to them. If these people had been rounded up directly from a town, they'd be wearing more diverse clothing, and the clothes would probably be in better condition. Alicia, do you have any idea what your sister was *specifically* looking into?"

"No. But like I said, she tends to focus on sex trafficking. Telling the stories that our media are paid to ignore."

Mason sat on the edge of his desk and folded his arms. "Torres, what else have we been hearing out of that part of the world?"

"Most of the communication has been pretty normal— until kids began chasing people down and biting their faces off," Torres said. "The standard rumors. A strong military presence, heavy censorship, the usual stuff about prisoners, and lately some talk about scientists and experimentation. This is mostly pieced together from voice calls—the censors do a good job of squashing anything in print, even in texts. And of course most Chinese are very careful about speaking overtly about anything that casts a negative light on the government."

"In other words, nothing new."

Torres shrugged. "I'd say kid zombies is new."

Alicia almost laughed at the absurd comment, but saw neither Mason nor Torres were laughing. "Are you serious?"

Torres looked her in the eye. "Tell me a kid eating the face off of another person doesn't scream 'zombie' to you."

"Let's not call them the walking undead just yet," Mason said drily. "Judging from the way they're acting, I'd guess their biochemistry has gone awry. Drugs, poisons. Back in the Middle Ages, there was something called dancing mania where groups of people would start dancing or moving around erratically, until they dropped from exhaustion. Sometimes entire villages would be affected. Current conjecture is that it was caused by ergot poisoning."

"Ergot? I've heard of it... isn't that some kind of fungus?" Alicia said.

Mason nodded. "Historians believe that the supplies of rye got infected with the fungus and caused entire populations to get poisoned." He pointed at the screen. "This, too, could be some mania caused by drugs or poison."

"But if so," Alicia said, "why shut down the entire communication network? It's just a few kids." She paused. "Unless it *isn't* just a few kids."

"Okay," Mason said. "What do you have in mind?"

"Virology. What if the Chinese government was doing biological experiments, and they got out of hand? We're all too familiar with what happened with Covid. Doing live experiments on human subjects wouldn't be out of the question for them, especially if those subjects are prisoners—or other people the government doesn't think of as human anyway."

Mason nodded. "Go on."

"So let's say these kids have been exposed to some kind of virus. The virus causes this manic behavior, attacking whoever's nearby, and then possibly spreading the infection."

"So we're back to zombies," Torres said.

"No zombies," Mason said firmly.

"It doesn't matter what we call them," Alicia said. "Most diseases can be transmitted by blood and saliva. If people bitten by these... victims... become infected by the same virus, the question is, will they begin doing the same thing as the kids? And if so, how quickly?"

"So according to your hypothesis," Torres said, "the comms blackout is because the military presence there fears this will become more than a few kids attacking people. You think they've been ordered to shut everything down because this thing that's *totally not zombies* will spread."

"It's a possibility," Alicia said. "But let me ask another question. Why aren't some adults *already* infected? If in fact there are viral experiments underway, why would the scientists use only kids as subjects? That wouldn't make sense. So where are the infected adults? Are they going nuts as well?"

"All very good questions," Mason said. "And not easy to answer. If China has proven anything, it's that they will cover up anything that might cause them to lose face." His normally unreadable face took on a grim expression. "The idea that this is a communicable virus worries me greatly. Another Covid, an experiment that got loose, but with much worse side effects."

"Worse than death?" Torres said, looking dubious.

"Eye of the beholder. All I know is that we need answers."

Alicia closed her eyes and rubbed her face. Gigi and Curt were caught up somewhere in that nest of madness. She opened her eyes to find both Torres and Mason staring at her.

"My sister is over there," she said. "I need to bring her home."

Mason raised an eyebrow. "And how do you propose to do that?"

Alicia steeled herself and took a deep breath. She wasn't going to let her sister down. "I don't have a plan yet. But I just found out my sister is in the middle of a violent outbreak. She's dealt with more than enough horrors to last a lifetime, without adding to it now. So get me over there, and one way or another,

I'll get her out. Her and her fiancé. Can you support me on this?"

Mason stared at her with his silver-hued eyes and remained silent for a few long seconds before nodding slowly. "I was going to send you anyway. Our agents need to have a measure of passion for their assignments—it ensures they'll push harder, go beyond their limits. And you did good work for us in Taiwan and China. But this? Alicia, we'll be dropping you into full-on hostile territory."

"I understand that."

"Good. And another thing. I know you're determined to get Gigi and...?"

"Curt."

"Yes. You'll get Gigi and Curt out of there. I'm confident in that. But that's only part of your objective. We also need you to gather intel. From your sister and fiancé, from their local contacts, from whoever you can trust. We need to understand what's going on there. And Alicia... no detection. We *can't* have the Chinese government knowing we're involved."

"If I'm caught?" Alicia asked.

Mason met her eye. "You're easily deniable. We'll bury your clearance, and there's no record of you with any of the other agencies. You'll get locked in a hole somewhere in China. And you'll probably be first on a list to be experimented on next. This isn't a joke, Alicia. If you're going, this is a black bag operation. We don't acknowledge it."

Alicia had expected this, but hearing it out loud still felt like a slap to the face. *Doesn't matter. I'm going with or without his help. The risk is the same.*

She forced a smile to her face. "Then I suppose I should try not to get caught."

"We'd all prefer it," Mason said. "Go home, get your gear, and be at Joint Base Andrews by 0500. Torres will work up a full briefing package for you." He looked to Torres. "Usual info, Lara. Known military assets in the area. Include the full package on General Liang. I already gave her the basic package. Give her the full analysis you briefed me on. Territory issues, maps, all of it."

"On it," Torres said. "But it's a lot to go over."

"I'm a fast learner," Alicia said. "I'll also need credentials in case I get stopped at a checkpoint."

"Of course." Mason waved a dismissive hand. "I'll make sure to get some Chinese identification to you before departure. Now get out of here. Pack for hiking. I don't know how close we can get you to Yichun. It'll probably be like last time, we have a station exit in Heilongjiang Province, but we'll need to get creative from there. I'll have Brice pull up satellite reconnaissance and see if we can tell whether the roads are locked down or not."

Alicia nodded. "Train ride?"

"Yes. I think the most direct way will be to get you to Taiwan. It'll be a familiar trip for you, except getting the two hundred or so miles from Harbin to Yichun. That part will need some investigation."

Alicia felt the reality of the situation settling on her. "Nothing is going to keep me from getting my sister."

"And the information we need," Mason added.

"And the information," Alicia agreed. "Where will I get supplied?"

"I'll arrange for what you need to be made available at the safehouse in Taiwan. If you have any requests out of the ordinary, get me the list and I'll do what I can." He gave Alicia a long look. "Alicia, are you ready for this?"

Alicia took one last look at the screen showing the video and photos taken by Gigi and Curt. Cold, iron resolve filled her.

"I'm ready."

CHAPTER
SIXTEEN

Fifteen minutes after arriving home, Alicia had her bags packed. Bagel sat on the bed, watching the process with confused interest.

A normal backpacking bag with an internal frame held a few changes of clothes, some dark, others in the mottled colors of the season, mostly browns and greens. Her duffel's workout gear had been emptied out and replaced with a low-profile ballistic vest and a collection of well-balanced throwing knives.

She glanced at the clock on the wall and realized she had a full twelve hours before she had to go to Andrews.

Bagel walked up to her, put his paws up against her leg, and tapped and squeezed a rudimentary message.

"Sit. Eat. Sleep."

Alicia looked down at the cat and nodded. She must be giving off huge amounts of weird vibes for Bagel to be, in effect, telling her to chill.

She plopped herself onto the sofa, turned on the TV, and tried to relax. Bagel settled onto her lap. She did need to chill for a moment and plan out what she was going to do.

Al Pacino's voice came over the television. *"There's the boss, and under him, there's the skipper."* Along the bottom of the screen, the cable box said *Donnie Brasco* was playing. She'd never seen the movie, wasn't big into gangster films, but just as she was about to change the channel, she saw Johnny Depp and grinned. Alicia had always thought he was gorgeous in an unconventional way.

"Yeah, it's like the army," Depp said.

"Bullshit." Pacino waved his hand dismissively. *"The army is some guy you don't know telling you to go whack some other guy you don't know. Listen here... when I introduce you, I'm going to say, 'This is a friend of mine.' That means you're a connected guy. Now if I said instead, this is a friend of ours, that would mean you're a made guy. Capiche?"*

Alicia sat upright, her eyes widening as the phrases "friend of mine" and "friend of ours" replayed in her head.

She'd heard those phrases before. She was sure of it. It had been at Denny's place, her father's tech guy. He was supposedly an MIT graduate, but she knew him only as the owner of a bar in Little Italy, a place her father had taken her to plenty of times when she was in the city. They had good food, and lots of Dad's friends hung out there.

It was there that she'd heard that phrase. She remembered one time when a huge guy named Gino Romano came over to their table—the man was nearly as wide as he was tall—and introduced some spooky-looking guy who spoke to Dad in Italian. Gino had definitely used the phrase "friend of ours" when introducing him.

She'd thought it was a weird thing to say, since Dad obviously didn't know the man, so how could they be friends?

"Bagel..."

The cat raised his head, the tip of his tail practically in his mouth as he meowed forlornly. Tapping and squeezing her thigh, he spelled out in Morse code, *"Sleep."*

"No, I can't sleep."

Alicia tried to remember other times she'd heard those phrases used. She knew she'd heard both of them before, and always when someone of Italian descent was introducing someone to her father. But her father wasn't Italian. The name "Yoder" was about as far from Italian as possible. But then she remembered Uncle Vinnie, the guy who, as best she could figure, Dad worked for when not doing stuff for the Outfit.

"I'm an idiot."

Alicia shook her head as it all fell into place. She'd even confronted her father about it on her eighteenth birthday. She'd done a reverse-image lookup on Vinnie and found a news article about Vincenzo Bianchi being the head of the Bianchi crime family out of New York.

She remembered the conversation as if it had happened yesterday. They were driving in her convertible...

"I've known Vinnie for almost thirty years," her father said. *"The rumors in the newspapers about him are all junk; don't give it a second thought. As to what I do... I have some colorful friends."*

"I met some. They're all Italian, right?"

"Not all." Her father laughed. *"But a good number of them are. You've been to my place on the Upper East Side. Not many Italians there. And you've met Denny—he's about as Italian as you are Jewish. But Vinnie and I and lots of his folks, we all came out of a part of New York City called Little Italy. Anyway, I don't tell you exactly what I do, because sometimes what I do is classified."*

"Classified? You mean like government classified?"

It was at that point she ended up first hearing about Dad's work for a secret organization, which turned out to be the Outfit. Her father didn't exactly lie to her, but he'd deftly avoided admitting to something that she now knew had to be true.

"My father is a member of the mafia." She whispered it to herself, weighing how the words felt to her ears.

Bagel tapped and squeezed. *"Good man."*

Alicia looked down at the cat, and her vision blurred with tears. "I know he is... but this is all... I don't know. I guess I was blind to what was right in front of my face."

She thought about her father's associates. Denny had been a lifelong friend of her father's, and he was hard to associate with the mob. A black guy, some kind of electronics genius from MIT, with a Puerto Rican girlfriend. Hardly the usual mob stereotype. But she'd heard there was a back room in that bar that she'd never been in, and she now wondered what went on back there.

And then there was Esther Rosen. She owned a sporting

goods store, but she had a back room too—and this back room was one Alicia had been in. Esther was a weapons expert and had given Alicia shooting lessons. She'd certainly be useful to someone with ties to the mob. It was hard to imagine the zaftig grandmotherly type being associated with something nefarious, but Alicia had seen the woman shoot a six-inch target from nearly a mile away.

Then there was Tony Montelaro. Just thinking about the Italian brick wall brought a smile to Alicia's face. He'd taught her an important lesson early on: technique didn't matter much when the other guy outweighed you by two hundred pounds of muscle. Her dad had made her spar with Tony to teach her that lesson, and he'd thrown her around like a rag doll. She'd since been invited to his home to eat with Tony's wife and kids, and she felt almost like a little sister to the big guy.

The people she'd met, the way they'd treated her father with surprising respect... it was the kind of respect a mobster would demand.

Because Dad *was* a mobster. It was a hard pill for her to swallow, but it made so much sense.

Alicia picked up her phone and called her father, not really expecting him to answer, but hoping he might. Between her sudden realization and Gigi's circumstances, she really wanted to talk to him.

The call went straight to voicemail.

"Dad, I need to talk to you. Gigi's in trouble. She's involved in some crazy stuff in China. I'm going over there to get her. She needs my help. I wish you could come with me." She paused, feeling the first tremor of fear settle in. "I could really use your advice. Your help. But I'll handle it. I'll bring her back. I'll be radio silent for... well... I don't know how long. I leave tomorrow morning. Love you."

After she hung up, Alicia stared down at the phone, then immediately called her dad's number again.

"You and I are going to have a long talk about some stuff when I get back."

She hung up again, then looked down at Bagel. "All right, you. I guess I'll have to ask Becca to watch you while I'm gone."

Bagel jumped up instantly and ran to his BabbelPet buttons. He spammed the "No" button twenty times before she could reach him to pull him away.

She lifted the cat up in front of her face. "No arguing. She'll take good care of you."

He swatted her on the face five times.

"Hey!"

Bagel did it again, but this time he pressed his fuzzy mittens into her face and began pressing her face in Morse code.

"No," he tapped.

"What am I supposed to do, Bagel? Take you?"

More of the pressing and kneading. *"Yes."*

Alicia dismissed the thought instantly. Taking a cat to China was stupid. Reckless. Impossible.

Unless it isn't.

Alicia stared at the cat. The little beast had serious attachment issues. But Narmer's words rang like a warning—and a piece of ethereal advice.

I suggest keeping him with you whenever possible.

Alicia owed this cat her life. He'd saved her from a disease that could have been fatal. She pushed her face into Bagel's and rubbed her cheek against his.

"I'm sorry, little buddy... I need to treat you better, don't I?"

Bagel pressed his face back against hers and purred.

Having an ally with her would be... comforting. The transportation from Andrews Air Force Base to the Far East would be via military transport, so normal baggage rules would be waived. As long as Mason didn't know she had Bagel with her, she could pull it off.

Better to ask forgiveness than permission.

"Okay, Bagel," she said. He licked his lips in expectation. "If we do this, you have to listen to me. You'll have to hide until we're on the plane and in the air. And you do what I say, or I'll leave you in China to be turned into street food. Will you do what I say?"

From Bagel's bored expression, she knew the threat meant nothing to the cat, and he probably knew she'd never go through with any of it. Nevertheless, he tapped out *"Yes"* on her face.

"I'm probably going to regret this," Alicia said. She set Bagel down, then crossed to the kitchen to grab a few packs of tuna. She couldn't bring much with her, so either the cat would have to find some rodents to eat while they skulked through the Chinese countryside, or she'd have to find something for him at their destination.

She walked back to the bedroom, Bagel following closely,

and shoved the tuna packages in her backpack. She pointed a finger at the cat. "You'd better carry your weight over there."

Then Alicia had a sudden idea. She threw open the doors to her closet and dug through a stack of Pelican cases. She found what she was looking for in the last case, and turned to grin at Bagel.

"Bagel, this is going to be *awesome*."

CHAPTER

SEVENTEEN

In the predawn gloom, Alicia turned right off of Dower House Road and passed a sign that read *Pearl Harbor Gate Hours 0500 – 2100*. Moments later she'd arrived at a well-lit security outpost.

She lowered her window as she pulled to a stop. She handed the guard her ID, and after a quick check he handed it back and waved her through.

"Thank you," Alicia said, and drove onto the base.

She went past the East Perimeter Road, her headlights illuminating the road ahead, which soon curved around past several hangars. Some held planes that were in need of repair and maintenance. Most were closed.

In the distance, the form of a C-5M Super Galaxy transport plane stood like an enormous shadow on the tarmac. Nearly two hundred and fifty feet long, the plane weighed almost six hundred thousand pounds when loaded. Alicia only knew the specs because of her sister, Samantha. The contractor Samantha worked for helped maintain the avionics systems.

Alicia drove closer, and a soldier waved her to the gaping maw of an open hangar. She pulled in next to a row of cars and military vehicles.

"All right, Bagel." She opened the duffel. "Time for you to hide. And keep quiet, you hear me?"

Bagel looked down into the bag, somehow managing to look put out, then crawled inside. Alicia zipped the bag up nearly all the way, but left a gap for air. She got out of her car and pulled out her backpack, slinging it over one shoulder, then carefully lifted the duffel over the other.

The airman who'd waved her in strode up to her, all business. "Ms. Yoder?"

"That's me."

He held out a silver coin to her, pinched between thumb and finger.

Alicia realized what he was doing—he was a member of the Outfit.

On the face of the coin was a familiar pyramid featuring the Eye of Providence—one of the Outfit's IDs. As the airman continued to grip one half of the coin, Alicia gripped the other half. A second later, the Eye lit up.

The airman pocketed the coin and gave her a nod. "I've got a seat for you on the C-5, destination Taiwan."

"Any refueling stops?"

"No, the C-5 is capable of in-air refueling. May I take your bags for you?"

Alicia shook her head and tightened her grip on the bags. "No thanks. I've got them."

The soldier nodded respectfully and held out a hand. "Your car keys, please. In case of an emergency. We'll have them stored securely in a safe inside the hangar's office waiting for you upon return. Do you know your return date?"

"Not yet," Alicia answered. She dropped the keys into his palm. "Hopefully not too long."

"Excellent." He pointed to the ramp at the back of the plane where a fleet of forklifts must have been used to load all the pallets currently in the cargo hold. "You're good to go, Ms. Yoder. Have a pleasant flight."

She smiled her thanks and walked across the tarmac to the plane.

From the deep shadows under the wing of the C-5, two figures emerged. Mason and Torres.

"Thank you for being on time," Mason said, checking his watch. "You still have nearly an hour before the plane departs. Lara, her package."

Lara held out a small Pelican case. "Inside you'll find a tablet with all the files we have on the situation in Yichun, plus everything we have on General Liang, and a summary of other things from our discussion yesterday. We've arranged for you to get equipped at the safehouse in Taiwan." She pointed at Alicia's duffel. "You'll want to figure out what you need and don't need once you're in position and can assess things better."

"What's my itinerary?"

"You're going to Taiwan first," Mason said, "though unlike

last time, there will be no customs interaction, as this is a black operation. A commercial jet will be shadowing your flight into Taiwan airspace, and your flight will be diverted into a secluded part of the tarmac where transportation will be arranged to the safehouse. But from there, there's a slight change of plans. It turns out Harbin is under lockdown, and getting you out of that city might prove challenging. So we've adjusted things a bit. You'll go to Shuangyashan instead. It's about two hundred seventy miles east of your target."

Alicia nodded. "So from there I just have to arrange transport to a city gone wild."

"We have some assets in Shuangyashan that might be able to help," Lara interjected.

"The situation is fluid," Mason said. "We'll have to play a lot of this by ear."

Lara pointed at the Pelican case. "When you get to the safehouse, leave the tablet there. You don't want that on you when going into China. So while you're en route, study it like your life depends on it."

"Her life *does* depend on it," Mason said. Alicia heard the worry in his voice. He pulled a phone from his pocket and handed it to her. "It's a miniaturized satellite phone. The latest and greatest encryption that should allow you to phone home base even if cell towers are offline. I want regular progress updates, Alicia." He pointed at her. "*Regular updates*. No exceptions, unless doing so puts your life at risk."

"Okay," Alicia said, pocketing the phone.

"Any questions?" Mason asked.

"Do we have an exit strategy for when I find my sister and Curt?"

"Not yet," Mason admitted. "We don't know their condition or the situation on the ground. Once you find them, and find out more, we'll figure out the best way to get them out."

"I guess I better get on board then. Thank you both for everything."

Mason held out his hand, and Alicia took it. Her boss let out a long, tired sigh. "Your father is going to lose his mind when he finds out what I've sent you to do."

Alicia smiled. "With any luck, I'll be back before he even knows I was gone."

Before the ramp had even closed all the way, Bagel was out of the bag and on Alicia's lap. She'd put a small, collapsible carrier in the bottom of her bag, but didn't pull it out. Instead, the cat curled up on her lap.

The seats inside the C-5 sat mostly empty. A quick count showed the plane's passenger capacity to be seventy-three. Alicia had secured her backpack and duffel in the bins for personal baggage, after pulling out her various IDs and the iPad-like tablet.

She felt herself pressed into the seat as the plane took off. The way the jet ambled down the runway, she could almost feel the jet struggling with its heavy load of cargo. The C-5 lifted slowly, ponderously, and banked in the air the same way.

She kept firm hold of Bagel until they reached cruising altitude.

Then it was time to study.

She turned on the tablet, which only unlocked after she swiped her finger across the built-in reader. Only one folder showed on the screen, so she tapped on it.

The folder contained several subfolders, the first of which was titled "Liang." She spent the next several hours reading the data gathered by Lara and the others in the analyst crew. At first, the collection of documents looked and felt scattered and barely connected. Receipts found in General Liang's waste bin, old personnel requests for soldiers and scientists, and so on. Each piece of information on its own meant little, but in aggregate, they pointed to both a geographical location in China, as well as a plan years in the making. A plan begun by the same general who had orchestrated the New Arcadia conspiracy, and whom Chris Xiang had killed.

And now a protégé of that general—that deluded *psychopath* who'd nearly manufactured a war to cause the hostile takeover of Taiwan—had somehow slid into the vacuum left by General Hong Zuocheng.

Liang Feng. What kind of madman had stepped into the old monster's shoes?

Alicia found herself wondering if Liang's goals were a continuation of the ones she'd nearly died to thwart, or if the new general had all-new horrors in mind. Judging from what she'd seen, courtesy of her sister, this new terror in China was a different flavor of evil.

The most interesting facet of Liang's file was its thinness.

She'd read the basics in an earlier dossier, and the full version honestly didn't add much more color. Liang barely registered, other than a few brief mentions in political and military memos. To Alicia, that lack of public notice felt intentional.

She sat back in her seat, scratching absently under Bagel's chin. She often wondered how the world would be if places like China and Mexico weren't run by absolutely corrupt governments. China was already one of the top economies in the world. Mexico would be in the top five if not for the cartels.

She pushed the dour thoughts away. The beginnings of the mission were simple. Get to Yichun undetected, with whatever transportation she could find. On foot if she had to. Get close enough to see the state of things. Evaluate the military presence. Look for regular traffic patterns that might point to the location of a nearby lab.

And... find her sister.

Unfortunately, Yichun was big enough to make that no easy task. And if the city was under lockdown, it might be an almost impossible task. The more she thought about it, looking for Curt might be easier. Gigi was just another Chinese girl in a city full of Chinese citizens. Curt, though? A big, white American? He couldn't help but stand out. Especially with that blond hair of his.

As she thought about this, Alicia heard a clank on the roof of the plane. She looked up at the ceiling and wondered if that was the sound of them refueling. Unlike a commercial jet, military transports didn't have much in the way of feel-good communications to tell passengers what was going on.

She looked back at the tablet. So much more data to go

through. Then again, she had another ten hours before they landed.

She petted Bagel between his ears. "You get yourself good and rested. I've got some studying to do, and I want to make sure I don't miss any details."

The cat yawned and went back to sleep, something Alicia wished she could do.

CHAPTER

EIGHTEEN

It was a gloomy morning as Alicia once again entered a part of Taipei that no tourists would normally go to. The area was a bit rough around the edges. The streets were so tightly packed it was impossible for two cars to drive side by side without one of the vehicles pulling onto a walkway. Only three months earlier she'd taken this same ride into a downtrodden part of Taiwan's capital, and now, as she studied her driver's profile, the man looked familiar.

"Are you the same person who drove me here last time?"

"Yes, I believe so." The middle-aged man was a part of the Outfit, and he hitched his thumb back to where they'd come. "However, last time I did not get you from the airport. You were in the downtown US embassy."

"You have a great memory." Alicia panned her gaze across the crowded streets. "It's amazing that anyone can find anything in this place. All the streets look the same."

"You said the same thing last time." The man cracked a smile and patted the side of his navigation system. "Most taxi drivers nowadays don't remember the streets like they used to before the computers. Now all you need is the overhead map, and it can guide you. But I'm older and had to learn how to navigate without using a map or these machines. I know this area very well."

He pointed. "The signs are always between buildings if you know where to look. You see there, there's a sign hidden between the awning of the Hot Pot and Pho restaurants. We're heading south on Lane 123 off East Nanjing Road."

He took a left, and somehow the street got even narrower. "This is Alley 4." He pointed up at a streetlamp with a barely visible number stenciled on it. "Very simple."

Alicia shook her head and thanked all that was holy that she didn't have to navigate these streets.

Last time she was here, it had been night, and there had been a number of prostitutes and street toughs around. She didn't see so many now—perhaps they just weren't as visible during the day—but there were plenty of homeless people shuffling about. The Outfit tended to have properties in rundown parts of cities. She'd once asked Mason about that, and his response was fairly sensible: nobody expects to find a spy center in the middle of a slum.

"We're almost there," her driver said.

Alicia didn't even recognize where they were until the driver stopped in front of a plain-looking building. Two large Asian men stood on either side of a set of double doors, protected from a light drizzle by a red awning.

Alicia grabbed her bags—one of them had Bagel poking his head through an opening—and stepped out of the car. The minute she closed the door behind her, the driver revved the engine and vanished from sight.

Alicia stepped up to the two men, who were the size of sumo wrestlers. The sound of techno music thumped from the door behind them. "Hi guys," she said in Mandarin.

"I'll need to see some ID, Miss Yoder," one of the men replied, in English. His voice was so gravelly and deep that it was hard to understand what he was saying.

Alicia dug the coin out of her pocket and held it out. The man grabbed the other side of the coin, and the Eye lit up. The two men stepped aside and motioned for Alicia to enter.

Alicia opened the door and walked into the building. The inside of the building was utterly silent. Only when she shut the door behind her did she hear the muted sound of the techno music—now appearing to come from outside. The music came from the door itself.

But she'd been here before, and this time the place's tricks and unusual characteristics held a different meaning to her. It was almost like walking into the *Cheers* bar and getting a greeting from the same patrons who were always there. The first time it was unnerving, but now it was somewhat like home.

And yet, as Alicia panned her gaze across the lobby, she was convinced that she'd once been to *another* place that had almost the same appearance. But that memory was vague, hazy. Even though her recent memory was now perfect, the nanites had done nothing to restore the gaps in her memory from before. Now those gaps hinted at something, but it was just out of reach.

The lobby was wood-paneled, with the scent of pipe tobacco. A reception desk across the room was manned by a short, matronly Asian woman with her hair bundled up with an elaborate set of clips.

Alicia smiled. "Mrs. Yang, it's so nice to see you again."

The woman returned her smile and motioned for her to come closer. "Come, come, Miss Yoder, I was told you would be arriving before noon, and before noon you have arrived." She spoke English with a light British accent. With her gray-streaked hair and wrinkled face, she had to be in her late sixties at least—but her voice was strong, she had perfect posture, and she gave off a youthful energy.

Yet despite her smile and pleasant manner, she also held a pistol, which she aimed directly at Alicia as she added, "ID, please."

Bagel hissed at the woman, and Alicia patted his head. "It's okay. The Outfit takes their security very seriously."

Alicia held out her coin, and when Mrs. Yang grabbed the other side, the Eye glowed.

Mrs. Yang put away the gun and gave Alicia a wink. "It's very good to see you again, miss. I believe you have a new set of needs." She looked down at the black cat poking his head out of the duffel. "Mr. Bagel, I apologize for having upset you. I hope you can understand that I was doing my job."

Bagel let out a five-second-long meowing sound that rose

and fell in tone, almost as if he were communicating in cat-speak.

"I completely agree, Mr. Bagel." Mrs. Yang reached under the counter and produced an ornate silver bowl filled with some form of kibble. Bagel scrambled out of the duffel, hopped onto the floor, and began chowing down.

How does this woman know Bagel's name? Alicia wondered. She must have mentioned it at some point, and now it was on file in her HR record at the Outfit. These people knew entirely too much for her comfort.

Alicia pointed to a solid wall to her right. "I recall this place being like a haunted mansion with moving walls and such. If I'm not mistaken, that's the way to the stairs leading down to the train."

"All things in their proper order, Miss Yoder." Mrs. Yang's posh accent didn't match her appearance. "This establishment meets the needs of those who seek its assistance. You are here with such a need, and I am here to help you fulfill it." She motioned to a hall on Alicia's left. "Director Mason left me with some specific instructions to exercise on his behalf. Please, follow me."

The hallway was lit by old-fashioned sconces with light-bulbs that flickered as if they were aflame. At the end of the hall a door stood slightly ajar.

"This is our quartermaster's section," Mrs. Yang said, "as I'm sure you recall. Your arrival unlocked this wing." She stopped before the door, stepped to one side, and motioned grandly. "After you."

Alicia pushed the door open, and it moved very slowly due to its immensity. It was a good six inches thick and probably weighed a thousand pounds, yet even so, it moved easily and soundlessly on well-oiled hinges. As she stepped through, lights flickered on, revealing a room filled with unmarked lockers, with no obvious way to open them. She felt like she was in some secret lair in a *John Wick* film.

Mrs. Yang motioned to a pole in the center of the room. At about eye level was a visor, like one might see on a submarine's periscope. "If you will, Miss Yoder, please peer into the biometric scanner."

Alicia put her eyes against the visor. A green light flickered, and a series of clicks followed. She stepped back and looked around. Several of the lockers had popped open.

"Let's start with this side of the room, shall we?" said Mrs. Yang, gesturing.

Alicia went to the first open locker. Inside was a camouflaged military uniform from the PLA, the Chinese army. The insignia on the collar indicated that the uniform belonged to a staff sergeant. Included with the uniform were black leather boots, socks, bra, and underwear. Underneath the clothes were all the IDs and papers Alicia might need. In addition to her red passport for mainland China—complete with her picture inside—she had been provided with a military ID, a Chinese driver's license, and a wallet stocked with a large quantity of Chinese money and a Bank of China Union Pay card.

"Very much like in your last mission," Mrs. Yang said, "you will find it useful to look like a member of the military. Satellite reconnaissance shows military personnel in the area equipped with battle gear, including the Chinese equivalent of a battle dress uniform. This uniform will give you freedom to navigate situations that a civilian might not. I would advise you to change into your uniform now. Let's make sure everything fits properly."

Mrs. Yang motioned to a table next to the biometric scanner. "Please keep your Outfit-assigned ID, since it is keyed to your biometric signature. The rest of your US IDs you must leave with me, along with your other things. I will take care of it for you."

Alicia reluctantly left her items on the table, then went to the next open locker, which contained a padded vest.

"It won't stop all rifle rounds," Mrs. Yang explained, "but it will stop most small-arms fire."

Alicia removed her military jacket and shrugged into the vest. She adjusted the straps and put her jacket back on. As she turned toward the nearest mirror and looked at herself, this was no longer a joke. She looked every part the PLA soldier, minus the battle rifle.

The third locker contained a plastic case made of the same impervious stuff that Pelican cases were made of. It was the size of a briefcase, but had no handle or lock. The Eye of Providence was molded into the plastic in two places.

"Contained within this case are military uniforms for your sister and her fiancé, including the necessary identification," Mrs. Yang said. "Based on the Outfit's research, the uniforms should fit them perfectly. The case also contains hair dye and

bandages for Curt, so that you can make him look less...
conspicuous."

The idea of disguising Curt was a sound one. It might be
the only way to get him out.

"But how do I open it?" Alicia asked.

"Just put your thumbs on both logos at the same time. They
are keyed to your biometrics. Hold them there until it clicks open."

Alicia picked up the case; it was heavy for its size. "What
happens if someone else tries to open it?"

"Hopefully that will not happen, but if it does, I suggest you
step back. The case will explode with enough force to shred
anyone within a thirty-foot radius."

The look of brief amusement on Mrs. Yang's face sent a chill
up Alicia's spine.

She moved to the next locker, which held a backpack.

"This is a standard three-day assault pack that most PLA
soldiers deploy with when on a combat mission. You'll find
several standard-issue items inside: compass, flashlight, other
such bits and bobs." Mrs. Yang's voice lowered for emphasis.
"And this *is* a combat mission. The number of soldiers deployed
in your target areas is the largest the Outfit has seen since the
so-called peacekeeping efforts of Hong Kong." She pointed at
the case that Alicia held awkwardly under one arm. "You'll find
the case fits nicely inside the pack."

It did, with room to spare.

The next locker contained a holstered pistol with a belt that
already had several magazines clipped onto it. Alicia wrapped
the belt around her waist and threaded the holster in place.

"This is a QSZ-92 Chinese-issued pistol," Mrs. Yang said. "It uses a Chinese proprietary 5.8x21mm 46-grain armor-piercing round, twenty rounds per magazine. The projectile is faster than the larger grain nine-millimeter, but the muzzle energy is a little less."

Alicia pulled the gun out of its holster, popped the magazine, and gave the gun a quick once-over. She seated the gun back into its holster and went to the final opened locker, which contained a small case, which she popped open to reveal a pair of goggles.

"Miss Yoder, that's a state-of-the-art set of night-vision goggles with a spare battery pack. Director Mason sensed you might have a need for it."

Bagel let out a meow and tapped on Alicia's leg. *"Food?"*

As if anticipating the request, Mrs. Yang pointed at the sealed package on the top shelf of the locker and said, "This is three days' worth of Chinese MREs. You'll also find several packages of tuna for Mr. Bagel."

The elderly woman then knelt down and offered the cat a piece of some kind of jerky. Bagel sniffed at it, then snatched it away and chewed on it, purring.

After taking inventory of everything in her pack and hefting it up onto her shoulders, Alicia took a moment to adjust some straps and was surprised at how evenly balanced the weight was.

"What's next?"

"Follow me, Miss Yoder."

Mrs. Yang led her back down the same hall, but instead of leading to the lobby, it took them to stairs going down.

Alicia shook her head. This had happened the last time, too, so she had been carefully looking to catch the sight of a wall moving on rollers or something, but she hadn't seen a thing. Somehow the straight hall got her turned around again and the lobby had vanished.

Mrs. Yang motioned toward the stairs. "The train is waiting for you."

Alicia heard a click behind her and turned back—only to find Mrs. Yang was gone and Alicia was facing a blank wall.

"How do you guys do this?" She spun around and let out a growl of frustration. Then she looked down at Bagel. "Did you see where she went?"

Bagel advanced toward the stairs, looked back at her, and meowed impatiently.

"Fine, fine, I'm coming." Alicia descended the stairs. They led to a tiny train platform, no more than ten feet wide, where a sleek railway car was already waiting, its doors open. Alicia had no choice but to board.

The doors slid closed behind her, and a disembodied voice announced, *"The train will be departing in ten seconds. Please hold on to a rail or you will likely be thrown backward. This is your only warning."*

Alicia took a seat and gripped one of the poles.

Bagel jumped onto her lap and flattened himself as he held on to her with his claws. Luckily, the fatigues were made of a thick material that helped limit the stabbing effect.

"Five seconds. Four. Three. Two. One."

Alicia and Bagel slid backward as the train accelerated at a rate rivaling that of a race car. Within seconds, wind keened loudly outside as the train flew through the darkness.

It was then that Alicia realized she wasn't one hundred percent sure of her destination. If she was still going to Shuangyashan, as Mason had said before she left the States, that was a fifteen-hundred-mile trip—and judging by the pace of the train on her last visit here, the journey would take about six hours.

She petted Bagel. "Let's get a little rest. This might be the only time we can get any shuteye."

Alicia rested her head on the back of her seat, and the rhythm of the train made sleep come quickly. She must have really been exhausted, for she didn't wake again until the train decelerated and the disembodied voice returned.

"We will be arriving at the Shuangyashan safe house in approx-imately five minutes. Please disembark only after the train has come to a complete stop."

Alicia checked her phone. Sure enough, the trip had taken six hours. In that time, she had traveled beneath the East China Sea, under the Koreas, and all the way up to Shuangyashan. If only such trains were more readily available, this would be an awesome way to get around. So much better than the airport congestion and security hassles everyone else had to deal with.

When the doors opened, Alicia stepped out. An elderly man wearing a surgical mask waited on the platform. He greeted her with a salute.

"Miss Yoder," he said with a thick Chinese accent, "can I please see your ID?"

After Alicia went through the process of mutual identification using the coin, the old man handed her a mask. "There are new rules in Shuangyashan. Everyone must wear a mask. There is fear of a new round of Covid."

"Covid?" Alicia scoffed as she donned the mask.

"That is what they say." The old man shrugged and gestured to the stairs behind him. "Welcome to Shuangyashan, Miss Yoder. Transportation will be waiting outside to take you where you need to go."

Alicia climbed the stairs into the dimness of an abandoned building. She followed exit signs until she found herself on the streets of Shuangyashan.

A man in a PLA uniform walked up to her immediately. Though his face was partially obscured by his surgical mask, she recognized him.

"I bet you didn't expect to see me here," he whispered.

Alicia blinked away tears of happiness and surprise. "Chris, is that you?" she whispered back.

Agent Chris Xiang had been with her at the worst of her last China mission. They'd saved each other's lives. He was the last person she'd expected to see.

He nodded to the truck on the other side of the street. "You're taking my place as a military witness. Basically, the PLA needs some supplies brought in, and you're there to make sure the driver makes it and doesn't chicken out." He made a hurrying motion. "Go. We'll see each other again soon."

As Alicia crossed the street toward the truck, the driver yelled at her in Mandarin, "Get in the back! You people filled even the inside of my truck."

She climbed onto the back of the large pickup, which was piled high with fifty-pound bags of quicklime.

Quicklime?

It was then that Alicia realized she understood what was going on. Quicklime was often used to help slow the decay of, or limit the smell of, dead bodies.

A chill raced through her as the driver put the truck into gear and they lurched toward their destination.

CHAPTER
NINETEEN

Once the truck had crossed through the military checkpoint just outside of Yichun, Alicia waited for the right moment. When the pickup slowed to take a turn, she scooped up Bagel, hopped out of the back of the truck, and watched as it continued driving toward the city. It was just after midnight, local time.

Out here, away from city lights, the stars in the sky shone brighter than she'd ever recalled seeing. She took a moment to just take it all in, letting peace and calm settle over her. Alicia wasn't good at the whole meditation thing, like her dad was, but looking up into these heavens, she understood what Grandma Yoder meant by "God's wonders." Even Bagel seemed mesmerized by the sight.

The moment passed, and she was about to dig out the local map that she'd brought with her when she realized she didn't need it. All she needed to do was bring up the image in her mind's eye. But she did pull out her compass to get her bearings. The soft green glow of the needle and compass rings helped her orient herself in the direction of Yichun. From what she'd gathered from signs while riding in the truck, she was about twelve miles from her destination. She figured she could make it to the city outskirts in three hours if she jogged some of the way.

"First things first, Bagel," she said, dropping her pack to the ground. She opened the top and pulled out a cat collar. Simple and black to blend in with Bagel's fur, with no nametag. She clipped it around the cat's neck and felt for a subtle widening in the material. When she found the spot on the collar, she pushed it and heard a light beep. "GPS for the kitty. Don't worry, Bagel. Now if we get separated, I can track you with my phone."

The cat looked dubious.

"No need to look at me like that," Alicia said.

She picked up Bagel and started off at a light jog, not wanting to push too hard until she could figure out how she tolerated carrying the pack. Arriving in Yichun exhausted wouldn't accomplish much. Bagel scrambled up her shirt and perched on the top of her pack, lying across it and her shoulder.

Running in the dark was usually ill-advised, but Alicia found that the starlight and crescent moon provided just enough light for her to see where she was going and not take any missteps. Perhaps the nanites were giving her eyesight an extra boost. Either way, she left the night vision goggles in the pack, not needing them.

No one she knew actually enjoyed running. No one she

considered human, anyway. A friend from college once told her there were two types of people in the world. The first ran only as a necessary evil. The second were psychopaths. At the time, Alicia had agreed. But since receiving Narmer's gift, things felt different. The simple act of running, once a bore and a chore, now felt liberating. And to run outside under the panorama of the open sky brought calm to a stressful situation.

For the next three hours, she alternated between jogging and walking, taking small sips of water to keep herself hydrated. Finally, the apartment buildings of Yichun sprouted on the horizon. Alicia continued forward until she was only a few hundred yards from the city's fringes.

Sunrise wouldn't grace this part of China for another ninety minutes, and there were no lights on in the city—none at all. The buildings at the city's edge stood like lifeless monoliths proclaiming...

Proclaiming what? Alicia wondered.

Death, her mind whispered back to her.

Alicia lowered Bagel to the ground, and they both crept closer. The distant sound of a scream broke the night's silence, then cut off abruptly after a single gunshot.

Alicia dropped her pack and removed the Chinese pistol from its holster. She adjusted the holster into its appendix position, racked the pistol's slide, then re-holstered it. She only had three magazines with twenty rounds each. Not enough for long-term use, but perhaps she could find more ammo in the city. Better yet, she wouldn't need it at all.

Alicia scanned the tops of the buildings for silhouettes

standing out against the star-filled sky, but she spotted nothing. The city was dead and still, a necropolis.

She leaned down and whispered to Bagel, "Stay close."

They ventured into the city, moving cautiously from street to street. At each intersection, Alicia pressed herself against the corner and looked for movement. Shadows flickered in alleys and doorways, and once she thought she caught the stirring of a dark curtain in a darker window, but nothing more.

The faint smell of smoke reached her. Without the nanites she doubted she would have noticed it all, as even now the scent was too faint to make out what was burning or in what direction it was coming from.

From behind her, Alicia heard the scrape of a shoe on hard-packed dirt. She whirled, drawing her pistol, but nothing greeted her. No soldier, no citizen, no... something *other*. Only blackness stared back. She flicked her eyes down at Bagel. His hackles were raised, and he stared into the gloom and backed away a single step before looking up at her with golden, worried eyes.

She took the warning and backed away alongside the cat, though she still couldn't see anything in the shadows.

And then Bagel suddenly relaxed and turned his back on whoever—or *what*ever—they'd heard.

Alicia took as straight a path as she could toward the city's center, not deviating down side streets. As badly as she wanted to find her sister, her first goal was to understand what was happening here.

None of the streets had signs naming them. It made for a

monotonous sort of hell with every street looking the same, each building looking similar to the one on the street before.

When Bagel paused and sniffed at the air, Alicia did the same. The scent of smoke was stronger here, and with it came the smell of burning meat.

"Please be bad barbecue," she whispered to herself. "Or just dead, burning animals. Don't be anything else." But she didn't believe it. The sickly-sweet aroma was unlike anything she'd smelled before, and Alicia suspected she knew what it was.

Just like she'd known what that truckload of quicklime was for.

Up ahead, the blackness brightened to gray and then a flickering orange. Someone had a small fire going, or maybe the feeble glow came from the leftovers of a guttering flame. It was coming from inside a darkened building, visible through a metal roller grate pulled most of the way down.

Alicia gave the opening a wide berth as she moved on.

But as she came around the corner of the building, she found the road blocked by cement barricades, each about four feet tall. The body of a young girl was draped over the barricade furthest from her, with a gaping red hole in the back of his skull. Bone fragments and brain matter decorated the wall of a six-story apartment building just behind the corpse.

Alicia approached the body with as much caution as she could manage. She reached out and prodded the shoulder of the corpse. No reaction... thank God.

She hadn't forgotten Torres's paranoid craziness about zombies.

The corpse's skin felt cool beneath Alicia's fingertips, but it also felt *spongy*. She lifted the girl's head to get a better look at her face. The clinical part of Alicia's mind took over, shutting down the emotions that could keep her from being able to look at the corpse of a little girl. *She isn't a little girl anymore*, her detached mind said. *The girl that once was, thankfully, is long gone.*

Normally she would have gloved up, like in her anatomy classes back at Princeton, but she'd gotten what was probably an unhealthy dose of brazenness because of Narmer's gift. Anything that could wipe out cancer could probably keep her from catching whatever cooties were around here.

The girl looked to be no older than around ten. Blood stained her lips and chin. Alicia pushed the girl's pale lips up, exposing her teeth, and felt a chill race through her.

The girl had bits of torn flesh stuck in the gaps between her teeth.

Alicia pulled out her flashlight and shone it in the girl's mouth. The back of her throat looked gray and lumpy. She then checked the girl's eyes. One was the entry point for the round that had taken off the back of her head, and prying open the other proved difficult, as a thick, sticky substance leaked from it. At first Alicia thought the eye had melted and was dripping from the socket, but when she finally got the lids apart, the eye was still present, just with unrecognizable growths on it.

"What in the world?" she muttered.

She prodded under the girl's armpits and found a few large lumps. They reminded her of cancer, but these nodules were significantly softer than the ones she'd discovered on herself before going to the doctor.

Alicia then illuminated the hole in the girl's skull. Whoever had blown the girl away had done it with the gun angled downward, ripping away both bone and flesh in the place where the spine connected to the skull. The remaining flesh in that area felt far too soft, and when Alicia pressed on it, a thick, white goo seeped out.

She took out her phone and snapped pictures of everything, then took a short video as well.

As she wiped her hands off on the girl's pant legs, she noticed that the pants were stained halfway to her knees. This girl had almost certainly come from the rice paddies outside of town.

The girl's body held no more clues. Alicia climbed over the barricade, Bagel leaping over to stay close.

A pile of smoldering logs lay some distance before her, three or four feet high. But they weren't logs. The smell gave that away. Thin branches weren't branches at all, but arms with the flesh burnt away. Walking around the burning pile—the acrid smell of burnt hair made Alicia's eyes water—she counted six burned skulls. Five had bullet holes in them, and the sixth showed blunt-force trauma so intense that the entire side of the skull had been caved in.

The orange glow of predawn lit the horizon. Alicia didn't want to get caught out in the open in daylight, especially if the military still ran the show in Yichun. The mouth of a dark alley opened near the pile of burning corpses, and in the depth of those shadows, she spotted an emergency ladder scaling the back of a building. She ducked into the alley and set Bagel on her shoulder before jumping up to grab the bottom rung on the ladder.

As she climbed, Alicia noted how few windows there were here. Not that the view would have been anything to brag about, but still. The few windows the building did have showed no light or movement.

When she reached the top of the ladder, Bagel jumped off her shoulder onto the roof, and she pulled herself up after him. The roof had an easy sloping grade up to its middle, to allow rain and snow to run off. Alicia kept low, crawling up the grade then back down to the opposite edge. She crouched down against the lip of a low wall, poked her head over the edge, and took in the city of Yichun.

Though the sun had now lightened the sky, there was no bustle of people moving to get their shops ready for the day. No workers hurrying to jobs or fields. No late-night workers shambling home from the graveyard shift. Even the birds had forsaken the city.

Lampposts lined the streets like statues, but they were still and dark, like the windows. Alicia closed her eyes and focused on the sounds around her. No telltale buzz of electricity. The entire town felt like a mausoleum. It reminded her of when the power went out in her apartment, as it had done once or twice, and the strange silence that followed. Until it was gone, it was hard to realize how noisy electricity really was.

"There's got to be something out there, Bagel," Alicia whispered.

In the distance, across the city to the southwest, she heard the low rumble of engines starting. Alicia doubted the military had a legit installation in a town like this, which left the takeover of a large business or apartment complex. Questions nagged at her mind. Why had they holed up at night? If things were truly as bad as they seemed from the outside looking in, why were they still here? Cleanup?

In the air, the hum of electricity suddenly started and increased, but then cut off abruptly in a shower of exploding lampposts as they overloaded.

Alicia stared at the showering sparks and shook her head.

"This place has some serious issues, not the least of which seems to be a flakey power grid," Alicia muttered to Bagel. The cat cocked his head to the side with a look that said, *You think?*

Control. The word forced its way into her consciousness. From her time on the streets, Alicia knew the score. At one point or another, she'd had everything controlled for her. Food, water, where she slept, basic healthcare. Her body. When someone could control another person's basic human rights—life, liberty, and pursuit of happiness—nothing else mattered. She'd lived that life, and to see it enforced on an entire city sickened her.

A small convoy of personnel transport vehicles—trucks and jeeps—turned a distant corner, coming into view a few blocks to the west. They screeched to a stop in front of a five-story apartment building, and soldiers piled out of the trucks in riot gear. Helmets, body armor, shields. Most carried rifles or shotguns. Alicia pulled binoculars from one of the outer pouches of her backpack and focused on the troops. She couldn't see anything, and then realized the binoculars had a button, which she pressed. Suddenly she saw clearly through the device, and overlaid in her vision was a symbol that indicated the binoculars were recording. She wasn't sure if this was standard for a PLA device or if the Outfit had juiced up the equipment.

She watched the troops gathering in front of the building and wondered, *Why so many?* The force numbered at least two dozen, and most were stacked up on either side of the single door to the building, while the rest trained their rifles on the bar-covered windows. Alicia zoomed in on the front door, which had a padlock on the outside, trapping the residents inside.

On an unheard signal, the lead soldier cut the lock and pulled the door open, allowing the troops to rush inside.

For a few moments, the world went still and silent again. Then gunfire ripped through the air, and bright flashes lit the apartment building's dark windows. Alicia covered her mouth to stifle a gasp. She saw the sparks of gunfire through some windows and followed the progress of the soldiers from floor to floor and room to room. On the third floor, glass shattered outward from one of the apartment windows as a body was thrown into it. Dark clothes marked the person as a soldier. His body hit the metal bars so hard they partially ripped from their anchor points in the concrete.

An access door on the roof burst open, and a woman in ragged clothing ran out into the early morning light. Two soldiers followed, one with a rifle, the other a shotgun. The fleeing woman reached the lip of the roof and looked over the edge at the remaining military force. One of the soldiers below aimed upward and put three shots into the concrete wall beneath her.

Alicia trained the binoculars on her. She looked filthy. Her dank hair hung in tangles to her shoulders and her clothes were stained and ripped and hanging off her. Some of the stains had the telltale color of dried blood. With a panicked look and a hopeless scream directed at her pursuers, the woman sprinted for another edge of the building, obviously intending to jump the gap to a lower, neighboring structure. But when she planted her bare foot on the lip of the wall to leap, a three-round burst from one of the soldiers behind her took her in the back. She still leapt, but she didn't make it across the gap. Her head struck the edge of the other building with a thud that Alicia felt more than heard, and her body pinwheeled to the ground. Blood splashed everywhere.

One of the soldiers stationed at the base of the building jogged toward her, leveled his rifle, and put half a magazine into the unmoving corpse for good measure.

"What the hell is happening here?" Alicia said aloud.

Some of the soldiers exited the building. All their nervous energy from before had evaporated. Now they looked defeated, shoulders hunched, heads hanging low. One staggered behind the vehicles, removed his helmet, and threw up onto the street.

They didn't bring out any prisoners with them.

The last soldier threw himself from the entryway into the street, turned, and emptied his semi-auto shotgun into the building's darkness. Two other soldiers slammed the door shut, bracing themselves against it while another wedged a riot shield under the handle to keep it closed. Then two more men ran up with welding gear and began welding the metal door to its frame.

The shotgunner who'd thrown himself clear of the building used the butt of the shotgun to push up to his feet. He pressed a hand to the side of his neck, then pulled the hand away to look down at his palm. Alicia couldn't see anything on his hand, but the soldier's neck was covered in blood. The others around him backed away, raising their rifles. The wounded soldier held a hand out, pleading. Alicia couldn't hear what he said, but his actions told her everything she needed to know.

He whipped his shotgun up and pulled the trigger, but nothing happened. He stared down at the empty gun, then dropped it and held up his hands. He fell to his knees, waiting to be taken prisoner.

Instead, a man with a captain's patch stitched to the shoulder of his uniform walked up behind the wounded soldier, drew his pistol, and shot the man in the back of the head.

The single report of the pistol cracked in the still air, an exclamation point on the horror show Alicia had just watched.

Until now, Alicia had only had an educated guess at what was going on here. Now, she was sure.

"They're terrified of infection," she said to Bagel.

The cat turned his large eyes to her, somehow looking as stunned as she felt. Alicia began to feel a bit less brave. Were her nanites enough to protect her from this?

"How bad must this infection be for them to shoot up an entire apartment building, weld the door shut, then execute their own man?"

She zoomed in on the faces of the soldiers. Maybe after she got home the Outfit could do something with this recording.

Over the next few hours, she watched as the soldiers methodically went from building to building, breaching and clearing. They lost five more soldiers in the process. One was dragged outside by one of his compatriots, only to be shot in the face by the same captain. The others never made it outside of the buildings they infiltrated.

Every door had a lock when troops went inside. Every door was welded shut when they finished.

Alicia knew that somewhere in this town, Gigi and Curt were huddling in an apartment, hearing the same gunfire. Probably locked inside. She ran the binoculars across the tops of buildings. Most had roof access doors, and many had emergency ladders. Escape was possible. Not everyone would try, but certainly some would have the courage.

So why weren't they?

As she monitored the progress of the troops, Alicia ran through possible scenarios.

There were two fairly obvious answers. First, there might be far more soldiers around than Alicia realized. If this had been the norm for a while, by now the people would know that successful flight was an impossibility.

The second answer was even worse. The people feared something else in the town *more* than they feared the soldiers. To leave their homes would mean putting themselves at even more risk.

So the big question remained: Just how bad was this infection?

Alicia retreated away from the lip of the building and climbed back down the ladder. With the sun high overhead now, she felt exposed. As she moved, she kept herself pressed to the walls of the buildings when she could, darting from alley to alley when she couldn't.

There were a number of abandoned military vehicles dotting the streets, making the place look like a post-apocalyptic war zone. She ducked behind an old American-made Jeep with a rear-mounted fifty-caliber machine gun, and rifled through the back, under the seats, and the glove box, the last location rewarding her with another QSZ-92 and an extra box of ammo. She ejected the magazine, pocketed it, and stuffed the extra gun and ammo box in her bag.

She considered calling Mason on the sat phone, but he'd just ask her questions she didn't yet have answers for. Despite the horrors she'd witnessed, she didn't have any more actionable data than before.

When she felt like she was a safe distance from the roving death squad, she slowed her pace to look around more fully at her surroundings. Residential buildings were all locked down with heavy padlocks and the occasional length of wood bracing them for extra support, but most of the businesses had their doors wide open, exposing their abandoned interiors to the elements. There wasn't a living person in sight. But piles of burnt bodies were stacked in most intersections.

She moved deeper into the city. The eerie quiet gave way to low voices and the scraping of something being dragged across the ground. Alicia ducked quickly into the shadows and moved toward the sounds. She hid behind a stack of wooden pallets and peeked through the slats out into a wide plaza. Husks of empty food carts lay tipped over, contents spilled around them.

Across the way lay a small park with old playground equipment, largely in disrepair. It reminded her of a scene from the second *Terminator* movie, just after the bombs had fallen.

Still following the voices, Alicia crept out from behind the stacked pallets and poked her head around the edge of the alley she was hiding in. A short distance away, three soldiers were struggling to move a waist-high concrete barrier.

"This is pointless," one of the soldiers said in Mandarin. "We should be running, not fortifying a stupid building."

"Keep your voice down, Jun," another said. "If the captain hears you talking, you know what will happen." He pointed his fingers like a gun and mimed shooting Jun in the head.

The third soldier sighed. "The captain is busy clearing buildings, Hao. And Jun is right. This is madness. We should have run days ago."

"Run where, Aang?" Hao leaned against the concrete barrier and wiped a hand across his forehead. "They'd just hunt us down. Or they'd go after our families instead. I've got a sister in Beijing who I'd rather not see tossed into a reeducation camp. And isn't your mother just down the road in Harbin? She'd be the first killed. Or worse. You saw what happened to all those people we took to the facility. Do you want your mother to end up like them? I know I don't want my sister that way."

Aang kicked a small rock, and it bounced across the pavement. "I don't want *myself* to end that way. And if we stay here, that's what will happen. And then the captain will *definitely* shoot us."

Jun sank to the ground and took a drink from his canteen.

"If we run, we get shot. If we complain, we get shot. If we stay and keep our mouths shut, we'll get bitten, go nuts and attack everyone... and get shot."

"We do our jobs," Hao said firmly. "That's all we can do."

"What if the captain had an accident?" Jun said. He spoke the words so quietly, Alicia wouldn't have heard them if the rest of the town hadn't been dead silent.

Hao reached down, grabbed Jun by the front of his shirt, and hauled the man to his feet. "Don't even say something like that. Aang and I will be shot just for hearing it."

"I'm just saying," Jun said. "With the casualties we had at the facility, and the ones we lost here cleaning up the general's mess, one more wouldn't even get questioned."

"Oh, sure," Hao said. "We'll just go get the infected kid from the lobby"—he tilted his head toward the apartment building they were blocking off—"then we ask the captain to hold still while Dr. Shen's failed experiment chews on his face."

Jun pulled Hao's hands away from his shirt. "There are infected everywhere. You act like we couldn't find one on any block."

Aang looked around, and Alicia could see the worry etched on the man's face. "You both need to shut up. Come on, let's just get this barrier into place, or the captain will put us on building-clearing detail again."

The other two grunted in agreement, the traitorous dialogue dying away like everything else in this God-forsaken town. They pushed and pulled, sliding the massive triangular piece of concrete where they wanted it, though Alicia didn't see how it would help against any of the infected. Then Hao and Jun went inside, leaving Aang alone outside.

The fat soldier leaned against the barrier and pulled a pack of cigarettes from his pocket. He withdrew one and lit it with a cheap plastic lighter. Alicia watched the soldier puff on the cancer stick for a few moments. With his friends gone, the rotund man sagged, the weight of the world he lived in settling heavily on his shoulders. As he looked down at his cigarette, it looked almost as though he hoped it would somehow show him a way out of this mess.

It wouldn't. And his day was about to get much worse.

Alicia leaned down and whispered to Bagel. "Walk out there, get his attention, then come back. Get him to come into the alley. Do you understand?"

The cat licked his lips, then walked out of the alley and meowed.

Alicia backed deep into the shadows and hid in a small indent in the building's wall, behind a large pile of trash.

Bagel meowed again, closer this time, and Alicia heard Aang say, "Hey there, little guy. You can't be running around in a town like this. The things here will get you."

The cat passed Alicia's hiding spot without looking her way. Aang followed, hands empty and pistol holstered. The poor fool couldn't know the cat was leading him right into a trap.

"You're way too nice a cat to be wild," Aang said. "Come back with me. I bet I can find some tuna for you. Maybe some chicken. It'll be canned rations, but still. Come on, little guy. Let's go ba—"

His words died as Alicia stepped behind him from the shadows and pressed the barrel of her pistol to the back of his head. Aang froze and held his hands wide to the sides, away from his sidearm.

"You move and I'll shoot," Alicia said in Mandarin.

CHAPTER
TWENTY

Alicia pulled Aang's pistol from the holster and shoved it in the back of her waistband. "Another gunshot in this town won't draw anyone's attention. You're going to answer some questions for me. If you do, you live. If you don't, I'll hand you over to the infected you seem so worried about. Do you understand?"

"Yes."

"Good." Alicia pressed hard with her gun into the base of his skull. "We're going to walk out the other side of this alley. On the right, a few doors down, I saw a noodle shop with a red door and broken windows. The door is open. You and I are going to go inside and have a little chat. Am I clear?"

"Yes."

"Excellent. Walk slowly, and pause a few paces from the street. Please don't try and be a hero. Your country doesn't care if I shoot you, and it seems your captain somehow cares even less. Let's go."

Aang walked forward slowly, his steps measured. Not once did he look back. Bravery, in the traditional sense, didn't seem like a trait of the soldier's, but it could have all been an act. Alicia lowered the gun to press it against his lower spine. She watched his movements and surmised he couldn't move quickly. But if he did, she had faith in her own reflexes to pull the trigger before he could do anything to her.

Bagel walked ahead and turned right at the end of the alley. The PLA soldier followed Alicia's instructions and stopped a few steps from the corner.

"Good," Alicia said. "Turn and face the wall, hands pressed high against it. Don't move, and don't say a word. Got it?"

Her hostage nodded slowly and deliberately.

Alicia backed away, then glanced quickly in each direction down the adjoining street. It stood empty, and Bagel sat patiently in front of the door to the shop.

"All right. Walk to the street, but keep close to the buildings. Walk quick, we don't want to be out in the open. If I start getting shot at, my first bullet cuts your strings."

Alicia winced. She could easily imagine her father saying something like that. How many times had he used phrases like that when dealing with people?

But Aang simply nodded his understanding and turned right out of the alley, hurrying to the door. Alicia followed him into the vacant noodle shop, glass from the shop's shattered window crunching under her boots.

Inside, the tables were tipped over, the chairs broken, the

floor smeared with old, dried blood. One of the legs from a chair lay cast aside, with blood staining the jagged, pointed end; it had obviously been used to stab someone.

For the first time, Aang looked back at Alicia. His flat look of fear changed ever so slightly to curiosity when his eyes took her in. She waved the barrel of the gun for him to go through a curtain made of hanging beads leading to the back. Half the strands of beads were on the floor.

Aang walked to the back, Alicia close behind. She spied an open door to the right. "To the right. Walk in and stop in the center of the room."

Her prisoner did as instructed. The room had a small cot in the back corner, with bags of flour stacked to the right.

"Have a seat on the cot."

Aang turned and sat down, still keeping his hands out to his sides. Alicia appreciated the compliance, and figured she'd measure all future hostages against him. She suppressed a laugh at the thought of what Grandma Yoder would think of her taking someone hostage. The stress of this town had wormed its way into her.

"Okay, Aang. I want to know what's going on in this town, and why your captain has turned you all into a roving death squad."

"You don't already know?"

Alicia snarled as she steadily aimed her gun at his bulbous chest. "If I knew, would I be asking?"

"I'm sorry." Aang's brow furrowed in confusion. "The way you're dressed, and the way you act... I assumed you were from headquarters and already knew."

Alicia pressed her lips together. "Maybe I am. Maybe I'm just making sure what you say matches previously gathered intelligence."

He shook his head. "If you say so."

"I say so. Answer the question."

Aang sighed and leaned against the wall. He closed his eyes for a moment. "Can I smoke? It calms my nerves."

"Move very slowly." Alicia kept the business end of the pistol level with the center of the fat soldier's face. "If you try anything, I promise you I'll wipe out your entire family."

It was a threat that she'd never follow through on, but if he believed she was with HQ, he wouldn't know that.

Aang slowly pulled out a pack of cigarettes and a lighter. After lighting one and pulling hard on it, he shook his head. "The nicotine doesn't work like it used to. Though I guess that's probably a problem with me, not the cigarettes. You don't need to keep the gun pointed at me. I'll answer your questions."

Alicia didn't move a muscle. "What happened here?"

"The general and his pet scientist screwed up."

"General Feng?"

"Yes."

"How did they mess up?"

He shrugged and took another drag on the cigarette. "I'm not a scientist. We delivered a bunch of terrorists and dissidents from the camps to a facility. Shen—he's the doctor at the facility—has been injecting them all with something."

"What?"

"I'm not a scientist," Aang said again. "A red liquid. I only saw it once, and I don't think I was meant to. Dr. Shen slammed the door in my face when he saw me looking inside."

Bagel patted Alicia on her leg. To the soldier, it would look like Bagel was merely stretching and kneading on Alicia's calf, but to Alicia it was a message.

"I warn."

The cat headed out the door, looked back at Alicia, giving her a meaningful look, and headed to the front of the store.

"Describe the red liquid for me," Alicia said.

"There really isn't much to describe."

"Then it shouldn't take too long."

"Honestly, all I can say is it's red. I don't know. Not solid red like blood. Kind of clear red, like fruit juice?"

Clearly this was getting Alicia nowhere. "Tell me about the circumstances where you saw it."

Aang sighed and rubbed his eyes. Up close, Alicia saw the telltale signs of sleep deprivation. Deep bags under bloodshot eyes. The skin on his face was pale and hanging with more slack than it probably should have. "In a facility north of the town. We deliver the prisoners there. I passed a room, and against the wall opposite the door was a line of chairs. The doctor's assistants had a person in each chair, and they were injecting the prisoners with the red fluid."

"Where were the injections administered?"

"Back of the neck," Aang answered, tapping at his own neck for reference. "Does it matter?"

Alicia didn't answer, but she wondered why anyone would inject something there. It wasn't a natural place to give a shot —unless you were giving a shot into the spinal column?

She lifted her pistol a fraction of an inch. "Go on. What else did you see?"

Aang sighed. "They were moving the prisoners through like an assembly line. I saw some lab equipment, but I couldn't tell you anything about it. Then Shen saw me, and he ran over to slam the door in my face."

"What does the injection do?"

"No idea."

He'd answered too quickly, and Alicia caught an almost imperceptible tic at the corner of his left eye.

"Aang, I don't have all day. And to be honest, neither do you." She took a step closer and waggled the pistol. "I'd planned on letting you live, but I don't really care either way. You brought men, women, and children from concentration camps to an illegal facility to be forced into human experimentation. Shooting you might just do this world some good."

Aang looked panicked and scooted back on the cot until his back hit the wall. "I didn't know it's illegal. I just do what I'm told. I'm a good soldier." The man was practically blubbering. "I swear I don't know what it's supposed to do, but... but I saw some of the effects."

"Tell me."

Aang took in a shaky breath. "We made a delivery a few weeks ago. I assume they all got the shot. When we made another delivery about a week ago, we drove by some rice fields, and I recognized a few of the earlier prisoners, working in the water. I just happened to remember a few faces. And they... I don't know. They weren't acting right."

"I don't know what that means, Aang," Alicia said coldly. "Explain."

He pressed a hand to his forehead in frustration. "I don't know. Just... they all seemed... stiff and weird. They moved with strange jerky motions."

"Maybe they were exhausted from being worked excessively?"

"No, that's not what I mean. They were working quickly, just... the way they moved wasn't right. It was like they were robots. Never pausing. They didn't talk, didn't make any noise at all. I'd never seen such a thing."

"They probably didn't want to get shot by the prison guards who'd brought them to those fields."

Aang's frustration came out in a hiss of air between gritted teeth. He banged the back of his head against the wall. "You ask questions but you won't *listen*. I'm telling you, the prisoners didn't react to *anything at all*. Not to the guards, not to each other. They didn't speak or even *look* at each other. They just worked, robotically. It was like their personalities had been removed. I think the shot did that to them."

"You think it made them more... compliant?"

Aang shrugged. "Maybe. Maybe more than that. It felt like... they had lost their humanity."

Alicia clenched her jaw as she recalled images of Uyghurs enslaved for being the wrong kind of people and not thinking the Beijing government was everything. Lost their humanity? The Chinese government had never thought of these prisoners as humans anyway.

"We've all been talking about it," Aang went on, "and some

of the other guards have said the prisoners don't take breaks. At all. Ever. They don't eat. They don't sleep. It's like their minds have been erased. Some of the soldiers call them 'thralls.'"

"And how does that relate to what happened here in Yichun?" Alicia asked. "How did this city get to be the way it is?"

Aang shrugged. "No one knows. One minute they're all peacefully working in the fields, and the next they lose their minds. General Feng and Dr. Shen came running back to the facility from the fields with the prisoners chasing after them. We didn't get the doors closed in time."

"Your slaves got into the facility? The guards didn't shoot them?"

"Oh, they did. But it didn't stop the rush of prisoners. They fell on the guards... they... it was terrible."

"What happened when they attacked the soldiers?"

Alicia thought she already knew the answer. But if the attack matched the one she'd seen in her sister's video, it would start solidifying details and behaviors that she could then report back to Mason.

"We couldn't tell at first. There were so many swarming the other men... my friends. But then our lieutenant went down, and the prisoner that tackled him bit into his neck. Blood went everywhere. And the prisoner, he..." Aang closed his eyes, maybe to forget, but quickly opened them again. His face was pale and his lips were trembling as if he was reliving the horror all over again. "The prisoner *chewed* on a piece of the lieutenant. I shot that prisoner a dozen times, but it didn't matter."

"Keep going," Alicia said. "I want to know how you got out, and why you all started locking down buildings."

"We ran," Aang answered. "Simple as that. I'm sure the captain would call it a strategic withdrawal or something, to help him save face, but we ran for our lives. We didn't even leave with all our men. Some were trapped back in the holding areas with the prisoners."

Aang tried pressing himself into the wall to get further away from the muzzle of Alicia's pistol. "Honestly, I don't know anything else. And I don't know if they're still doing experiments there or not. I only know that the general went there. His orders to the captain were to secure Yichun and... well, you saw."

"So you all got back here and what?"

"Pure chaos. The streets were filled with fleeing people. We could barely tell who was attacking who. Then one of our men got his ear bitten off by a little girl. He couldn't bring himself to shoot her. I don't really blame him. Shooting adult prisoners who are attacking you is one thing. Children... not many are capable of killing a child. The girl ripped a chunk of his cheek off. That's when some of the other soldiers opened fire. The girl took a few rounds, but ran off. Some of us recognized the girl as being from one of our earlier prisoner transfers. And the people we rescued told us that children were the first to... to begin attacking people."

Aang looked at Alicia with pleading eyes. "Look, I've told you everything I know. I don't want to get executed for abandoning my post. If I go back right now, I can make up a story. Say I saw one of the infected running around. Please, I—"

"You call them 'infected,'" Alicia said. "Does this infection spread?"

Aang licked his lips, and drops of sweat appeared on his forehead. Alicia could somehow smell the fear emanating from him, and she knew she'd arrived at the heart of their little chat.

"I'm not sure. Again, I'm not a scientist. I—"

Alicia brought her pistol in close and pulled the slide back just enough to give the appearance she was checking to see if a round was chambered. She nodded to herself, all part of the act. When Alicia carried, she always carried with a round chambered. Her dad had drilled that habit into her. Then she extended the pistol again and took a step forward, her finger in the trigger well.

"Wait, wait, wait!" Aang threw his hands up in front of him and squeezed his eyes shut. "We received orders. We were told to lock down the whole town and to shoot anyone who had been bitten—citizen or soldier. So that's what we did. The captain made us all strip to prove we had no bites. If you had one, you were executed on the spot, then thrown into a pile to burn."

"How'd you lock the city down?"

"We told the truth. We announced over the city-wide speakers that there was an infection, and to stay inside. Anyone caught outside would be shot."

"Did anyone test the lockdown?"

"Of course."

"And?"

Aang didn't answer, but the way the light in his eyes died, Alicia knew the answer. In a town already cowed by a military presence, a few people shot as examples would do most of the job. China already had a healthy dose of paranoia from dealing with contagions over the years.

"I'm going to ask you one more time, Aang. Is this infection contagious?"

"Yes."

"You're certain?"

"Yes."

Alicia waited for more. Silence stretched between them. Then Aang licked his lips and took a long pull on his forgotten cigarette, which had nearly burned down to his fingertips.

"We encountered some infected adults just a couple days after the outbreak," he said. "Not prisoners from the facility—people from the town. They had bite marks. Some had chunks missing from their faces and necks. And they all had the same empty expression as the infected prisoners. They attacked us just like the others. So we put them down. Burned the bodies in the street. That's been going on ever since."

"I saw the piles," Alicia said.

She didn't understand why the newly infected had changed so quickly. It was natural for viruses to evolve once they raced through a population, but that usually took time. This whole thing had started less than a week ago.

Aang looked spent. Even the fear of having a gun pointed at him no longer carried the threat it had when she had originally jabbed him with the muzzle. His hands drooped and his posture sagged.

Alicia considered what to do with him. She couldn't just let him go back to his fellow soldiers, no matter what she'd promised. Yet she didn't want to shoot him. Not only would the sound draw attention, but he'd been helpful, at the very least.

She pulled off her backpack, took out her map of the region, unfolded it, and brought it forward to lay in Aang's lap. "Where's the facility?"

Aang frowned down at the map. With the hand holding the smoldering cigarette butt, he pointed at a spot northeast of Yichun. "Here, but it's just a crypt now. Everyone there is dead... or infected, I guess. You aren't thinking of going there, are you?"

"We'll see," Alicia answered, pulling the map away to refold it. "I need to find two people first. A Chinese woman and a big white American. Have you seen them?"

"There are lots of women here," he said, looking at Alicia like she was stupid. "But... there was some talk about an American."

"What did he look like?"

"I don't know. I just heard about it in passing. We were locking up a building to the south of here, and one of the guards made a joke about getting to finally lock up some Americans. It was just a passing remark."

"Where's this building?" Even if it wasn't the right building, or the right American, at least it was a lead.

"I don't—"

Alicia pressed the gun to his forehead hard enough to slam the back of his skull into the wall. All her stored-up anger and worry broke through the dam she'd built inside herself to keep it in check. "If you say 'I don't know' one more time, your fellow soldiers will be scraping your brains off that wall when they eventually find you."

"A-all I remember is a gray apartment building." Aang closed his eyes, and from the way he scrunched up his face, Alicia could tell he was desperately trying to remember. He stiffened, then opened his eyes and looked up at her. "It was above a chicken restaurant. I don't remember the name, but it had a chicken breathing fire on the sign out front."

"How far from here?"

He pointed to the south. "I think, maybe five or six blocks? I can take you there. Maybe you could help me get out—"

Alicia held up a hand as Bagel came racing into the room. The cat's hackles were up, and he spun around to look at the door. Alicia put a finger to her lips and waved Aang down. He slid quietly off the cot into a crouched position, a look of confusion on his face.

Outside, Alicia heard the faint crunch of a boot stepping on broken glass. Just a month ago, she never would have heard it, but now it was clear as day.

The question in Alicia's mind was whether this boot belonged to a soldier, or an infected.

Gunfire answered her question as it tore through the thin walls of the noodle shop.

CHAPTER
TWENTY-ONE

Pieces of wall and plaster dust filled the air as Alicia threw herself to the floor. Bagel flattened himself so close to the ground that he was practically invisible in the shadowy corner of the room. The booming shots sounded like rifles, probably their absurd-looking bullpup QBZ-95s. Alicia had taken too long questioning Aang.

She rolled to her side to look at her prisoner.

He hadn't gotten down quickly enough.

Aang's body still sat upright, leaning against the cot he'd crouched beside at her warning. But the entire left side of his face was gone, and he had taken another half dozen rounds to the upper torso and neck.

Pity never entered Alicia's mind. The soldier had transported slaves and prisoners to a facility where they were experimented on, and he had welded doors shut on apartment buildings, just like soldiers had done during Covid.

But still.

After a brief lull, a fresh stream of gunfire tore through the building. Alicia couldn't stay here; the soldiers were probably spraying and praying so that any infected were taken out and they didn't have to deal with them, and eventually they'd just throw a grenade in. Or they'd grab a few more guys and storm in.

She yelled, "What the hell are you guys shooting at? I just arrived from Beijing!"

There was a moment of silence, then someone yelled back, "We have standing orders! Anyone rummaging around in an unsealed and quarantined building is assumed to be infected and will be shot. Come out with your hands up!"

Fat chance she was about to do that.

With her heart racing, Alicia crawled forward, keeping low to the ground. Across the hall she spotted another open doorway leading into a kitchen.

She edged out, still pressed to the floor, and caught a glimpse of someone in the doorway leading to the street. She popped off two shots to keep the soldiers from swarming the shop, then crawled back to Aang's body as more bullets fired in return. He had a Velcro ammo pouch on his left hip that held two spare magazines for the Chinese QSZ-92.

She shoved the two extra magazines into her pocket and crawled forward again, Bagel edging up with her. Alicia gave the little guy a reassuring pat on the head, then popped out and put two more rounds through the open door. One hit the metal doorframe with a *ping*, and the other caught one of the shooters in the shoulder as he leaned in to shoot another burst from his rifle. He screamed in pain as the bullet hit high on his left shoulder, and he fell back outside.

Alicia jumped up and threw herself across the hallway into the kitchen, Bagel scampering after her.

A body lay slumped in the back corner of the kitchen, a cast-iron pan in her lap and a single bullet hole through one eye. The brown blood splatter on the wall behind her was at least a day old.

There were no other exits.

Bagel faced the kitchen doorway, his hackles up, his tail swishing impatiently.

Alicia crossed to the wall opposite the door and picked up a discarded kitchen knife to scrape at the plaster. It fell away with little effort, exposing wooden beams. No insulation or visible wiring. She couldn't tell what was on the other side of the wall, but it couldn't be worse than staying here.

She launched a burst of gunfire to cover up the sound of her smashing at the wall with a heavy pan. Large chunks of wall fell away, and she ripped away the rest with her hands.

Just to be sure she had a few extra moments, Alicia emptied the rest of the magazine through the wall in the direction of the shop's entrance. She didn't expect to hit anything. Time was all she needed.

Her gunshot provoked another round of heavy rifle fire. While the soldiers shot blindly into the building, Alicia kicked out the old sheetrock on the opposite side of the wall, making a hole just big enough for her to crawl through. She sent Bagel through first, then threw her pack in before pulling herself to the other side.

Dim light from newspaper-covered windows barely pene-trated the gloom, but Alicia's eyes adjusted quickly, and she found herself in a small warehouse with simple metal racking, though the shelves stood mostly empty and covered in dust. There was only one door, and judging by its location it opened back onto the street.

The light coming into the dark space from the adjoining restaurant flickered. Alicia stepped back, training her gun on the hole. The light flickered again, and she heard yelling.

Gunfire erupted in controlled bursts, and Alicia threw herself down onto the dust-covered floor. A line of bullet holes stitched their way through the connecting wall, allowing spears of light to pierce the shadowed darkness.

The gunfire cut off suddenly. The screams didn't.

Something, or someone, hit the shared wall hard, making dust and plaster fall to the floor on her side. The screaming grew louder.

"No, no! Help! God, no!" a voice shouted in Mandarin, clearly terrified. Three gunshots, from a pistol this time, accompanied the screams. Another thump shook the wall, then a second.

On the third thump, the sheetrock exploded in a shower of dust and plaster as a person's head broke through. It wasn't a soldier, and he wasn't dead.

Vacant eyes rolled up and stared at Alicia.

One of the infected.

The man pushed away from the hole, and through it, Alicia saw a bloodied soldier—it was one of Aang's friends, the one named Jun—pick up his rifle from the floor and point it at the infected. Jun had bites on his arms and a chunk torn out of one ear. He slammed a new magazine home.

Alicia ducked again, covering her head for all the good it would do if one of the soldier's stray rounds hit her. Even her vest wouldn't stop a rifle round at this distance.

The roar of the Chinese bullpup filled her ears, and rounds tore through the air above her, ricocheting dangerously off of the metal racking.

Then the gunfire stopped once again, leaving only a ringing in Alicia's ears and the sound of Jun screaming his fury at the infected. Alicia dared to get up and peer through the small hole the man's head had made in the wall. She saw Jun frantically trying to reload his rifle as the infected staggered toward him. He wasn't fast enough. The infected lunged and took Jun to the floor, ripping chunks out of his neck.

Jun's screaming stopped as the life leaked out of him. His killer chewed, then took another ravenous bite. The infected— the *thrall*— wore the remnants of a black business suit, white shirt in tatters and stained red from earlier violence. Alicia could see bites on his neck. Somehow, after everything he'd been through, he still wore his tie.

A woman in a floral-patterned lounging robe stepped into the kitchen doorway. Her face was smeared with blood and gore, and she, too, chewed on something. *Someone.*

Aang's other friend had been named Hao. Alicia suspected he lay in a pool of his own blood out of sight.

A piece of plaster chose that moment to fall to the floor. Both infected turned slow, empty gazes toward the sound— and saw Alicia.

They charged.

The businessman slammed himself at the hole his head had made, trying to force his way through. His hands tore at the fragile sheetrock, widening the gap, but he made no sounds, and his expression was slack and emotionless. Up close, the thrall's eyes had a thin, semi-opaque layer over them, just like the eyes of the dead girl Alicia had examined this morning. But one of his eyes also had a small white growth coming from within.

The infected businessman managed to push one arm through the hole.

"Sorry," Alicia said to the man. "I hope you go to whatever afterlife you believe in."

She raised the pistol and shot him in the face from point-blank range.

He twitched once, then collapsed, his body halfway through the hole. Behind him, the infected woman scratched and pounded.

Alicia felt no guilt for putting the man out of his misery. She pitied him, unlike Aang. And now she had ended his torment.

The woman didn't have the strength of her male counter-part, but she had the same determination as she pounded on the wall. Apparently her brain couldn't comprehend that her best move would be to pull the dead guy's body out of the hole and leverage that opening—or use the opening that Alicia herself had made.

Alicia moved to the warehouse door. It was a sliding door, on caster wheels. She pushed it to the side, but the casters were rusty, and it moved only one agonizing inch at a time. Then it stopped altogether, held closed by a chain on the outside of the door, bound by a simple padlock.

The pounding sounds continued as the infected woman persisted in battering herself against the wall.

Alicia fished the lock closer. Her dad had taught her to pick locks, basic ones anyway, and had encouraged her to keep a set of lockpicks with her at all times—which she did. She pulled her set from a pocket of her bag, and within a minute—which felt about thirty seconds too slow in her mind—she had the lock open.

"Okay, Bagel," she whispered. "We may have to run quickly, so get ready."

The cat slipped through the gap, then looked back with a pleased smirk.

With the chain removed, Alicia strained to get the rusted wheels moving again, and they shrieked as they rolled, impossibly loud in the quiet afternoon. The pounding on the wall behind her stopped, and she heard the pounding of running feet.

The door ground to a stop. The gap still wasn't big enough to squeeze through.

"You've got to be kidding me!"

Alicia grabbed the door's edge, planted her right foot against the door frame, and strained against the rust-locked metal track. It edged a fraction of an inch.

The infected woman in the robe burst from the front of the noodle shop.

Alicia set her other foot high against the frame and angled her body so she was nearly parallel to the ground, heaving with every bit of strength she had. The wheels shrieked again, then the door flew open as the rust gave way. She hit the ground hard, barely having time to get an arm up before the thrall jumped on her. Snapping jaws tried to clamp down on Alicia's nose, missing by only millimeters.

Alicia brought a knee up as a wedge between herself and the infected housewife. The woman's fists battered and clawed at Alicia's exposed skin, digging furrows and drawing blood. Alicia levered her left forearm under her attacker's chin, forcing it up and away, then drew her pistol and punched forward with the muzzle as hard as she could into the woman's eye socket. Bone crunched and gave way, and Alicia pulled the trigger.

The bullet took off the back of the woman's skull in a shower of brain, blood, and bone, and the thrall collapsed.

Alicia's ears rang from the blast. Breathing hard, she shoved the corpse off her and pushed up to her feet.

She looked down at the scratches on her arms. They were almost certainly teeming with whatever virus that woman had running through her. She hoped to all that was holy that the nanites would be able to fend it off.

Bagel meowed loudly, and Alicia didn't need a translation. That gunshot would bring soldiers, maybe even more thralls. She hurried away from the plaza, as quickly and silently as she could.

She moved south where she could, looking for the chicken restaurant Aang had described, but finding nothing but progressively worsening urban conditions. Trash littered the dirt roads, with the occasional bird picking at spoiled goods. Every building she passed either had a lock on the door or stood open like a beckoning tomb. How many people lay dead or dying in those locked edifices? How many infected crawled around inside?

This place was a nightmare straight out of a horror movie.

She looked down at Bagel walking silently beside her. "What do you think, Bagel? Can you magically sense where Gigi might be?"

Bagel's golden eyes panned the street, his tail swishing.

On the next street, most of the buildings were smoking ruins. Alicia's heart sank as worry squeezed her from the inside. What had happened here? Too many infected, so the PLA just burned the whole street as a precaution?

She looked for some indication that one of these buildings had been a restaurant. She didn't think so, but she couldn't be sure.

Please, no.

She moved on, hoping. And dreading.

She almost missed the fire-breathing chicken logo. A dirty red awning had been ripped from its moorings and hung against the face of a building, covering the sign. She had already passed it when a breeze lifted the edge of the awning. She happened to glance back at that moment, and caught a glimpse of red and yellow painted flames.

She turned around. "Did you see that, Bagel?"

Beneath the tatters of the red awning lay a broken body in a pool of dried blood. Bagel hung back as Alicia went to the corpse's side. At first Alicia thought Bagel was scared by the corpse, but he wasn't looking at the mess, he was looking up at the building.

"It's okay, Bagel. You can stay there."

Alicia looked down at the body. Twisted and shattered bones told the story of high impact. "Don't tell me..." She lifted her gaze up the face of the building until she saw a broken window four floors up.

She pried the man's eye open. No growths. And she didn't see any bite marks. Not infected. Probably.

She looked up again. There were bars on the lower windows, but none on the windows up that high. After all, who would jump out a window four floors up?

Someone desperate.

She moved to a door beside the chicken restaurant. It was held shut by a padlock and a wooden board wedged tightly under the handle as extra enforcement. It seemed the death squad hadn't yet been back this way to weld it shut—but it was only a matter of time.

Alicia kicked the board away, then picked the lock. She slipped inside, with Bagel at her feet, and closed the door softly behind her.

CHAPTER
TWENTY-TWO

Alicia didn't breathe. Didn't move. Bagel stood motionless, body pressed against her leg.

Her eyes slowly adjusted to the dark. The entry space wasn't a foyer with a reception desk like the apartment buildings she was used to back home. Instead she stood in a narrow space with mailboxes mounted on the wall to her left, and a door into the chicken restaurant to her right. She knew it went into the restaurant because it had a sign on it that said only "Fried Chicken" in Chinese lettering. Directly ahead were stairs leading up.

She knelt down and felt around Bagel's neck to ensure the collar hadn't fallen off in all the running. Then she took off her backpack, removed a hand-sized black case, and opened it to reveal a tiny camera. The Outfit's version of a GoPro, it was only an inch long and encased in a clear, waterproof, plastic shell. If there was one thing the Outfit did well, it was technology, and that was largely thanks to Brice, the head "gadget guy." Before her departure, she'd given him the rundown on this camera, and she remembered his words perfectly:

"It communicates using the 802.11ax protocol, more commonly known as WIFI6. With the 802.11ax, you have a range of up to three hundred feet, and even at its edge, the data throughput is quite good, sufficient to return a compressed video signal. You'll also notice a solar cell on top of the camera which helps trickle-charge the lithium-ion battery, helping it maintain power to the transmitter and camera operations for up to an hour."

She clipped the tiny tube-like camera to the underside of Bagel's collar. "All right, Bagel. Ready to do some reconnaissance? Don't worry, I'll come up behind you. I just want a look down hallways and in open doors before I come up. They won't notice you as quickly as they'll notice me."

Bagel's golden eyes narrowed with suspicion as he looked up at her.

"It'll be fine. If you see anyone, I'll see them too, and you can come back." She turned on her phone, which was already connected to the camera. "Okay, Bagel. First step is up the stairs. Go on ahead. I need to see how the camera does in the darkness."

Bagel gave her one last look, then darted up the stairs. Something in the way he moved gave the impression he was sulking.

Alicia lowered the brightness on her phone and watched the screen. The camera performed marvelously, coloring the world in shades of night-vision green. Seeing the world from Bagel's lower perspective was strange, but the camera had a fish-eye effect so she could nevertheless see all the way to the ceiling as the cat reached the top of the stairs.

In green, artificial coloring, she saw the hallway stretching ahead of Bagel, losing texture and depth in the distance. Dust particles floated in the air, far more than seemed natural.

But Bagel didn't move. He stood rooted in place, fixing the camera down the long, dark hall.

A chill inched its way up Alicia's spine. She was somehow reminded her of her years on the streets. Most of the girls from those days developed a sixth sense. Some people, some cars, some buildings, some streets... they just exuded a feeling of *wrongness*. Of... evil.

An evil that many foolish people in this world didn't believe in.

Evil doesn't exist, they might say.

Or: *That's just superstition.*

Or even: *Evil is just misunderstanding another's point of view. Be more tolerant.*

All of them were wrong. Evil existed. Alicia didn't doubt it for a minute.

Looking at the feed down that hall, she got the same feeling she used to when the *wrong* kind of car pulled up and asked her to get in. Down that hall lay despair. In other circumstances, she would have called her cat back down and run in the opposite direction. But that choice wasn't available to her. Not as long as the possibility remained that Gigi and Curt were here.

She walked softly up the stairs. They were concrete, so she didn't have to worry about them creaking. She kept one eye ahead, and one on the screen, watching for anything unusual.

Bagel turned as she came up behind him, and the camera turned with him, revealing more stairs going up to the third floor. This building had six floors, and presumably this stairwell climbed all the way to the top.

Bagel turned suddenly to look down the hallway.

Something had changed.

At the far edge of the camera's view... stood a child.

Alicia felt her breath seize in her throat.

The child—a little boy of maybe eight—stood completely still. A long nightshirt covered him down to just below his knees. Hair covered most of his face, and it looked stringy and dirty.

But his eyes were visible, reflecting the infrared light coming from the camera.

Bagel hissed and backed up a step.

The boy cocked his head to the side, his expression unchanged. He took one halting step forward, then another.

Bagel backed up another step, and now Alicia could see the cat's tail over the edge of the top step.

Careful to remain soundless, she crept up a few more steps, then stretched up on her toes so she could just see over the top edge of the stairs. The little boy had moved closer, head still canted to the right. Alicia crawled up the last few steps, then reached out to put a light hand on Bagel's back, intending to pull the cat back.

At that moment, the infected boy charged.

He was unnervingly quiet, but his bare feet slapped on the concrete floor. And he covered the distance so quickly, Alicia barely had time to react.

She ducked to the right, avoiding the boy's grasping fingers as he leapt. As she dodged, his momentum took him right past her, tumbling down the stairs. Had she not gotten out of the way, he would likely have taken her with him.

Alicia turned to see the boy already scampering back up the stairs, moving on all fours like a possessed creature out of some horror film. Bagel retreated up the stairs to the next floor, but before Alicia could follow, the boy grabbed hold of her leg. His fingers dug into her skin as he clawed his way up her leg, then her torso, and in an instant his gnashing teeth tried to take a bite from her face.

Alicia pressed her left forearm up under the boy's chin, straining to keep the bloodstained teeth away from her. His strength made no sense to her. No child could be this strong.

Her arm slipped. It went over the thrall's chin, and he bit down, hard, into the skin above her wrist.

All her pity and hesitation vanished. This wasn't a child. This was a threat.

She punched the infected as hard as she could with her right fist, which did nothing but bruise her knuckles. Then she took him to the ground, wrapped her legs around him, and rolled him over so she had leverage. She lifted the thing's head and bashed it twice against the concrete floor. The science experiment didn't yell, scream, or even grunt in pain. Its vacant eyes merely stared up at her, as expressionless as the rest of its face.

She bashed its head on the concrete a third time, even harder.

The thrall shuddered and went still beneath her.

Alicia clenched her jaw tightly. The bite on her arm throbbed. The whole fight had been nearly silent, and had lasted under a minute, yet with the rush of adrenaline, she felt like she'd been fighting for hours.

She pushed herself up against the hallway wall and opened her bag to pull out the first aid kit. Using the light from her phone, she checked the scratches she'd received from the woman at the noodle shop. They looked angry and red, but they'd stopped burning and didn't seem to be bleeding. The fresh bite near her wrist was a different story. If Narmer's little gift didn't handle this virus, she was a dead person. In the meantime, her tendons were her main worry. She flexed her hand and rotated her wrist a few times. Nothing felt torn or outside of the normal pain from having been bitten by the infected kid. Still, she poured some hydrogen peroxide from her kit onto the wound, wiped it clean with some clean gauze, then wrapped it up. There was no point in taking more chances than she needed.

Bagel hadn't moved from his spot on the stairs, but his golden eyes were fixed on Alicia.

"I'll be all right, Bagel," Alicia said with a whisper. "Though maybe we should avoid fighting these things. Or dispatch them before they get close. I'm done playing games with them. Aren't you?"

These infected people... they weren't human anymore. Earlier, she'd been appalled by the PLA kill team, but now, after seeing what she'd seen... those soldiers were probably doing the right thing.

The question really came down to whether there was a

stage between getting infected and turning into a mindless zombie. No, not *zombie*. That wasn't what these things were. They weren't undead, or supernatural. Though after seeing them up close, she couldn't blame Torres for *calling* them zombies.

Alicia stowed the first aid kit, stood, and hoisted the bag back over her shoulders. "Let's go, Bagel. This might sound crazy, but let's start knocking on doors."

Bagel padded past her down the hallway to its end, so Alicia could see it was empty on the camera feed. As Alicia followed, she noted splashes of blood on the walls, punctuated by bullet holes. Yet somehow there weren't any corpses in the hall... other than the one she'd just left behind.

At the end of the line of doors, she found one open. Perhaps the thrall Alicia had just killed had come from here. A sweet rot wafted from within the opening. Alicia had picked up the same scent earlier, from an open door of a shop when she'd first entered Yichun.

Bagel edged up to the doorway and peered inside, giving Alicia a view through the camera. No movement, but the dust motes in the air swirled even more thickly here. She drew her pistol and checked the magazine to make sure she had a full one. She didn't remember reloading during the shootout with the soldiers, but was grateful for the muscle memory.

She kept the pistol close to her body rather than extended forward, using the tactics her dad and the Outfit had drilled into her. The last thing she needed was to have someone inside see her pistol and knock it from her hands. She should have asked for a suppressor back at the safe house. Given how the

Outfit operated, Mrs. Yang might have had one in her back pocket or something. Alicia vowed silently to never go on assignment again without one.

The apartment had only one room. The dead body of a woman lay propped against the wall opposite the entryway, a hole in her forehead and a bloodstain on the wall behind her. But Alicia's attention was drawn to the second corpse: a child, lying face-up on the floor.

She couldn't tell if it had been a boy or a girl. Just a vague shape covered in rags. Small hands that hadn't succumbed to... whatever had happened to the body. A tuft of black hair. Pants stained nearly up to the knees, and a threadbare smock spattered with old blood on its front. A child from the rice fields. Alicia knew in her gut this was one of the original subjects from the facility. One of the first recipients of the red serum Aang had mentioned.

The pants had stretched and ripped open as the body beneath expanded, revealing tattered remnants of skin. A normal dead body would have been a bloated, fly-covered mess. But here, where the skin sloughed away all that remained behind was a white mass that, in the dim light coming in through the covered windows, reminded Alicia of sprouting mushrooms.

Most noteworthy were the strange dust motes, which completely filled the air around the body, like a tiny cloud. Alicia pulled a spare shirt from her bag and tied it around her face. Immunity wouldn't save her from suffocating to death if the stuff in the air clogged her lungs.

She grabbed a long-handled wooden spoon from the

kitchen counter and knelt down near the child. When she poked the white mass, it didn't give like she expected. Instead of the spongy texture of a mushroom, the outer layer felt hard and brittle. Where the spoon touched it, the white growth broke off and hit the floor, exploding into puffs of thick, white dust, like chalk dust, but with thicker flakes.

This was the source of the dust motes in the air. The thickest flakes gently settled on the floor like snow.

No... like pollen. Like... spores.

Whatever this was, it had taken over all the child's internal organs. The face, too, was mostly a white mass splitting through the skin. The mass had eaten the brain and eyes. A small, red point of flesh stuck out from the chalky lump. The tip of the child's tongue.

"What is in that serum, Bagel?"

When the cat didn't meow, Alicia looked over her shoulder and found Bagel staying by the door. She couldn't blame the little guy.

Alicia pulled out her sat phone and called Mason. He picked up on the first ring.

"Did I not tell you to call me on a regular basis? Holy crap, you —" There was silence on the line for a second. *"Sorry about that. I'm glad you're alive. What have you got for me?"*

"It's a mess here, sir. They've been testing a serum on prisoners and people bused in from other parts of China."

"How did you get confirmation?"

"I interrogated a soldier, who explained it all. He trafficked the test subjects himself, and saw the injections being administered. Sir, it's really bad. Way worse than we thought."

"Hold on, I'm putting you through the office speakers so Torres can join in." Alicia heard a few clicks, then Mason said, *"There we go. Okay, Yoder. What do you mean by 'bad'?"*

"General Feng and his people are testing some sort of serum. He has an assistant by the name of Dr. Shen. No first name. The serum makes the subjects extremely docile and compliant. The soldier used a Mandarin word that roughly translates to 'thrall.' It sounds like they're trying to make obedient slaves. They were evidently working them like crazy out on the farms."

"Those people on the videos didn't look 'docile' to me," said Torres.

"No, they didn't. And they aren't. The soldier said they unexpectedly went crazy and started attacking everyone at their black-site facility north of town. They're super aggressive, and they don't go down without headshots."

"Ha!" Torres said. *"Zombies. I told you all."*

"Enough with the zombies." Mason sighed. *"They're infected by something. This... serum, whatever it is. And what about the military response, Yoder?"*

"They've locked down every building." Alicia took a few steps away from the body and the thick cloud of spores. "Welding doors to the frames of apartment buildings. Shooting anyone who resists, and anyone who's been bitten by an infected person—and that includes other soldiers. There are piles of burnt corpses in the streets. It's a hellscape over here."

Neither Mason nor Torres spoke for a moment, or maybe they'd put her on mute. Then Mason said, *"You said the military are executing anyone who has been bitten. Is that paranoia on their part, or is the contagion communicable?"*

"It's communicable, and their paranoia is justified. Sir, whatever is in that serum clearly had some unintended side effects. When those patients started biting people, the virus spread to them. And the cycle repeats itself, with the bitten eventually going crazy and trying to bite others. It's a plague, but more violent."

"How long before the bitten ones go crazy?" Torres asked, all traces of humor gone.

"I'd have to guess within days, at most," Alicia said. "But... I just found something else."

"What?" Mason asked.

"I think the effects of the injection have a limited shelf life," Alicia said. "I just found the body of one of the children. I can't tell if it's a boy or a girl, but it definitely worked in the rice fields. And I'm pretty sure it got the serum."

"What makes you think that?"

"Because it looks like the kid was consumed from within. I'm just hypothesizing, but it looks like the infection eats away at their insides. Maybe when it gets to their brain, that's when they go nuts. It's like a parasite eating its host, eventually killing it. The kid in front of me... there's this white stuff inside of them that's basically burst from the kid's skin suit. It looks like a giant spore or some kind of messed-up mushroom. The outer layer is chalky and fragile, and it crumbles into a thick fog of pollen or spores."

"Alicia," Mason said, sounding concerned. *"I want you to be*

extremely careful around this. You haven't allowed yourself to be touched, or... bitten by any of these infected, have you?"

"I'm fine," Alicia lied.

"Good. Because this sounds like a doomsday virus."

"Yes, sir. I guess it does. If it isn't stopped, it will eat through the population. All of it. Not just Yichun, and not just China."

"Alicia, I need you to listen to me very carefully. I'm going to get you out of there. You're not equipped to handle something on this scale. You can't—"

"Sir, I mean no disrespect, but I'm going to find my sister, one way or another. Even if I have to disobey any order you give me."

"One second." The line remained quiet for a few seconds, and this time Alicia was sure she was on mute. Finally, Mason got back on the line. *"I just sent Torres away. It's just you and me. Alicia... I know about your condition."*

Alicia said nothing. Better to wait and see what Mason thought he knew.

Mason continued. *"Your father and you... you both have some funny business going on that I don't fully understand. Before you were even in the picture, Levi defeated a cancer that should have taken him out. I know about your recent diagnosis and about the miraculous cure. Would you care to fill in the blanks?"*

Alicia's heart thudded loudly in her ears. *How the hell can he know—*

But of course he knew. This was the Outfit, after all. Anything that was put into the doctor's computers would end up in their hands. There were no secrets from the Outfit.

But she tried to keep one anyway. She told Mason her first whopper of a lie. "No offense, sir, but I don't know what you're talking about."

"*I see.*" Mason grumbled something under his breath. "*Okay, you're there, and I understand your desire to stay. But consider the facts, Alicia: your sister, if you find her, will either already be dead or infected. I'm just trying to be realistic with you. So I think for everyone's sake, you need to augment your mission goals.*"

Mason's words were like a stab to Alicia's heart. The idea of her sister dying or turning into one of these things was more than she could take.

But she kept her voice calm. "Augment my goals?"

"*There must be a vaccine. A cure, an antidote, whatever. You need to get your hands on it.*"

"What if they don't have one?" Alicia asked.

"*The first rule in biological warfare is to create the vaccine as you create the virus,*" Mason said. "*These scientists may be evil, but they're not stupid. They'll have made one. I'm working on getting more resources in your area, but it's going to take some time. In the interim, you're going to need to handle this alone.*"

"I understand."

"*Good.*" Mason paused. "*Have you made progress in finding your sister?*"

"A little. I'm in a building I think she might be in, but I've already been attacked once—"

"*I thought you said everything was fine.*"

"I'm dealing with things."

Another pause. "*Be careful, Alicia. If you find your sister, and she's okay, try to exfiltrate her from the city. But she and her fiancé aren't the only people who need rescuing. We need you to find that vaccine."*

"Understood. I'll call again when I have more."

"Be safe," Mason said again, then hung up.

Bagel moved into the gloomy hall when Alicia approached. He took off down the hall and waited for her at the base of the stairs leading to the third floor. The cat looked like he wanted this whole business over with just as much as she did. His tail swooshed back and forth.

"Lead the way," Alicia said.

Bagel bounded up the steps, leaving Alicia to follow his progress through the green-tinted night vision of the camera. She took the stairs slowly, phone in her left hand, pistol in her right.

The cat ran down the third-floor hallway, making the feed bounce like a shaky camera in a bad action movie. But when Bagel stood still, she saw nothing out of the ordinary. There were more dark splotches accompanied by bullet holes, but not as many on this floor. And none of the doors were open.

When she reached the third-floor landing, Bagel padded back toward her, pausing briefly at each of the closed doors to sniff. Then he ran past her and up the stairwell.

Bagel again "cleared" the hallway, but this time Alicia decided to knock lightly on a few of the doors. There were fewer signs of violence here, which might mean there were healthy survivors.

If there were, she didn't find them. The third time she tapped, something heavy slammed into the door from the other side. No grunts of pain or effort accompanied the sound, and no words were spoken. The thump came two more times, and Bagel backed away quickly.

Apparently an infected was inside. Soon it would fall to the floor, the mysterious contents of the virus turning its victim into a chalky white mass.

The cat backed away another few steps, looking up at Alicia, then ran back to the stairs. His steps were quick, his tail flicking in excitement. With one last glance back at Alicia, he took off upward.

Alicia looked at her phone screen and saw the camera bouncing wildly as Bagel ran down the hall, stopping at each door to sniff like he had before. She followed cautiously, and when she reached the landing, she had to squint into the gloom to see where her cat had gone.

She checked her screen. To her surprise, she saw herself; Bagel was looking back at her. Her shirt was ripped in a dozen places, and she had bloodstains in a dozen more. She looked every bit the infected... except that her eyes didn't have the same dead shine.

And she held a gun.

She picked her way down the hall and found Bagel standing in front of a door. He looked at her, looked at the door, and meowed.

Alicia rapped on it with her knuckles. "Anyone home?"

Nothing.

She sighed and looked down at Bagel. Whatever he thought he'd found, there was no one here. She started back down the hallway, ready to explore the final floor above them.

Bagel meowed again.

She turned back to the cat, who looked at her as he scratched at the door, forcefully.

"You sure, Bagel?"

Alicia went back to the door and knocked again. Then she closed her eyes and pressed her ear to the door, listening.

"Shh. Someone is there." Female. Spoken in Mandarin.

"The army?" Male. Alicia smiled when she heard him speaking in English.

Alicia knocked again, louder this time. "Gigi? Are you and that boyfriend of yours inside?"

A moment of silence preceded the sound of someone running to the door. The doorknob rattled, then the door jerked inward. Gigi stood in the doorway, eyes wide. Tears instantly filled those eyes, and Gigi threw herself into Alicia's arms.

"You're here! You made it!"

CHAPTER
TWENTY-THREE

Alicia squeezed her sister tightly. Gigi seemed thinner, but not unhealthy.

Gigi pulled away and looked down the hallway. "Come on," she said. "Get inside, quick."

"I already took care of an infected boy wandering the halls," Alicia said.

"What about the other ones?" Gigi asked.

"Others?"

As soon as she said the words, Bagel hissed, looking farther down the hall. Four thralls exploded out of the darkness, running at full speed.

Alicia shoved Gigi inside and followed right after. She slammed the door shut, locked it, then braced her back against it as the infected rammed into the other side. Gigi leaned her shoulder into the door too, and a Chinese man Alicia didn't recognize ran up to add his weight in support.

Gigi put a finger to her lips, and Alicia nodded her understanding.

The thralls outside rammed into the door countless times. Moments stretched into minutes, then an hour before they finally slowed and stopped.

Gigi pushed away and walked backward slowly, never taking her eyes from the door. The Chinese man did the same and motioned for Alicia to follow. Bagel stayed close, looking around the apartment with unease. Then he stopped and froze. Alicia followed the cat's gaze.

Curt.

He lay in the corner, pale in the soft candlelight. Sweat streaked his face and plastered his blond hair against his scalp. One leg of his athletic pants had been cut away, and a thick bandage had been wrapped around his calf. Even from across the room, Alicia could see angry red lines of infection running from underneath the bandage.

He lifted a trembling hand in greeting. "Hey, Alicia," he said. His voice was a dry croak. "Tell me you brought the entire US military with you."

Alicia put on her best false smile. "I'm all you guys need." She winked at Curt and turned away so he wouldn't see her fear for him. Gigi saw—but Alicia felt certain her sister already knew the score.

"How did you find us?" Gigi asked.

"A rumor from a soldier led me to the building," Alicia answered. She pointed down at the cat. "Then Bagel must have sniffed you out. He's a very resourceful cat. That's why I brought him with me from home."

Gigi's eyebrows climbed. "You brought a cat to China?"

"Couldn't find a sitter," Alicia said. "Who's your friend?"

The Chinese man smiled and extended a hand. "Song Wen-gin," he said in accented yet clear English. "But you can call me Wes."

Alicia took the man's hand. "Of course. Curt's college friend, and Gigi's inside man here in Yichun. Is this your apartment?"

"It is." He held his arms wide to encompass the place. "Welcome. Make yourself at home. Please ignore the... undesirables outside."

"I'll try," Alicia said.

"It's really just you?" Gigi asked. "Dad isn't here?"

Alicia shook her head. "Sorry, sis. I called him, but he's unreachable at the moment. I came as soon as we saw your video, and the messages you sent."

"I'm so sorry. I didn't mean for you to come here and get yourself trapped in all this. This place has become one of the inner circles of Hell."

"Yeah, you definitely chose the wrong day to visit Yichun," Alicia said. "But we'll do what we can to get you out."

"We? You mean you and Dad?"

"Not Dad. Let's just say that... I was sent here as part of my job."

Gigi furrowed her brow. "What do you mean—like working for the CIA? And why are you dressed up like a soldier in the PLA?"

"It's a long and complicated story." Alicia shook her head.

"What matters is I'm here to help figure out a way to get you guys out of here."

Gigi let out a low whistle. "That's the kind of crazy stuff I expect Dad to say. Not you."

Gigi didn't know half of how crazy it was. But Alicia couldn't tell her about the Outfit, so she ignored the implied question.

"Let's start with you telling me what you know," Alicia said. "Can you do that for me?"

Gigi's eyes slid to Curt, then back, and she nodded. "Sure. I can do that."

Alicia pulled off her bag and sank to the floor, keeping near the door in case the thralls came back. Gigi didn't sit down with her like she'd hoped. Both her sister and their Chinese friend, Wes, had way too much nervous energy about them. As for Curt, he looked like he was dealing with the worst fever of his life.

Gigi began pacing. "I was out buying supplies to get out of town with a few of the people we'd interviewed. They were going on record about the military abuses here, the corruption, the trafficking. Everything I came to expose. Which meant we had to get them out. We were going to take them into South Korea."

Alicia smiled up at her sister. That sounded just like her. Come for the story, stay to help free the truly oppressed.

"That's when I took that video," Gigi continued. "Those kids attacking everyone. Biting them." She glanced at Curt, and Alicia felt her heart sink.

"I watched the video," Alicia said. "What happened after that?"

"I ran." Gigi threw her hands in the air. "What else was I going to do? I'm not a damn ninja or whatever, like Dad. I ran as fast as I could back here. It was barely fast enough. One of the children, a boy, chased me. Silent, but incredibly quick, and determined. He chased me right into the building and up the stairs. He almost got me while I tried to unlock the door, but thankfully Curt heard me screaming and opened it."

"That's when I got bit," Curt said weakly. Alicia turned to face him. It seemed to take all his effort just to talk. "Little guy was really strong. I kicked at him to keep him outside while Gigi came in. I didn't even realize he'd bit me until I felt blood trickling down my leg afterward."

Alicia frowned. That meant Curt's bite was already a couple of days old—which meant he should have already turned. Was it because the bite was on the leg? Most everyone else had bites on the neck and shoulder. Maybe it took longer for this infection to hit the brain if an extremity was infected. Or maybe the infection's slower progress was because Curt was substantially bigger than the other victims.

"The gunshots started pretty soon after that," Gigi continued, staring off into the distance. Alicia could tell her sister was only looking at bad memories. "A few at first, then more. Then we heard the PLA trucks and jeeps. More gunshots, more screams. When we heard screaming and fighting in the hall, even right outside our door, we decided we weren't going anywhere. Good thing, too. The next day, the military burst into the building and shot up the first few floors. Almost as quickly as they came in, we heard them shouting to 'disengage.' It sounded like things were going poorly. We spent the better part of that day flat on the floor in case bullets came through the walls. We've been hiding out here ever since."

Alicia hated to think of her sister living through that nightmare. Alicia's training with the Outfit had mentally prepared her for... well, not for this situation specifically, but she had been prepared to handle seeing people gunned down in front of her—and putting them down herself. Gigi didn't have that preparation or mentality. She didn't have the ability to switch off her emotions and compartmentalize like Alicia did. How was Gigi even sane at this point?

And on top of all of that, her fiancé now lay in the corner—where he was almost certainly dying.

Or worse.

Gigi was in the middle of the worst day of her life.

Narmer's words came back to Alicia. He'd said he had faith in her ability to be a force of good in the world.

That started here. Now.

"Hey," Alicia said. "You guys did better than almost anyone could in your shoes. I know Dad would be proud of you, Gigi. Once we get out of here and back stateside, he'll probably brag about you to all those friends of his at the social club. So let's just focus on getting you guys out of this hellhole. Sound like a plan?"

The others nodded.

"Okay. I'm going to tell you what I know." She pointed to the door. "Those kids you saw, Gigi—they were being experimented on at a hidden government facility to the northeast of here. Injected with some serum. It gave them some sort of virus, which at first made them docile, hard workers. But something went wrong, and they became violent. And now, when they bite other people, they transmit that virus... and the victims suffer the same fate."

They all looked at Wes.

"How do you know this?" he asked. He was probably hoping she was wrong.

"I captured a PLA soldier and asked him a few questions."

"And he just answered you?" Curt said. "How do you know he wasn't lying?"

He took a deep breath and let it out slowly. Alicia recognized the attempt at covering for pain and nausea. He looked like how she'd felt when cancer was running through her body.

"Because he was terrified," Alicia said. "And I had a gun to his head."

Curt started to say something more, but then he must have seen from Alicia's expression that she wasn't joking, and he fell silent.

Alicia pulled the map from her bag and unfolded it. "Wes, the soldier told me the facility was right... here. Do you know what's out that way?"

Wes crouched down next to her and looked at the place she pointed at. "Nothing, really. A few rice fields. But that *is* the direction the PLA vehicles have been taking the prisoners when they drive through Yichun at night."

Alicia frowned. "I'm certain there's a testing facility out there. How can no one know about it?"

Wes shrugged. "People don't wander in this part of the

country. Especially around Yichun. We've had curfews for a few years now. If you get caught outside at night, the military makes you disappear."

A few years? Alicia had been in this town only a few months ago, and she hadn't been aware of this. Then again, she'd only been here during the day. And apparently the Chinese were good at keeping their military presence under wraps.

"Why are you interested in the facility?" Gigi asked.

Alicia looked her sister in the eye. "Because I'm going to break in."

Gigi's eyes widened. "You're serious."

"I am. I told you I was sent here for my job. That's where they need me to go. But I'm not leaving you in this apartment, trapped like sardines. Is there somewhere safe, somewhere outside of Yichun, I can help you get to?"

Wes pointed to a blank spot on the map, to the east of Yichun, but not that far out of Alicia's way. "The map doesn't show it, but there's a small village here. I have friends there who were already expecting us because of our original plan to escape. But can we even get out of Yichun?"

"We have to," Alicia replied. "But I won't sugarcoat it. It's a war zone out there. What they did to your building was done all over the city. They're welding doors shut. Burning bodies in the streets."

Wes covered his face with his hands. "This is Covid all over again."

"What do we do?" Gigi asked. "Just tell us what to do."

"You come with me," Alicia said. "I'll do everything I can to get you to safety."

Wes uncovered his face. "We have to get the others. The ones we were going to escape with. If we can find them."

"No," Alicia said firmly.

Gigi and Wes both flinched. Curt had closed his eyes, but he shook his head slowly.

"I'm sorry," Alicia continued. "We don't have the luxury of looking for anyone. Besides which, the chances of them being alive are, unfortunately, low. And... this virus has a ticking clock."

Curt opened his eyes, and Alicia saw he already knew the truth.

"What do you mean?" Gigi asked.

Alicia didn't mince words. "The virus is lethal."

In the silence that followed Alicia's proclamation, Gigi went over and sat by Curt, taking his hand in her own. "How long?"

"I don't know for certain," Alicia said. "I think the original carriers are already dead. I saw a few of them around the city. From what the soldier told me, it looks like the original carriers took weeks to turn aggressive." She paused. She wished Curt had weeks, but she had to be truthful. "The bitten... they seem to be succumbing more quickly. As in, days. So when I say we have a ticking clock, I mean it."

"Is there a cure?" Curt asked.

It was the question they all had on their minds.

"Maybe," Alicia answered. "My boss believes that anyone developing such a virus wouldn't do so without having a vaccine. That's why I'm going to the facility—to find out."

"A vaccine prevents disease," Curt said. "Will it reverse the infection in someone already bitten?"

"Curt, I'm sorry, I just don't know. I wish I could tell you, but I can't. All I can say is, we need to get out of here, now."

"We tried last night," Wes said. "But the army had torn down the fire escape, and we didn't dare go down through the building, not after all we'd heard down there. We thought we could quickly get to the roof and jump to the building next door. But the infected were in our hall, so we couldn't even do that."

"And those thralls are probably *still* out in the hall," Alicia said, frowning.

"The... thralls?" Wes asked.

"That's what the soldiers are calling them," Alicia answered. "In any case, we'll have to risk it. Pack up whatever you think you absolutely need, but pack light. I recommend food and water. Maybe one set of clothes. We have to be able to move quickly."

"We already have all that packed," Gigi said. She pointed to three backpacks resting against the wall. "Food, water, first aid, and our camera gear. We didn't bring much, and we're leaving a lot of the clothes."

"Good." She checked her watch. "It'll be dark in about an hour. Let's wait until then. We'll be able to move faster in the dark, without worrying so much about the PLA." She felt forced to look at Curt again. His skin looked an even lighter shade of white. "Curt, you can stand and walk?"

"Sure thing," he said, not moving. "I'm just saving my strength. Don't want to show any of you up."

Alicia smiled. *Dad was wrong. Curt is a good guy.* "Good stuff. I'm going to have Gigi and Wes holding you close in case that leg gives you any trouble. And I need my hands free. For now, everyone should get in a few minutes of rest, because I don't know when we'll get any more."

Gigi stayed sitting by Curt, and Wes sat next to Alicia. Wes gave her a quick smile, then closed his eyes and leaned his head back against the wall.

"Alicia, I need to ask you a favor." Alicia barely heard Wes's question, asked in a whisper.

"Okay."

"Can you get me back to the States?"

She looked at him out of the corner of her eye. "No family here?"

"They're all gone."

Alicia knew she should say no. She had no business making promises of amnesty to foreign nationals. But Wes—Song Wen-gin—would be killed if left in China. General Feng, or people like him, would hunt down anyone who lived in Yichun to silence them about the virus that had been let loose. Even if he managed to escape for a short time, once Gigi's piece went live he'd be found and executed for treason. All his future options in China ended with him being put against a wall and shot.

The man had let Gigi and Curt stay in his home. A refuge against all the insanity. He'd protected them.

So Alicia replied in the only possible way she could. "You bet. Though when you get stateside, you'll need a new identity. My dad knows a few people who can probably make that happen."

"I understand," Wes said. "An easy sacrifice in trade for a future."

"I guess it is."

Alicia closed her eyes and took a deep breath. Her dad would have easily fallen into some sort of meditative trance in a situation like this. She would have preferred to just sit back and listen to music. Bagel crawled into her lap, curling up to take a quick nap, and she absently scratched his neck. So far, the little guy had been a good companion. She let the cat's calm breathing relax her, and she drifted.

"The sun is down," Wes said. Alicia flinched as his words shattered the silence of the small apartment.

"Already? What time is it?" Alicia looked at her watch. Half past six. She'd dozed, and looking across the room at Gigi and Curt, they had, too. "Well, I guess this is it. Grab your stuff."

She stood and threw her pack over her shoulders. Wes and Gigi did the same. Wes took the third bag, Curt's, and slung it across his chest.

Alicia crossed to Curt and helped pull him up. When she took his hand, it felt like cold wax. His skin looked a shade whiter than before, if possible, and his breathing was ragged. Worse than all of this, he was rubbing at his eyes. Up close, Alicia saw a light film covering them.

"You all right, Curt?" Alicia asked.

He rubbed his eyes again. "Can't seem to focus. It's like I need glasses."

"I'm sure it's nothing," Alicia lied. "You just need some rest."

"I'm sure a vaccine would do some good, too." Curt chuckled, his lungs rattling with fluid, making him hack.

When the coughing subsided, Alicia said, "Don't worry. I'll take care of it." She looked at Wes and Gigi. "You two have him? I'm going to check the door."

Alicia crossed the apartment, Bagel at her feet, and pressed her ear to the door. When she didn't hear any steps or scratching after a few minutes, she carefully grabbed the handle and pulled the door open an inch. No thralls pushed in. Unprompted, Bagel stepped out into the hallway, making his way into the darkness. Alicia turned on the phone to get a look at the hallway through her cat's camera, and found the space empty and still as a mausoleum.

Where had the thralls gone?

She waved the others forward and stepped into the gloom. She lifted the Chinese pistol in one hand and kept her eyes on the phone screen. The dim glow of the camera feed barely illuminated the area around her, but her eyes could pick up details easily enough.

Taking the lead, Alicia led the group down the stairs. She'd liked the idea of going to the roof and jumping down to the next building over, but it was clear that Curt wouldn't be able to jump any distance at all. Their only way out was the front door.

They descended the stairs with no issues, the thralls conspicuous by their absence. Yet the building still felt *wrong*. Like the air was heavy with dread.

Alicia closed her eyes for a moment, focusing on the silence, listening for the static that meant someone or something had a bead on her. But she heard nothing except the ragged sound of Curt's labored breathing, and she felt nothing but the nagging feeling that an important detail eluded her.

On the ground floor, Alicia followed Bagel outside into the night. The cat seemed unconcerned, which took a little of the edge off Alicia's worry. She took a moment to orient herself. The stars above shone bright, promising hope and a future. Lies, maybe. But maybe this was a good omen.

Alicia turned in a small circle, then stopped short when she caught a red and orange glow off in the distance in the northern part of the city. A fire. Straining her ears, she caught the faint sounds of faraway screaming. Then the popping of gunfire, loud enough for all of them to hear. All from the same direction.

She waved the others closer. "That fire may be why we aren't seeing any thralls. They may have been drawn north by the light. Let's take advantage and move quickly to the edge of town. There were some abandoned cars and motorcycles on the outskirts. We'll need to get one running."

Curt clearly wasn't going to be walking all the way to another village. By the looks of him, she wondered if he could even stay on his feet for two blocks.

Gigi glanced at her fiancé, clearly thinking the same thing. "Can we just find a car nearby and make a break for it?"

"Unfortunately, no," Alicia answered. "There are concrete barricades on almost every road. The PLA made sure no one would be leaving by car. We'll have to do this on foot. Let's head roughly northeast, but stay wide of the fire. I've already walked most of those roads, so I know them pretty well."

"You walked them *once*," Gigi said. "There's no way you remember them *that* well."

"Trust me, Gigi. I've had some pretty good training from Dad, and from my new job. Between me and Wes, we've got this. Right, Wes?"

Wes nodded.

Gigi began to protest. "But—"

"There's no time to argue," Alicia said, cutting off her sister. " The quicker we're out of the city, the quicker I can look for the facility and some sort of vaccine or cure."

At the mention of a cure, Gigi nodded.

Alicia set a brisk pace as they wove through the streets and alleys. Or at least, as brisk as Curt could manage in his condition. Alicia hoped the movement wasn't making the infection move through his body faster. But it was a risk they had to take. If they didn't get out of the city soon, they'd all die anyway.

The light from the fire grew as they drew nearer. The screams became audible to everyone, and the gunfire came more often. Alicia picked out shouted orders from a superior to his subordinates, and the voice sounded frantic. Whatever was happening over there, the soldiers were in a bad place.

Alicia steered clear, not only of the fire and whatever chaos was going on over that way, but of the piles of burned corpses, to the extent that she could. Gigi and Curt didn't need to see that. Unfortunately, avoiding *all* the carnage simply couldn't be done. Under the burned and tattered awning of a seamstress's storefront, a bloated corpse lay face-down in the dirt, a small but dense haze of spores enveloping it like a personal cloud. The flesh had begun melting into the ground, and small white growths protruded from the spine and the base of the skull.

Gigi stopped cold. "Is that what's going to happen to... us?"

Alicia didn't need to read minds to know that wasn't how that question was initially going to end. She wasn't asking about *us*. She was asking about *Curt*.

"I don't know." Alicia waved them forward, out of the street where a trigger-happy sniper could end all their worries with a few well-placed shots. "Let's keep moving. The sooner we get out of here the quicker I can find the cure."

"What if there isn't a cure?" Gigi asked.

"There will be. The Chinese military may be dishonest and brutal, but they aren't stupid. They'll have... something, even if it's just a prototype. Probably the same thing they did during Covid and a dozen other outbreaks. You let me worry about that. You and Wes worry about keeping Curt upright. We're almost to the edge of the city."

The blaze seemed to have spread, but the screaming and gunfire had lessened. Alicia could no longer pick out shouted orders. She felt no pity for those military leaders, but she did pity their subordinates who had to blindly follow orders or get shot through the back of the head. They deserved better. Everyone here did.

China should have been a land of hope and prosperity. With a less corrupt government, it could be the jewel of the East. Instead its people suffered indignity after indignity. Slave camps. Human trafficking. Poverty. Technology stolen rather than invented and advanced. And now genetic manipulation and experimentation.

When Alicia had been in this part of China a few months earlier, she'd focused on the job. To do anything else at that time would have led to her death. But now she saw things clearly. Her country of birth couldn't be saved. Not truly. At least not in her lifetime.

Well... not in a normal person's lifetime. If what Lorna had said was true, maybe *Alicia's* lifetime would actually be long enough.

They soon found themselves on the fringes of Yichun. Alicia started checking abandoned cars, and more than a few still had the keys in them. They opted for a small van, and Wes and Gigi began helping Curt into the back seat.

That was when Alicia's ears picked up the faint pounding of boots. She lifted her pistol, aiming at the dark mouth of a nearby alley.

A soldier broke free from the darkness, running right at them. Had he heard them, or was his appearance here just bad luck?

When he looked frantically over his shoulder, Alicia had her answer.

"Get in and drive!" she shouted.

Alicia grabbed Wes by the back of his collar and shoved him toward the driver's seat. She then turned and put two rounds into the oncoming soldier. Gigi flinched, hands flying to cover her ears as the pistol roared.

Alicia took a few steps forward, putting herself between the van and what she knew was about to come out of the alley. The soldier fell to the dirt, then pushed himself back up. Alicia knew she hadn't missed, but for now the soldier's adrenaline and fear kept him going. With good reason: behind him, half a dozen thralls spilled out into the moonlight.

Shooting them all wasn't an option. So Alicia did the next best thing. The best bad choice she could make.

Alicia aimed again, pumping several rounds into the soldier's legs.

He fell hard. Not dead, though he soon would be. The decision made her want to vomit, but she knew she needed him alive for the moment. Alive but unmoving.

As bait.

"Shit!" Gigi screamed behind her.

Alicia spun around to see Gigi struggling against Curt, who was seated in the van but had leaned out to clamp his teeth down on Gigi's side.

Alicia rushed in and punched Curt in his temple with everything she had, knocking him out.

Clutching at her bleeding side, Gigi met Alicia's gaze with a look of pure panic. "Sis? What... am I going to do?"

"You're going to get in this van." She took off her pack and handed it to Gigi. "There are zip ties in here. Tie him up while Wes gets you both to safety."

"You're not coming?"

"We were always going to split up." Alicia nodded to a nearby motorcycle with the keys still hanging from the ignition. "Best we do so while I have my own ride."

"But how will you find us?"

"There's a tracker in my bag too. I'll find you." She pulled Gigi into a quick hug. "I'll figure this out. Just go."

Gigi ran around the van and got in the other side, and Wes

wasted no time. Dirt and gravel kicked up from the spinning tires as he sped away.

Alicia looked back at the thralls. They had fallen onto the dying soldier, their teeth ripping into him. The man's screams quickly turned into gurgles as his throat was torn apart in spurts of arterial blood. Alicia had sentenced him to death. Now she had to make sure it hadn't been for nothing.

She holstered her pistol and sprinted to the motorcycle. As its motor growled to life, the thralls looked up from their feast. Faces smeared with blood and flesh, they stood and rushed her.

Bagel jumped onto Alicia's shoulder as she revved the engine, and the bike peeled away, leaving the thralls in a cloud of dust.

She was safe... for now. But Curt was infected... and Gigi was now on her way to the same fate.

Alicia prayed she'd find a cure at the hidden facility. It was her only hope of preventing Gigi from turning into a thrall.

TWENTY-FOUR

Between rice fields illuminated in moonlight, the door to the underground facility stood open, an ominous welcome to the depths of a hell Alicia wasn't sure she was prepared for.

Bodies of soldiers littered the ground like broken action figures. Among them, Alicia also saw the corpses of workers who'd been shot by the facility's guards. None had the cloud-like spores surrounding them. The clinical part of Alicia's brain wondered if the death of the body served to kill the continued metamorphosis of the infected.

She crouched down, hand straying to scratch behind Bagel's ears. The cat stood rigid, tail upright and frozen in place. He was on edge just like she was.

"What do you think, Bagel?" Alicia whispered. Her enhanced vision didn't detect any movement. She had to fight her impatience to rush inside. Running headlong into the facility wouldn't help Gigi or Curt if it got her killed in the process. "I'm thinking the virus or fungus or whatever it is, doesn't keep growing if the host is killed before a certain point. Maybe it needs a certain amount of warmth or specific conditions that a living body provides. That would explain the girl we found on the barricade, and all these corpses. It all tracks, but we still don't have all the information."

Bagel didn't take his eyes from the open door.

"Fine. Ignore me then. Do you see anything?"

Bagel circled back to stand right next to her feet, and batted out "*No*" on her foot.

"Okay then. In we go."

As they crept toward the entrance, she ejected the partially spent magazine from her pistol and inserted a fresh one she pulled from a pouch on her belt. She looked down at the pistol and frowned.

"What am I doing? There've got to be dozens of perfectly good rifles out here."

She walked to the soldier farthest away from the facility entrance and took his rifle. When she pulled the magazine free, she saw he hadn't even gotten off a shot before the thralls had ripped out his jugular. Alicia looked back away from the building entrance, following a trail of trampled footprints back toward the rice fields. It all matched the story told by the soldier she'd interrogated back in town. She then gathered a handful of full magazines from the fallen and half-eaten soldiers, stuffing them into pockets and pouches.

At the door, Alicia paused. It was massive, made from nine inches of solid steel, but stood open because it was blocked by the mangled corpse of a field worker. The worker's head had been mostly blown away by gunfire.

Alicia tried to think of the dead in terms of thralls and soldiers rather than men, women, and children. Tried not to imagine the bodies of trafficked little boys and girls superimposed over the corpses of the smallest of the thralls. She didn't need her picture-perfect memory to remember all those children. Those images would be with her until the day she died.

Bagel jumped over the corpse, paused, then headed down a sloping rampway.

"After you," Alicia muttered.

The term "facility" didn't accurately describe the building. It was more like a bunker. The downward angle of the pathway was wide enough to drive a truck down, and it obviously led underground, beneath the low hills.

Doubt I can blow up this base like I did the last one.

Bodies lay unmoving down the concrete pathway like a trail of morbid breadcrumbs leading to the laboratories she knew waited for her ahead. *Maybe they'll be empty.*

As if reading her thoughts, Bagel looked back at Alicia with a look that said, "*Are you kidding me?*"

The subterranean road led to a truck dock. The only vehicle present was a military transport truck, which looked mostly untouched. The dock had a single, built-in bay door that currently stood closed, and a smaller, regular door that led further into the installation. The latter stood open, partially broken from its hinges and smeared with blood. Streaking red handprints dragged away from the biggest of the splotches.

Just three months ago, Alicia would have turned around

and called for backup. Maybe even three *days* ago. But the bite mark on her sister's side had turned desperation into courage.

Lights flickered on the other side of the doorway, and sparks fell from exposed, shredded wiring. Alicia moved around them with caution. She didn't want to test her supposed longevity against the threat of electrocution.

The hallway looked cheaply built. No recessed lighting like the passages at the Outfit's HQ. Just hastily built walls of concrete and harsh fluorescent lights.

Made in China.

Her nerves almost caused a hysterical giggle to bubble up out of her, but she managed to keep it down.

The single pathway led to a T-intersection. At the junction, Alicia looked down at the cat with a raised eyebrow. Bagel looked left, then right before choosing the left hallway.

No bodies here. The corpses outside had been terrible, but now the lack of dead bodies was somehow even more disturbing. Especially with generous pools of blood on the floor, and red spatter on the walls with bits of hair and bone stuck in it.

Alicia raised the rifle and thumbed the safety off.

At the end of the hallway was another doorway, but the door was long gone. Alicia half-expected a torrent of thralls to burst through the dark portal, and she had to take a steadying breath to calm her shaking hands. Even Bagel hesitated to walk forward. But nothing jumped out at them as they passed through the doorway into a lab.

It stood in shambles. Broken glass littered the floor, and scattered papers were everywhere. Still no bodies, though.

Alicia couldn't figure out how the underground complex

was organized. There must be other passages that led to the barracks and the holding cells. The warehousing area might be on the other side of the loading bay door she'd passed. But most importantly, somewhere there was an office for this General Feng who was overseeing the project.

Slinging the rifle over her shoulder, Alicia began grabbing papers, looking for anything that jumped out. As she put the pieces together from multiple documents, her blood turned to ice in her veins.

"No. No this isn't possible."

The documents spoke of a biological weapon stolen from Taiwan that had been genetically modified to cause death to anyone who breathed in its fungal spores. The dates matched up to the torching of that lab months ago. The lab that had nearly given China the excuse it needed to take over Taiwan.

All that effort. All that progress. All the pride she'd felt, the praise she'd had heaped on her. None of it had meant a damn thing. She hadn't succeeded three months ago.

I failed.

The Chinese had taken that biological weapon and had been manipulating it for their own benefit.

From a tipped-over filing cabinet, Alicia found a folder that gave her a better understanding of what she was dealing with. *Massospora cicadina.* A fungal infection that took over the bodies of a specific type of cicada and drove them to mass-produce to continue the spread of the fungus. Eventually it turned the bodies of the bugs into a white, chalky substance from the inside out.

The bug wasn't the important part of the equation, though.

The chemical release of cathinone was. The scientists had found it was easily absorbed into the system, replacing dopamine. Together, the fungus and the chemicals it released served as a wicked antidepressant—and after being modified, the scientists found it completely shut down the hosts' ability to think for themselves, turning them into...

"The perfect slaves. This... this is monstrous."

She didn't know what had gone wrong, but that hardly mattered at the moment. The subjects had all turned, and they were hyper-violent. Something in their altered body chemistry must have driven the thralls to want to pass on the fungus.

Alicia grabbed a few of the more salient documents, folded them, and stuffed them into a pocket.

Refrigeration units lined one wall, and she looked inside them all. Their shelves held row after row of small vials containing a red serum. Each was labeled "Serum 613" with the date of production.

But none of the cold-storage units held anything marked "anti-serum" or "anti-virus" or anything that might be indicative of a cure.

Alicia wanted to scream in frustration. Her watch showed she'd already been inside for two hours, and she was no closer to finding something that would help Curt and Gigi.

A soft metal tapping pulled her attention to a shadowed back corner of the lab. Alicia pulled the rifle back up and walked as silently as she could toward the sound. It had been so quiet, nearly indiscernible from the sounds of falling glass fragments and the creaks of the bunker settling, that doubted she would have even noticed it if not for her exceptional hearing.

Bagel cocked his head at her in curiosity. Even the cat hadn't heard the sound.

As Alicia got closer to the darkened area of the lab, she saw why it was dark—all the lights in the ceiling had been shattered. She spotted an injector on the ground in a pile of broken glass. Almost as though the injector had been thrown up at the lights to break them.

She picked up the injector and pocketed it. She'd need one if—no, *when*—she found the antidote.

She stood silently and strained her ears. The tapping had stopped, but she heard the faint sound of shallow breathing.

She followed it to a cabinet in the corner of the lab. Someone was hiding here. She was sure it wasn't a thrall; they weren't the hiding type. Which left soldier or scientist. Either of which could be dangerous in their own way.

She yanked open the cabinet door quickly, revealing a cowering man in a bloodstained lab coat.

"Out," Alicia said, keeping her voice down. "And stay quiet."

The man slid from his hiding place, keeping his hands up. His eyes frantically darted around the room like he expected a thrall to pop out of thin air.

"Are you here to extract us?" the scientist asked.

"Only if you know where the antidote is."

"There isn't one," he replied, but far too quickly.

Alicia smiled and used the barrel of the rifle to lift the scientist's chin a little. "We both know that's not true. No way you make a weapon like this without having a way to counteract it."

"I swear I—"

"What's your name?"

"Uh… Dr. Shen Ping."

"Shen? Interesting. Your name is all over the reports I've found in here. Interesting stuff. So you're the one who took the Taiwanese samples we thought we destroyed and altered the weapon for your own use?"

"There's no weapon." The man shook his head vehemently. "I'm afraid you don't understand the science here. That's not how—"

"I studied neuroscience at Princeton, Doctor. Don't patronize me." Alicia felt the smile, false though it was, fall from her lips. "How about I go find one of those thralls out there and let it bite you? Since I don't understand the science, that would be fine, wouldn't it? Nothing would happen, right?"

"You… but… you wouldn't…"

"I would. I've made a lot of decisions today that I'm not particularly proud of. But feeding the designer of a slave fungal concoction to the monsters he created wouldn't even make the list. Antidote. Where is it?"

"I don't have it."

Alicia pressed the rifle barrel a little harder into his throat. "That wasn't my question."

Shen licked his lips and squeezed his eyes shut. "It's untested. It kills the virus, but it may kill the host too. I haven't done a full study on it yet."

"*Where is it?*" Alicia repeated.

"The general keeps it in his office."

"General Feng? Where's his office?"

Shen pointed back the way she'd come. "Straight down the hallway, at the far end."

"Great. Let's go."

Shen shook his head. "The hall is filled with subjects. Besides, the general barricaded himself in his office with one of his soldiers."

"There aren't any thralls in the hall. I just came from there."

The scientist's eyes darted behind her to the room's other door. "Then they're all back there. I hid here while the soldiers fled deeper inside the facility. The... thralls, as you call them, must have followed them back there."

Alicia grabbed Shen by the collar and pushed him toward the entrance. The scientist took one step, slipped in a pool of liquid, and crashed to the floor. He hit a chair on the way down, which spun and hit the open door of a supply cabinet, dumping its contents onto the lab's floor.

The sounds were loud in the quiet facility, and in the moments that followed, Alicia heard the distant patter of bare feet on concrete.

She yanked the doctor up with one hand. "Well, now we've definitely got to get out of this room."

Shen clearly agreed, as he practically ran back into the hall, Alicia on his heels, Bagel running beside her. They got back to the T-intersection and kept going. At the end of the hall, they stopped before a closed door with a numeric keypad on it.

Nothing announced that this was General Feng's office, but Alicia shoved Shen toward it.

"Open it."

"But—"

"No choice, Shen. Get us in there, or the thralls will find us out here. They're already headed this way."

Shen tapped at the keypad with a shaking hand. His first attempt made the pad beep loudly, and a red light blinked. He tried again, getting the combination wrong a second time.

"Shen..." Alicia said coldly.

The doctor whimpered and punched the buttons again, only to get the blinking red light a third time.

A thrall appeared in the hallway behind them. It stared their way for a long moment, then burst into a run toward them.

"*Now*, Shen!"

He entered the wrong code yet again. Was he truly that scared, or had someone changed the code?

If it's the latter, we're dead.

Alicia raised the rifle and put a three-round burst into the charging thrall's chest. It hit the floor hard, but pushed right back up to its feet. Alicia hit it with another burst, this time to its face, dropping it permanently. Her ears rang from the roar of the rifle in the confined space, but it cleared quickly.

Now an entire swarm of thralls appeared. Their clothes identified them as a mix of rice field workers, PLA soldiers, and scientists. No one here had been spared the transmission of the fungus.

The beep sounded once more behind her, but this time it was a different tone.

"I got it!" Shen yelled.

As he threw open the door and rushed inside, Alicia dove after him, tucking into a roll. She was just about to kick the door shut behind her when a gunshot went off, a spray of blood hit her across the face, and Shen's lifeless body fell on top of her.

Bagel hissed.

The dead weight of the scientist pinned Alicia to the ground. She pushed at the body, trying to lever Shen's corpse off her. *Why couldn't those nanites have given me super strength?*

More gunfire erupted from deeper in the room, cutting down the first wave of thralls as they tried to pile into the general's office. Shen's legs had blocked the door, keeping it open, and now the thralls clawed over one another in an attempt to get through the doorway.

Alicia managed to untangle herself from Shen's lifeless limbs and scrambled away from the door. She ducked behind a desk and peeked around it to see who was holding the infected at bay.

At the back of the room, two men alternated fire, covering for each other whenever one stopped to reload. One was an ordinary soldier, teeth bared in defiance as he sent controlled bursts from his rifle. The other man wore a dress uniform, resplendent with a wall of medals pinned to the front of his jacket, and general's insignia on his cuffs and shoulders.

General Feng.

One of them had killed Shen. Maybe they thought he was

infected. Or maybe they just had a shoot-first policy in the middle of an outbreak.

A gun safe stood open behind the men. It stood empty, but Alicia saw the brackets for holding pistols and rifles. The two men were practically bristling with weapons and ammo; clearly they'd loaded up with everything they could.

But next to the empty armory was something of even greater interest to Alicia: a glass-doored refrigeration unit.

Feng *had* to be keeping the anti-serum in there.

"Get ready, Wong!" General Feng dropped a magazine and slapped a fresh one into his rifle. "I'll clear the way for you. We are the last hope of the program. We'll show the world China's power. You know what to do."

"Yes, sir!" Wong put a fresh magazine in his own rifle, then picked up a bag from the ground at his feet and hoisted it over his shoulders. Alicia had seen enough refrigerated transport bags from her days at Princeton to recognize it for what it was. Feng had one at his feet as well.

Perhaps they'd already been about to make a break for it when Shen opened the door. Which meant the anti-serum was no longer in the refrigerator—it was in those transport bags.

We'll show the world China's power.

You know what to do.

Despite the push of the thralls, Alicia hadn't gone unnoticed by the general. He spared a moment to send a three-round burst her way. She ducked behind the heavy desk just in time.

"Ready?" Feng shouted. "Go, Wong!" He opened up with a

continuous barrage of rifle fire, giving Wong a window to dart through the door.

Alicia leaned out and took a wild shot at the escaping soldier, but missed. What if that soldier was the one with the antidote?

"I don't know who you are," Feng yelled at her between rifle bursts, "but you can't stop this. I won't allow you to. This formula will make China unstoppable."

Another quick burst hit Alicia's cover. There wasn't any point in replying to the madman. He'd used a fungus to turn prisoners into mindless slaves. Attempting to reason with him would get her nowhere.

Thralls continued to push forward, but there were fewer now, and Feng was able to take more measured, accurate shots. Soon he'd be relieved of their threat, momentarily anyway, and would come after Alicia—or merely escape.

Alicia drew her pistol and flattened herself to the ground, looking under the desk. Through the gap, she had a clear view of the general's boots.

Taking a steadying breath, she aimed and pulled the trigger twice.

Feng screamed as one of her bullets took him in the side of his right foot and the other shattered his ankle. He dropped to the ground, losing his grip on the rifle, and Alicia popped around the side of the desk, pistol ready.

The world around her seemed to move in slow motion. A thrall climbed over the corpses of the others, eyes locked on the fallen general. Feng's hand dipping to his waist, drawing a pistol. The refrigerated bag lying open next to him. In it she caught a glimpse of a few vials of liquid. Some were red... but others were blue.

That has to be the antidote.

The general lifted his pistol, his teeth gritted, his eyes filled with pain and hate, and pointed it not at the thrall, but at Alicia.

Her compassion left her, shut away like it had been when she'd taken down the man in her apartment complex. She made no conscious decision as she put five rounds into Feng's chest. It just... happened.

The world had devolved into pure threat assessment. And she'd put down the threat. Not just to her, but to the world.

Feng blinked up at her, pistol sliding from his limp hand. He tried to talk, mouth moving soundlessly, blood spilling from its corners.

Alicia almost put a bullet through his eye. Instead she spun to the thrall and emptied the rest of her magazine into its legs, shattering bone and spraying blood. It hit the ground hard, rolled, and came face to face with the dying general.

Reap what you sow.

The thrall had once been just a child, a boy of maybe eight or nine. But as Feng looked it in the eye, the general's expression of hatred turned to one of fear.

Looking away from the general and his grisly fate, Alicia grabbed the medical transport bag. The blue serum was in a transparent case labeled "Antifungal 613."

Three doses. Curt. Gigi. And one for analysis.

One more thrall was coming through the doorway. Alicia pointed her pistol at the thrall's face.

"I'm sorry," she said as she pulled the trigger.

Distantly the *feeling* part of her, the part that had been pushed aside by the cold, analytical side, wondered who she had become. Wondered why she'd allowed an organization to put her in a situation where she was a trigger-puller.

She ran down the hallway, taking headshots at the two thralls who came toward her. Bagel ran at her side, effortlessly avoiding the infected.

She took a left at the intersection, sprinted down the hallway, and burst into the loading dock area just in time to see the transport truck's glowing taillights as it drove away up the ramp. The soldier was getting away, and he posed a massive threat. Given what Feng had said—*We'll show the world China's power; you know what to do*—she had to assume his bag held the red serum.

She couldn't allow him to leave this facility. If he got away, he could go anywhere, and this threat needed to be contained. Now or never.

Alicia ran after him, but as slow as the truck was, she couldn't run fast enough to catch it. She looked down at Bagel, and she had an idea. Not a great one, but all she'd had today were bad options.

"Bagel, I know you can catch that truck. I need you to jump into it. Stay hidden. I'll catch up."

Her cat didn't hesitate to sprint after the military vehicle. Bagel caught up to the truck quickly and leapt into the back just before it left the facility, the door having opened for it automatically.

Alicia watched as the truck, the soldier, the serum, and Bagel vanished into the darkness.

Then she pulled out her phone and opened the GPS tracking app. Two red dots showed on the screen: one directly ahead and moving away from her, and the other stationary to the southeast. Bagel and Gigi.

"I'm coming, sis. Hold on."

Alicia tore through the Chinese countryside on the motorcycle. She stuck to the roads where possible but used her memory of the terrain maps to take small shortcuts across open fields where she could without risking the bike or herself.

The village Wes had shown her on a map wasn't very far away, and she made it there in under an hour, keeping the bike at full throttle the whole time. She blew past the small wooden homes at the edge of the village, skidding to a stop in front of a shack where the GPS signal from her bag originated. The van was parked outside, too. Alicia dropped the bike onto the dirt and ran inside, pulling the medical transport bag off her shoulders.

The shack was a single room, and Alicia took it all in. Curt lay on the ground in the middle of the space, arms zip-tied behind his back, his ankles similarly restrained. He now had the same vacant look as the thralls, and he bit at the air between them. Beyond him, against the wall, sat Gigi, with Wes beside her.

"You look like hell, sis," Gigi said, then coughed.

Alicia dropped to her sister's side and forced a smile. "It's been a tough day at the office." She put her hand on Wes's shoulder. "How is she?"

"Not good," he replied. "She's getting sicker much faster than Curt did."

Alicia pulled up Gigi's shirt to see the wound. "Infected. Look at the black lines coming off it."

"Did you find... anything?" Gigi said. The pleading tone in her voice nearly broke Alicia's heart.

"I did." Alicia opened the bag and pulled out the case with the blue vials. She extracted one, took the injector gun from her pocket, and attached the vial.

"Curt first," Gigi said.

"Gigi, I—"

"Curt first," Gigi said firmly. "I can hold on for a few more minutes. You need to fix him."

Alicia nodded and crossed to Curt's side. She jabbed the needle into his neck and pulled the trigger, injecting the full dose into him.

Curt immediately began to convulse, and his mouth opened in a silent scream. The lack of sound disturbed Alicia, and she nearly looked away. But almost as quickly as the convulsions began, they stopped, and Curt collapsed.

"Is he okay?" Gigi asked.

Alicia reached out hesitantly, keeping clear of his mouth as she felt for a pulse.

Nothing.

White fluid leaked from his mouth, nose, ears, and eyes,

bubbling like hydrogen peroxide. Just like Shen had said, the treatment had killed the fungus.

Had it also killed the patient?

Or, Alicia thought, *the patient was already beyond saving.*

If the fungus had grown in the same way that *Massospora cicadina* did in cicadas, it had already eaten most of his internal organs. There was no coming back from that.

Curt's face went slack and sank in on itself. Alicia felt again for a pulse, but she knew she wouldn't find anything.

She looked over at Gigi and shook her head.

"But he... but you..." Tears fell from Gigi's eyes. She tried to get up, but she didn't have the strength to move.

"It's an antifungal," Alicia said, her voice sounding hollow to her own ears. "It kills the fungus, but it can't undo the damage that the fungus did. He was too far gone, sis. The Curt you knew was already gone."

"I didn't even get a chance to..." Gigi broke into sobs, and even Wes began crying.

"I'm so sorry," Alicia said. She pulled the empty vial from the injector gun. "And Gigi... I don't know if this stuff is safe for you either."

Gigi choked out a few words. "Kill me then. It's better than being turned into one of those *things*."

"Gigi—"

"Just get it over with."

Alicia knew her sister was right, even if at the moment Gigi wasn't thinking clearly. But after seeing Curt die right in front of her, she felt a stab of fear.

She inserted a second blue vial into the gun. "Are you sure?" she asked.

"Either it works, or I die from it. Better than dying like... like that." Gigi nodded to Curt's body. "He deserved better, Alicia. So much better."

"I know he did." Alicia put the gun to Gigi's neck, then paused. "You should lie down first. So you don't hurt yourself."

Gigi didn't say a word as she lay on the dirt floor. She never took her eyes off Curt.

Alicia put the injector gun to her sister's neck again, and pulled the trigger.

Just like Curt before her, Gigi's body flew into immediate convulsions. Her mouth stretched open, jaw popping under the strain. Her eyes rolled upward until only the whites were visible, and her back arched, leaving only her head and feet touching the ground.

Then she collapsed.

But unlike Curt, she didn't fall still.

She coughed violently, then began choking, and Alicia rolled her sister onto her side. The same foaming white liquid spilled from her mouth and nose, but in quantities far less than from Curt. With a heave, she vomited up gobs of white goop. She heaved a second time, then sagged, her eyes closed.

Alicia pressed her fingers against her sister's neck. She felt a pulse, steady but weak. With a sob of relief, she sat back.

"Is she okay?" Wes asked.

Alicia couldn't answer that. "She's alive," she said.

The bite mark still showed, raw and deep, but the lines of infection had begun to slowly fade. Alicia could only hope that the fungus hadn't done too much damage before it was stopped.

She took a deep breath. "I can't stay, Wes. You need to watch her until I get back, or until I send someone for you."

"You're leaving? You can't leave. Gigi isn't... she needs you here."

"This isn't over," Alicia said. "There's still a soldier out there with a bunch of the fungal serum. I need to stop him."

"Go." The word, barely a whisper, came from Gigi's mouth. Her eyes fluttered open, and her mouth twitched in what Alicia thought was a tiny smile.

"Sis?"

"I'll be fine." Gigi didn't make a move to get up. "Get out of here. Go do what Dad would do and save the world or something. For me. For Curt." Tears spilled from her eyes.

"I'll send help." Alicia put her hand on her sister's face, then stood up. "Just rest, Gigi. I'll finish this."

The GPS signal from the truck hadn't stopped moving. It was making slow, steady progress southeast. Alicia took the motorcycle again, speeding across northern China, making ground quickly against the slow-moving military transport.

As she took the bike through an open field, standing up on the balls of her feet to let her knees absorb the rough terrain, she pictured the map of the surrounding area in her mind, and compared it to the direction the soldier had traveled.

The closest city in that direction was Jiamusi.

She had expected him to go to Harbin. It was a much bigger city. What did Jiamusi have that Harbin didn't?

When she was within fifteen minutes of the truck, it stopped, just outside of Jiamusi. She checked the GPS and noted its location.

The soldier had stopped at a commercial airport.

Of course.

The general had wanted to "demonstrate China's power." The only way to do that was by releasing that "power" on their enemies.

She gunned the bike, tearing down the road until she arrived at the airport. It wasn't large, but it might be large enough to support an international flight. She looked up the airport on her phone and found only one departing flight to somewhere outside of China.

It was headed for Honolulu, Hawaii.

And it was departing... *right now.*

Alicia looked up and saw a large airplane taxiing down the runway. She could only look on helplessly as it took off.

The tracker on Bagel was still stationary, however; thankfully the cat hadn't somehow snuck onto the plane. Alicia drove the bike right up to the low fence surrounding the airport, ditched it, and hopped over. Apparently airport security wasn't at the top of the local military's priorities.

She followed the tracker to the military truck and climbed into the back of the vehicle. Bagel looked up at her, his gold eyes glowing in the darkness.

"All right, Bagel. Let's get out of here."

The cat followed her out of the truck and back to the abandoned motorcycle. She took out the sat phone and dialed up Mason.

"*Status?*"

"We've got a problem, sir."

"*Did you find the virus?*"

Alicia found herself nodding even though she knew Mason couldn't see it. "It's not a virus, but a fungus. It's a long story, but I have a sample of the antifungal."

"*That's great news. But I can tell from your tone of voice there's an issue. Did you find your sister?*"

"I did. She got bit, and I gave her the antifungal. I think it got the virus out of her system, but she's still in bad shape." She didn't mention Curt. It was too hard to say the words out loud, and there was nothing that could be done for him now, anyway.

"*Give me the coordinates. I have agents now in country.*"

"Sir, there's another problem. Multiple problems, actually. There's a research facility northeast of Yichun full of more of the virus. The city itself is filled with infected, and needs to be contained. And a soldier carrying vials of the virus just took off on a plane to Honolulu."

"*Where's it departing from?*" Mason asked.

"Jiamusi. It took off just minutes ago. I'm sorry, sir. I couldn't stop it."

"*Alicia, you've done everything you can. You did more than anyone could have hoped. Text me your sister's coordinates, then get back to her and her fiancé. Agents will be there in a couple of hours.*"

"Yes, sir."

"*And Alicia, one last thing.*"

"Yes?"

"*Did you find General Feng in all of this? Or any sign of him?*"

"I did." Alicia wondered if the image of leaving the general to die at the hands of the monsters he'd created would haunt her dreams. "He's not going to be a problem anymore, sir. Ever again."

CHAPTER

TWENTY-FIVE

"A passenger plane out of Jiamusi, China, crashed in the Pacific Ocean, just an hour away from its intended destination of Honolulu," the news anchor said. *"The US government has been coordinating with the Chinese government for search and rescue, but there is little hope of finding survivors.*

"The news comes hot on the heels of a reported explosion that practically leveled the Chinese city of Yichun near the border of China and Russia. Chinese authorities are calling it one of the most tragic accidents in their country's long history, and are blaming the blast on a local power plant explosion. No word yet on the death toll, but it is rumored to be staggeringly high.

"In other international news, the Italian authorities have had little luck with a string of missing priests—"

Mason turned off the panel display in his office and tossed the remote onto his desk. He pointed up at the blank display.

"This could have been a lot worse, Alicia. I know we've told you this a dozen times already, but well done."

Alicia shook her head in disbelief. "An explosion? Seriously? Is that what we do any time we're involved in something—blow it up?"

Mason waved the comment away. "We didn't do it this time. Believe it or not, there are some sane people even in the Chinese government, and I managed to inform the right people of what they were facing." His silvery eyes flashed with amusement. "It seems that the powers that be weren't big on what General Feng was up to, and as is the style of the Chinese government, they got rid of the problem, with prejudice."

"I'm surprised they didn't nuke the place," Torres said, shaking her head. "From the data I was able to gather, the folks out of Beijing carpet-bombed that area with thermobaric bombs that made the folks at the Pentagon take notice. Our generals in DC are privately flipping out over the saber-rattling, but they don't understand that the Chinese probably did the right thing."

Mason nodded. "It seems like everything is now secure."

"You guys took care of the lab?" Alicia asked. "You sure you got it all?"

"Our guys made sure the lab was wiped with our own version of hell on earth. The heat was evidently so high that even the metal doors melted. That's the second Chinese military installation you've helped us put out of commission in the last few months."

Alicia shook her head. "Whoever you sent as cleanup did the real work."

Mason pulled a folder from the bottom of a stack on his desk and opened it. "It says here that your sister Gigi will make a full recovery."

"Physically," Alicia said.

"Physically," Mason agreed. "But if she's half as tough as you and Levi, she'll get there eventually. Give her time. Again, I'm sorry to hear about what happened to her fiancé."

Alicia swallowed the lump in her throat. She'd been ambivalent about Curt until she'd seen him at the end. And it was devastating to see how wrecked her sister was over his death.

"It'll be a long time before Gigi is back to normal," she said, "but at least she's out of that hellhole. And if my father and I have any say in the matter, she'd going to be a lot less adventurous in the future."

"Amen to that." Mason pulled out another folder and tapped it. "This is all the paperwork for a Mr. Song Wen-gin."

"He goes by 'Wes.'" Alicia gave Mason a smile. "Thank you for getting him out of China. He was instrumental in keeping Gigi safe."

"We have retained a new identity for him," Torres said. "As far as the *pendejos* in the PLA know, he died like everyone else in Yichun."

"And the people on the plane," Alicia said. "Was that the Outfit's doing?"

Mason shared a look with Torres. "I'm sorry, Alicia, but it had to be done. You did everything you could. But the risk was too great. The moment that soldier got on the plane with the potential to spread that virus, those passengers were already dead."

"I killed them," Alicia said quietly. "I could have gone after him first, instead of going to Gigi."

"You saved your sister," Torres said. "And killed a Chinese general hellbent on releasing a world-killing virus."

"Yeah," Alicia said, closing her eyes. There was no point in debating *what-if*s. Not now. But the situation tore free that metaphorical scab she'd been itching at since getting back from China for the first time a few months ago. A singular thought nagged at her mind.

The Outfit isn't for me.

"Sir, I... I think I need some time."

"Of course," Mason said. "I'd say you've earned it. You've been through two high-stress assignments in a very short time. Take some time off. How long do you need?"

"I don't know," Alicia said. "I just don't know."

EPILOGUE

Alicia took another sip of her Mexican Coke, which had gotten warm.

"You're nursing that thing like it's a bottle of tequila," Torres said. She looked around the bar. "I dig the place. How'd you find it?"

"Friend of my dad's owns it. Good food. Great place to meet privately or to just sit around and think."

"Yeah," Torres said. "You're having second thoughts, aren't you?"

"Am I that transparent?"

Since getting back from China three weeks ago, Alicia had spent most of her time alone, barely leaving her apartment. And even before that, she had never spoken much to Torres beyond passing her in the hallways of the Outfit, so it was a big surprise when out of the blue, Torres had called her and asked if she wanted to talk. Alicia shocked herself when she said yes.

"You've gone dark," Torres said. "And you didn't look like you had the warm fuzzies when you left HQ."

"Mason's worried?"

"Maybe. I haven't asked. *I'm* worried. After everything you've been through the last few months, you looked like you could use a friend who understands how crazy this world really is. You're tough as nails, Yoder. I like you. Anytime you need to talk, I'm here. Just wanted to tell you that."

"Thanks." Alicia smiled. "I appreciate it."

"Hey, anyone who understands the benefits of Mexican Coke is someone I want in my corner." They laughed together for a few moments, then Torres asked, "How's your sister?"

"Coping. It can't be easy to lose a fiancé, much less the way she did."

"Yeah," Torres said. "I have a small understanding of that kind of loss. Different situation. Same end result."

"I'm sorry. I had no idea."

Torres waved a dismissive hand, but Alicia saw the pain in her expression. "It was four years ago. It was a cartel hit in Mexico."

"He was the target?"

Torres shrugged. "I don't know." She cleared her throat. "Look, give Gigi some time. She'll get through it."

"You're not over it?"

"No."

They sat in silence for a few minutes, enjoying the quiet of the bar. Finally Torres leaned forward like she was about to bring Alicia into a conspiracy.

"Yoder, do you like working for the Outfit?"

"I don't know. That's the question I can't shake."

Torres nodded her understanding. "Don't get me wrong. The organization does a lot of good. Advances in science, technology, and medicine. We've kept the world from going all World War III on each other more than a few times. But it isn't for everyone."

"Are you thinking of leaving?"

"No. But we're not talking about me. You're good at what you do, Yoder. *Really* good. You could help the Outfit accomplish a lot. But..."

"But what?"

"I don't know. I've got a sense for these sorts of things. At least that's what my *abuelita* always said. I've just got this feeling that you like helping people. Am I right?"

Alicia nodded.

"Yeah, I thought so," Torres said. "You can do that at the Outfit. But... it will always be at arm's length, if that makes sense. With your skills, you could... well..."

Alicia almost laughed. "Come on, Torres. Just spit it out."

"You could go private."

"Like a private detective?"

Torres shrugged, but didn't say anything.

"What's bringing this up?" Alicia asked. "Have you been talking to my dad?"

"Nah." Torres smiled. "That dreamboat is out of my league. No, it was something in your expression when you left. Like I said—"

"Your *abuelita* said you had a sense for these things. I'll think on it. To be honest with you, I've been having second thoughts about a lot of things for months now. Just... don't tell Mason."

"Wouldn't dream of it." Torres rapped her knuckles on the tabletop. "I have to catch the train back to DC. Keep me in the loop with what you decide, one way or the other." She slid out of the booth but paused before walking away. "I have a good feeling about you, Yoder. Whether at our current place, or out in the wild, I think you and I are going to be working together for a long time." She waved, then walked out the front door.

Alicia laughed in disbelief, but somehow felt better.

"It's about damned time she left." Tony Montelaro slid his considerable bulk into the booth where Torres had just been sitting. "I know your father's out of town and you're crashing at his pad, but why are you ducking his calls?"

"Hey, Tony, good to see you too." Alicia sat back in her bench seat. "He put you up to talking with me?"

"Maybe." Tony shrugged.

Alicia couldn't help but smile at the man's look of discomfort. She knew that he was probably one of Dad's mafia soldiers or whatever they called them, and he'd probably done some terrible things, but she couldn't help but see him as a jovial uncle of sorts.

"I told him I was fine," she said. "He knows I'll call when I'm ready. I'm just dealing with some things."

"I understand." Tony leaned forward and spoke in a conspiratorial tone. "Hey, I've been hearing things... You thinking about quitting that job you just got?"

"Not you too, Tony. Look, I just need some time to sort this all out. I've taken a month off. I'm going to use it to get my head right and make a decision, okay?"

"No, that's not going to work," Tony said. "A month, you said?"

"Yeah. Why?" When he didn't answer right away, Alicia sighed, leaned forward, and pushed the Coke bottle to the side. "What's with the hesitance from everyone today? *Spit it out.*"

"It's a family thing. Kind of delicate."

"What kind of family thing?"

"A 'missing person' kind of thing. I've got family back in Italy. A priest assigned to the Vatican. He's gone, and no one knows what the hell is going on." Tony paused, then nodded to himself as if he'd made some sort of decision. "Look, you want to help people. Really help actual people without an agenda. Right? So help *me*."

"You want *my* help?"

"No," Tony said. "I *need* your help."

A strange feeling of release grew in Alicia's chest. It was almost as if God himself had come down from heaven and put an angel in front of her to guide her next steps. She gazed at Tony's sincere expression... and it felt right.

She never could have imagined that her angel would come in the form of a three-hundred-pound mafioso named Tony.

"Okay, Tony. Tell me everything."

AUTHOR'S NOTE

Well, that's the end of *Operation Thrall*, and we sincerely hope you enjoyed it.

This is book two of a writing collaboration between Mike and Steve, where we're formally introducing Alicia Yoder to the world. If you didn't catch the author's note from New Arcadia, book one of the Alicia Yoder series, then the next couple paragraphs should serve as a way to introduce ourselves, give you a little insight into who we are, what our thought processes were regarding this book, and maybe even where we're going with the series.

We are authors with a rather lengthy list of books to our names, but we are by no means similar in how we became authors or in the types of things we normally write. I guess the easiest way to introduce ourselves is just by diving in, so let's start with the Rothman portion of the Rothman/Diamond duo.

I started this author thing accidentally, and by that, I mean years ago I had two young boys who enjoyed their bedtime stories. And my attempts to create off-the-cuff stories were pretty elaborate and to remain consistent I began to write things down. That was the beginning of a slippery slide into authordom for me.

As to my background, I've worked most of my life in various engineering disciplines, with my formal education in the hard sciences. I've spent most of my career in Silicon Valley companies as a designer and inventor of cool things. During that long career, I've traveled the world and seen many things that help bring color to my work. My writing has naturally evolved to focus on stories heavily laden with science, action, and adventure.

Now, I'll hand the virtual microphone over to Steve so he can introduce himself:

I think I've always wanted to tell stories. One day I looked up at my mom's bookshelf, and I saw Tolkien, Lewis, and Brooks up there. Terry Brooks, in particular caught my eye, because the books looked so massive next to the others. I had to know what those were. I read Sword of Shannara when I turned 10-years-old, and never really looked back. Fantasy, Science Fiction, Westerns, and Crime Thrillers. And somehow, all of those led me to Horror. The end result of all that reading? I love mysteries and thrillers.

My background is all over the place. I'm an accountant by

trade. I lived in Mexico for a year. I've been an editor, book reviewer, art director, and publisher. I love sports almost as much as I love cooking BBQ. When it comes to writing, I tend to focus on character. What they love, hate, hope, and fear. I love writing characters that "solve problems" like Repairman Jack or Harry Dresden. I also like showing heroes placed in situations that push them to the limits. But most of all, I hope the stories I write (or co-author!) entertain.

With the introductions out of the way, let's move on.

We both both enjoy the idea of writing thrilleresque stories, and while Mike's approach brings with it heavy amounts of science and international intrigue, Steve has a way with bringing the dark side of human nature to the fore, up to and including elements of the paranormal. You clearly saw some of that in the events that occurred in China during this story, and you might believe that was heavily influenced by Steve (the horror guy), but would you believe the idea all germinated from a real-life biological event that is based on real science? See the addendum where Mike puts on his science lecturer hat and explains some of the weirdness you folks just read.

I suspect that in this title, you saw the results of a melding between the strengths of both authors to produce something that further challenges the audience. As this series develops, you will see elements folded in that test our preconceived notions of what's real and what isn't. Could things that we believe to be figments of our imagination actually be elements of science reality? Could we "sciencify" (a technical term) a novel that had what we've always considered to be paranormal elements in it, and puncture that gauzy veil between make-believe and reality? We believe we can, and it remains to be seen whether that works out as planned or doesn't.

It's arguable that this book was in part a zombie novel—it wasn't really, at least in the traditional sense where supernatural elements were involved. This will be clearly explained in the addendum, but we think it's an example of what we mean when we want to challenge people's preconceived notions of what's real and what isn't. What's possible and what isn't.

In our minds, we saw the conclusion of Operation Thrall as sort of a two-book introduction to our readers of who Alicia Yoder is, and to give you a feel for her personality and how she might differ from her adoptive father.

Those of you who've read the ongoing Levi Yoder series will certainly see resemblances between the two, especially now with the advent of Narmer's unexpected appearance in her life, but who she is and how she views the world is quite different than her mobster/agent father.

With our backgrounds, we fully intended to give you a story that combined aspects of Michael Crichton-like novels with technical aspects that might be somewhat unusual along with a darker streak and sensibility, akin to some stories that might be reminiscent of Stephen King or F. Paul Wilson. Can aspects of traditional thrillers and horror combine to create an entertaining yarn? We certainly hope so and ultimately you as the reader will be the judge.

So, where are we going with this series? The ending was

something that left a few things dangling. Alicia is having mixed thoughts with regards to the Outfit, and her last-minute interaction with Tony promises something unusual. We do plan on taking this series in a very specific direction that for some may mimic areas that have been trodden before by authors such as Dan Brown, Lee Child, or David Baldacci—but as always, we have our style and sensibilities that are different than any of the aforementioned authors.

And we can't forget Bagel. Our cat who seems to be a bit more than just your average cat. How did you folks like his inclusion? Want more of him? Less? We would definitely like to hear your comments on the stories and characters.

We expect to have a lot of fun writing this series, and we hope you all enjoy the ride... it's going to be a tumultuous one.

Thanks for reading *Operation Thrall*, and there's lots more where that came from.

--Mike and Steve

We should note that if you're interested in getting updates about our latest work, we have links below so you can join our mailing lists.

M.A. Rothman: https://mailinglist.michaelarothman.com/new-reader

Steve Diamond: https://authorstevediamond.com/newsletter/

P.S. – The next title is Vatican Files - and to get a taste of that novel, below is a description that will hopefully give you a feel for what's to come. We hope you enjoy it.

Uncover the Vatican's Darkest Secrets in "Vatican Files"

In the heart of the Vatican's secret archives lies a mystery that could shake the foundations of faith. When Father Alessandro Montelaro unearthed a cryptic manuscript alluding to a missing Gospel of Mark and its ties to the ancient Essenes, he vanished without a trace, leaving his nephew, Tony, desperate for answers and the Church unresponsive.

Alicia Yoder, a brilliant yet disillusioned government agent, is drawn into the enigma by Tony's plea. She embarks on a perilous journey to find the missing priest, following his footsteps through an intricate web of historical puzzles. Little does she know, a covert organization, the Custodes Veritatis, the Guardians of the Truth, are also in pursuit, sworn to protect the ancient covenant of Christ.

As Alicia races against time, she's pursued by both the Guardians and shadowy figures from within the Church. Her quest takes her from the echoing catacombs beneath Rome to the sun-baked sands of Cairo, where the line between truth and deception blurs. In "Vatican Files," follow Alicia's gripping adventure as she seeks to unveil a truth so profound, it could alter the course of history. Will she find Father Montelaro and the secrets he sought, or will the truth remain buried forever? Prepare for a thrilling journey into the heart of mystery and faith.

<Scene 1>

Father Alessandro Montelaro sat hunched over the ancient manuscript, the soft glow of the desk lamp cast eerie shadows across the vaulted ceilings of the Vatican's secret archives. His eyes strained to decipher the faded Latin text, his gloved finger tracing the delicate curves of the script. The silence that enveloped the underground chamber was broken only by the occasional rustle of parchment and the muted ticking of a distant clock.

In the depth of the night, when the world above ground was lost in slumber, a door at the far end of the archives creaked open. The priest's head snapped up, his heart quickening with a mixture of curiosity and trepidation. The dim light flickered as a group of Swiss guards wheeled in a series of crates, their expressions showed a combination of exhaustion and surprise at seeing him at such a late hour.

"Father Montelaro," one of the guards said, his voice hushed but urgent, "these boxes contain items from a site revealed by a nearby landslide."

"Landslide?" The priest frowned. "Is this from the tremor I felt earlier today?"

The taller of the two guards nodded. "Yes, Father. The earthquake unveiled a previously unknown cavern on one of the hills about four kilometers away. It turns out that items had been hidden away in this place and the prefect was afraid that looters might disturb the site."

Intrigued, Father Montelaro rose from his chair, his curiosity piqued. He followed the guards, his footsteps echoing in the vast chamber. The two large men carefully placed the crates on the metal shelves reserved for holding items that need to be catalogued, and left the underground archives as quickly as they appeared.

Retrieving a nearby crowbar, he pried open the first crate and Father Montelaro's eyes widened in astonishment. The air was thick with dust and the scent of age wafted up from the wooden box.

Inside were relics from a time long past, items adorned with the unmistakable chi-rho symbol, the intertwined letters '☧' representing Christ.

His white-gloved fingers brushed over a seemingly ancient chalice; its surface adorned with intricate engravings. There were brittle scrolls and carved wooden boxes, all of them adorned with iconography from a time long past, and as he carefully retrieved items from within the crate, the priest spotted hints of hand-written text in both Latin and Aramaic.

His heart raced with excitement and reverence. The items before him were evidently from the early days of the Church, a tangible connection to the roots of his faith. The mild earth-quake, it seemed, had unveiled a trove of history, hidden for centuries beneath the earth.

Father Montelaro carefully lifted an ornate box from the crate, its lid adorned with the chi-rho symbol inlaid with precious gems. He opened it with trembling hands, revealing a collection of delicate jewelry—rings, pendants, and bracelets, each bearing the same ancient symbol. The flickering lamplight danced on the polished surfaces, casting a warm, golden glow.

It was easy to understand why such things might have been hidden in those early years. If indeed it turned out these items were from the first century, it stood to reason why such identi-fying markers would have been kept hidden. In the first hundred years of the faith, it was a secret sign for Christians to identify themselves to each other.

It was at that moment, Father Montelaro felt a profound sense of awe and responsibility. He was entrusted with preserving these artifacts, these tangible links to the dawn of Christianity. The discovery filled him with a renewed passion for his work, a deep appreciation for the intricate tapestry of history that he was now a part of.

As he emptied the last item from the first crate, he noticed that one of the scrolls he'd placed on his table had opened up on its own volition.

The priest stared at the ancient object and muttered a prayer under his breath, making the sign of the cross.

Scrolls that seemed to be as old as these items *never* will-ingly opened themselves to scrutiny. After centuries or even millennia, such things became impossibly brittle and only through the miracle of modern technology could the contents of the scroll be extracted, without ever having to unroll the item.

Father Montelaro was seventy-five, and even though he understood the concepts behind what the technology did, how the CT scanning device or advanced computer software worked were well beyond his comprehension.

The priest put on a surgeon's mask, fearing that even the slightest breath might damage the ancient object. He stared at the flowing, handwritten message from another time.

It was perfectly preserved, and the priest's heart raced as he shook his head, knowing how impossible such level of preservation was.

His eyes darted across the page and he quickly realized this was some form of eloquently-written testimonial from a man named Gaius.

An ancient Roman name, yet the language descriptions read almost as if written by a person from modern times.

In the dim flicker of candlelight, I find myself huddled with fellow believers, our faces illuminated by the soft glow, and our hearts alight with an unwavering faith. Among us sits Mark, the very disciple whose words had earlier painted the story of Christ's life.

The priest gasped and his eyes widened at the impossibility of such a find. He was immediately torn between running out of the chamber to alert the prefect and continuing. It was past midnight, and the scroll pulled at his attention.

His eyes, usually bright with enthusiasm, now held a somber depth as he unrolled a scroll before us. The parchment crackled softly, echoing the anticipation in our hearts. We were about to witness a profound secret, a revelation intended only for the most steadfast among us. I am Gaius, and this moment will be etched into my soul for eternity.

As Mark began to read, the words that flowed from his lips were not the familiar verses we had known. They were different, profound, and laced with mysteries that seemed to unlock hidden chambers of understanding. The Gospel we knew, the one that had been cautiously circulated among us, suddenly felt like the outer courtyard of a grand temple, and what Mark shared was the sacred sanctum, the holiest of holies.

In this new Gospel, Jesus' teachings were not mere stories but profound discourses, weaving together threads of wisdom that resonated with the very core of our beings. The words were bolder, daring to challenge the status quo with a fearless spirit. They carried the weight of revelation, hinting at the divinity of Christ in ways we had scarcely dared to ponder.

As I listened, my heart swelled with a mixture of awe and trepidation. These words were revolutionary, capable of transforming the souls of those ready to receive them. Yet, they were also dangerous, like a blazing torch in the heart of a dry forest, waiting to ignite a conflagration.

As the echoes of Mark's voice faded into the silence of the chamber, he fixed his gaze upon me, his eyes reflecting a blend of wisdom and urgency. In that profound moment, he entrusted me with a sacred task, a responsibility that weighed heavy upon my soul.

349

"Gaius," he said, his voice steady, "these words are not for the present, but for a future yet unseen, a time when our faith will flourish without the shackles of fear. You, my dear friend, are the keeper of this hidden Gospel. It is your charge to safeguard these revelations until the world is ready to receive them with open hearts."

His words hung in the air like a solemn oath, binding me to a destiny I could not yet comprehend. I nodded, my heart pulsating with reverence for the trust he placed in me.

"Find a place, a sanctuary far from prying eyes and seeking hands," Mark continued, his tone measured and deliberate. "A place where the wisdom of these teachings can rest undisturbed, shielded from the storms of persecution. Bury this scroll deep within the earth, beneath the roots of an ancient tree or within the heart of a hidden cave. Let the earth itself become its guardian."

I nodded again, my hands tingling with the gravity of the task. Mark's gaze bore into mine, his faith in me unyielding.

"When the time is right," he said, his voice carrying a note of hope, "when our faith stands tall, unbroken by the chains of oppression, and when the hearts of humanity are ready to embrace the full brilliance of Christ's teachings, then, and only then, shall this hidden Gospel see the light once more."

With shaking hands, I took the scroll from him, its ancient parchment rough against my fingertips. As I clutched it to my chest, a profound sense of purpose settled within me. I would honor Mark's trust, protect these sacred words, and await the day when they would illuminate the world, guiding humanity toward a future of enlightenment and spiritual awakening.

Mark laid a gentle hand on my shoulder, his touch imbued with *a silent blessing. "May your faith remain unyielding, Gaius," he said, his voice carrying the weight of centuries yet to come. "And may you find the strength to guard this treasure until the appointed time."*

With a final, lingering glance, he turned away, leaving me alone with the scroll that held the secrets of a future yet unwritten. I tucked the precious document into the folds of my robe, my heart resolute, and set forth to find the perfect sanctuary for this hidden Gospel, a beacon of hope awaiting the dawn of a new era in our faith.

Father Montelaro looked at the array of tightly-bound, brittle scrolls on the table and wondered aloud, "Could a new gospel of Mark be sitting right in front of me?"

Noticing a scrap of vellum partially hidden underneath the bottom end of the scroll, he grabbed a pair of tweezers with trembling hands and retrieved the fragile item.

The archivist's eyes widened with astonishment, noticing the Latin script etched in a handwriting starkly different from Gaius's elegant script. The message was concise but laden with urgency: *"The Romans have vowed to eliminate us. The Gospel has been moved to a place of safety."*

The priest's heart raced with the weight of the revelation, realizing that even in antiquity, there were guardians, unknown and unsung, who valiantly safeguarded the sacred words, ensuring that the light of truth would endure against the tides of persecution.

With tears welling up in his eyes, the priest stared at the hastily scrawled message.

Pulling in a deep breath, the septuagenarian slowly let out

his breath and gazed at the ancient scrap of animal hide. Still holding the item with his tweezers, he looked on the flipside of the brittle object and noticed more hastily scrawled Latin.

"In the land where the river's gift meets the sun's eternal gaze, beneath the guardian palm's shade, the hidden words shall find sanctuary."

Father Montelaro stared at the message and wondered what it could mean.

ADDENDUM

Even though *Operation Thrall* is very much a mainstream thriller, we definitely took our readers through some scenes that likely stretched credulity and even though in the story, we gave nods toward science in one form or another, we feel somewhat compelled to either explain some of what was covered or maybe give a bit more detail than the story otherwise demanded.

Obviously, our goal in this addendum isn't to give you a crash course on science, or a dissertation on current events, but instead give you enough information or keywords so that you have the data necessary to do more research, if you're interested.

Nanites:

Though the specific applications of nanites in *Operation Thrall* are fictional, nanites themselves are not a thing of fiction. The engineering world has had the ability to create things at the molecular level for quite some time.

The best example of this is in computer CPU manufacturing. Today, we are mass-manufacturing electronics with processes dealing with trace widths as low as 1.8 nanometers. That's more than a thousand times smaller than the width of the finest hair. An atom averages anywhere from 0.1 to 0.3 nanometers wide.

We've even been able to manufacture tiny machines at the nano-scale. Think of a nanite as a tiny robot. A nanorobot, if you will. Molecule-sized robots have been the promise of medicine for quite some time. The concept used in this novel, where these "tiny doctors" are able to repair the body (within reason), and fend off sicknesses, is not really as ridiculous as it might seem.

Today, it is already possible to synthesize nanites that can determine where they are, and deliver minute units of a medicine to the correct locations. For instance, if one of these nanites was carrying a drug meant to treat a specific form of cancer, it would also carry a sensor that would help it identify its molecular target.

The advantages of such a precise approach are obvious. Chemotherapies, by contrast, blast the entire body with poisons, damaging healthy cells along with the cancerous ones. Nanites could be "programmed" to target only the unhealthy cells.

Yet today we are not using nanites as tiny doctors. Why?

Many challenges exist—among them, the ability to manufacture these nanites in a sufficient quantity to do clinical testing. This is hugely expensive today, and frankly, that's the biggest technical hurdle.

But once that hurdle is crossed, the field is open for what could be a revolution in medicine, generating entirely new methods of treating cancer, other diseases, and even possibly halt the aging process.

Zombies - are they real?

Zombies, as they are commonly understood in popular culture, are often associated with the undead, reanimated corpses that hunger for human flesh. However, the concept of zombies has a different and fascinating origin in Haitian folklore and Voodoo tradition. These traditional zombies are distinct from the fictional creatures depicted in horror films and literature.

Haitian Zombies:

1. **Origins in Voodoo:** The concept of zombies in Haiti is deeply rooted in Voodoo spirituality and folklore. In Voodoo, a zombie is believed to be a person who has been reanimated by a sorcerer, known as a "*bokor*," through a combination of herbal concoctions and ritualistic practices. For reference, Wade Davis an ethnobotanist, explores the phenomenon of Haitian zombies in his book "The Serpent and the Rainbow." He delves into the

cultural and spiritual aspects of Voodoo and the use of neurotoxins derived from pufferfish to induce a death-like state in victims.

2. **The Process:** According to Voodoo tradition, a person can become a zombie through a series of steps. First, the *bokor* uses a powerful substance to induce a death-like state, making the victim appear dead. The victim is then buried, and after being exhumed, they are subjected to further rituals that strip them of their will and consciousness, effectively turning them into a mindless servant. For more information on this, see Richard P. Metzner academic article 1999 called "The Ethnobotany of Zombies." It discusses the ethnobotanical aspects of zombie creation in Haitian culture, exploring the use of natural substances in the process.

3. **Purpose of Zombies:** In Haitian folklore, zombies are not typically depicted as creatures craving human flesh but rather as individuals enslaved by the *bokor* to perform labor or carry out tasks against their will. They are considered to be soulless and trapped between life and death. Maya Deren is an ethnographer and filmmaker who wrote a book called "Divine Horsemen," and it provides a comprehensive exploration of Haitian Voodoo and its rituals. She also discusses the cultural significance of zombies within the Vodoo tradition.

4. **Cultural Significance:** Zombies are deeply ingrained in Haitian culture and spirituality, reflecting beliefs about life, death, and the power of sorcery. These beliefs have been passed down through generations and continue to play a significant role in Haitian folklore. In the book "Rara!: Vodou, Power, and Performance in Haiti and Its Diaspora." Elizabeth McAlister explores the role of Vodou (Voodoo) in Haitian culture and its diaspora, shedding light on the cultural significance of practices like zombification within the broader context of Voodoo rituals and performances.

It's important to emphasize that the Haitian concept of zombies differs significantly from the fictional, flesh-eating creatures commonly associated with the term in Western popular culture. Haitian zombies are deeply rooted in religious and cultural traditions and are associated with spiritual beliefs rather than horror or entertainment.

In Operation Thrall, we took an approach that somewhat resembles aspects of the Haitian tradition, leaving aside the undead popular culture aspects, and focusing more on the slave-like behavior of the so-called zombies. And of course, we twisted the concept up a bit further by the introduction of science into the mix.

Science and zombies don't seem like the kind of thing that would be a natural mix...

How many of you have heard of *massospora cicadina*?

Likely not many, so let me introduce you to a humble, yet real, fungus that is somewhat terrifying in what it does.

Massospora cicadina is a parasitic fungus that infects cicadas, particularly the species *Magicicada septendecim, Magicicada cassini,* and *Magicicada septendecula.* This fungus is also commonly known as the "flying salt shaker of death" due to its distinctive appearance when the fungus erupts from the abdomen of infected cicadas.

This fungus is known for its unusual and gruesome life cycle, making it a fascinating subject for scientific research.

Here are some key points about *Massospora cicadina*:

1. **Infection and Life Cycle**: *Massospora cicadina* infects periodical cicadas during their nymphal (underground) stage. The infection typically occurs during the cicadas' final molt before emerging as adults. The fungus penetrates the cicada's abdomen and begins to grow.

2. **Conidia Production:** As the fungus matures within the cicada, it forms structures called conidia, which are essentially spore-filled sacs. These conidia contain the fungal spores and eventually erupt through the cicada's abdomen, creating a powdery substance that looks similar to white mites or mold.

3. **Zombie-Like Behavior:** Once the conidia-producing stage is reached, the infected cicada undergoes behavioral changes. It becomes hyperactive, and its abdomen may start to

disintegrate as the fungus continues to grow and produce conidia.

4. **Transmission**: The powdery spores produced by the infected cicadas can infect other cicadas. These spores contain the fungus, and when they come into contact with healthy cicadas, they can initiate new infections.

5. **Sexual transmission**: In addition to infecting other cicadas through spore transmission, *Massospora cicadina* has a unique way of ensuring sexual transmission. Infected male cicadas often engage in "wing-flicking" behavior, which is attractive to healthy female cicadas. When a female mates with an infected male, she can become infected herself, thus transmitting the fungus sexually.

6. **Effect on Cicada Populations:** *Massospora cicadina* is known to have a significant impact on periodical cicada populations. While it doesn't typically cause mass die-offs, it can reduce the fitness and reproductive success of infected cicadas, which can have population-level effects over time.

7. **Fungal Adaptations:** Researchers have found that *Massospora cicadina* has evolved specific adaptations to manipulate the behavior of its host cicadas. It's believed that the fungus somehow influences the cicada's mating and wing-flicking behaviors to enhance its chances of transmission.

8. **Scientific Research:** *Massospora cicadina* has attracted the attention of scientists and researchers

studying parasitism, fungal biology, and insect-fungus interactions. Its unique life cycle and effects on cicada behavior make it a compelling subject for scientific investigation.

Overall, *Massospora cicadina* is a remarkable example of parasitic fungi adapting to exploit and manipulate the behavior of their hosts, in this case, cicadas, and eventually leading to their death. It serves as a fascinating case study in parasitology and entomology.

Just imagine that this fungus literally eats the cicada, which looks very much like a cricket, from inside out. It ultimately takes control of its body and in effect creates what arguably would be a zombie-like insect that's been hallowed out by the parasitic fungus. Especially in the later stages of infection, the cicada is still mobile, even though most of its internal organs have been consumed by the fungus, and its erratic behavior and jerky movements are directly attributed to the fungal infection.

It's nature's version of a real zombie, in insect form.

You can easily imagine how this story was inspired by such a nightmare-like fact of Mother Nature.

Thankfully, there is today no *known* fungus that does this to humans, but you could imagine that with some genetic manipulation, it wouldn't be out of the question that such a thing could be developed. We could see an event such as what had been described in Yichun happening in reality—which is a very sobering thought.

Gun Stuff

Like most aspects of this novel (and all our novels), accuracy and plausibility are extremely important to us. From the plausibility of zombies—or at the very least using the wild reality of nature and playing "what if" with the story—to the details on the type of cancer Alicia has that manifests at the end of NEW ARCADIA, we want things to be fairly grounded in reality. Guns are no different. Whether or not you, the reader, have a personal stance on guns doesn't change the fact that we want them to be accurate.

For starters, you may be wondering why Alicia carries a Sig. Well, that's simply because Steve Diamond carries a Sig. There is a familiarity to that particular brand of pistols... and maybe he's secretly hoping if he puts them in enough novels, Sig will take note and send him a nice P226!

One of the questions Steve frequently gets with respect to pistols, is "Why do you carry your gun 'appendix?'" This means carrying your gun, concealed, inside the waistband, close to your front belt-buckle. In OPERATION THRALL, Alicia mentions she carries this way, and there are a few reasons. First, it makes the pistol easier to maintain 100% control over. It doesn't get caught on chairs, and it's easier to make sure the concealed weapon is covered by a shirt. Second, it makes drawing from concealment easier, and faster. Lastly, drawing from appendix produces less strain on the shoulder.

Strain on the shoulder? What? Is that a thing? Yes, it turns out it really is. Steve had two shoulder surgeries within the span of a few months. Torn rotator cuff. Torn labrum. Torn cartilage. Bone spurs. The surgeons clipped his bicep tendon and moved it (biceps tenodesis). In short: Steve's shoulder was a disaster. Once healed, he found carrying his pistol in the appendix position made it so he barely had to use his shoulder to draw at all, and came with all the earlier mentioned benefits.

When Alicia is qualifying with her pistol at the Outfit's HQ, the tests may seem a little over the top. They are... for most people. The sad reality is that most agencies and militaries around the world only need to show basic proficiency. Steve has been fortunate enough to shoot with some of the best shooters in the USA (of which, he is not one!). The types of tests and standards they put themselves through makes Alicia's qualifying test look fairly tame. But really, the entire purpose of that section of the novel is to show how much improved vision, muscle control, and heart-rate control, affect Alicia and her ability to shoot better.

The pistol Alicia uses in China is the QSZ-92. This is a real pistol, and it is the gun used by the People's Liberation Army of China, as well as their law enforcement agencies. It may seem like a trivial detail to include, but think about it from the perspective of a "spy." Using a gun foreign to the country being infiltrated puts the spy at greater risk of discovery. And more importantly, in the case of this novel, it meant she could scavenge ammo and spare magazines for the pistol once in-country.

Bagel - surely that's just made up nonsense, right?

Training pets to communicate with their owners via pre-recorded push-button voices is a fascinating and innovative approach to understanding and enhancing human-animal communication. This method involves teaching pets, typically dogs, to press specific buttons that emit pre-recorded vocalizations to convey their needs, feelings, or desires. While this approach is relatively new, it has gained popularity through the efforts of pet owners and researchers who are exploring its potential.

An example with Bunny the Dog:

Bunny, a Sheepadoodle (a cross between an Old English Sheepdog and a Poodle), is one of the most well-known examples of a pet trained to communicate using pre-recorded buttons. Her owner, Alexis Devine, began teaching Bunny to use the buttons to express herself. Over time, Bunny learned to press buttons associated with words like "outside," "play," and "love." Through this training, Bunny has been able to communicate her needs and preferences, giving her owner valuable insights into her thoughts and feelings.

Here are some key points about this training method:

1. **Button Training Process:** The training typically involves introducing the pet to a set of buttons, each with a different word or phrase. The owner or trainer encourages the pet to press specific buttons in response to different situations or cues.

2. **Positive Reinforcement:** Positive reinforcement, such as treats or praise, is often used to reward the pet when they successfully press a button to communicate their intent.

3. **Building Vocabulary:** Over time, pets can learn to associate specific buttons with certain actions or needs, effectively building a vocabulary of words they can use to communicate.

4. **Complex Communication:** Some pets, like Bunny, can develop the ability to string together multiple button presses to form more complex sentences or express nuanced feelings.

5. **Ongoing Research:** While many pet owners have embraced this training method, ongoing research is being conducted to understand its potential and limitations. Researchers are exploring how well pets can truly understand and use language.

Below are some resources with bibliographic citations that provide more information on training pets to communicate with pre-recorded buttons:

"The 'Talking' Dog of TikTok"
- **Source:** New York Times
- **Citation:** (https://web.archive.org/web/20230922125010/https://www.nytimes.com/2021/05/27/style/bunny-the-dog-animal-communication.html)
- **Summary:** Bunny, an internet-famous sheepadoodle,

has brought attention to a new area of study within animal cognition: the use of assistive technology for language acquisition.

"Can Dogs Use Language?"
- **Source:** Scientific American
- **Citation:** (https://web.archive.org/web/20230922125619/https://www.scientificamerican.com/article/can-dogs-use-language/)
- **Summary:** The "button dogs" of TikTok seem to be learning human words. What's really going on?

To what extent can our pets communicate is a topic that science is still chewing on. It should be noted that Bagel, our spunky little fur ball, seems to be a bit above average for your average pet—and it shouldn't be unexpected, given his mysterious origins. We'll see how robustly that communication develops over time. You never know, future readers might be surprised what Bagel is capable of.

Uyghurs - is what's been said real?

In this novel we made references to Uyghurs and implied that they were political prisoners and abused. Even though our novels don't generally try to talk about today's politics, at times we will reflect on things that are happening.

Since we used the Uyghurs as an element in the story, we felt it only fair to list the facts as being reported in the media.

The imprisonment and human rights abuses against the

Uyghurs, a predominantly Muslim ethnic minority group in China, have been widely reported and condemned by various international organizations, governments, and human rights groups. These actions have led to significant concern and scrutiny from the international community. Below are some key points about the Uyghur imprisonment issue, along with relevant bibliographic citations:

1. **Detention Camps:** The Chinese government has established a network of detention camps in Xinjiang, where Uyghurs and other Muslim minorities are held without trial. These facilities are often referred to as "reeducation camps" or "vocational training centers" by Chinese authorities. (https://web.archive.org/web/20230922132130/https://www.hrw.org/report/2019/05/01/chinas-algorithms-repression/reverse-engineering-xinjiang-police-mass[1])

2. **Human Rights Abuses:** Reports and testimonies from former detainees and international observers suggest that the conditions within these camps are deplorable. Detainees are subjected to forced labor, religious restrictions, forced assimilation, and psychological and physical abuse. (https://web.archive.org/web/20230923154824/https://xinjiang.amnesty.org/[2])

3. **Mass Surveillance:** China has implemented a comprehensive surveillance system in Xinjiang, utilizing advanced technology such as facial

recognition, predictive policing, and big data analysis to monitor the Uyghur population. (https://web.archive.org/web/20230922132220/https://www.hrw.org/news/2018/02/27/china-big-data-fuels-crackdown-minority-region[3])

4. **Forced Labor:** There are allegations of forced labor involving Uyghur detainees, who are often subjected to factory work under exploitative conditions. Some of these products have made their way into international supply chains. (https://web.archive.org/web/20230922132804/https://www.aspi.org.au/report/uyghurs-sale[4])

5. **International Response:** Several countries and international organizations have criticized China's treatment of the Uyghurs and have called for investigations into the human rights abuses. However, China has denied the allegations and defended its actions in Xinjiang. (https://usun.usmission.gov/joint-statement-on-behalf-of-50-countries-in-the-un-general-assembly-third-committee-on-the-human-rights-situation-in-xinjiang-china/#:~:text=We%20are%20gravely%20concerned%20about,predominantly%20Muslim%20minorities%20in%20Xinjiang.[5])

6. **Legislation and Sanctions:** Some countries, including the United States, have implemented sanctions and legislation aimed at addressing the human rights abuses in Xinjiang and holding Chinese officials accountable. (https://web.archive.

org/web/20230922133708/https://2017-2021.state.
gov/the-united-states-imposes-sanctions-and-
visa-restrictions-in-response-to-the-ongoing-
human-rights-violations-and-abuses-in-
xinjiang/[6])

7. **Ongoing Concerns:** The situation in Xinjiang
   continues to be a subject of ongoing concern, with
   international efforts to raise awareness and
   advocate for the rights and well-being of the
   Uyghur population. (https://web.archive.org/web/
   20230922133811/https://www.cecc.gov/
   publications/commission-analysis/hui-muslims-
   and-the-%E2%80%9Cxinjiang-model%E2%80%
   9D-of-state-suppression-of[7])

The Uyghur imprisonment issue remains a complex and
deeply troubling human rights crisis, with ongoing efforts by
various stakeholders to address the situation and advocate for
justice and accountability.

---

1. **Bibliographic Citation:** Human Rights Watch. "China's Algorithms of
    Repression: Reverse Engineering a Xinjiang Police Mass Surveillance App."
    May 2019.
2. **Bibliographic Citation:** Amnesty International. "LIKE WE WERE
    ENEMIES IN A WAR: China's Mass Internment, Torture and Persecution of
    Muslims in Xinjiang." June 2021.
3. **Bibliographic Citation:** Human Rights Watch. "China: Big Data Fuels
    Crackdown in Minority Region." May 2017.
4. **Bibliographic Citation:** Australian Strategic Policy Institute (ASPI).
    "Uyghurs for Sale: 'Re-education,' Forced Labor, and Surveillance Beyond
    Xinjiang." March 2020.

5. **Bibliographic Citation:** United Nations. "Joint Statement on Behalf of 50 countries in the UN General Assembly Third Committee on the Human Rights Situation in Xinjiang, China." October 2022.

6. **Bibliographic Citation:** U.S. Department of State. "U.S. Imposes Sanctions and Visa Restrictions in Response to Ongoing Human Rights Violations and Abuses." July 2020.

7. **Bibliographic Citation:** Congressional-Executive Commission on China. "Hui muslims and the 'Xinjiang Model" of state suppression of religion." March 2021.

Printed in Dunstable, United Kingdom

68867001R00214